The Blackbird

 HENNINGHAM
FAMILY
PRESS

First published in 2020 by Henningham Family Press
130 Sandringham Road, London, E8 2HJ
henninghamfamilypress.co.uk

This is a work of fiction. Names, characters and incidents
either are products of the author's imagination or are used
fictitiously. Any resemblance to actual persons, living
or dead, is entirely coincidental.

Illustrations © David Henningham, 2020

Printed and bound by T.J. International Ltd, Padstow
& Henningham Family Press, London

Printed on Gmund Urban Cement Grey 310gsm and
Munken Lynx Smooth 90gsm

ISBN 9781999797409

Supported using public funding by
ARTS COUNCIL ENGLAND

G . F
S M I T H
1885 ONWARDS

The Blackbird

Claire Allen

HENNINGHAM FAMILY PRESS

London

2020

for Sam and Rosa

Chapter One – 1941

HE was scowling, one hand shielding his eyes against the sharp morning light as he squinted up at the steeply-angled shadow on the transept roof, which was all he could see of the opening in the tower wall. Any moment now, the first of the men would emerge.

To start with, it hadn't been certain they would go up at all. Half an hour earlier, they had been standing ready in their overalls, waiting, some huddling together by the chapter house wall rolling thin cigarettes and muttering, the rest picking their way up and down the length of the cluttered yard as they smoked. Every few paces, they had to stop and step around the slabs of red sandstone which were stacked two and three high in every available space, each with its carved mason's mark and, carefully scratched on in pencil alongside, a series of numbers and letters giving its final position on the tower. So much stonework was ready to be lifted and fixed into place, there was no more room left under cover. Finished pieces were being brought outside and left in the open until their time came to be strapped into the lifting gear at the end of one of the cranes and winched towards the heavens. The stones, too, had been waiting for a decision.

Thomas glanced up again. It was impossible to see anything. The sun was still climbing and hung low in the sky, right behind the tower. It threw everything into such stark contrast all he could make out was the dark, familiar silhouette. He gave up and looked away, blinking, the outline of the unfinished building swimming drunkenly in front of his eyes like a piece of coloured cellophane. Craning up had reawakened a twinge in his neck. He rubbed at it, cursing.

It was Jenner who really made him want to curse, though. There was a man with a talent for complicating things. Whether or not the men went up wasn't his decision to make. Mathieson & Sons had been contracted to do the work and it was up to them to decide. But Jenner and Caldwell, the clerk of drawings and the clerk of works, had the architect's ear, and – give Jenner his due – he'd always been fair and diligent. He and Caldwell, working together, trod conscientiously across the hazard-strewn ground between those who had designed the building and those who were actually building it. It was no easy job keeping both sides happy, and the master masons knew that, so were obliged, at the very least, to hear Jenner out, in the absence of the clerk of works himself.

And Jenner hadn't wanted the men to go up. Not with so many missing and everyone so exhausted. It wasn't only Caldwell they were without. The masons were having a run of serious bad luck. Last week, Barker had lost his wife in a raid and was in no state to work. They were down to just eight now, including Thomas himself, and eight men were just not enough.

Thomas knew all of this. Still, he had found himself trying to change Jenner's mind. The men were already here, he'd pointed out. They were willing. Surely it was better to get something done than nothing. He didn't usually get involved – he knew his place – but he'd noticed something recently and it had been bothering him more than he realised. Jenner was getting above himself. Nothing he could pin down. It was just in the way he carried himself, the way he inspected their workmanship so meticulously, now that he had taken on the clerk of works' reponsibilities in addition to his own. Of course, Caldwell had inspected their work too. But he did it differently. In a way that didn't make the hairs stand up on the back of Thomas's neck. He'd been trying to ignore his irritation for weeks, but this morning he couldn't keep his mouth shut.

He had other, more selfish motives, too, of course. At the prospect of being forced to return home early again, he had felt the already too-familiar prickle of dread. He saw the empty flat in Hunter Street, the unmade bed and unwashed dishes and everything just the same as he'd left it.

So, he had nudged Jenner towards the decision he wanted. And slowly, Jenner had warmed to the idea of the men going up. The prospect of reporting some progress to the architect in London, no matter how slow, was clearly tempting. With Caldwell away, he was probably anxious to prove himself up to the task. And at least the men would get a day's pay. Thomas knew Jenner cared about that and made sure to mention it.

Still, he was surprised at how easy it was. Jenner didn't come across as the kind of man who could be persuaded. He had a clamped way of speaking; he used his hands in rigid, jerky movements, for emphasis. He seemed an immoveable sort. And yet, he had been manoeuvred with hardly any effort at all.

And with Jenner on side, any debate about the men's fitness for work was over. This was the biggest contract the company had ever had. They weren't keen to get on the wrong side of the architects. The men were sent up.

Finally, they emerged, one by one, onto the transept roof, like a series of shadow puppets, and started the ascent up the framework of ladders and scaffolding around the outside of the half-built tower. The younger men went up ahead – Riley, Kinsella, Jones – even in silhouette he recognised their leaner outlines, their agility as they moved up the ladders. Less affected by the lack of sleep, they were keen to get the day's work begun so that it would be sooner finished. Thomas watched through eyes narrowed to slits as they zigzagged upwards.

The raw edge of the unfinished tower waited for them. Soon, he would be up there too, craning down to watch the inch-by-inch ascent of the first blocks of stone, their almost imperceptible progress, until they were there level with him, cantilevered out over the drop. Everything working in harmony. The rest of his life would be down here, safely out of reach, out of his thoughts. Working took all his concentration as the blocks, one at a time, were slowly swung into position. Eight palms flat against the grain of the stone as four men oriented each piece by hand, a fraction of an inch of air becoming a hairsbreadth becoming nothing at all as the stones were lowered and fixed into place. Well, he had got his way this time. He shrugged and squinted up at the tower again.

Jackson was back at work this week. Thomas had been watching him as they crossed the central space to the stairwell together. Even before he'd started climbing his breathing was ragged. He had a hand-kerchief clenched in his fist, ready to clamp against his mouth if the coughing started up again. Thomas had half-heartedly tried to persuade him to go back to his doctor, and, seeing him standing there so hollowed out, he knew he ought to have been more forceful. But the truth was, they needed him. And Jackson was a grown man, capable of making decisions for himself. Thomas found refuge in this thought and tried to put the sound of the older man's heavy, rasping breaths to the back of his mind.

He was waiting for Jenner to bring the updated schedule before he followed them up. Jackson was the last to reach the foot of the ladders, though Murphy was almost as slow. Murphy was fifty-nine and, though he was a strong and precise fixer mason, he'd been having trouble with his knees and the climb wasn't getting any easier as the tower grew. Thomas sighed: it felt like the whole bloody lot of them were there on borrowed time.

The men were hollering down at him to hurry up. They weren't supposed to climb the tower without a supervisor. Stupid, of course. The oldest of them had twenty years' experience over him. He waved at them to go on up. He would follow once he'd spoken to Jenner. But where the hell was he? At this rate, they would never get started. 'I'm right behind you,' he shouted. 'Give me five minutes,' and he gesticulated again that they should make their way up without him.

He was just turning away when it happened. A sudden quick movement, a blur in the corner of his vision, and he looked back towards the tower. Johnny Kinsella was already up, his slender, frizzle-headed silhouette pinned onto the impossibly blue sky. He stood there, oblivious, unable to see what was happening, as his young friend, Dan Riley, lost his footing on the ladder.

Everything stopped. The men who had been behind Riley froze where they were; they could do nothing but watch him fall. Riley straightened out and for a moment seemed to be standing in mid-air, his arms held out at right angles. Thomas couldn't reckon the fact of him as flesh and bone and blood. Their lives were so much taken up with stone, he could almost persuade himself that this was a stone figure, some forgotten statue, accidentally dislodged from its niche.

When it met the lead roof it was falling towards it would perhaps cause some damage; it might smash into pieces and be broken and that would be that. Another one would have to be carved. More time and money lost, but not the mess and horror of a living body falling from that height.

Daniel Riley. Thomas's mind whipped through what he knew about him as if a sudden breeze had riffled through the pages of a book left open. Twenty-two years old. Spared conscription because of a collapsed lung, the result of a childhood illness. Other than that, as fit as a fiddle, and a focused, careful worker. An invalid father and younger sibling, a sister, who had epilepsy. The mother had it tough, looking after them both. The girl was more or less an invalid, too, because of the fits, and she was sometimes violent. Riley had badly wanted to join up, but he put it to the back of his mind and made the best of things. It seemed like something he was used to doing. Even as an apprentice, he'd felt the pressure to support his family. Thomas remembered the tall fifteen-year-old of seven years ago as clearly as if they had just met that morning.

When he hit the roof of the eastern transept, he didn't break into pieces, but struck it like something flung in anger, limbs splayed and awkward, just short of the apex, then slid down, rolling over himself, his limp arms tangling round his body, until he disappeared from view behind the parapet that rose from where the sloping roof met the transept wall.

It was a long journey to his side. Thomas heard

his own voice bellowing out for someone to call an ambulance as he ran across the masons' yard. For someone to get the lad's mother. For someone else to fetch blankets. And then he was taking the spiral steps three at a time, circling up through the darkness to the narrow, bright opening at the top. Blinkering his thoughts, not allowing himself to consider what he might find when he got there. He'd been for a drink more than once with Riley, and sensed that the lad looked up to him a little. He hadn't wanted him to. Riley could find a better man to be his role-model. Thomas didn't want to take him on in that way. He wasn't the mentoring type.

He reached the doorway and burst out into the light, clutching hold of the stonework as he tried to catch his breath. He couldn't see Riley for the men. They had all clambered back down the ladders onto the roof and he could see Jackson and Kinsella crouching over him next to the parapet. Kinsella, kneeling at the head end, was bending over the boy, but lifted his eyes at the sound of Thomas's boots, and Thomas saw his stricken, grey face. Jackson, at Riley's feet, didn't look round. His head, too, was bowed, as if he were praying. The rest of the men stood or squatted on the steep slope of the roof, forming a silent semicircle around the tableau. Still breathing heavily, Thomas approached. Riley had come to rest on his side, with one arm sticking out oddly behind him, the other thrown across his face which was turned towards the parapet, away from the men.

He crouched down in the gutter between Jackson and Kinsella and put his hand, gently, on the boy's outflung arm. Moved it gently to the ground, elbow bent, so that he could see his face. He leant over him, close, his head pressed against the stonework. He was breathing, at least. In the shelter of the low wall he could hear the shallow sips of air, and could see, now, the rise and fall of the boy's side. Next, he felt for a pulse at his wrist, and it was there, flickering unsteadily under his fingers. But his eyes were closed. Thomas closed his own eyes for a moment, still holding the warm wrist in both hands. Thank God he was alive. Although... No. He mustn't think that. It would not have been better. Let his poor mother have some hope of getting her son back. At least for a while.

He opened his eyes again. He didn't know what to do. He started talking, his voice quick and low. He was just speaking words, nonsense words. He had no idea what he was saying. Out it babbled. About Riley's mother, his kid sister and how they both needed him to get through this, but not to worry, they'd all look out for them for in the meantime. He could take as long as he liked to get well again. Someone had gone for his mother – they lived in one of the roads off Canning Street – and she would be there waiting for him when they came down. He didn't stop to think how they would get him down. But already the ambulance was here – he could hear the siren wailing, and Murphy and Jones sprang to their feet and called down and within moments, it seemed, the ambulancemen were emerging onto the roof. He stood there, mute and helpless, as Riley was gently lifted and strapped onto a stretcher. He could do nothing. And then the slow, awkward progress down the spiral steps. He followed, in silence, with the rest of the men.

When they carried him out, his mother was there beside the ambulance with the epileptic girl by her side. She rushed forwards when she saw her boy, a great sob heaving out of her. But some of the men managed to catch hold of the sister and persuade her to stop with them and she watched from a distance as Riley was loaded into the back of the ambulance. Not that he looked a mess. There was no blood, nothing was crushed or twisted out of shape, but some of the men knew the family and said it was best to distract her if they could – she was very sensitive to shock.

There was something of a disturbance going on outside. Jenner put his pencil down on the desk. He listened. He couldn't tell whether it was something or nothing. He was annoyed with himself, on edge. How the hell had he ended up going along with Shaw? He'd been dead set against it at the start. The fixers weren't in any shape to be up there; he knew that. But, somehow, he'd been talked into thinking it was for the best.

He sighed. He and Caldwell together understood the opposing tensions better than any of them. From their isolated positions – Jenner preparing and adjusting the architect's drawings for the masons to work from, and Caldwell inspecting the finished construction, they could see both sides clearly and were often caught between them. For the masons, building was by necessity a slow process; they lived a cathedral into being. But the architects came at it with a sense of the whole thing fully-formed. Their familiarity with the countless intricate drawings of the finished elevations and details clouded the reality of construction. In their minds, the building already existed, and its actual incompleteness irritated them. Any kind of delay was intolerable. Jenner knew the nature of a building's growth – he had been a mason for almost twenty years himself – but his own feelings tended towards the architect's. He, too, was impatient. It was, after all, no longer the Middle Ages. They ought to be able to make swifter progress.

It was also true that if construction slowed too much, the inevitable questions would start to be asked higher up. It wasn't inconceivable that the work could be stalled completely until the end of the war, and that might be years. They'd been given a slim enough allowance of materials as it was, and those could easily be reallocated. If that were to happen, what would the men do? They were too old to go off and fight. Even the younger ones weren't fit enough. That was why they were here. What else was there for men whose whole working lives had been spent working on this one building? They couldn't all make a living from headstones, even in wartime. It was in all of their interests to get on with the work. He knew this.

And yet, he was uneasy.

He wasn't fully certain how, or even why, Shaw had done it. Shaw was a mason through and through – happy with the human pace of construction, the contact of hand with stone. He wasn't in a hurry. So why push the men up when they were understaffed?

Jenner knew he wasn't usually so suggestible. But there was something about Shaw; he'd noticed it once or twice before. A magnetism that drew him the kind of attention and friendship from other men that he himself had never known. Had he been more inclined to feel the lack, he might have envied his easy popularity. As it was, Jenner needed very little from other people, and what he did need, he took from his wife and the companionship she gave him.

Had he, then, been drawn by this peculiar appeal Shaw had? Or was the truth plainer? Had he simply let his guard down and allowed himself to be persuaded? Either way, it had set him on edge. He didn't like the fact that his clear judgement had been clouded, and that it had happened without his noticing.

What was going on outside? He pushed back his chair and strode out of the makeshift office next door to the chapter house, making his way round to the first transept crossing and then to the central space, directly beneath the tower. A figure flitted across an open doorway, making the sunlight blink. And another. Surely the men had already gone up, so why the milling about down here? Another figure appeared at the doorway and this time came inside. One of the apprentices, approaching with an avoidant, unwilling look about him.

'What is it?' he called out. 'Have the men gone up?'

The milk-faced lad stopped in front of him. ''S'been an accident, sir. Riley's fallen, sir.'

Jenner clenched his jaw, feeling a sharp, familiar ache in one of his back molars. The pain gave him the comforting spur to self-control that he needed. What new horror was this that they must absorb? Slowly, he released the pressure on the tooth before speaking.

'How bad is it?'

The boy shot a look at the doorway he'd just come through. 'It's bad, sir. Ambulance is comin', sir, but it looks bad. He–'

'–Where's Shaw?'

The lad looked at Jenner, then looked away. 'He's with 'im, sir.'

The messenger scurried away. Jenner watched the daylight blink again as he disappeared through the doorway. Slowly, he leaned his head back and gazed up at the stone ceiling high above him. The elegant rib-vaulting curving up and in towards the bell trap at the centre of the vast, domed space directly beneath the tower. The height was dizzying. He lowered his head and stared hard at his shoes, firmly planted on the flagstones, trying to quell the sudden nausea he could feel rising up his body. The low sun was slicing an oblique girder of light through the stained glass at the other side of the crossing. He saw now, that it had spattered the nearby paving and wall with patches of watery colour, one of which fell across his shoe. Another mingled the grey of his trouser leg with emerald, and a purplish-blue had lighted on the back of his hand like a bruised butterfly. He flinched and gasped, and had to stop himself from trying to shake the colour away.

What had they done? What kind of broken mess had they caused by sending the men up the tower? A brutal picture was already fixing itself into place in his mind, seeding questions. How high had the unfortunate mason been when he fell? Was there any hope for him? He tried to block it all from his mind but he couldn't pull free of it. He knew he should go outside, offer his help, bear witness, but he couldn't move.

Thomas found him hunched over his desk, scribbling in the margin of a typewritten sheet. The door was open so he'd walked straight in without knocking, glad not to have to feign a deference he didn't feel. Now he cleared his throat and waited.

Jenner looked up. Gestured for him to come further into the room, possibly sit down. It was difficult to tell. Thomas guessed that it was deliberately vague. Jenner had always seemed a little uncomfortable around the masons and Thomas assumed he felt himself superior, since his work was based here, at a desk. He would never cope with it, he thought. Face to face with the elements day after day, a hundred and sixty feet up at the growing edge of the tower, with the stone-cold air blasting in from the river. He might have been a mason once-upon-a-time, but he'd never done work like this.

Either way, Thomas preferred to stand. He watched Jenner screw the cap carefully back onto his fountain pen before standing up.

'How is he, the er...?'

'Riley,' Thomas said. 'His name's Daniel Riley.' There was something chilling about Jenner's non-appearance outside. As if what had happened mattered so very little he couldn't be bothered to stir himself. But that was Jenner all over. Just sitting in here, coolly doodling at the margins of his beloved plan of works. There was something inhuman about it. Nothing really mattered to Jenner but the tower. The men existed only in the abstract, no matter how much he spoke up for them at meetings. He didn't see them as individual people, flesh and blood.

Jenner nodded. 'I know who he is. Is he badly hurt?

Thomas looked at him. 'I don't think,' he said slowly, 'that he'll be coming back to work any time soon.'

He saw the expression in Jenner's eyes – one of almost pure animosity. And then he turned away and stood with his back to Thomas, apparently debating with himself. Perhaps trying – and failing – to hide his contempt. Undismissed, Thomas waited.

When Jenner turned to face him again, he seemed to have come to something. His face was closed and composed. 'I'll recommend that the men go back up,' he said quietly. 'I think it's for the best.'

It wasn't for the best. Not at all, and Thomas said so. The men needed to go back to their families and try to banish what had happened from their minds. The morning was half gone already; what difference would the rest of the day make? 'For God's sake,' he said. 'Let them go home.' But Jenner couldn't be shifted. He made his recommendation, and Thomas went outside to tell the men.

He watched from the transept roof as they climbed the scaffolding for the second time. The six men had been standing in the cold for almost an hour, waiting to be told what to do. He felt for them as they beetled their way stiffly up the ladders once more. The fall was probably playing on all their minds, as they went rung by rung, past the place where Riley had fallen, up to the uneven rim at the topmost point of the tower. He certainly couldn't get it out of his own mind – the out-stretched arms as he dropped, the way he rolled down the roof, and the ungainly shape of his body, bundled against the parapet.

He put his hand on the first of the ladders and grasped the rung. For himself, he wasn't so bothered. He preferred it this way. Keeping busy. Avoiding the alternatives. Only when he was up above the city could he begin simply to be. He was at his best when he was working. Everything else was just the murky complication of human relationships. He shook his head. He'd been a good husband for a long time before he strayed, and he'd never been anything but a decent father to

his daughter. But he didn't know how to fix the things
that had gone wrong. He started to climb.

He had tried to soften the news. A day's pay in their
pockets. Jenner wasn't a monster, he'd said, trying to
sound like he meant it. It was probably for the best
to keep going and not dwell on what had happened.
But they mocked him, told him he'd gone over to the
other side. Sticking up for the gaffers, now, are you,
they'd said. They didn't mean it, of course. They knew
he was one of them through and through and always
would be. Still, it grated on him that he'd endured it
on Jenner's account.

He had an uneasy feeling that Jenner was punishing
him. Pulling rank. Reminding him that he, Jenner,
was of more consequence. As if he needed to be
reminded: the man was omnipresent – looking over
their shoulders every minute. Assessing, advising,
poking his nose in. Reporting his findings back to the
architects. None of the masons was ever allowed to
forget that he was more elevated than they were.

But he only worked for the architects because he was
a mason and knew the trade, not because he was one
of their own rank, no matter how fine his draughts-
manship. He was really not so different from the men,
despite the advancement of his career. And, in a way,
he was caught, with fellowship offered by neither
masons nor architects. He was on his own.

Thomas reached the top of the tower and climbed up
over the lip of stone and brickwork onto the temporary
wooden platform built on the inside. Periodically, as

the walls of the tower gained in height, the platform would have to be dismantled, raised a little, and set down again. It was due to be lifted – there was now quite a drop down from the working edge. Yet it gave them a good deal more shelter when it was like this than when the drop was shallower. He crouched in the bowl of it now, his back against the brickwork, his shoulder hard up against a wooden joist, catching his breath. Already, the first pieces of stone on the ground were being prepared for their ascent. He could see the cables tautening and slackening where they ran over the wheels at the end of the jib.

The shout came from below and he waved at the crane operator to start hoisting. He pulled himself to his feet and touched Jackson on the shoulder. 'You pair up with me this side,' he shouted, over the noise of the winch. That way, he could keep an eye on him, make sure he strained himself as little as possible as they pulled the pieces into position. Opposite, Kinsella and Doran were pulling on their gloves. As he peered over the edge to watch the slab's slow progress up the side of the tower, he leaned on the stones they'd fixed into place yesterday, and thought back again to the night a few months back, in the autumn, when the raids first started up in earnest.

He had been walking home after spending a few hours with a girl he'd been seeing – Merle, her name was, like the film star – and had paused to smoke a cigarette in the darkness of a doorway, when the sirens began. He was in one of the roads that ran parallel to the cathedral. The chief engineer lived on this road and Thomas remembered talk about a meeting that was being held at his home that evening. Almost directly opposite where he was standing, a door opened abruptly. It seemed the meeting was right there, and breaking up as he watched. Through the open door he could see dark figures hastily shrugging on coats. He watched shadows emerge and move down the steps, hunching their shoulders with unconscious, skyward glances, as if they were expecting rain. Hurrying, but trying to look as if they weren't. He saw Jenner appear and cross the road towards him, conscientiously not looking up into the sky before striding off into the darkness. Within a couple of minutes, the street was deserted, the door closed and sealed up. Not a chink of light escaped. In the still air, the approaching planes nothing more than a tense, half-imagined hum, just beyond the periphery of hearing. Reluctantly, Thomas dropped his cigarette end and scuffed at it with his boot, then started walking.

Twenty minutes later, the house would take a direct hit. The meeting had been attended by every single person of consequence involved with the cathedral. The architect and his advisers, the various parties involved on the money side of things, representatives of the diocese. Old and young Mr Mathieson, too, had been there. All escaped without a scratch. All save the chief engineer and his family.

Emboldened, the warmth and pleasure of Merle's bed still fresh in his mind, Thomas had stared directly at the planes, daring them to do their worst, determined not to be cowed by them. He smoked another cigarette as he made his way through the city centre. The raid was in full force, but he knew the streets so well he could have gone blindfolded. He walked deliberately in the middle of the road, taking his time. Not another soul out of doors. Even the wardens had taken cover, and he was yelled at only once, the man gesticulating towards a shelter, opening and closing his mouth at him, his voice swallowed up in the roar and smoke and din of it. Thomas shrugged him off when he tried to push him towards the shelter, and kept walking. He felt untouchable. He didn't look behind him. When he got to Hunter Street he strutted through the archway that led to the flats and winked up at the hod carrier set into the brickwork above his head. The figure was one of a pair – on the other side was an architect – the two of them, he supposed, being necessary for the creation of buildings. When his wife and daughter were still with him, he liked to imagine the statue watching over the place, keeping it safe. But he didn't need its protection: he was indestructible.

He learnt about the chief engineer's house next morning, but it was several days before he found out Merle's house had also taken a direct hit. She must have been dead before he even reached home.

Since that raid, Thomas hadn't been able to forget the miserable folly of his walk home, the utterly delusional sense of his own agency, whilst his lover lay beneath the broken tiles of her fallen-in roof, and the engineer's whole family was wiped out in a moment. Merle had wanted him to stay but somehow it was her attachment to him that had made him leave, and so had spared him.

He'd started to dislike himself. At the same time, he began watching Jenner – he didn't know why exactly, but he'd had the uncomfortable feeling they had been pitched into something together since that night. He wondered whether Jenner's brush with mortality had affected him at all.

Perhaps it had. What he had seen flare in Jenner's eyes earlier was surely the will to control, to master the situation. He could understand it. But he didn't agree with it. Sending the men back up the tower in anger, because he'd been swayed against his better judgement, was ridiculous. A man had fallen. Accidents happened, he knew that. Everything came down to chance – who died, who survived. You could go through your prayers, your rituals to try to save yourself, if it made you feel better, but none of it made any difference. One false footing and that was it. You fell or you didn't, just as the bombs would either do for you or they wouldn't. There wasn't any way of controlling it. But sending the men back up: that was just plain wrong.

Chapter Two – 2014

THE kitchen window opens onto the walkway outside. As she forks a sausage out of the grill, there is the scuff of someone walking past, the momentary blink in the daylight as they pass. She can't see who it is because of the frosted glass – just a person shape. The walkway is narrow and their coat, or bag, drags against the wall. Louise winces, remembering Jake's grazed knuckles yesterday, as he tried to pedal next door's tricycle to the end of the row of front doors.

She spoons a dollop of mashed potato next to the sausage and puts the plate in front of him, reaching over his head to chop the sausage into slices while he jiggles his legs in the high chair, watching her hands. When she's finished, she pushes the miniature fork into one small fist, the knife into the other, and sits down next to him.

Their flat is on the third floor of a U-shaped block which wraps around three sides of a patch of grass with a tiny kids' play area in the middle. A climbing frame with a kind of Wendy house on top, and a couple of animals on springs that rock backwards and forwards. No swings, though, or slides, which Jake likes best. Still, it's better than nothing. And she finally feels settled here. It's home.

There's a knock on the door, followed almost immediately by a more peremptory rattling of the letterbox. Probably Minaz from the end flat has forgotten his keys again. She glances at the clock on the cooker. If it is Minaz, he's late. He should have been back from school an hour ago. But sometimes he hangs around down in the kids' playground after school with his friends – sitting inside the little den eating chicken and chips from boxes. Climbing on the roof and dangling their long legs down before jumping off. But she hasn't heard them down there today.

She helps Jake steer his fork to his mouth as she stands up. 'Back in a sec,' she says.

She isn't surprised when it isn't Minaz, but the fact that it's Benny standing there does take a moment to register. She doesn't quite manage to say anything at all before he has taken control and started speaking himself.

'I've been thinking about you,' he says. 'I wanted to say hello. How've you been?' He gives her a broad smile and swings his bag to the ground. It seems heavy. She notices that it lands half over the threshold.

'I'm fine,' she says. 'How did you...?'

'Find you?' He grins again. 'Oh, well. Easy when you know how, isn't it?'

Her hand is still on the door. She waits. He sniffs.

He is looking at her, waiting too. She glances up at his face and looks away. It was always his eyes, the intensity of his gaze, that drew her in. Seeing that look again stirs something.

'So,' he says. 'Are you going to ask me in?'

His clothes look dusty and he is wearing heavy boots. He's probably been labouring again. Which means he's back living in London. She looks at the bag, the boots, the heavy overcoat he's wearing even though the weather is warm. She doesn't want to ask him in. He has never been here. This flat is entirely her own. She doesn't like the idea of him coming inside, seeing the life she has made for herself. It would spoil it.

'I'm busy, Benny.'

He doesn't react immediately. And then he nods slowly, as if he'd known it would be like this. He turns and looks down into the playground below, gripping the railings with both hands, arms spread wide apart. When he turns back to her, there are tears in his eyes. 'I just want to see him,' he says.

Bang on cue, Jake totters into the hall from the kitchen. He is still clutching his knife and fork and his open, about-to-cry mouth is full of mashed potato.

'Christ!' he says. He lowers himself onto his haunches and stares at the child. 'He's grown.'

'Kids do that,' she says.

Jake lets loose a wail and some of the mash drops from his mouth onto the floor. Louise bends down to cuddle him then steers him back towards the kitchen and lifts him into his chair. 'Finish your dinner, sweetie. There's a good boy. I'll be back soon.'

'Aren't you going to tell him who I am?' Benny says when she comes back to the door.

'No. I'm not planning to.' She faces him, her gaze as level as she can make it.

'Do you think that's fair?'

She doesn't answer.

There is a crash from the kitchen. She turns towards the sound, is going into the kitchen, when she sees Benny reaching down for his bag and stepping into the hall.

'No,' she says, stopping. 'I said don't come in.' She can hear Jake whimpering in the kitchen. She stands, blocking the hallway. She can just see into the kitchen. Jake's food is on the floor, the plate lying in two pieces.

She waits until Benny has shouldered his bag and stepped back out onto the walkway before she moves. Then she reaches for the door and closes it behind him.

With a fresh plate of food and a change of clothes, Jake is back to his cheerful self again. It was the interruption that bothered him. And being left alone. He has never been happy on his own. She wishes she could be as easily placated. How the hell did Benny find her?

Well, he isn't going to mess things up for her this time. Last time he came back she made it so easy for him. She asked for no explanations, nothing. She simply took him back and fell in love with him all over again. It was just after she'd had the first letter from the council about the redevelopment, and she was frightened. It was like he had known, holding off, waiting to come back to her when she was at her least resistant. And then there he suddenly was again, with his reassurance, his glib pronouncements that it would be years before the council actually did anything. That, by then, they probably would have moved on anyway – they weren't planning on staying here for the rest of their lives, were they? She'd thought, but hadn't said, that she'd already lived there for most of her life, and it suited her just fine.

She trowels some mash onto the end of a chunk of sausage and holds the fork out. It hovers in front of Jake's face. He makes a half-hearted lunge and then, abruptly, changes his mind and opens his mouth, as if all the fight's suddenly gone out of him. She feels a stab of pity, recognising the mute acceptance, the defeatedness. The decision just to go along with things. 'Here,' she says, nudging the bit of sausage into the middle of the plate and pushing the handle of the fork into his potatoey hand. 'You do this bit.'

It had been good, at first, having him back. She hadn't started seeing anyone else when Benny left, and neither had he, he said, even though he'd been gone for months. Somehow that made a difference. As if it proved something about their feelings for each other. After all, the strength of his love was what had brought him back to her. That was what he'd told her. And the redevelopment notice gave everything an electricity. They didn't know what was going to happen, how long they'd have until their lives were thrown into the air. That he had chosen such instability showed that what they had together meant something. It didn't occur to her until much later that it might have been the temporariness that appealed to him.

She'd felt proud to be with him, then. Had forgiven him for leaving her. She can't remember when it was, exactly, that she knew she was pregnant for certain. She had known for quite a while anyway, without needing the test kit to prove it. Since his return, she'd been wilfully reckless about sex. She'd come off the pill after he left and hadn't started it up again when he came back. Part of her wanted it to happen. Maybe she saw it as a way to cement what they had, to keep him close to her. And it seemed so right, the carelessness, the thrill of it, the connection she felt to him. Everything about that time was to do with herself in relation to him. She stopped seeing her friends as much. Cut down on visits to her own family. She needed to be near him, to have him in sight. He, too, would catch at her fingers, or stroke the back of her neck, whenever she came within his orbit. As if he, too, needed the contact, the affirmation of their togetherness. He had made her feel that she was the queen of his life, and, with the slow suspicion, which grew into a certainty, that she was carrying his child, she had felt life was at its zenith.

When the meal is finished, she runs a bath. Jake wants to go on the tricycle out on the walkway again, but she feels unsettled. Not that she thinks Benny's still around, but she'd sooner keep the door firmly closed. She gets Jake interested in his trains and he busies himself building a track down the hall while the bath fills. She stands in the doorway watching him. He's humming to himself now, tricycle forgotten, as he joins the wooden sections together with urgent fingers, in a race to build as far as the front door before he has to get undressed.

She has never regretted having him. Not once, even when Benny left again, when Jake was still only weeks old. She loves him solidly and without question. A love so different from what she once felt for Benny, it is hard to give the two things the same name. When he left for the second time, she knew she would never allow herself to get so lost in someone again. Neither Benny nor anyone else. Everything changed for her when her son was born. She felt herself adjusting, settling, the different elements shifting position and pulling into place. A tighter, more pared-down self, like a freshly weatherproofed house. Everything that mattered safe inside, shuttered against the outside world, yet standing squarely slap bang in the middle of it. That was how she felt after Jake arrived. Perhaps Benny had recognised the transformation, and realised his time was up. Maybe that was why he left when he did.

She turns off the hot tap and swirls a bit more cold in. 'Come on, Jakey. It's bath time.' She steps over the section of train track he has built across the doorway and picks some lengths up from the floor to help him. 'Let's join it up,' she says. 'Then you can watch Percy from the bath.' They finish it together, building it all the way down the hall and back, and set the little train going round with an assortment of carriages and coal trucks in tow. He is pleased with it. In the bath, he chuckles each time he sees it trundle past the doorway. 'Toot toot,' he crows, and she rubs at the dried mashed potato crusting his cheeks.

Weird that he has no idea who that man was. Knew he was no good, though. Why else would he throw his dinner on the floor? She dips one of the stacking cups into the water and holds it up high, and they watch the water spray out through the holes in the bottom. 'Have shower,' he cries, so she does it again and holds it over his head. He lifts his face, open-mouthed, to the falling water. Drops cling to his eyelashes. With a rush of anger, she sees again Benny's big work boots stepping into the narrow hallway. As if he really thought it was as easy as that. Just walking back in. She isn't going to let him. She can't. She has her life the way she wants it, now, and she isn't going to let anyone wreck it for her.

'Again, again!' She dips the cup and holds it over Jake's head. The fine, wet hair plastered to his scalp. Boots, she thinks. Just there, where the train track stops.

When he abandoned them, it was a pair of boots that alerted her to the fact that he'd gone. Jake was six weeks old, maybe eight. She can't remember exactly. Old enough for them to have got into a kind of routine, anyway. She'd be getting up every couple of hours through the night, sometimes every hour, to feed him, so in the mornings, when he seemed to have his longest sleep, she'd stay in bed, and Benny would be gone when she finally woke up. At the time, he was labouring on a building site somewhere. He'd been to university, but hadn't done anything with it. He had ideas but no focus. He never seemed able to settle at anything for long enough. He would say stuff about how good it felt to do work that felt like work, that used your whole body instead of sitting at a desk all day. She hadn't questioned it, but afterwards, she wondered whether it was more to do with avoidance than anything else. Labouring wasn't something he could fail at, the work so short-term and irregular he didn't have time to get bored with it.

Anyway, he'd be gone when she got up, and she'd spend the day alone with the baby. There were still a few people left in the flats on their floor, but the nearest neighbour was the other side of the stairwell, so in their section of walkway they were on their own. It was nice, when the sky was clear and blue, to wrap a blanket round the baby and just walk up and down until he fell asleep. It saved having to wrestle the buggy down the stairs, because they'd more or less stopped fixing the lifts, now the estate was less than half-full. Last time she'd gone out, someone had laid a turd on one of the half-landings and she'd almost gone through it with one of the buggy wheels. It wasn't fair. They were running the estate down deliberately, leaving it half-deserted, and then they used it against the place, saying it's just as well we're knocking it down if people can't respect the place they live in, when it was smackheads and truanting kids coming in from outside who were leaving all the crap. She'd seen the groups of boys in grey trousers with their school blazers stuffed into bags, whooping and shrieking, high on something they'd brought here to mess around with, pushing each other up and down the corridors in trolleys they'd nicked from Tesco's. And she'd seen the desperate-looking figures skulking around one of the empty flats that had been broken into, with their hollow, grey faces and unwashed clothes, waiting for their dealers to show up.

That day, it was only when Jake had fallen asleep and she came back inside that she noticed Benny's other boots were gone as well as the work boots. He normally left them in the hallway. She'd laid the baby in the Moses basket and carefully unzipped the fluffy all-in-one he was wearing, in case he got too hot. She hadn't panicked. Her mind was perfectly blank as she lay down on the bed. She had closed her eyes and lain still for a long time before getting up again and looking

in the cupboard. When she did, she saw straight away that the backpack was gone. His two drawers of clothes had been emptied, and there was the swipe of his hand through the dust on top of the bedside table, where he'd swept the loose change, a half-packet of fags and her spare earphones into his bag. He had gone.

She was numb for about a week. She didn't leave the flat except to go out on the walkway, startling the pigeons that strutted along the top of the railing and huddled on every ledge they could find into sudden, noisy flight. It was January, and she would stay out there in the cold, walking up and down, up and down, until, one by one, the pigeons returned, eyeing her half-heartedly as if they knew she was no threat to them. She would listen to their soft gurgling coos as the baby slept. She wrapped him up carefully enough each time, but she didn't bother about keeping herself warm. She wanted to feel something: anger, hurt, cold, anything. Nothing got through. She gazed out numbly over the estate. Its huge trees were bare, and the enveloping green she remembered from summers past seemed like something that would never return. Up against a huge oak, someone had dumped a sofa. It lay there, tipped on its back, cushions sodden and scattered amongst the tangled tree roots. The branches were filled with birds, though, and with less human noise to drown them out, their song seemed louder, the liquid burbling of a robin somewhere out of sight, brittle and clear in the frosty stillness.

Eventually she had to go further afield because

she ran out of food, and that jolted her back into a semblance of living. She hadn't been down the stairs for more than a week. There was more graffiti, more rubbish strewn about. A broken kitchen chair blocked one of the landings and, further down, there was the blackened evidence of a tiny bonfire in a corner of the stairwell.

When she got back from the shops she rang his mother before she'd even put the shopping away, standing in the hallway with the bags at her feet, Jake still strapped in his buggy. She didn't want to lose her nerve. Benny had given her the number, once, for some reason, and she'd saved it on her phone. She said who she was – they had never met – and that she was only ringing because she was worried. She explained how he had left without warning, and hadn't returned any of her calls.

Benedict isn't here, his mother had said, accusingly, and she knew straight away that he was. She knew already that she was disapproved of. Benny was rather proud of the fact, as if it gave him credibility. It was childish, really. And it had once or twice made her wonder if her difference from him was all that had drawn him to her in the first place, as a way of scoring points, proving his independence, his lack of prejudice. He tended not to say much about his parents, about his background, but she'd figured out enough to know that she probably ticked all the wrong boxes. Anyway, the mother had gone very quiet when Louise mentioned the baby, and it was only after she'd put the phone down that she understood why. He hadn't told her.

She lifts Jake out of the bath and wraps him in a towel and they watch the water gurgle down the plughole before putting his nappy and pyjamas on. She pours some milk into his Tommee Tippee while he crouches in the hall in the middle of his train track, watching the train go round and round. He picks it up and caresses it while he has his story, touching its little grey, plastic face. Running the wheels along his palm. He drinks his milk and she feels the heaviness in his body as he leans against her, falling asleep. She gets up carefully and lifts him into the cot. Uncurls his fingers from around the toy train and puts it where he can see it when he wakes up.

She's tidying some toys away in the living room when she hears footsteps on the walkway and stiffens. Please not again, she thinks, listening, tiptoeing into the hall. She glances in at Jake. Please no. But then it comes. A restrained knock on the door. He's going to try again. He really means to work his way back in. She is going to have to be careful, and strong. She pulls the bedroom door almost closed and takes a couple of deep breaths. The knock comes again. More insistent, but still controlled. She opens the door.

He's had a drink. Enough to soften the sense of urgency. He used to do the same when they were together. He hasn't changed, then. Still has too many things buzzing round in his head. He used to say being with her calmed him down.

He smiles at her apologetically. 'Lou,' he says. 'I'm

really sorry about earlier. Stupid of me to just turn up out of the blue like that. I should've thought. That's why I've –'

'– Benny,' she says, her tone immediate and sure. 'I'm not interested. I want you to go away and leave us alone. We don't want you here.'

He puts his face in his hands and shakes his head, as if he can throw off her words. 'No,' he says. 'It's not…. It's…' He takes a deep breath and pulls himself up straight.

He is struggling – she can see that. It must have taken some guts to come back. Almost three years. Although, for Benny, perhaps such things are easier. Self-doubt was never something he was troubled by. Briefly, she wonders how he has spent the time, where he has been living, but she cuts the curiosity dead. She won't let herself feel anything.

'Lou,' he says again, reaching across the threshold and touching her arm. She shakes his hand away. 'Don't be like that,' he says, a querulous note escaping and catching at the edge of his voice before he can suppress it. He takes a deep breath and exhales strenuously, puffing out his cheeks. 'I know… Christ… I know how it's been. What I've put you through. All of this.' He gestures vaguely with his arm. 'On your own.' He moves his head closer to her and drops his voice. It comes out slightly husky. 'I should have been here.'

'Well,' she says. 'You weren't –'

'– Everything's changed. Things are different now.'

'Yes.'

'It won't happen again.'

'No.'

'I won't leave you again.'

He means it, too. She knows he does. He always did believe what he said when he said it. It would be so easy, she thinks, even now, just to slip back, to believe it, too. But she won't. He has no more chances.

'You're leaving now,' she says. 'And you're not coming back.'

After he's gone, she checks on Jake. Fast asleep. She bends down low over him, notices his hot little breaths, the slight flush on his cheeks. When he was a baby she would sit and watch him as he slept for hours at a time, preferring to be with him, quietly, in the room rather than alone in front of the television.

She would like to kiss his warm cheek, or brush it with her fingers, but she doesn't. She undresses quickly before climbing into her own bed and turning off the light immediately. Just don't think about it. Benny won't come back again. She lies down and stares up at the ceiling in the dark. It had been so difficult to keep control of her voice. Everything felt like it was welling up at once – anger that he was there at all, trying to wheedle his way back in; anger at herself, too, because it was her own fault he expected it to be so easy. He'd managed it before, after all – getting her so caught up in him again after his first disappearance that she'd felt she was the luckiest woman alive. And a tiny part of her, even after everything he's put her through, was glad to see him. But things are different, now, and she is frustrated, too, that he hadn't been able to see that. He had always been self-centred; it was part of the boyishness that once won him such appeal, and gave him the confidence to throw himself so wholeheartedly into things. But it was also part of his problem. He fed on attention, liked to be amongst people who put him at the centre and bolstered his self-image. He hadn't grown up enough to cope with anything else. It was always easier to move on, reinvent, rather than stick around and adapt. He hasn't changed, and he was too busy with what he had to say about himself to notice that she has.

There is also a little kernel of anxiety. She knows it's nothing, but can't quite make it disappear, especially now, lying in the dark. It hadn't been easy to make him go away. She'd had to keep on with the calm, quiet voice, saying no, and eventually he'd twigged that things weren't going quite as he'd planned. He hadn't had the bag with him, the second time, but it occurs to her now, he'd probably just hidden it round the corner. It was when it started to dawn on him that he was unlikely to be spending the night there that his tone grew a little darker. Not threatening. She wasn't actually scared – or even close. He is a coward at heart. She almost pities him. He is so unprepared for rejection. No, he hadn't gone so far as to threaten her. But there was something. She feels wide awake. She sits up and switches the bedside light back on.

Chapter Three – 1941

MARY glanced at the clock. He should be home any minute. He was always regular about his timekeeping. Their dinner was keeping warm in a low oven, ready for the moment she heard him come in.

Mrs Hayes from downstairs had given Hope a game of snakes and ladders. One that she had from when her own children were little. Hope had been in the habit, recently, of going down to the old lady's flat for an hour when she came in from school, and sitting with her in her basement kitchen. When Mary asked what they did, what they talked about, Hope said she mostly talked about her children. Showed her photographs. Some had Mrs Hayes in them, she said. A young woman, holding chubby toddlers on her knee and smiling. There was one, she said, taken by the seaside. Mrs Hayes and her young man. Only that was before she was married, so she wasn't Mrs Hayes yet. She had on a white dress with a little matching hat. So smart, and the young man looking so handsome. She talked about the cathedral, too, sometimes. She told Hope she could remember before the building started. A big bare empty patch of earth, with a fence right around, and they dug great holes to lay the foundations in. Imagine that! Nothing there but a load of big holes. And now!

The old lady was full of stories and Hope loved going downstairs to spend time with her. William, too, was fond of the old lady. They had rented the upper floors of the house from her eight years ago. Somehow, Mary had struggled to get on so well with her. She sensed disapproval. She had tried. In the first year, especially, seeking her advice about the kind of things she was likely to know about – even if she didn't actually want the advice. Offering to do bits of shopping for her. Buying an extra chop once a week and having Hope take it down for her to cook for her supper. It never made any difference. Her efforts were always received with good grace, but Mrs Hayes continued to hold herself aloof and nothing with any vigour had ever taken root between them.

With all her preparations made for the meal, Mary sat down at the kitchen table opposite her daughter and their unfinished game. She picked up the eggcup they were using for the two dice, and gave it a shake.

'Seven! Ha! Down a snake, Mother! Look!'

Mary counted out the seven squares.

'Bad luck!' cried Hope, delighted.

Mary laughed, and whizzed her counter back to a square on the bottom row. 'If I carry on like this, I've no chance!'

Hope scooped the dice back into the eggcup and quickly took her own turn. 'Three!' It was all she needed. She had won, and was skipping around the table, victorious, her mother laughing, too, to see her so happy, when the front door opened and closed. It was a heavy sound. Hope sat down at the table, panting slightly. Mary stood up and lit the gas ring for the cabbage. She could hear her husband in the hallway, taking off his coat and jacket before carrying his leather document case into the front room. She gestured to Hope to tidy the stray wisps of hair that had straggled across her forehead during their game. Hope tucked them behind her ears and straightened her pinafore.

He was at the kitchen door just as she opened it to go out to him. It startled her. She was still too much in the earlier moment to hide her pleasure, and she smiled a broad, happy smile at him.

He broke the spell. It wasn't his fault. He was tired. He needed to have his dinner, and some peace and quiet. She knew that. And yet, it was always the same. She could never quite relax when he was home. His hours at the cathedral were the hours she counted as her own, and so she felt her life was divided, and this made her feel she must be doing something wrong. It oughtn't to feel like that, she was sure, because she wasn't doing anything wrong. She knew she was at heart an honest, faithful person, yet it felt somehow disloyal to prefer the time she spent away from him. It wasn't because she didn't love him. She did. But she sometimes got the feeling that he loved her too much, and wanted her to be as reliant on him as, in some ways, he still was on her, and it weighed heavily.

He sat down at the table. He looked very tired.

'Hope and I were playing a game,' she explained, unnecessarily. 'Snakes and ladders. Mrs Hayes is ever so kind. She gave it to her. Isn't that –'

He nodded slowly. 'I hope you haven't been tiring our neighbour out.'

The little girl shook her head. 'I don't think I have,' she said under her breath, and went to fetch the cutlery from the drawer and started, methodically, to set the table.

Will was protective of the old lady. She was the age his mother would have been. Mary had found the two of them, once, with their heads together in a cone of light from the standard lamp in the old lady's airless sitting room, looking at pictures. Mrs Hayes needed no excuse to drag out her photograph albums – she was always showing them to Hope – but Will was not usually so free with his memories. Mary hadn't seen the drawings for years. He had drawn them as a boy, when his mother was still alive. She had watched as he passed them, one by one, into the old woman's trembling hands. His mother, standing, one arm outflung, throwing seed for the birds. In another, her arm lifted, her head raised, and the dark, complicated blur of a bird unfolding as it took flight from her pencilled hand.

Mary tried hard to smooth out her irritation during

the meal. High spirits, frivolity, often grated with Will. He was a serious man. It vexed her that she had been caught in a light-hearted moment. She usually kept herself more in check. She had high standards for her

own conduct. She wanted to be the best she could be, and this included tying down the loose ends of herself that were a hindrance to her husband's peace of mind. Because she knew how slowly peace of mind came to him, how precious it was. And she knew that she could be a balm to him now, as she had been in the past. Yet, try as she might to train her vexation on herself, little bits of it kept whipping out and flicking at Will. Was it really such a terrible thing for a little girl and her mother to be happy together?

It was a tense meal. He was generally quiet, unde-monstrative, but this evening he seemed more drawn into himself than usual. As she tipped the drained cabbage into a bowl, placed the tureen of potatoes on a trivet, set each dinner plate in its place, he sat silent and preoccupied, the muscle in his jaw flickering.

Hope was always different, too, when her father was at home. She acted as if he were half-stranger, and he seemed to have no natural feeling for how to behave with her, either. The previous evening, Mary had looked on as he asked what she was drawing. Patiently, politely, the little girl explained the various elements of her half-finished picture and he sat near her, listening. Yet he was unable to catch hold of the threads she left trailing and twist them together with his own experience into something they could share. The moment passed and Hope continued with her drawing. It saddened Mary that he seemed so unable to relax into fatherhood. He bore the responsibility with grace, and would say, she was sure, that he loved his daughter without question. But he seemed to get no pleasure, no lightness of heart, from her presence in his life.

She watched the precision with which he sliced a potato into three, speared one of the pieces on his fork, and dipped the clean, cut edge in the small pool of gravy he had poured at the side of his plate, before eating it.

When she married Will, she had made a promise to herself, in God's hearing, that she would be the best she could possibly be. Her family had disapproved of her marrying outside the faith, but she had known that God would always be God and would not abandon her.

Looking at Will, she remembered the months that had followed their marriage. The baths she made ready for him each evening, in the tiny worker's cottage in Derbyshire. Sitting beside him on a kitchen stool as he soaked.

'Tell me about your day,' he would say. 'What did you do first when I was gone this morning? Did you go out? Did you talk to anyone? What did you eat at lunchtime?' And she would tell him. There was nobody else who cared as much as he did. She would watch his face as she spoke. Eyes closed, head resting on the back of the bathtub as he concentrated, travelling by her side through the day they had just spent apart, and it seemed to do him good.

And then, after she had helped dry him and he was dressed again, she would take off her own clothes and climb into his bath, feeling that she was anointing herself with his industry as she listened to his account of his own day. She grew to know the men he worked with before she had met a single one of them. Occasionally, her attention would drift but she was careful that he didn't notice. She imagined how his face might fall if he knew the ritual wasn't as necessary for her. She didn't feel the pinch of apartness as keenly as he did.

He didn't raise his eyes, even after he had emptied his plate and pushed it away from him. How troubled he seemed, and how very distant those shared baths felt now. It was unfortunate that she and Hope had been in such high spirits when he came home. She berated herself for resenting him for it. So thoughtless of her, when, with the approach of each night, came the renewed, terrible threat. Would the planes come? If they came, where would they strike? What would be lost? Everything, in a moment, wiped out somewhere. And the great cathedral, shrouded in scaffolding, standing in the midst of it all. But how refreshing it was to forget. She hated to have the burden of worry constantly dragging at her. So much better to be able to put it out of your mind. But then, when she did that, afterwards she would feel guilty, as if it were somehow a betrayal.

'May I leave the table, mother?'

Mary stood up to clear the plates. With a nod from her mother, Hope took her schoolbooks to the other side of the room and began to read. Mary carefully piled plate on top of plate, and tried to keep the scraping and clanking to a minimum. She knew the sound annoyed him.

And yet, the bunched knives and forks, slick with gravy, slid out of her grasp, and in trying to stay them with her hand, she let slip one of the plates. It broke wholeheartedly on the tiles, and the knives and forks clattered their accompaniment. She was down on her hands and knees immediately, restoring order.

He winced when the plate hit the floor. A controlled shudder which seemed to travel from his shoulders outwards. She sensed he would like to explode with fury. But he wouldn't. He would suppress it.

She wrapped the broken fragments in a sheet of newspaper and carried them out to the dustbin. It was a cold evening, with a misting drizzle that hung almost motionless in the air. Too fine to fall. The dustbin lid was velvetted with minuscule beads which turned to water at her touch. The sky looked safe. It was packed tight with cloud; there wasn't a single bit of it that showed clear. Perhaps, then, they could relax a little. Will's mood might improve once he had digested his meal and smoked his pipe.

She hoped so. It was too tense otherwise. She knew Hope felt it, too. When the plate fell she had flown to her mother's side and silently helped collect up the scattered cutlery. Mary wanted to take her in her arms and never let her go. She was too devoted. Too preter-naturally watchful. Mary wished she would go and sit with her father and let her clear up the mess alone.

Upstairs, she watched Hope undress and helped her wriggle into her nightdress. Together, they huddled at the bedroom window, with the curtains drawn around them, and looked out at the cloudy sky. Easily visible across the rooftops stood the hulking shape of the cathedral, the stump of the tower that was growing slowly upwards. Hope reached onto the top of the window and took down the measuring device she had twisted from a length of wire. A straight piece with a small loop at one end, the size of a farthing. Carefully, she positioned it, with the loop uppermost and the bottom end touching a spot she had marked on the windowsill. Having done this, she stooped slightly so that she could see through the loop. Mary watched as she took her pocket knife and, still holding the wire device with one hand, with the other scratched a mark on the side of the window frame. Then she stood up straight and examined the scratch.

'It's the same as last time,' she said. 'It's still no taller.'

Mary shrugged. 'It will be,' she said. 'You have to be patient.'

Hope folded up her pocket knife and replaced the wire hoop on top of the window sash. So like her father, with her precision, and her sense of urgency that the tower should grow. Mary sat on the edge of the bed, feeling suddenly weary. Even if the weather did mean the planes stayed away for another night, they were pushing against the tide trying to build that thing at all. It troubled her that she felt like this, sometimes. Surely she, of the three of them, ought to be the most eager for this great cathedral to be completed. Will wasn't doing it for God's glory, that was almost certain. And she suspected her daughter's faith – so ardent when she said her prayers – was only a child's unquestioning acceptance of what others tell her is so.

She watched as Hope pulled her dressing gown more closely around herself and tightened the cord before kneeling beside the bed. Mary knelt next to her and closed her eyes as Hope sent up her whispered prayer. 'God bless our home and keep us safe. God bless Mother and Father and Mrs Hayes. God bless Emily and look after her in heaven…' Emily was a schoolfriend. She had died in a raid just before Christmas.

She kissed her goodnight and straightened the curtain, looking out again, briefly, at the ugly, attenuated silhouette of the half-built cathedral. It was for this building that they had come here, to live in this city. In the days before Hope was even born. It was harder and harder to remember any other life, now. She pulled the bedroom door gently closed and crept downstairs.

He hadn't moved from the table and here Mary was coming downstairs again already. It felt like only minutes since she had taken the child up to bed. He felt a strong lurch in his stomach. Of course, he would have to tell her about the accident. He had never really thought to keep it from her. And yet. She was so easily upset. So attuned to the significance of what seemed otherwise arbitrary things. He had never been able to take any comfort from a belief in God's great plan, as she could. He had, at one time, tried, but it had been a long time ago, when his mind was still pliable, and even then, he couldn't do it. Now, he made no pretence.

He knew two things would happen when he told her about the accident: she would be horribly upset, and she would try to find reasons. Both of which he would have to scrape together the patience for. He could understand that it was upsetting, but he had spent all day with it churning round his own head. He couldn't face her sorrow on top of his own turmoil. And the searching for reasons was likely to frustrate him the more, because, with Mary, it was a habit that was so stubbornly backwards-looking. The thing had happened. It was terrible, but it had to be absorbed. Life had to carry on. For Christ's sake – they were in the middle of a war. Terrible things were happening every day, and the world didn't just stop and gape and hang its head. He had been carrying this suppressed outburst around with him all day, sitting uncomfortably with the sense of shame that had begun almost immediately to purple and was now an almighty bruise on the pale expanse of his conscience. He had seen the looks he got after the masons went up the second time. It was their beloved Thomas Shaw they should be taking their grievances out on, not him, he'd wanted to shout. If they thought he was callous for saying they should go back up after the accident, what would they think if they knew it was Shaw, not he, who had wanted them to go up in the first place? How was it that he had ended up with all the dirty looks and Shaw had got off with nothing? A quick change of mind and he had sidestepped out of shouldering any of the blame. At least Jenner could say he had the men's interests at heart in sending them up the second time, even if it wasn't actually true. The fact was, he had made the recommendation only out of spite for Shaw. Still, it remained true that they wouldn't thank him if everything ground to a halt and they had no wages coming in. Mary came back into the room and he straightened himself in his chair.

As he told her, he watched her face. It was like a painting: mouth slackly open, eyes wide and unblinking, as if Saint Sebastian stood bristling with arrows right there in front of her, or each hammer blow that drove the nails through Christ's palms was reverberating through her body. Just standing there, in the middle of the kitchen, as if she were, in that moment, watching the young mason fall. Jenner's irritation flared at once, but he held it in check.

'Will he…' she faltered. Her words were on the verge of a sob. 'Will he… I mean, is he… Will he die?'

'I don't know,' he said. 'I didn't see him myself. One of the men told me. I've only got his version.' He paused. He could feel her watching him.

'Whose version?' she whispered. 'Who saw?'

Thomas Shaw, he wanted to say. Thomas Shaw.

I allowed myself to be persuaded. I let myself be tempted, steered by him, because in my heart I wanted the work to go on, I wanted them to go up, and it happened because of that. It was Thomas Shaw. But he shook it away, waved her question aside. 'Just one of the masons,' he said. 'I don't know his name.'

He stood up and the chair scraped against the tiles, an ugly, forlorn sound. It matched her tragic face. He pulled her to him. He had known the news would upset her. He hadn't predicted how much. It wasn't as if she knew the lad who had fallen. She rested her head against his chest and he stroked it. Her hair smelt of soap.

He needed to be alone, to get out of the kitchen, out of the house altogether. He hadn't had the time to think all day, and he needed it. Badly needed it, because he still couldn't work out how it had happened. Not the fall – the fall, he could understand well enough. But Shaw. He couldn't think with her there, obliviously sorrowing for a boy who had fallen because of her own husband's bad advice. It rubbed his nose in his error too much. He needed to get away from her to put his mind straight, to calm his anger with himself.

His father had been persuasive. Had chipped away at him, after his mother was gone, until he had him in the shape he wanted, apprenticed to the son of the same Derby master mason who had taken him on forty years earlier. The early talent for drawing which his mother had nurtured through his boyhood, Will's father quickly repackaged as a hobby. His ability to caricature was the only aspect of it that was valued and openly encouraged, as a means of gaining popularity. Not that it ever helped.

He kissed the top of her head, as if to dismiss her, and turned to fetch his boots.

She sprang after him like an echo. 'Are you…?'

He shook his head. He knew the track her thoughts were following. And no, he wasn't. The injured man didn't need him fretting at his hospital bedside. What good could he do for him, now? It was too late. And he would be getting care enough. He probably wouldn't live, no matter what they did for him. But then, nobody could say that, nor even think it. In any case, he couldn't bear the idea of seeing him. The brutal reality of what his advice had caused to happen. His massaged, no longer impartial, advice. How had he not seen that he was being worked on, just as his father had worked on him? 'No,' he said. 'I'm going back to the cathedral.'

Without a word, she went to fetch his heavy coat. He allowed himself to be ministered to, pushing each arm into the outheld sleeves, standing for a moment whilst she crossed his scarf over his chest and buttoned the coat over the top.

He kissed her lightly on the forehead and held her face for a moment, trying to see into it. Would she forgive him, he wondered, if she knew? But as usual, her eyes veiled themselves almost immediately. Where was the direct, unwavering gaze he had once so cherished? Where had his receptive young wife gone?

The early days of their life together had faded so incrementally he hadn't noticed; he could only see the difference now, the absence of what was once there.

He took his notecase from the front room, noticing the damp chill in the air. They no longer lit a fire in there during the week. It would be cold at the cathedral, too. But at least he would have the space to think clearly. He could cope with the cold; it was people that clouded things.

He stepped out into the night, habit making him glance up at the sky, even though, with the bad weather holding, there was no danger of a raid. She stood at the door to see him down the front steps and across the street. He listened for the sound of it closing, but it didn't come. She must still be there, watching him. He didn't turn to look.

Chapter Four – 2014

'HAVE you finished, my love?' Hope doesn't expect him to answer, but she asks anyway. More and more, nowadays, she finds herself holding up both ends of the conversation. It's one of the things she misses most – talking together. He was once such a vivid communicator. But the disease is eating out his tongue. He speaks less and less. She smiles as she takes the fork out of his hand and puts it on the plate. 'Ice cream? I thought we might. For a treat. It's the caramel one you like, with the chunks of chocolate.' She spoons a ball into each bowl and sits down again, opposite him. The ice cream brings a smile. There are still some pleasures.

When he's finished, she escorts him to the sofa and turns the television on. He likes watching TV. He never used to, but now it absorbs him. Once he's settled in front of it, she can get things done which would be impossible otherwise.

The local news has just started. A feature about the Blackbird. She glances at Robert. Not a blink of recognition. She turns sadly back to the screen. He likes it best with the sound off, so they watch in silence. A red banner with bold, white type comes up across the bottom of the screen: Blackbird Estate, Southwark – final leaseholders evicted. So that's that. It's all over. They've certainly put up a fight, but what chance had they ever stood? She looks at Robert again. He has a bead of ice cream at the corner of his mouth. She wants to tell him to lick it away, but he won't do it. She'll have to wipe it for him. She feels in her pocket for a tissue.

He watches. He gives the screen his full attention, but she can tell he doesn't know the place any more. She can scarcely blame him: it looks in a sorry state. Most of the flats are boarded up already. Like a ghost town. Or some kind of post-apocalypse nightmare. Well, he's in as bad a state himself. And he'll be levelled to a pile of rubble, too, by the end of it. Nothing left to show that there was ever a functioning, thinking mind inside that hollowed out skull.

Years ago, she remembers, he shook his fist at the TV screen in anger. *Hide and Seek* had just been stolen. That sort of thing suddenly seemed to be happening a lot – months earlier, a Henry Moore had been pinched from somewhere else and melted down for scrap. *Hide and Seek* was a series of bronze figures Robert had been commissioned to make for the estate when it was built. Seven figures of playing children, all of them different, dotted amongst the trees and between the huge blocks. Lifesize figures doing everyday things had been Robert's trademark for a time – he'd made similar things for quite a few other new estates over the years, but *Hide and Seek* had always held a special place in his heart, and its theft enraged him. The estate was already earmarked for redevelopment, even then. It was being deliberately neglected, he had growled. Set the place up as a failure, let a bad reputation gradually accrete around its name, and it would become a failure. They knew exactly what they were doing. It was social engineering of the nastiest kind, as if there had never been any other choice but to pull the place down.

It was shortly after they moved into this flat that

people started being moved out of the Blackbird, and the estate was on the news again because some of the leaseholders were refusing to go. She remembers it so precisely only because of the packing crates and the chaos and how frustrated she had been feeling about her own situation at the time. Yet again, he had been angry and she had wondered how he could stand there in all the unnecessary mess of it, getting so worked up about other people's upheaval, when he had forced exactly the same thing on her. She hadn't wanted to move. That had been at the nub of it. Theirs had always been a relationship built on talking things through. She couldn't remember one single other occasion when he had made a significant decision without consulting her. Not once. And yet, here they had been, two years ago, in this first floor, purpose-built flat. All very nice, of course. She had no complaints about the quality, the location, or anything like that. But why had they had to move here at all? What had been wrong with their old house, all of a sudden? It had suited them very well through almost fifty years of marriage. She hadn't quite believed the odd change in him; it had happened so suddenly. He had been so rigid that she hadn't been able to bear opposing him. She just closed parts of herself off and let him have his way, hoping they would be able to weather it out. He must have his reasons, she told herself. But her resentment had simmered for a long time, and was certainly bubbling as they watched that news report. She, feeling that he cared more about the displaced residents on the TV screen than he did about his own wife. She had thought him so selfish. And then, over months, had come the creeping realisation that he wasn't being selfish at all. Quite the opposite. He had known what was coming and had summoned all his last hold on things to effect this move, so that, when the inevitable happened, she would be able to manage.

And now. She reaches across to him and wipes the blob of ice cream away. He barely registers that she has touched him. She sighs. Would she really have preferred to know sooner? Knowing would have made no difference.

Well, now the Blackbird really has reached its final chapter. With every last person out, there's no stopping the demolition. She imagines huge wrecking balls swinging on chains. Whole terraces folding in on themselves, watched by grubby children in too-big shorts, and women with aprons over their frocks, but she knows she's got the wrong era. She's thinking of the demolition after the war, that made space for a lot of the housing that's now going the same way. They'll probably use dynamite. Each of the huge blocks crumbling to the ground in seconds. She's seen them doing it on TV. And then, she thinks, in forty years' time, they'll probably be at it again, knocking down the stuff they'll build in the Blackbird's place.

When the report has finished she gets up to make them a pot of tea and tidy the kitchen. He should be happy enough left on his own until the end of the news, and then they can sit and watch something together.

She is part way through the washing up when she hears him calling, not from the living room but the bedroom. He calls again, and she can hear in his voice the high-pitched, tremulous note of panic.

She rushes to him, peeling off her rubber gloves as she goes, keeping her mind calm, as she has trained herself to do. She stops in the doorway. His face peers at her palely from the middle of the room, where he is standing with his trousers down. He looks frightened and shamefaced and utterly defeated. Something smeared with brown hangs from one dangling hand; she recognises the blouse she had left out on the bed earlier, so that she wouldn't forget to iron it. In one corner of the bedroom stands the Ercol easy chair they bought for his father after he had to stop work. It had sat in his parents' flat, in his father's favourite spot next to the gas fire, until he died. Robert couldn't bear the idea of parting with it. Well, now he has relieved himself on it. He must have thought he was in the bathroom.

She tries not to recoil as the smell hits home; his bowels haven't been very good lately. She digs her nails into the paintwork of the doorframe trying not to retch as the full-throttle stink of warm, liquid shit roils over her.

At some point, he must have guessed things weren't quite right, and in his panic to reorient himself, to clear up a mess he knew shouldn't be there, he has smeared his mistake everywhere. She spots one of her cashmere jumpers crumpled on the floor next to the bed. The pale green duvet cover has smudgy handprints across one corner and there are more on his shirt front; she can see the rising panic in the long traces his fingers have streaked across the fabric. Wiping his hands there over and over, trying to make it go away. Now he is frozen in terror, his eyes on her. Waiting to be told what to do. She notices he is shivering, his bare legs puckered with goose-bumps.

'Dear me,' she says, keeping her voice level. She mustn't get flustered. It will only make him difficult, and she needs him to co-operate. 'Dear me. Let's try to get you sorted out. Come on.'

She puts her hand on his shoulder, helps him step out of his trousers and underwear, and steers him gently to the bathroom where she carefully removes the rest of his clothes and throws them, one by one, into the bath. She has to pull to get her blouse out of his clenched fingers. He is still a strong man. A head and shoulders taller than she is. She swallows hard and pulls off a length of toilet roll.

'Sit down, my love,' she says, once she's wiped away the worst of it and flushed it away. 'Here, look. I've put a towel across the toilet seat so it won't be cold. Just while I fill the basin.'

And then she washes him. He sits there, as biddable as a sleepy child, standing and turning round when she tells him to. Watching the magic as her hands dip into the water, wring out the flannel, and bring it, warm, to his translucent skin. Wiping, soothing. Slow and methodical. She drains and refills the bowl, refusing to be disgusted. Her wedding ring glints in the soapy water as her hands dip in and in and in. When she has finished, she helps him into clean pyjamas and sits him back down in front of the television.

The tea is overstewed. She pours it away and makes a fresh pot. Whilst it brews, she returns, still calm, to the bedroom. The sickly smell is filling it now, pressing into every square inch of air, touching against their pillows, her half-read book on the bedside table, her water glass. She twists the net curtain into a rope and ties a knot at the bottom so that it hangs free of the two opening sides of the window, and then she swings both windows open, fixing the hinged arms on the very last notch, so that they are open as wide as they will go. She imagines the smell unrolling itself down the wall and spreading like mist along the street below.

She picks up her rubber gloves from where she dropped them on the hall floor, and goes back to the kitchen for a bowl of soapy water. She looks through the serving hatch: Robert is staring, enraptured, at the television screen. She runs the tap as quietly as she can. She doesn't want him all agitated again, getting in the way while she's cleaning up.

Once she's stripped the bed and spread the duvet cover on the floor, she pulls the cover off the chair cushion and throws it on top of the bedding. This done, she bundles everything up and goes to the bathroom for his clothes and her blouse, and puts the whole lot straight in the washing machine. Back in the bedroom, she gets down stiffly onto her knees to scrub the carpet and wipe the chair legs. The wood is mercifully smooth and free from awkward cracks and crevices. She thanks heaven that it hadn't happened with the wicker chair. The carpet takes more work. She gets out what she can, and then hauls herself up using the edge of the bed. It will have to do.

The smell, at least, has begun to fade. But there is still her cashmere jumper. Wearily, she carries it into the bathroom and sits on the side of the bath to swill it in the basin with some wool wash. She rubs at the marks. It is a lovely Easter chick yellow. He bought it for her the birthday before last. She feels the prickle of tears and presses her lips together, forcing herself to look up at the ceiling until they subside. She does the best she can, but even after three changes of water, she can still see traces. Sadly, she drains the bowl and squeezes the water out of the wool. Maybe it will look better once it's dried. She props the airer across the bath and gently hangs the jumper over it.

The tea has gone a bit stewed again but she can't face making a third pot. Quickly she pours him a cup and carries it through with a couple of biscuits in the saucer. She doesn't pour herself one. She needs to get out of the flat. Just for a few minutes. A breath of fresh air.

Without disturbing him, she makes sure the balcony door is locked, and quietly removes the key. In the kitchen, she unplugs the kettle and toaster and flicks the master switch on the wall that powers the oven. The key for the balcony door she puts in an eggcup on the windowsill. He won't look there. In the bedroom, she closes and locks the windows and unties the knotted net curtain.

She stands in front of him to get his attention. 'That's the last of the milk, Robert! I don't know how we've managed it! I need to go to the shop. I'll be five minutes.' They haven't run out of milk. She hasn't gone out for a pint in years. It's delivered to their door every morning. But somehow, she feels this will make more sense to him than anything else.

He looks at her for a moment, then his attention slips and he peers round her, trying to see the screen. She steps out of the way.

She locks the flat door behind her. She feels as guilty as if she were a mother leaving a baby locked in a flat, but it is only for a few minutes. She crosses the road. One of the lovely things about the flat – and this was one of the ways in which Robert had constantly tried to quash her objections to moving there two years ago – is the fact that it is almost opposite a park. She has only to walk to the corner, cross the road and she is at the railings. Good, old-fashioned park railings, too, tall and black with a gate at each corner that is closed each evening at dusk. She hurries, now, to the nearest gate. It won't be dark for a good while yet – there is still a lot of light left in the day, and warmth with it. There are one or two people dotted about. A young couple sitting on the nearest bench. She walks quickly past, and sits down well away from them, a few benches further on.

As soon as she sits down she feels herself crumple. The tears come without warning, and she gives in to them, sobbing for a good minute or more into her palms before she can start to take control of herself. Afterwards, fumbling in her pocket for a tissue to blow her nose, she feels a little better, but so exhausted, she feels she might never get up. She leans back and closes her eyes. The blackbird they always hear from the flat is singing. She can see it – up on the chimney pot of one of the big houses facing the park.

It isn't so much the shit that has got to her. That, on its own, she could have dealt with. It's his attempt to clear up – the fact that he had known something was wrong, but not known how to fix it. He has always been such a capable man. Always with the right words ready, whatever the situation. Seeing his pathetic attempts to restore order, and the fear in his eyes. He was so utterly cut adrift.

She blows her nose again and squeezes the damp tissue into a tight ball in her hand. Shakes her head. Not a blink of recognition, she remembers, when the estate came on the news. They'd even shown the block his parents used to live in. And on the shelves above the TV, the old photo of that same building, taken in 1974, with the three of them standing smiling beside the little bronze figure who had just been installed, peeping around the outside wall of his parents' ground floor flat. Robert with one arm around each of their shoulders, his father's hand resting on the little bronze boy's head.

There will come a time, she thinks sadly, when he won't know me either.

She allows a thought to unfurl itself carefully. She is half-afraid of it, but the truth is, she needs some help. That first time they saw the specialist, after Robert's diagnosis, it had been mentioned how the disease might also affect Hope. She hadn't allowed much of what was said to penetrate at the time. She had been far too caught up in Robert and what was happening to him. Yet apparently the words had sunk in anyway.

How the slow creep of the dementia would make it more difficult for her to notice it worsening. It might be hard to recognise when you need help, the specialist had said. Because you will have managed up to now, and nothing will seem to have changed.

I do need help, she sobs now, the confession bringing back her tears. It's true. I do. The prospect of asking for it frightens her. She is still very able; she will manage at home if she has some help. But she sees that asking for any help at all, no matter how little, is the beginning of losing him. Once his care is devolved somewhere else, and her grasp on it slips. He is only going to get worse, and she is only going to grow less able to cope. There is going to be no grand reversal of fortune, no peripeteia, in this drama. She sees it all ending with him going into a home, and this she must avoid at all costs. She couldn't bear it. She knows how much he hated the idea. He'd kept his father in his own home right up until the end. Visiting him twice a day for years. Reading to him. All those books they got through together. She sighs. She has been trying to do the same with Robert, reading to him sometimes in the afternoons. But he won't settle. Unable to lose himself in a story he can't follow, he doesn't seem able to take anything else from it. She remembers him telling her how his father seemed sometimes simply to lose himself in the sound of the words. But Robert grows restless, gets up and walks around, as if he feels locked out and resentful. It stirs him up, rather than calming him. He prefers to tinker with things. She has given him old clocks to take apart. Once she gave him a cassette tape that had tangled in the works of an old tape player. She had no idea why it hadn't been thrown out years ago. He spent all afternoon at the dining table, with it spread in front of him on an opened newspaper. First pulling the yards of stuff free from the machine, and then untangling it all and spooling the coils of mangled tape back inside the plastic casing. She hadn't had the heart to throw it away after that. She still has it somewhere – stashed in a drawer. A tape of Bach's *Goldberg Variations* that they long ago replaced with a CD.

She needs to get back. She has been out too long. It is so wonderful just to sit here, listening to the blackbird. They are far enough away from the main road at the bottom of the hill that there is no traffic noise. Just the occasional bus, hauling itself up to the roundabout at the top, its engine straining. If Robert wasn't so restless, she could keep the balcony door open, and they could sit out in the wicker chairs of an evening. There is room for the two of them and it is pleasant to sit there. They used to, when they first moved. The summer before last, before all of this. Although even then, it was already happening. She thinks of it as before only because she didn't yet know about it. For him, the horror had already begun. She wonders whether it had given him any comfort, sparing her for those few more months. Or whether the agony of concealment, and the fear of what was to come, left him no room for anything else.

She stands up: it is time to go. She thinks, suddenly, of her mother as she straightens her skirt and starts to walk back down to the lower gate. She rarely thinks of her. A woman she knew for such a short time. Yet she remembers her faith. That it had seemed to offer her something. Some kind of comfort, or certainty, perhaps. A sense of solidity underpinning all of life's rampant non-sequiturs. She wishes she could believe in something other than Robert's slow decline and death, and her own powerlessness. She reaches the gate and walks back up the street, along the outside of the railings, until she is opposite her own road. She waits at the kerb, even though the road is empty of traffic. There he is, up there. She can see the end of their balcony. If he were well, and sitting out with his tea, she would be able to call and he would turn and wave to her. But she has locked him inside. How different their lives have ended up from how they might have been. And the thought of her mother disturbs her. She feels herself becoming fearful, again. Worried that if she says anything to anyone about not being able to cope, she will set some awful wheels into grinding motion that cannot be reversed and she will lose him.

An approaching car slows and beeps at her. Jolts her out of her thoughts. She gives the driver an apologetic wave and hurries across the road. At the door, she types in the code and pushes as the lock releases, noticing the change in the air as she steps inside the cool hallway.

Chapter Five – 1941

SHE started praying for the man. Daniel Riley. She couldn't stop thinking about him. He appeared in her dreams. True, she had never met him, but she knew the family a little. Will was unaware of this, because she had taken care to conceal it from him. He would try to stop her going. She had been helping out once or twice a week at the Salvation Army Mission, and Mrs Riley often came along with her grown girl in tow. She was a desperate-looking woman, older than her years, lined and sinewy from a lifetime's hard work and worry. She smoked almost continuously. The girl liked it at the mission. She looked at picture books and sometimes played by herself with some of the children's games they had there. It was one of the few places her mother could leave her on her own for a while without her getting het up and causing trouble. Mary had spoken to Mrs Riley a few times. She liked her. For all her hard-edged appearance, she was softly-spoken and kind. She had tried with the girl, too, but there was something closed about her that made Mary feel oddly self-conscious. She didn't know how to speak to a girl like that. How the mother managed to eke out her son's earnings to feed them all, she didn't know. They must barely have been managing, as it was, with so many unwaged days when the raids were bad. Now he was in hospital, it didn't bear thinking about.

Since the accident, Mrs Riley hadn't been to the mission. At first, Mary asked Will for news each evening, but questions seemed to anger him. His nerves had grown more and more jangled in the days that followed, and so she stopped asking. All he would say, in any case, was that there was no change. But the more time passed, the more concerned she grew that the family was suffering and that she ought to do something to help.

Even Hope felt her anxiety. Mary had been so careful, not saying anything to William until the child was safely in bed at night. Yet she knew. Perhaps Mrs Hayes had told her. Last night, as they knelt together at her bedside, she had offered up '...and Mr Riley,' as an addition to her usual list of people to whom God was being asked to pay special attention.

Mary tried hard not to think badly of her husband but her mind kept going back to the night he had told her about the fall. How distracted by his work he had seemed, even in the face of something so terrible. Scurrying off back to the broom cupboard of a room near the chapter house where he had his desk. His head full of those confounded drawings and calculations he was always making and remaking, trying to make sure that the recipe of manpower plus stone came out with the expected result and the tower rose at the predicted rate. It was all so much dead stuff – stones and money and paper. Did he have no feeling to spare for poor Daniel Riley?

After a full week of asking him nothing, she could stand it no longer. Hope was in bed. He was sitting at the kitchen table tapping out his pipe and refilling it as he read the paper. She saw a scene of domestic contentment, and with that thought scarcely shaped, the question was asked and everything changed.

He stood up so suddenly he tipped his chair over. Quickly she ducked behind him and set it right again.

'I cannot allow you to keep on with this,' he said. His voice was only a little above a whisper. Unnecessary noise was something Will never had been able to abide. He wore an expression of weakening self-restraint and what swirled behind it, she could see, was pure undiluted feeling. He seemed like something caged and tormented. He actually paced up and down the kitchen, before coming back and facing her. The table was between them and he placed his hands, carefully, side-by-side, palms down on the table top.

'I must insist,' he said, in the same low voice, 'that this is the last time you ask me these questions. You must not ask me again. I don't want to need to say I forbid it, but…' He lifted his palms from the table and released a long breath. 'I would like some tea,' he said. 'Upstairs.' and he went up to his study room where the desk was littered with his papers.

That night, she couldn't sleep. The more she tried, the less sleepy she felt. Yet her body was heavy with an aching weariness, and she dreaded the day to follow, if sleep wouldn't come. The night silence felt tight around her limbs, stifling her movement. Will was a light sleeper, and she knew that if she so much as sat up, let alone got out of bed to go to the window, he would stir.

Still, he was at least sleeping. Not sitting hunched over the desk in his study, or dashing out to the cathedral at the sound of planes. The planes had been over so little since Christmas, it almost seemed as if the worst was already over. Perhaps it was, and they had all survived it intact. All of them except Daniel Riley. She closed her eyes again. It was so much better not being torn every night from sleep by that ghoulish wailing from the sirens, struggling down the stairs and out into the shelter in the back garden, swaddled in blankets. He never came with them. If he wasn't running to the cathedral with his coat flapping, he would simply take to his study room and sit out the raid in there. He always dressed and put his boots on, but he refused to come inside the shelter. She, Hope and Mrs Hayes always had to sit and wait without him, praying to God that he would be safe. Hope folded inside herself in silent terror. Mrs Hayes silent, too, with her hot water bottle clutched against her chest. Mary guiltily wishing he could be an easier man to understand.

When she looked at the alternative, she could see it

was far better to have these muffled-up, quiet nights of cloud. Yet, for all that, she would have liked, at that moment, to climb out of bed and see a clear sky, a bright moon, sharp-featured and alert as a hawk. She felt closed in, as if she were struggling to breathe. She knew a few clear nights would bring more raids, but she craved the deep blue-black of a frosty sky, pinpointed with stars.

Holding her breath, she withdrew herself, limb by limb, until she was out of the bed. She picked up her slippers and crept barefoot around the bed, avoiding the creaky boards, carefully unhooking her dressing gown from the back of the door.

In the kitchen, she ran the tap and waited, thinking. If she went to the hospital tomorrow, she would be able to find out for herself how Daniel Riley was. She wouldn't need to involve Will; she could bypasss him altogether. She held a glass in the stream of water and allowed it to fill. She knew he would not want her to do this. It would make him angry. And yet, he had not actually forbidden it. It was her questions which had so incensed him. Well, if she didn't ask the questions, then she would be doing as he wished. Or at least she would not be doing what he did not wish.

She drank the water, feeling its coldness through the glass. It calmed her – trying to find the holes between his words where there was space for her to make her own decisions. He had always been a man who liked to stick close, to know where she was, what she was doing, but it was becoming something else, now. He had never before spoken to her like this. How did he dare threaten her with 'forbid'? She was only asking questions. What was happening to him that he used such words, like a weapon, against her?

She sighed as she held the glass underneath the tap and refilled it. He hadn't forbidden her from going. Well, then, she would go. She held the water up to her face and looked at it. Transparent. Her fingers gripped the other side of the glass, the pad of each of her fingertips made white with the pressure.

Thomas was exhausted. For two nights in a row he had been up on the temporary platform of the tower, firewatching. One was his own watch, but the previous night's had been Riley's. He had taken the poor lad's place quietly, without mentioning it to the rest of the men. He sensed it would be awkward to. Some of them were superstitious – or had become so, working on this great barn of a church, growing slowly taller whilst the rest of the city disintegrated at its feet. He understood their anxiety. It was true, there was something back-to-front in it. That it should continue in such rude health. It was arbitrary, of course, but some still comforted themselves with the belief that the cathedral was spared because it was a house of God. It flew in the face of reason – they had only to remember Coventry – but reason didn't concern them. Increasingly, the war seemed to bring out something more primitive. He had picked up, over the past few days, an earthier, heathen feeling in some of the men, who sensed bad luck hovering about the place, and feared it might be contagious. There were dark mutterings about which unlucky family would be following the engineer and his household, and Barker's wife and children into the grave. And which of them would be the next to fall from the tower. There were even those – he had heard them – who feared that because the cathedral didn't lie east to west as it should, its misalignment doomed it to failure. It was only a matter of time. Of course, it all boiled down to the same thing in the end: gut feeling based on nothing at all and a gnawing sense of instability. Thomas didn't himself know what he believed. Didn't care, most of the time. On the whole, he felt the world was what you saw and did, not what you believed in. Still, he had assumed no-one else would want to volunteer to sit up there through Riley's watch, blinking in the darkness, waiting, and so he had gone up himself.

Nothing happened. For most of the night the clouds had been low and fog hung over the city. He had been feeling for weeks, now, as if he were on a kind of precipice from which, if he lost his balance, he would fall into a pit of such deep exhaustion he would never be able to climb out. But there were worse ways to spend a night. After a time, the waiting and the tiredness merged into a serenity of sorts. He had come down just after five, as the fog began to lift and the river crept into view – a wide, flat stripe of grey.

Against it, the familiar skyline grew distinct and the spire of St Michael's a few streets away sharpened against the surrounding rooftops.

He didn't go home. There was a nurse, Sally, who lived not far from the cathedral. She would let him into her bed for a couple of hours. It was preferable to the walk back to Hunter Street and his empty flat. She was kind. She understood that sometimes it was just the warmth of another person he wanted. She left him sleeping when she went off to start her shift, and it was after nine o'clock when he reached the hospital himself.

Riley was just the same. Although he was sometimes awake, he had still not really regained consciousness. There were times when he seemed to be struggling to break through, but he knew nobody, said nothing. His eyes had a strange emptiness, although they followed movement. Because of his injuries, he could not sit up; he had to spend his time flat on his back. How they managed to feed him, Thomas had no idea. From what he'd seen, most of the time he just slept.

Thomas spoke to him. Told him how the watch had gone. Told him about work – the section of octagonal turret Riley had been working on before he fell was now ready for the scaffolding to be built higher and the men had moved to the opposite corner to bring that turret up to the same height. He laughed. Said with any luck the wind would be at their backs instead of in their faces as they worked, if the weather stuck. He told him about the baby one of the bricklayers' wives had just had. A little girl. Strong and doing well. Riley's eyes were mostly fixed on the ceiling, but occasionally, if Thomas leaned forwards, or creaked in his chair, they would flick sideways, before returning to their scrutiny of the stained paintwork above their heads.

She appeared just as he was thinking about leaving. Riley had drifted off to sleep, and he knew the family would be along soon. He liked to keep his visits separate, to allow them their private time with the boy. He recognised her at once: she was Jenner's wife. He had seen her before, once or twice. He couldn't remember where or when. Strange that she was here, after Jenner had taken so little interest.

She was certainly coming over to Riley's bed. The sister at the desk at the head of the ward had pointed it out to her. So she wasn't here for anyone else.

'Hello,' she said, and he noticed a slight tremor in her voice. As if she were afraid. Perhaps she was worried about seeing the injuries. But there was nothing horrible to see. All the harm was on the inside.

He stood up and offered her the chair.

'It's alright,' he said. He couldn't help noticing how she held back from the bedside. 'Really. He's sleeping now.'

She stepped closer and looked down at Riley's face. He noticed her nostrils flare briefly, and she swallowed a couple of times. Her face looked young, delicate. She couldn't have been as young as all that – she had a child older than his own daughter – but she looked it.

She was terribly nervous and her emotion seemed to be brimming over. He caught the telltale brightness in her eyes as she looked up at him, her forehead wrinkled with concern.

'Is he…? Will he…?' She couldn't say it.

'Will he live?'

She nodded.

He looked down the ward and back at her. 'I hope so,' he said.

He had been about to leave, but now she was here, he felt he ought to look out for her. Ridiculous thought, because she was a grown woman and had come here under her own steam. She was perfectly capable of managing by herself. And yet he stayed and they talked.

He couldn't make her out. When she understood that he had been there, had witnessed the actual fall, she seemed spellbound. 'Tell me,' she said, and her body seemed to ready itself, as if she would feed on the details. He felt a little repulsed. Her attention seemed too much like rapture. But he was being foolish, of course. She was terribly concerned, that was all. Tears kept threatening and the tremor in her voice grew each time she looked at the prone figure in the bed.

'How far did he fall?' she asked. Since Riley was sleeping, he drew up another chair and sat down. Again, it struck him how young she seemed. Almost like a child being told a story. Her attention to what he was telling her seemed so unabashedly eager. It was like there was some absence of lived experience which she was seeking to fill. It made him angry, all of a sudden. He wanted to shake it out of her. This is real life, he wanted to say. This man's life is destroyed, shattered. There's not a blind thing anyone can do about it. Everything's over for him. Even if he lives. Can't you see that?

But he did it gently. 'He fell a very long way,' he told her. 'His spine is damaged so he may never move any part of his body again, let alone walk. And the head injury is bad. I don't know how bad. It's nothing you can see, of course. But...' He looked at her, worried he might have gone too far. But he couldn't help wanting to jolt her out of herself. 'Brains are... well. They have to have this hard case to protect them.' He knocked his knuckles against his own head. He felt again as if he were talking to a child. 'But it's as much use as an eggshell with a fall like Dan Riley's had. Terrible things can happen inside a man's head, dropping that distance.' He stopped and looked again at the sleeping figure. He shook his head.

She said something, but her voice was low and he didn't catch it.

'What did you say?'

She looked at him and repeated what she had said. 'And a woman's,' she said quietly. 'A woman's head. Terrible things could happen to a woman, too.'

He didn't understand her. It irritated him – a foolish comment like that, as if he didn't know. What exactly did she mean by it? Her face gave nothing away. She was gazing intently at Riley again. She might have been willing him to wake, or to mend. Well, it would take more than hope and good intentions to fix what was wrong with him.

He looked at her again. She was right, of course. A woman's body would be damaged, too. Beyond repair, as Riley's most probably was. But when was a woman ever likely to go up those ladders? What was she was getting at?

He supposed she must live quite a circumscribed life. He tried to imagine it, how she passed her days, but he couldn't. Even trying to get an idea of his own wife's life was hard: he simply didn't know. It had never occurred to him to wonder. He didn't know why he was wondering now. What was it about Jenner's wife that had set him thinking this way?

'We should leave him,' he said quietly. Riley was beginning to wake, and he didn't think a stranger at the bedside would be the best thing for him. Although, probably, it would make precious little difference. Perhaps it was really Mrs Jenner he was worrying about. She might find Riley's strange detachment, his blank, untethered gaze, too distressing. And then, Riley's family would be coming along soon. He would rather not be involved in the discomfort of their all meeting in the corridor, and the necessary introductions he would have to perform. He felt unqualified to introduce Mrs Jenner to anyone else, seeing as he'd only just met her himself.

She stood up at once and followed him down the ward. The nurse gave them a curt nod as they left.

Outside the hospital, they shook hands.

'Will you be coming to see him again?' he asked. On balance, he hoped not. She had perhaps had her satisfaction, now. She had shown her pity and her curiosity was sated. He wouldn't be sorry if he didn't see her again. She had unsettled him. And he would rather visit Riley on his own. He didn't want her there, listening to him reading stuff out from the *Echo*. Some of the words he had to skip over and he didn't want her knowing that.

Something seemed to fall into place before she answered him and she relaxed a little, seemed to lighten and come into focus a little more. She nodded, pulling on her gloves. 'Yes,' she said. 'I'd like to. I feel so awful for him. And for his family. Do you think they would mind very much if I did?'

He shook his head slowly. 'No. I don't suppose they'd mind.'

Chapter Six – 2014

WHEN Carl arrives, she peers out onto the walkway, and down into the kids' playground below. It's well lit. There isn't anyone about. Across the road, once or twice, near the bin chute of one of the other blocks, she thinks maybe she has seen something. A movement, just a glimpse. But she knows she is probably being paranoid. There isn't anyone there now. She closes the door.

'I brought us a couple of cans,' he says, producing them from the plastic bag that hangs heavily from one hand. He places them carefully, side-by-side, on the table.

'Oh yeah? We celebrating?'

'As a matter of fact, yeah. We are,' he says, grinning. 'So I got you this, too.' He pulls out a bottle of rosé from the bag and sets it next to the cans. He looks at her, sheepish but proud, crumpling the empty bag into a ball and handing it to her. 'I'm back in the team,' he says. 'They said I'm fit enough, so…' He pauses, and then waltzes her around the kitchen, stumbling about between the table and worktop. She feels the handle of the fridge scrape across her back. Her feet are dangling.

'Put me down,' she says, laughing.

They look at the bottle of wine. She remembers they drank rosé the first time they went on a proper date. Back when they were still at school. Both feeling self-conscious because they'd known each other since they were kids. He'd been trying to impress her – most of her friends had been lucky to get a few swigs from a can of Strongbow on their first date.

He's brought a takeaway, too, so they sit in front of the TV with the foil trays open on the coffee table in front of them. He forks chow mein and fried rice onto plates and hands her one. The local news is on. A silent pan shot of the run-down Blackbird Estate switches to a talking head. The sound is off, but she can tell it's an impassioned outpouring from the way his mouth is moving so quickly, his forehead crinkling and uncrinkling, the edge of his gesticulating hand flicking blurrily into shot as he speaks. She unmutes the volume and catches the end of it, before he is cut short mid-flow. He's one of the leaseholders who hung on for as long as they could. He's just been evicted.

In a way, she won't be sorry to see the end of the Blackbird. She has happy memories, too, from when she was younger, but the last months after Benny left have pushed out most of the good stuff.

She glances at Carl. It's different for him. He was born there. For him, it's the whole of his childhood going. She knows he's had some stick about working on the demolition site. How could he? His old home. The kind of comments that can dig in and get to be an irritation. He's not said much about it, but she knows they have hurt him. Still, with all the time he's had off work because of his injury last year, he's lucky to have a job at all.

He unscrews the lid from the wine and pours each of them a glass. As always, his face is giving nothing away. She rubs his back. 'D'you think you'll end up actually blowing up your old block?'

He shrugs. 'They get explosives people in for that bit. We just do the donkey work before and after.'

She cuddles closer to him. 'You ok?'

'Yep.' He leans forwards for another helping of rice. The news report has finished and moved on to the weather.

She can't settle. She gets up to check on Jake. He's fine – lying in his cot with his arms flung above his head. He doesn't look like he's too worried about anything. Just to be sure, she creeps into the bedroom, pulls the curtain to one side and peers out. Nothing.

She looks at Jake's sleeping face. He won't remember those last months at the Blackbird before they got this place. In the end it was just the two of them and no-one else on the entire floor. So many people had already been moved out and rehoused, or evicted, or simply given up on the place and legged it, and there she still was, doing nothing. She had felt like she was living in limbo, waiting to have somewhere else to go, but with her arms and legs tied down so tightly she couldn't move.

It was a bad time. The place intensified every insecure feeling she had. The walkways were deserted, and at night she hadn't dared leave even a window open. There were noises – bangs and thuds deep in the fabric of the building. She couldn't tell which direction they came from, or even whether they were above or below. Everything started to feel unreal, as if she and Jake were floating in their flat untethered from the rest of the city. Like Dorothy and Toto flying up into the air in their little wooden house in The Wizard of Oz.

There were other kinds of noises, too, from the stairwell. More and more people came into the block and hung around there. Dealers, users, drifters. Howls and shrieks and scuffles. Sometimes fights broke out and there would be police sirens and shouting and people running up and down the stairs, along the walkways, past her door. She would stand tensed in the hallway listening, the sounds growing louder as they approached. She could almost feel their breath, smell the sweat as they passed on the other side of the door, inches away. Most of the empty flats had metal shutters, sealing them up against intruders, but when they were broken into, nobody did anything about it.

There were foxes, taking advantage of these new bolt-holes, ghosting along walkways and up and down the stairwell before disappearing through spaces that appeared overnight behind newly mangled shutters. Their ghoulish barking haunted the hours of darkness.

She began to imagine the place returned to nature: ivy and Russian vine twining up the banisters; squirrels rattling along shower curtain rails and pulling the stuffing out of mattresses; magpies nesting in cupboards; rats coming up from the sewers through the pipes and seething up the inside of the lift shafts like cockroaches; starlings congregating overhead at dusk and descending to carpet the roofs and walkways of the blocks with their oily iridescence, only to lift away as one at dawn, like a dark cover whisked from a birdcage. She saw mushrooms pushing up through plugholes; black mould swarming over bathroom tiles; chipboard furniture swollen with rain, doors hanging off their hinges; drifts of dead leaves in the corners of rooms concealing furled hedgehogs, hibernating dormice; woodlice hiding under damp cardboard boxes. Sycamore helicopters spiralling in and sprouting on living room carpets, buddleia growing out through glassless windows like flame.

She knew she had to do something, had to start bidding for a place to move to, but she couldn't face it. There would be endless stuff to fill in. She didn't have a computer so she would have to go down to the housing office and use one there. She would have to leave the flat. Week after week passed and she did nothing. Drawing further and further into herself. She never saw anyone any more.

One afternoon she was so disturbed by a rattling noise that kept starting and stopping that she left Jake sleeping in his cot, locked the flat, and crept up to the next floor to investigate. The noise was louder as she surfaced onto the ninth, but it was coming from higher up. As she rounded the corner on the final landing, a heady, aerosol smell drifted down to meet her, and then the unmistakeable dry hiss of spray paint. She was tempted to go back down again, she didn't want her presence in the building to be known about, but a figure moved into view, silhouetted against the skyline, and saw her.

'Hello?' he said. 'Don't be scared, please. Come and see. I'm creating a heaven up here.'

She went up the last few stairs. The aerosol smell was strong: even though they were in the semi-open air, it was trapped under the overhanging roof and it filled her head as she looked at what he was doing.

It was a picture – a dream landscape of lush vegetation, vines, vivid pink and yellow flowers of his own invention and everywhere amongst the leaves and flowers, half-hidden, were birds and animals. But although the plantlife was exotic, the creatures were not. They were the pigeons, the squirrels, the blackbirds, the foxes of the estate.

'It's lovely,' she said. There was nothing else she could say. Through the paint she could see the shape of the yellowish tiles he had sprayed over. The concrete floor was littered with coloured plastic lids and discarded spray cans. His sagging jeans, his hands, his T-shirt were flecked with colour.

'I didn't know anyone was still living up here,' she said.

He didn't say anything. Perhaps he wasn't living there. She hoped he didn't ask about her.

'Francis,' he said, and he held his hand out to her. An odd, old-fashioned gesture, but she took the proffered hand and shook it briefly. 'The pigeons, they come and chat to me sometimes,' he said, bending down and searching with his hand amongst the sea of upright and toppled cans at his feet. 'Cooing and that. They're good company, y'know?'

She nodded. 'Yeah.'

'And the foxes. There's a female I've been feeding.' He stood up straight again, a can in his hand, pushed up his beanie and shook the can experimentally next to his ear, maybe to see how much was left inside. ''Cos they need it, in the winter, don't they? Food and that.'

She nodded again. It was time to go. He didn't seem to mind. Already he was turning away from her, back to his foxes and pigeons. He was as locked away in his own world as she was becoming in hers. It was much easier to see it in someone else. Behind him was a clear view across to the City. They were above the trees here. The endless sky piled up with clouds. She said goodbye but he was shaking one of the cans energetically now and he didn't hear her. The hat was pulled down over his ears again. He was the first person she had seen, other than Jake, for weeks. Afterwards, she couldn't even be sure he had existed at all. Maybe she had imagined him. The next day she went up to the top floor again to check if she had dreamt the encounter, but the graffiti was still there, although someone had already spoilt it, spraying their name over the top in bulging, black letters, each one with a white catchlight so that they looked like letter-shaped balloons floating in front of Francis's heaven.

She got back in touch with Carl by accident. A friend of his lived in her block and she met him on the landing, staggering beneath one end of a mattress they were carrying down the stairs together. The friend had been rehoused and was moving out. Carl saw straight away she wasn't coping and started coming round quite a lot, doing bits of shopping for her, just to help out. Sometimes, Jake would be asleep in his buggy and she'd just stand on the walkway outside the flat, looking down at the buses, watching the trains on the bridge crossing over the top of them. Because there were no leaves on the trees to muffle the sound, when the wind was right she could hear the platform announcements from the station. That gave her a funny sense of having gone somewhere. The familiar place names. Most of them parts of London she'd never been to. But lots of people did go there, every day. She found it a comfort to watch the clockwork comings and goings. Everything ticking along as it should be. It was only for her that things had come to a standstill. Somehow, that made her feel better.

She had her first shag with Carl when she was fifteen. They waited until they could do it properly. Indoors, not in the faulty lift that you could jam between floors, or up against the wall of one of the empty garages. And then, just after they'd left school, she met someone else and Carl was dropped. The someone else was a mistake, of course, and plenty of others followed. Benny had been the last in a long line.

When, finally, she was able to face things enough to make a rehousing application, something came free in her and she saw what she hadn't known was there. She was still in the habit of loss – the assumption that things would be better if what was gone could be brought back. What she hadn't seen coming was the feeling that she didn't actually want Benny to come back, and she didn't want to live on the Blackbird any more either. Now she realised it had been staring her in the face for weeks, trying to catch her eye.

The morning after she and Carl slept together for the first time since they were kids, she was offered one of the flats she'd bidded for. It wasn't the one she'd wanted, but it was ok. And now, here they were.

She straightens the curtain and dims the nightlight. Why won't Benny leave her alone? Today's visit must have been the fourth or fifth time he's been back, and his tone was different. Maybe he's figured out that saying he's sorry, saying he loves her, saying he's changed isn't working, no matter how much he means it. He has started getting angry. Frustrated because she won't believe him. He can't see that believing him isn't the issue: what matters is that none of it makes any difference.

This afternoon, for the first time, she was frightened. What of, she doesn't know. He is a coward, always has been. Although she's starting to think there's more to it than just the fear of seeing things through. It's as if, deep down, he actually can't feel things at all. As if, at the root of him, something has been cauterised, and the passions and currents blowing around at the surface are all there is. Maybe it's the emptiness underneath that he's been trying to run away from.

She knows he won't do anything. First sign of any kind of hardship or accountability and he'll go to ground. Run off home to his mother. His problem is that he's never properly cut away from her. Has never needed to stay put and take what's coming because he has no other choice.

His current obsession will run its course, she's sure of it. And then he'll disappear again. There's no way he'll do any of the things he started threatening her with today. He hasn't any rights over Jake. It's all just hot air. Throwing his weight around. He likes the drama, the show of a fight, but he hasn't got the guts for it.

Nevertheless, she doesn't like this new tack he's been pursuing. It makes her uneasy. Even if it is all bluff and bullshit, and he doesn't really know anything more about his rights than she does, it's unsettled her.

She goes back into the sitting room and stands, indecisively, halfway to the sofa.

'What's up?' Carl asks.

She's told him, of course, that Benny's been back. But she hasn't said how many times. She doesn't want to make it into something it isn't.

'Come on,' he says. 'You've hardly eaten anything. It's gone cold now.'

She sits next to him on the sofa and buries her face against his shoulder. 'I'm not that hungry,' she says. 'Sorry.'

'Hey,' he says. 'Jakey will be ok, you know. It's not like he's going to be left with strangers, is it?'

She smiles. He thinks she's worried about leaving Jake with her mum when she starts doing some hours the care agency's offered her, after the weekend. Just in the mornings, but it's a big step, to leave him with someone else. He's probably right. Part of her anxiety about Benny is probably down to the new job and leaving Jake.

'He'll be fine,' he says again.

She nods. Takes a breath. 'Benny's been back again.'

Carl sits up then. He picks up the TV remote and mutes the volume.

She tells him about the visits – this afternoon's, and the rest. About how, each time, she has told him to leave them alone. And how he's been hanging around afterwards, not going away. She's seen him sitting in the kids' playground with his hands in his pockets, at least an hour later. And since last week, she doesn't know whether she's being paranoid or not, but she keeps thinking she's seen him, lurking around the place. Not even coming to the door any more, but just hanging around, watching.

'Where?' he asks.

'Oh, anywhere. In the trees, a few times, when it's been getting dark. And yesterday, I swear he was on one of the walkways opposite. It's like he's watching us. Waiting.'

'Was it definitely him?'

'I don't know. I think so.'

'What did he do when he saw you?'

'I don't know. I just peeked out the kitchen window, and when I saw him I went and turned the light off. When I came back, he'd gone.'

'Why don't you come and stay at mine for a bit? Not forever, if you don't want, but just till he gets the message?'

She sighs. 'That would be like giving in, though, wouldn't it?'

He shrugs. 'Dunno. Maybe. I can stay tonight, if you like.'

Chapter Seven – 1941

THERE was a knock at the door. Jenner lifted his head and waited for whoever it was to come in. A knock was just a formality; everyone knew that. But the door stayed closed. 'For God's sake, man,' he shouted out. 'Come on in, if you're coming.'

Slowly, the door opened. It was Shaw. His spirits sagged. He was too weary to have to deal with Shaw. At the same time, Jenner felt himself tighten. This fellow was more than intelligent enough to know he needn't stand on ceremony and wait until he was invited in, but there was impudence enough in the man too, to hold to his own rank, to put on show the kind of pride so many of the masons excelled in – a sort of held-apartness, as if to say they knew themselves better than their superiors but were keeping mum about it. He had seen it again and again when he was a young mason himself. He suspected Shaw used it to get the men on his side, to get them to trust him. There was no denying he had the common touch.

Jenner straightened up in his chair, feeling the

stiffness in his shoulders. He'd had precious little sleep for the past three nights. The raids had been bad. He had been here all last night, and most of the two nights before. He noticed that Shaw, too, had a heaviness about him, and a darkness around the eyes. He had probably been firewatching.

'So,' he said, eager to get the interview over with. 'What can I do for you?'

'Oh, nothing, exactly,' Shaw said, coming into the room only far enough to be able to close the door behind him. He seemed, on principal, to have decided never to enter a room as if he expected to be invited to sit down.

'For God's sake, man, come in properly, can't you? And sit or stand as you like.'

Shaw took a few more paces into the room.

'Well, what is it? What do you want?' Jenner was too tired to control his irritation. He wanted the man gone.

'I've a bit of news about Danny Riley, sir,' Shaw said. 'I thought you might want to know. I can, er…' He took a deliberate step backwards, towards the door. 'I can come back later, if you're too busy now.' But he wasn't fooling Jenner, who knew he hadn't an ounce of respect for him.

'No, now is fine. Go ahead.'

'Well, sir. I'm afraid the news isn't good for him. The doctors reckon he won't make it. Not after so many weeks with no change.'

Jenner frowned.

'They don't think he's going to live,' Shaw said, slowly and clearly.

'I understood you well enough,' he snapped. 'And is that all?' Jenner could feel the irritation rising in his throat.

'Yes, that's all,' he said. 'Thank you, sir.' He turned to go, and then turned back, as if he had remembered something else. 'I expect Mrs Jenner will be feeling pretty cut up about the news,' he said.

Jenner had already begun shuffling the papers on his desk, but he looked up at this. 'Meaning what?' he said.

Shaw cut him a quick glance. 'Meaning what I say,' he said. 'She's got quite fond of the lad, lately. I…'

Jenner saw the man look at him again as his words petered out. He knew he'd misjudged something and Jenner thought he saw a shadow of fear in his eyes. Just for a moment, he almost felt sorry for him in his blunder. But then his perception righted itself. No doubt Shaw would soon be regaling the workers with tales of how he, Jenner, didn't know what his wife was up to.

He kept his voice level. 'She has been visiting the hospital, then?'

Shaw nodded. 'She has, sir.'

'For Christ's sake, man. Will you sit down.'

Shaw walked back into the room and sat on the edge of the chair, leaning forwards slightly, his knees wide, like props. He was a solid, well-built, man, but he had an elegance of sorts: his unhurried movements were considered rather than clumsy.

Jenner cleared his throat. 'I knew, of course, that she wished to visit. It's…' He looked up. 'Well, as I have no time to go myself, it's…'

'She can report back, sir. On his progress, like.'

'Quite.'

The interview ended soon afterwards. When Shaw had gone, Jenner stood in front of his desk, looking at the strewn papers he had been working on. For a moment he couldn't recognise them. They might as well be the scrawlings of a lunatic. He felt himself sinking into a mire of figures and plans. No matter how neatly executed, how precisely worked out each drawing was, none of them could be held stable. Every day something changed and the plans had to be redrafted. What should have been a harmonious whole listed impossibly, first one way, then the other. Less than a year ago, there had been no stone because of delays at the quarry. Now, there was scarcely room to move anywhere there were so many pieces of stone blocking the way, waiting to be lifted up the tower and fixed into place. And every day's work they lost to this latest spate of raids only seemed to deepen the mire. Added to which, every night's rest that was lost, the more unreal the thing became, until the very idea of trying to build a cathedral tower in the middle of a city at war seemed ludicrous. He felt he had made an error of judgement in coming to this place at all. For a moment, as he stood, with his back turned on his work, he recalled his earlier life, now lost forever. Had he not been lured by the jewel of being involved in such a great project, he might be in Derby yet. Perhaps he had done wrong, bringing Mary here. Taking her from her family, forcing their child to be born in a city where her parents were strangers. Perhaps, in his ambitious striving, he had overreached himself. And now, with Caldwell on leave of absence, he was doing the job of two men.

He turned back to the desk, to the chaos of papers he needed to deal with. The raids might go on for weeks. There was no knowing. He sank into the chair he had bullied Shaw into occupying, and stared at the desk. It all seemed futile. He had no control over any of it, try as he might. And now his foolish wife had taken things into her own hands, going off visiting that boy in the hospital. What was she thinking? Why waste her time? He was dying in any case. She could do nothing for him. He took a deep breath and held it, lacing his fingers together and pressing them against his lips, as if in prayer. He felt everything was falling away from him. The tower might never be completed. The whole building could be turned to dust and rubble overnight. His wife would not keep to the house, but went wandering about the city visiting strange men in their hospital beds. And he himself couldn't be trusted to know his own mind. He tortured himself daily, now, over what had happened on the day of the accident. He had never known himself anything other than in full possession of his faculties. He didn't understand how he could have failed himself that day, failed to see how Shaw was working him, steering him where he wanted him to go. With such disastrous consequences. It terrified him. And he hated the complicity he felt. He wanted nothing to do with the man, and yet he couldn't escape what they had, together, caused to happen. It angered him, too, that Thomas Shaw seemed unconcerned on this score. Yes, of course, he gave a good show of things – visiting the boy in the hospital, bringing back reports. But where was his sense of his own culpability? It seemed he was untroubled by it.

He took her by surprise. Mary was getting herself ready to go out. She had her coat on and was checking herself in the hall mirror as he opened the door.

She looked horrorstruck. 'Is there a problem?' she whispered. 'Has something happened?' Her pale face, so ready to receive catastrophe. She had such a tendency to be drawn towards the negative, as if suffering were a necessary part of life.

'I don't know,' he said, closing the door behind him and standing in front of it. He felt he filled the narrow hallway, barring her escape, frightening her. The words came out blunt and harsh: 'You tell me. Is there a problem?'

Her mouth fell stupidly open. Her dark eyebrows pulled tightly together. The picture of innocence. 'I... I'm not sure I...'

'Don't play games, Mary,' he said. 'I know where you're getting yourself ready to go to.' As he spoke, he felt an odd mixture of anger and weariness.

Did he really need to come home when he'd been at work barely an hour to set her straight about her conduct? Was she really so naïve that she couldn't see it for herself?

'Will, I'm not at all sure I know what you're –'

'– So, you're going to deny it, are you? Play the innocent?'

She took a step backwards, away from him. It fuelled his growing anger. How dare she act as if she feared him.

'Are you?' he asked again.

'What am I to deny or confirm, Will? It's hardly fair to accuse me without telling me first what I'm accused of.' Her voice was low and calm, as ever. You had to concentrate, always, to hear what she was saying.

'Oh, you know,' he laughed. 'You aren't so very foolish, are you?'

She shook her head, tears starting into her eyes. She had it off pat, this act of hers. And yet. She did look genuine, the alarm in her eyes seeming to strip her face bare. He felt a pang of remorse and put out his hand to her, took her by the shoulder, and steered her down the few steps back into the kitchen. The lunch plates were set out on the table, and everything was laid ready for their midday meal, but it wasn't yet ten o'clock. She caught his eye. There was the gleam of fear again. He must try to be firm yet gentle. But here was the proof: she had planned her day around it. His ebbing anger paused and started to build again at the sight of such blatant intention to go against his wishes.

'I know about your visits to the hospital,' he said.

Her face seemed to close itself up, without changing at all. How frustrated it made him feel. This constant refusal to speak to him directly about what she was thinking. All of herself kept locked away from him. Sometimes he felt they were complete strangers to each other. And yet they had been married nearly ten years. They had a child together. Why must her God be her only confidante? And the child. He knew she talked to the child. Why not him? Why did she push him away? It was since they had come here she had been like this. Since the child had been born. Why had everything changed?

She nodded. 'Yes,' she whispered. 'I have been to see Mr Riley. I wanted to find out how he was. I couldn't stop thinking… And you…' She looked up at him, accusing. 'You wouldn't tell me.'

'Wouldn't tell you?' He pulled out a chair and sat in it heavily. 'Did you ask?' She nodded. He waved it away. 'I told you what I knew. The boy was badly injured. What else was there to say?'

'You told me nothing. I wanted to find out for myself.'

'You had no right,' he said. 'Not without consulting me first.'

'I don't see why not.'

He shook his head. What had got into her? She never normally spoke against him.

'For Christ's sake,' he said. 'You consult me first, and that's the end of it.'

She looked at him. That blank, closed look again. It frightened him.

'Anyway,' he said. 'Why waste your time on him? There's nothing anyone can do. It's tragic, I'll give you that. But these things happen. He has his family. You're not needed.'

'I wanted to see him.'

'Well, you've seen him. More than once, from what I've been told. You won't be needing to see him again.'

She didn't say anything.

'Do you hear me?'

She nodded.

'Look,' he said. 'I don't know what you're playing at. It's all very noble, very decent, I'm sure, but it's not wanted. Not by anyone. You needn't think the family appreciate it. They'd rather you left them to their misery. Believe me. They don't like us here. They won't want you poking your nose in.' He paused.

'How do you think I feel, finding out from another man that he's been meeting my wife at the hospital? And what the bloody hell do you think you're you playing at, meeting a man there, in the first place? '

'If you are talking about Mr Shaw, I can hardly avoid seeing him,' she said, 'since he also visits Mr Riley.'

'Of course I'm talking about Shaw,' he snapped. 'Who the hell else would I be talking about? And if he's skipping off there all the time, then all the more reason for you not to go again.'

'Why?'

'Why? For God's sake, woman!' He stood up. He

felt a sudden impulse to violence. He wanted to shake some sense into her. Cram some understanding into her naïve little fantasy of how real life worked. Did she not know what people would think? Did she not know what men were like? That man, in particular? He didn't listen to the gossip as closely as others might, but he'd heard enough. And he knew from his own experience: Shaw wasn't to be trusted. He would talk her into all sorts of things.

She sat there, still and silent, as he stared down at her bowed head, the wisps of hair at the back of her neck. His whole body was tensed as if waiting to dodge a blow. He felt the twinge of fear again. What was she doing to him? It hadn't occurred to him that she might take matters into her own hands in this way. Not without his knowing about it. What sensible married woman would make arrangements to meet another man in public without her husband's knowledge? What had she been thinking? Surely it was reasonable of him to expect that much. If she couldn't understand the world, couldn't see the results of her actions, of the inferences that would be made, and the laughing stock that he himself would become, then he would have to take control and do something to stop it. Suddenly, he could see the possibilities and passions in her, stretching towards the future like a series of cracks across damaged masonry. Haphazard and unpredictable, zigzagging outwards in all sorts of sickening directions at once. Utterly unstable. If she could do this without his knowing, what else might she do?

Was there to be anything left in his life that remained under his control?

'I forbid you,' he said at last. Calmer now, allowing his fists, his jaw to unclench, his stalled breath to release. Stepping away from her, his voice level. 'I forbid you from making any more visits to the hospital. I forbid it.'

When he was gone, she removed her coat and hat, and took off her good shoes. She put on her apron again and the shoes she wore around the house. She would not be visiting the hospital today. She tied the apron in a neat, tight bow.

The air raids had started up again, and they had spent the last couple of nights in the Andersen shelter. Mary wished he would come with them. She had a horror of pushing open the little door when the bombardments were over, and finding the place where the house should be filled with air and a clear view out to the street in front. He wouldn't come, even though he knew he tortured her. It was pointless, he explained, in his measured, scientific way. As if he had no feelings about it at all. A shelter offered no more protection than a house if there was a direct hit. He would rather take his chance in comfort. And there he sat, in his study. It was impossible to sleep through a raid, and surely just as impossible to work. But he sat there, at his desk, with his papers spread before him, nonetheless. Making his point, and declining to help as she bundled their bleary child down the stairs and out into the earth-smelling darkness.

She thought there was a chance Mrs Hayes might not have heard Will's raised voice. She was a little deaf, and kept her radio on during the day, with the volume turned up. Mary was used to the muffled voices and threads of song drifting up from the basement rooms. But she only half cared what Mrs Hayes had heard. Really, it mattered very little. She crept down the stairs to the basement anyway, to check she was alright as much as anything. The radio was switched on, but Mrs Hayes was asleep in her chair, a blanket over her knees. There was a low fire in the grate. Mary pulled the door almost closed so that she wouldn't disturb her: sleep was a valuable commodity. She envied the old woman her ability to rest.

She tiptoed back up the stairs and out into the garden. It was cold, but inside the shelter there was some residual warmth from the paraffin heater they had kept burning through the night. The bombs had been falling until around four, the drone of the planes sometimes subsiding, only to return, throbbing overhead, bringing the dull thunder of explosions closer again. The old woman always lay curled under her blankets on the lower bunk in a kind of mindless, inert terror while it was happening. She never seemed to get any more used to it. She was more childlike than Hope, in that respect. Mary and Hope pressed themselves together on the higher bunk, on the damp, narrow mattress. When the all-clear sounded, they had crept back to the house and managed a few hours' sleep. It saddened her that Hope had to be moved again, when she'd had so little rest. It was almost tempting to let her stay where she was. She always looked so pale, hunched inside her eiderdown, shuffling back to the house in a dream. But the air in the shelter was heavy with mould. It wasn't healthy for a child to stay there any longer than was necessary.

She sometimes felt that Will was entirely unsuited to family life. He was so shut inside his own thinking he didn't see how it affected them all. It didn't occur to him that he might carry Hope inside so that she wouldn't have to wake up. He should have stayed a bachelor. She wondered why he had wanted to marry her, why he had ever thought it was something he needed to do. But then, she remembered the young man she had bathed every evening in the little home they had in Derby. His need to be with her, to know how she had spent her day. He had never been able to exist without an anchor. When his mother was lost to him, he had been untethered for a long while, but he had met Mary when he was still young, and had latched himself onto her with the ferocity of a hungry child. Beneath all the ambition and the extra responsibility he now had, perhaps he hadn't changed so very much after all. Maybe she was still his anchorage.

Slowly, she pulled the sleeping bags off the two bunks and carried them back up the steps into her own kitchen to hang on the sheila maid. They would lose their dampness with the heat from the fire, and be dry by the time she needed to carry them out again, ready for another night. Then she dragged the two mattresses from the wooden bedframe and pulled them outside. They were too thin to be heavy, but they were unwieldy. She tried not to snag them against the sharp edge of the door as she pushed them up the ladder ahead of her, onto the grass. There wasn't much heat in the sun, but at least they would get an airing.

She went back into the shelter and sat down for a moment on the narrow plank bench that faced the two bunks, her knees almost touching the lower platform. So, he had forbidden her from going to the hospital. Carefully, she unscrewed the paraffin lamp and detached the canister. It was almost empty.

She picked up the paraffin bottle and, though she put her hand on the stopper, didn't immediately pull it loose. She allowed her thoughts a little room to grow. Would she obey him? Would she stop visiting Daniel Riley? She closed her eyes. For a moment, she felt she might sleep. If she stayed absolutely still, just as she was, and stopped her thoughts from tramping on ahead of her. But they wouldn't stop. She saw the lad's face. The closed eyes, the chin sunk down into his neck, when it ought to be standing out, proud and strong. He was twenty-two years old. Only a little older than Will had been when she first met him. She wondered who washed him. The nurses, probably. He always looked freshly shaved. And a little dark dimple in his chin, where the razor didn't reach. Slowly, she opened the bottle and topped up the lamp, filling the paraffin chamber almost to the brim before poking the rope of wick back into the liquid and screwing it all back together.

If she didn't visit again, what would it matter? She wasn't needed; she wouldn't be missed. Her husband was right, there. Maybe it would be better if she stayed away. But the image of the poor boy's thin face rose up again. Not to go would be like an abandonment of hope.

She would miss seeing Thomas, too. She could admit it to herself here, alone. It surprised her – she had been so focused on Riley. Quickly, she reckoned up the duration of their – what was it? Could she even call it a friendship? She had been visiting for three, almost four weeks. She never went at the weekends, it was true, but even so, she went every week day, and Thomas was there more often than not. Because of all the delays with the building work, he was barely needed at the cathedral during the day. Was a month enough for someone to become a friend? Often, he would leave when she did, and they would walk together through the hospital corridors, winding their way back to the entrance. She didn't hurry away; she enjoyed their slow amble. They talked, that was all. She had learned more about the tower in the past few weeks than she ever had from her husband. Thomas told her what it felt like to be up there, raised above the city, on a level with the birds. He made it real, as Will had never tried to. She could picture him, covered in stone dust, precarious yet sure. He had that contradiction in him. She had only ever touched him to shake him by the hand, but she had an immediate sensation of mass, of weight. So much more solid than Will. And with his direct way of speaking, there was something absolutely definite about him, yet he had lightness, unexpectedness, too. He could conjure a joke from nowhere, like twisting paper flowers from bits of newsprint, and just as easily, he could walk two hundred feet in the air, and be as nimble and sure-footed as a dancer. When she shook his hand, she noticed how calloused it felt, how scarred both of them were compared with her husband's. Will was physically so much finer. His narrow frame, his smooth, pale skin. And such precise, long-fingered hands. The hands of an artist. He had, in the early days, before they were married, drawn some very good pencil portraits of her. He had a strong eye for the chiaroscuro effects he could achieve and would arrange her always so the light fell across her, leaving pools of shadow, which he would render in the minutest cross-hatching. Looked at up close, his work was as precise as an etcher's engraving. He didn't draw any more. Not like that. His only outlet was the interminable diagrams of the half-built tower, which tortured him more than anything else, with their fitness for nothing but function.

Yes, she could see that Thomas had his own gift for fineness of a sort. It might not be as visible, but it was there. Up on the tower, he had told her, he could smell the sea when the wind came in from the river, and could tell which way the weather was tending. He knew of a pair of blackbirds nesting in the shelter of a window ledge hemmed in by scaffolding, and had carried up worms in a tobacco tin for them to feed to their hatchlings. He could identify birds – even the uncommon ones – simply by hearing their calls, having learnt how to do this as a boy. He had told her that blackbirds mated for life.

She kept a box of matches in an airtight jar. She had made it a handle of string and it dangled from one of the hooks she'd fashioned from bits of wire and attached to the bolts that held the shelter's corrugated ceiling in place. She took it down and unscrewed the lid, feeling the matchbox for signs of damp. The matches wouldn't light if they weren't dry, and she had taken to swapping them each day with a fresh box from the kitchen, for fear of the darkness and cold they would have to endure if the matches failed them. They seemed good enough, but she slipped the box into her apron pocket automatically, and exchanged it for the one she had brought with her.

She was starting to feel cold. The shelter smelled of soil and grass and damp, overlaid with the tang of the paraffin. Yet she couldn't quite make herself get up and leave. The smallness, the gloom, was consoling, in its way. Although she was sitting upright on a hard, wooden bench, she felt calm and absolved. As if she had been taken away from herself.

Step outside, and she would have to face her decision. Stay a while longer, and she could simply think.

Having summoned Thomas, she realised she wasn't

quite ready to shake him away. She hadn't realised how much she had been watching him. She surprised herself at how readily she could picture him. His broad shoulders, the weathered skin which was so much darker and coarser than her husband's. The reddish-brown hollow of his throat. She knew the way he moved, the slight catch in his voice at certain words, and the funny lopsided lilt of his accent, and all of it gave her more pleasure than she could admit, even to herself. She saw that she had been conscious of the male in him all along, without really knowing it.

She sighed and stood up, being careful not to catch her head on the sloping sides of the metal roof. Ought she to feel guilty? Had she gone too far in getting to know another man? She had done nothing, yet had she overstepped the boundary? She sat down again and didn't know.

Will was frightened of him. Whether it was because of what he might do, or what he might make her want to do, she wasn't sure. He said Thomas had a reputation. Well, she didn't know about that, but she understood something about the forces that might drive him. Will was a man in that way, too, sometimes, and when desire stole over him, he was in its grip. His grimacing, agonised face above hers, as if he were fighting his way through a wall of thorns. Eyes clamped shut as he ground into her, hating his own need, refusing to see the act they were performing together.

She opened her eyes. She didn't want to think about it any more. She stood up and emerged in a stoop from the doorway, blinking in the light. She looked up at the sky. It didn't look as if it would rain. The mattresses could stay outside for now. She propped the door wide open with a half brick, to allow the air to circulate, and clambered up the ladder.

Chapter Eight – 2014

SHE has helped him into his best trousers and a new shirt, ready for when the new person arrives. She is called Louise – that's all she knows. She has told him, of course. Yesterday, at teatime, she announced they'd be having a visitor today. She'd rather have left it until this morning, to save him being anxious about it overnight, but she knows from experience that the longer he has to get used to an idea, the more calmly he tends to take it. The information seems to lodge somewhere and bed itself in, so he's better prepared, even when he swears blind he hasn't been told anything.

Now that Hope has started down this route, she feels desperate for the help. She prays there won't be any problems. Louise is coming to help her in the mornings, and then there will be someone called Grace to help with putting Robert to bed. And at weekends they will have Ola on Saturdays, Bridget on Sundays. It's a lot of new faces for him to get used to all at once. They haven't met any of them yet. Louise is the first.

She is conscientiously punctual. A good start. Hope doesn't like people to be late, but neither does she appreciate it when they arrive much too early. It isn't necessary. And there are those who pride themselves a little too keenly on that sort of thing. She is glad Louise isn't like that. She shows the young woman into the sitting room and introduces her to Robert.

Robert is too busy examining his shirt cuff to notice their visitor at first. Hope can see a bit of cotton hanging from the button, where he's been pulling at it and made it come loose. With any luck, the button won't drop off until Louise has gone.

She is young. Pretty. Something serious about her, too. Hope watches through the serving hatch as the kettle boils, noticing how gently and unobtrusively she makes her presence known to Robert. He has stopped fiddling with his cuff and is holding out his hand to her, showing her the button, the loose thread, the nice shirt he is wearing. 'Bought it in Edinburgh,' she can hear him saying. 'Last summer. Do you get up to the festival much?'

They last went to Edinburgh more than twenty years ago. He's right about the shirt, though. They had bought him a shirt. She remembers it very well. For some reason they hadn't enjoyed Edinburgh very much that last time. Perhaps they were beginning to feel too old for it. Too out of touch. Anyway, whatever it was, he'd had the wonderful idea that they should jolly themselves up a bit and spend their last afternoon choosing each other a present. He had bought her a silver charm in the shape of a tiny bird with a worm in its beak – she still has it somewhere – and she had bought him a lovely shirt. Not this one though. The Edinburgh shirt is long gone. This is one she bought in BHS.

Well no, says Louise. She hasn't actually ever been to Scotland though she hears it's beautiful and she'd love to go. But she has been to Wales a couple of times, she says, and she starts telling him about the places she remembers. Seaside towns he might have heard of. Staying in a caravan with a leaky roof.

Hope likes her already. She can see how gently she is taking things. Putting Robert at his ease. Letting him know she is listening to him. Giving him time. It's a mothering skill, she thinks. Maybe that's why I'm not getting it right. I've never done it. I bet she has a child. She puts the teapot and cups on a tray which she carries carefully into the next room. She's feeling guilty again for that time she ran away and left him on his own. A mother would never have done that.

She pours out the tea and hands a cup to Louise. 'You seem to be getting along very well together,' she says.

Louise smiles. 'Robert was just telling me about your trip to Edinburgh.'

She seems trustworthy. Hope tests herself. If she had to, would she leave him with her, now, right away? If she had to – called away on some fictitious emergency. She imagines herself leaving the flat, saying goodbye to the young woman at the door and letting it close behind her. It is a strange feeling. She looks at Robert. He seems to be taking things fine. He is sitting back comfortably. His hands are still going, roving about as they always do, picking at his cuffs and fiddling at the piping around the arms of the sofa. The habit has become so ingrained his hands have become like separate entities. She sees him, sometimes, watching them as they jump about, with the intensity of a naturalist observing some minutiae of the animal kingdom, and she wonders whether he still understands that they are attached to him. But now, apart from his hands, he seems to be relaxed. Usually, if a stranger comes into the flat, he won't settle. He'll stand near a wall, as if he fears an earthquake is imminent, from which he'll need to take shelter. Or he paces, in his weaving, tottery fashion. Louise seems to have won him over straight away. Miraculously.

Hope mentions this. Louise smiles. She has a lovely, open face. Friendly and interested. It's nice to be smiled at. Hope can't remember the last time. She feels her eyes washing over with tears. It's relief, as much as anything, that she isn't going to be so alone with him from now on.

Louise asks about the photograph on the shelves above the TV. 'It's the estate I used to live on,' she says. 'The Blackbird. That block is Ashendene House, right? I recognise the little statue. There was another one sitting on a wall. They got nicked a few years back, though.'

What a funny, surprising world it is, Hope thinks. How often it happens that total strangers have some common thread. And she wonders whether it is the connection that draws them together – invisible wires, each exerting a pull until they are brought within range of each other. Or whether it is just part of the pattern. The small, arbitrary connections happening by chance, tiny spots of colour standing out from the grey weave of existence. Once, many years ago, she and Robert had holidayed in Brittany, and met a couple there who had taken the woman's elderly mother on holiday with them. The old lady turned out to have grown up in Robert's childhood home. And so, two strangers discovered they had been born in the same house, in the same room, fifty years apart. It was the highlight of the holiday.

'Yes,' she says. 'Robert was very upset when they were stolen. He made them, you see.'

She takes the photograph down from the shelf and hands it to Louise. Points out Robert and his parents, and the window of his parents' flat, behind them. They look at it together. Robert shuffles over, too, to see what they are looking at. He was such a tall, handsome man, then, with his unruly hair flopping over his face. So much of it and so dark. She looks at him now, his shoulders curving around the hollow of his chest. His hair still thick, but all grey now, and kept short, so that it's easier for her to wash.

Louise peers into the frame. 'That's so weird,' she says. 'I used to play around on that patch of grass when I was a kid. We all did, because of the statues.' She looks at Robert. 'I thought they were wonderful,' she tells him, and there is a wobble in her voice, as if she really means it. 'I was really sad when they were stolen.' She shrugs her shoulders. 'It was kind of like the beginning of the end, wasn't it? Everyone gave up on the place after that.'

Hope nods, smiles. 'He would have liked that, Robert's dad,' she says. 'Kids playing outside. He didn't go out very much.' She sits down opposite Louise again. 'He had a head injury,' she says. 'His life was pretty limited. But he would have liked to hear children playing.' She glances across at Robert. 'He was so worried about his father. He absolutely insisted his parents move, so that they would be near enough for him to go and see them every day and help his mother look after him.' She shakes her head, and the tears that threatened earlier, start their stinging at the back of her eyes again. 'It broke his heart, what happened to his father. He lost all his language. And then, when it started to come back, all the connections were damaged. He had the words, but he couldn't match them up with what they meant.' She gives a small, defeated laugh and looks up at Louise. 'And now Robert's no better off than his father was. It's cruel, isn't it?'

Robert had devoted himself to his father. The head injury reversed their roles: his father became the dependent child and Robert the provider. Bringing the newspaper every day and reading out loud to him. What was going on in the world, film and theatre reviews, incomprehensible articles in the finance

section. It didn't matter what it was – all of it was meaningless to his father. He would simply turn the pages, enjoying the thinness of the paper, the rustling noise it made, and the smell of newsprint. His memory might have been damaged but his senses were undimmed. If anything, they were sharper than ever. He seemed hungry for sensation, his eyes scanning the movement as each page was turned and came to rest, watching as his fingers skated across the print. Feeling the rough texture of the paper against his skin. And then something would catch his eye, and whatever it was, he would point to it and Robert would read it. They never discussed what was read – neither Robert offering nor his father asking for clarification. Robert had known the words mostly washed over him. But he enjoyed it anyway. The occasional times Hope had been there too, she had seen that. The affection in the old man's eyes, mingled with a sort of wonder, as he sat in his chair and listened to his son's voice.

The seven *Hide and Seek* figures – dotted around amongst the trees in the wooded areas at the heart of the estate – had been Robert's last piece of public art. There had been a whole series of commissions for housing estates before then, after he'd won an award for a piece he'd done for an estate in Wakefield. *The Alley Alley Oh*. A loop of children with linked hands, threading themselves underneath the arm of the child on the end, who had made an arch against the wall. Kids played games like that then, though they don't seem to any more. There was one in Stockport, of two children on a roundabout. One of them sitting, the other in a running posture, pushing it round as fast as he can, so that the pullover tied around his waist flies out behind him. The people on the estate used it as a bench to stop and chat. And Hope had always liked the one he made for an estate in Barnet, of two boys arguing over a game of conkers. The figures were always life-size, and Robert liked it when people sent him photographs of their families and neighbours living their lives around them. He didn't want them set apart or on plinths – he liked it if kids climbed on them or used them in games. For him, it was a measure of their success. But by the mid-seventies, council estates weren't being built any more, and he didn't fancy the idea of his work ending up in shopping centres and corporate lobbies so he had simply stopped, despite the offers that kept coming for private commissions.

Instead, he started working with people like his dad. Helping them find a route back into language. With some of them, it had helped. Slowly, the separate worlds of objects and words reconnected. But with his father, they never did. He had spent hours with him every day. He was convinced they could retrieve something. The links were still there, he said. The wrong words weren't so far away from the right ones. His father's under-standing wasn't completely gone. He made flashcards at home in the evenings – cutting pictures of fruit and vegetables, items of clothing, common garden birds, out of magazines and gluing them onto index cards. It had all made little difference.

'Do you have any children, you and Robert?' Louise asks. She has been talking a little about herself – about what it was like before she left the Blackbird. The isolation, the lack of heating and water. The rubbish everywhere, and the noises at night. Trying not to say too much about how difficult it all was, but she has clearly had a tough time, living through the slow dereliction of her home. Robert has got up from the sofa and is looking at the spines of the books on the bookshelf. He often does this, for an hour at a time. As if he is looking for a particular book and can't find it.

'No.' Hope shakes her head slowly. 'I don't know why not. We never decided not to.' She looks into the younger woman's face. 'But I don't know whether I would have been very good at it, you know. Being a mother. If it had happened.' She remembers, again, her shameful flight after the toilet incident. It comes back in fragments. The sound of the bus pulling up the hill. The long, burbling skein of blackbird song as she sat on the bench with her head in her hands. And the sight of her own two feet, poised at the very edge of the kerb, ready to cross. Rooted there, until the blare of a car's horn seemed to take her by the ears and drag her back into the moment and the terribleness of having left him in the flat, alone.

Of course, he had been perfectly alright. When she got back, he was sitting exactly as she had left him. He hadn't so much as lifted his teacup. She had plugged the kettle and toaster back in, and taken the key for the balcony door back out of the pot on the windowsill.

Louise uncrosses her legs and puts her empty cup back on the tray. Oh, 'I dunno. I think, when it happens, you just try and cope the best you can. I don't know whether anyone's good or bad at it. It's like how you've been managing with Robert, I suppose.' She pauses, twists her earring round in her ear. 'I was terrified when Jake was born, when he was handed to me, as if I knew what to do with him. I still get terrified, sometimes.'

She looks over at Robert, who has sat down again and started fiddling with the TV remote control. The back has come off, and he is trying to get the batteries out. She moves closer to him and watches him do it. When he has taken both batteries out, he tries to get them back in again, but he can't. He holds the contraption out to her.

'Maybe the other way around,' she says, taking the battery that's poking out and turning it round before giving it back. 'Try that.'

He gets it back in. And he's so pleased to have done it, that he allows Louise to slide the cover back on for him. Hope feels a sudden lifting away of her anxiety as she watches. This young woman, who loved *Hide and Seek* when she was a child, who has the courage and gristle to bring up a young son alone on a deserted estate, who has gentleness and patience beyond anything she could have hoped for, is going to help

them. It is going to be alright, she thinks. She has
made the right decision.

Chapter Nine – 1941

THE girl he was seeing, Sally, reminded Thomas of his wife. At first, he hadn't realised it at all. And then, when it struck him, he wasn't sure whether this was what had attracted him in the first place, or whether he liked her in spite of it. There was a physical similarity – both of them round-limbed, yet taut and compact. He had enjoyed his wife's naked body, and he enjoyed Sally's. But it wasn't only that. During the past few weeks, Sally had begun to assume things were a certain way, when nothing had been agreed between them. And in this, too, he felt the echo of his wife.

His wife had left him eighteen months earlier, after he had been foolish enough to go home with a girl he'd met. No second chance, no nothing. She'd just packed a case and off she'd gone to her mother's, taking their daughter with her and leaving him to manage as best he could. He didn't blame her. Not really. It was stupid of him to go with the girl. A mistake he needn't have repeated. It had never happened before. He knew how to control himself. It was just that, the one time, he hadn't.

As the weeks became months, and the months stretched into and then beyond a year, he had begun to understand that he was perhaps never going to get her back. And he thought that maybe it was inevitable. Her mother had never liked him. She didn't like men, full stop. And now she would be filling her daughter up with her hatred.

But he was free on his own, and he liked that, at least. He still loved his wife, but he had enjoyed neither her attempts to circumscribe his life, nor her assumption that she knew him better than he knew himself. For example, there was only one bedroom in the flat, and she had insisted they give it up for the child and set up their own bed in the living room. It was the way she assumed he would oppose the idea that rankled. He was happy to let the child have the room, but his wife's tone had been combative from the outset. He felt stifled and outraged. He wasn't good with words and he didn't even try to explain that she was wrong in so much of what she believed about him. He wouldn't say it right and she wouldn't understand him. It would only add fuel to the fire. Besides, when he didn't behave the way she expected him to, she didn't seem to notice anyway. She was all pre-emptive, blinkered retaliation, as if she had lost the ability to simply see and feel and respond. Was that what marriage did to people, he wondered.

Once it was clear she and their daughter weren't

coming back home in a hurry, he had moved the bed back into the bedroom, and after that it felt at least as if he had clawed back some control of the situation.

He never brought women back to the flat. That would be disrespectful. But there was a good half-dozen beds besides his own that he'd been sleeping in over the past year. Sometimes, feeling lonely, he'd roll up at one door or another, rather than go home and spend the evening alone, cooking his drab supper and eating it in the chair by the fire.

He was going to have to break things off with Sally, though. He hated this part of getting involved with women. Everything else he could manage, even the close shave he'd had a few months back with a typist hadn't particularly irked him. He would have liked to have carried things on with that girl. She was married to a serviceman, but she thought it was a fair game. She reckoned her husband was bound to be up to all sorts out there in North Africa or wherever he was, so why shouldn't she have her fun, too? She was right, of course, and he had been happy to oblige. But when the girl's mother found out, she'd written and told the son-in-law, and Thomas had decided he was better off out of things.

With Sally, there was none of that. There was nothing in her circumstances that might bring him more trouble. She wasn't married, and her parents weren't around either. It was Sally herself he needed to escape from. Her belief that he was now hers to lay claim to. Hers to know in advance what he would think about a thing – a film, a friend of hers, a story in the newspaper, anything – and broadcast as if he had actually spoken. And yet, here he was, hurrying towards the welcome she would give him. The open arms, the warm bed, the comfort of another person to spend the night with. He would miss all of that.

When he rang at the door, it opened immediately. The girl she roomed with was just leaving. She didn't look surprised to see him. 'Don't worry,' she grinned. 'I'm off for the night. Shift doesn't finish till six.' She held the door open for him. 'Enjoy yourselves!' She skipped down the steps to the street.

So, Sally was expecting him, then. Of course she was. If he didn't come, on the nights her roommate was working, she asked him where he'd been, what he'd been doing, that he couldn't come to see her. As if it was any of her business what he was doing. Half the time, he was up on the tower, firewatching. If not, then he crawled home and into bed, exhausted. But he was stubborn. Because she demanded, he wouldn't tell her, and it made her sulky.

She had already had her bath, and was wearing a silk dressing gown that showed her body in all the right places. It wasn't actually hers – it belonged to the other girl. A present from a boyfriend who had been in Japan. But they seemed to share all their clothes.

She wrapped her arms round his neck and pressed herself against him. 'The bath's still hot,' she murmured, and she was unbuttoning his coat, reaching inside, as she said it. He stood there, mute, allowing himself to be undressed, enjoying her gentle competence. Like her roommate, she was a nurse, and he supposed they were both good at undressing people. They shared a long, narrow room, which had a single bed at either end, and a fireplace in between, opposite the door. He glanced over at the other girl's bed, wondering how recently she had entertained her own lover there.

'Here,' he said. 'Let me do it.' He snapped back into himself, and took his half-unfastened belt from her hands. He wanted to take off his clothes himself, in the bathroom. He felt too much covered in stone dust and sweat, too conscious of himself and the smell of his work and his day, to meet her soft, sweet-smelling skin now. And if she went any further with her undressing, he would never make it to the bath before the water went cold.

Once there, he had some thinking time. He wanted to break things off, but hadn't thought how best he should. Now, he could see the likelihood of his doing it at all dwindling away to nothing. Banned from coming into the bathroom, she had taken herself off to the kitchen to make them something for supper. She was still wearing the silk dressing gown, but now with thick woollen socks pulled over her feet. The house belonged to the parents of one of the other girls who lived there, whom he'd never actually seen. They lived abroad and probably would have been appalled at the constant comings and goings, as if the place were some sort of knocking shop. It was impossible to know who lived there and who was just passing through. But it meant that he could soak in the bath without fear of some disapproving landlady hammering on the door, threatening to throw him out.

He didn't break things off. The next morning, he had to keep his visit to Riley short. Air raids had been less frequent for the past few weeks and progress on the tower was once again accelerating. He didn't have as much slack time to fill. Still, he felt a duty to see the lad, especially now he was worsening and the time for visiting would be ended soon enough.

Riley hadn't had a good night. The ward sister was there when Thomas arrived, checking up on him, writing on the chart that hung at the foot of the bed. He had an infection on his chest and didn't seem to be shaking it off. And yet he wasn't ready to let go of life just yet. His breathing might rattle and wheeze, but his chest still rose and fell steadily. The sister knew Thomas by now. They all knew him. She gave him a tired smile and left him with the patient.

Whatever the doctors said, Thomas tried to believe that there must still be a little space for hope. He looked at the boy's silent, closed face. It was a difficult belief to maintain. Already, Riley had gone away from them, was locked inside himself. Who could know what was happening in his mind? Had it really stopped working, as they were starting to say it might have? There he lay, still breathing, still warm. Was it possible?

He put his hand on the boy's arm and held it there

for a moment. 'I'm sorry not to stay for long, Dan. I'll come back tomorrow night, and I'll maybe bring a paper with me. Tell you what's been going on in the world.'

He looked urgently at the boy's face. Riley's eyes were open, looking at him. They seemed more focused, as if he could actually see him, recognise him. And the usually slack lips, surely, were smiling.

Where was the ward sister? She had to see this. She wasn't at the desk. He stood at the end of the bed and peered up and down the ward. Took a few steps towards the empty nurses' station, thinking perhaps she might have gone into the storeroom behind it, but the door was open and he could see no-one was there. If Dan was starting to come back to them, someone else needed to see. Damn it, where was the sister? Where were any of the nurses? He took a few more agitated paces down the ward before coming back to Riley's bedside.

He stood over him, breathing heavily. The boy's eyes betrayed nothing. They were still open, but had the same inward, glassy look they always had. The lips once again loose, incapable of speech. Thomas took a deep lungful of air and held it. Released it slowly, keeping his eyes fixed on the doughy face. Nothing. He sat down heavily and cupped his head in his hands for a moment, massaging the bridge of his nose with his two middle fingers. Nothing. It was nothing. He took another breath and stood up to leave.

Mary was there at his shoulder. He hadn't heard her,

hadn't sensed anyone behind him, as he usually could. Damn it, she's not like normal people, he thought, irritation springing from nowhere. She's like a bloody ghost. She looked like one, too, with her pale, troubled face. Dark circles round her eyes.

'Have you not been well?' he asked. 'I've not seen you for a while.'

'I'm fine,' she said, her voice sudden and breathless, as if it cost her a lot to speak. Had she already spoken to the sister, perhaps, and been told about Riley's decline? Or was something else troubling her? He glanced again at Riley's inanimate face, wondered how long she had been standing there, how much she had seen. He couldn't bring himself to ask. He would be late for work if he didn't leave, but he made no move to go. She still had her coat on, and her hat. She sat down, drawing her handbag onto her knee, both hands gripping the clasp. He could sense the tension in her elbows, drawn in tight against her sides. What on earth was wrong? He didn't move. He felt himself being held there in some kind of spell of Mary's, waiting.

The sister and one of the nurses in her charge had returned and were walking together down the centre of the ward, talking in lowered voices. Only the sibilants reached him. When they passed he knew he should tell them what had happened, how Riley had looked at him and smiled, but he knew he wouldn't. They reached the bottom of the long room, and he could no longer hear anything, though he could see their mouths were still moving. Then the nurse disappeared through a door in the far wall, and the sister worked her way back towards them, on the other side. She had a military eye. She scanned beds and occupants, lockers, and all the spaces in between, checking for anomalous items, visitors, patient behaviour, anything. Everything seeming to be in order, she took herself crisply away.

'I've been coming without my husband knowing,' Mary said. Her voice was barely audible. So small and tight, and there was a catch in it, as if she were hoarse from shouting or crying.

He said nothing. He continued to stand just behind her shoulder, looking at Riley.

'He has forbidden me from coming.'

'He found out, then?' His voice sounded loud and growling, compared with hers. He cleared his throat as discreetly as he could. He felt clumsy and ill-equipped.

She inclined her head. Once, twice. A nod.

'But you've come back anyway?'

Another nod.

He felt a surge of pity for her, remembering his last encounter with her husband, his cold reaction to the news he had brought about Riley. He was a good man, honourable, he knew that, but he made it difficult to build bridges.

He hadn't thought, before, of how it must be for this woman, having to live with a man like Jenner. It was alright for stone – that emotionless focus, the need for control. He knew the hours Jenner put in at work – knew how much of himself he put into the endless

133

revising of the planned schedule, as each day their circumstances slipped and slid. It was true – he had felt it, too – that nothing now could be said to be in the least bit stable or reliable. The money was unsteady and they had fallen victim to some of the worst luck imaginable. It wasn't surprising they were having more accidents. The men were exhausted. Nobody actually slept any more, even when the planes didn't come. They had got into the habit of fear. Thomas had himself sometimes felt as if the ground might liquefy beneath the foundations, and the whole cathedral slide into the mud. But that was the shape of things. There was no changing it. Jenner didn't seem able to see that. He needed to be on top of it all, taking control, willing the tower to completion. But stone was not a living thing. Stone could be transformed through that kind of precision and calculation. Thomas looked at Mary. She was malleable and warm. Her neck was thin and pale. A few stray wisps of kinked hair stood out from her head in a sort of halo. Jenner could bend her to his will, alright, but in doing so would turn her into stone, too. Something to be shaped, and chiselled and put into its place. The woman and the spirit and the gentleness would be gone.

'Does he know you're here now?' he asked.

She shook her head. He put a hand gently on her shoulder, just for a moment, and then took it away again. It was the first time he had touched her.

'I'm sorry,' he said. 'I didn't think. It was me that told him. Bloody big mouth I've got. I didn't know.'

Her head shook again. This time it didn't stop. She lowered it into her hands, her shoulders curving inwards, her rounded back bent over. She seemed to become as small as a child.

He reached out his hand again, and then changed his mind and let it drop. He wasn't usually so self-conscious with a woman. But there was something about Mary Jenner and it stalled him. He couldn't forget her fascination with Riley's accident, how she had seemed to be trying to picture it happening. And the way she looked at the still figure in the bed. He seemed to mean something more for her than simply a young mason who'd had a fall. Thomas couldn't understand her.

She stayed at the bedside for twenty minutes more, without speaking, barely moving. Her distress seemed to leave her and Thomas stood, forgotten, next to the curtain the sister had drawn around the bed. He couldn't just walk away without saying goodbye, but he felt unable to disturb her and take his leave. At the same time, he felt it was wrong of him to be hidden away with her behind the flowered curtains.

When she stood up, touched the boy's hand briefly, and then turned to go, she seemed both surprised and glad that he was still there.

In the cafeteria, he bought her a cup of tea and steered her to a table. She seemed unable to act without direction. He put the cup and saucer in front of her. 'Pity there's no sugar,' he said. 'You could do with some.' He paused. 'My grand-da used to keep bees,' he said. 'He used to send us honey when we were kids. Or sometimes he'd come over on the boat and bring pots of it in his suitcase. Packed with his shirts and spare pants. His wife wrapped them up first in greaseproof paper and string, but they leaked anyway. We'd lick his shirts, me and my brothers. Try to get the honey out.' He stopped and looked up at her. She was staring into the tea. 'Funny, isn't it,' he said, without conviction, 'the lengths kids will go for something sweet.'

She didn't move.

'Mary,' he said, as gently as he could.

At her name, she looked up.

He was afraid that her peculiar stasis was his fault. 'I'm sorry I told your husband. I didn't mean to get you into trouble.' He held both hands around his cup, letting the dry heat burn his fingers. 'I won't say anything about today,' he said. 'Or ever. If he asks. You must come and go as you please.'

'Thank you,' she whispered.

'Come on,' he said. 'Drink your tea.'

He watched as she sipped at it. Her hands were small, her wrists thin and white. He wondered, briefly, whether her husband had been rough with her. She seemed so much more cowed than he had seen her before. But Jenner wasn't a big man. He was almost as delicate as she was. He couldn't imagine it.

Still, she had come. Against his orders. Well, that spoke in her favour. She'd got an independent spirit, and it acted on its own sense of what was right, not his. If she could preserve that, then maybe she had a chance. Maybe Jenner wouldn't turn her to stone just yet. He knew what he would do, though. In her place. He'd leave. Take the child and just leave, as his own wife had done.

His thoughts snagged on something then, and jumped ahead, sensing a connection. His wife had left him because of his infidelity. Did Jenner, too, suspect infidelity? Was that what was going on? He felt stupid not to have thought of it before. It would explain Jenner's animosity towards him since the accident. Did he have some cock-eyed idea that he was getting up to no good with his wife? It wouldn't be the first time someone had suspected him. A reputation could stick.

'Did he say why you wasn't to come?'

She looked up sharply. 'Oh, yes,' she said. 'It's because of you. Because he thinks you're no good.' She put her cup down in its saucer. 'And because he thinks I'm wasting my time with Mr Riley.'

He nodded. 'And what do you think?'

She looked into his eyes urgently. 'I think that even if it helps, just a little bit, my being there… if he can hear me talking to him, then maybe it will be enough.'

That wasn't what he had meant. But of course she had misunderstood, had brought it back to the boy. He paused before he answered her. ' No,' he said. 'It won't make a blind bit of difference. Your husband's right there, at any rate. He's not going to make it. No matter how much you pray for him. You can't will him better any more than your husband can will that bloody tower into existence.'

'But the tower does exist. It's getting taller. You're building it!'

Thomas felt exhausted. Not for the first time, he noticed how stubbornly circular and childlike her conversation could be, and then immediately regretted the thought. It was too uncharitable. She was no child. She had preserved her sense of hope, was another way of seeing it. Wasn't that something to be cherished?

'Where did you come from?' he asked. 'Before here.'

'Derby,' she said. 'Or not far away. My family live in a village.'

'Do you miss them?'

'Yes,' she said, after a pause. 'Although I didn't see them so much. Once I was married.'

'Do you have any friends here?'

'No,' she said, flatly. 'Only you.'

She smiled, then, and her face was filled with something so tenderly offered that he had to turn away. She left herself too open. He felt afraid for her. She had no defences against the world. Or none that he could see, at any rate. He wondered how she would survive.

'How are the blackbirds?' she asked. He frowned. For a moment he had no idea what she was talking about. And then he remembered the nest, on a ledge in the stonework near the base of the tower. He must have told her about the tiny hatchlings he'd been feeding. He couldn't remember it if he had. The parents had been scared off, had abandoned their chicks. They hadn't lasted long. One day he'd gone up with a tobacco tin of worms and the nest was empty. Just the smooth, rounded inside, neat as a bowl, with nothing in it but a few downy feathers. Either they'd been taken by magpies, or by one of the falcons he sometimes saw, swooping from vantage point to vantage point across the city, or they'd fallen. He had gone down and searched the roof of the porch below but hadn't found anything. The magpies had probably got there first.

'Oh, he said, keeping his voice light. 'They're not doing so bad. Getting more feathers by the day. They'll be flying the nest before long.'

On his way out, he saw Sally, wheeling a trolley piled with starched and folded white sheets.

Aren't you meant to be at work?' she said, puzzled. Her hair was pinned up in a roll at the back of her head, with dozens of hairpins hidden underneath her nurse's cap. She had been busy pushing them in when he left her a few hours earlier, still swathed in that Japanese kimono. He wanted to pull them all out again, and watch her hair fall down onto her shoulders, the way it had been last night. He needed an antidote to the intensity of the past hour.

'Dan Riley's been taken bad,' he said. 'I stayed a bit.'

'Was that woman here, too?'

'Mrs Jenner? Yes, she's with him now.'

'I'll be getting ideas about you two. You're always slinking around together.'

'Don't be so bloody stupid. She's half out of her mind over the boy. Why would I –?'

She giggled. 'Why wouldn't you, you mean?' She jogged his elbow. 'Come on, it was a joke. No need to look so serious. I know you'd never do the dirty on a dish in a nurse's uniform.'

He scowled at her, and then pulled her roughly into his arms. 'No,' he said, kissing her hard on the mouth, feeling her teeth against his lips. 'No, I wouldn't.'

She pushed him away as he tried to kiss her neck. He didn't like women to pin their hair up, but he did like the way it exposed the pale, delicate skin behind their ears. She took hold of her trolley again and marched away down the corridor. 'I'll see you on Wednesday,' she called over her shoulder.

He was more than an hour late for work. Jenner interrogated him. He gave him a factual report on Riley's deterioration since his last update and, when the question about Mary came, he was braced for it.

'Were there any other visitors?'

'One or two. Not many. There never are, first thing. But yes, I think there were one or two.'

'You know exactly what I mean, Shaw. Don't play games. Were there any visitors for Mr Riley, besides yourself?'

'Oh,' he said. 'No. The family tend to come later.' He paused. Jenner clearly wanted more. 'And, I imagine it was a little early for Mrs Jenner. Perhaps she'll be going along later.'

'Mrs Jenner will be paying no more visits to the hospital.'

'Oh. I see.' He looked Jenner squarely in the eye. 'Well, that's a shame,' he said. 'But it's probably for the best, eh? It's not easy to watch a person die by degrees.'

Jenner didn't reply. He opened the door and Thomas walked out.

Chapter Ten – 2014

'You should do as I ask, if you want this to work out ok for you.'

Louise looks at him, unsure she has heard him right. 'What do you mean?' She is in her pyjamas and her feet are bare. She wishes she had thought to pull on her trainers and a hoodie before she went to the door. She feels more vulnerable like this. It's probably why he comes late, she thinks. He knows she'll be less prepared.

'I mean just what I say. Do as I ask.'

'Or?'

He doesn't like this. He never did like being put on the spot, or challenged. A brief spasm of anger contorts his thin face. He thinks he has the upper hand, but he doesn't. He is pathetic, she thinks. She isn't frightened of him.

'Or things,' he says with meaning, 'will start to get more difficult.' He takes a step forwards and glares down at her.

She laughs. 'Oh, right,' she says. 'I see.' It's like he's

been watching films of the Krays or something. Or reading a dummies' guide to doorstep intimidation. None of it is natural. He's got himself high on some self-righteous notion. And maybe something else as well – there's a slightly glazed look in his eyes that makes her wonder whether he's taken something – and then he comes round here night after night trying to bully her into doing what he wants. She speaks clearly, with as much assurance as she can. 'I've told you, Benny. It's no go. I'm not changing my mind. Not this time.'

He steps backwards, away from her. Like it's the first time he's heard this. Again, he overdoes it – raised eyebrows, mouth fallen slack. And then the expression melts into something else – his eyes soften and a knowing half-smile lifts one corner of his mouth. As if he knows full well she can't manage without him and this is just a preliminary to his being admitted. She feels her anger rising.

'I want you to leave now,' she says, trying to keep the same, level tone. He mustn't know he's getting to her. 'Go away, and don't come back. Ever. We don't want you here.'

He frowns. Pushes his hands deep into his trouser pockets. Looks up at the roof of the walkway, where the paint is peeling off. The light on the wall outside gives him a sickly, unreal pallor. She glances over at the flats opposite – the lights like neatly-spaced buttons studded along each walkway. She finds them comforting, sometimes, when she catches sight of

143

them through the window. Blazing away into the night in their steady rows. Switching themselves off when day returns.

'It's that old boyfriend, isn't it? From when you were kids?' he says at last. 'Making you think you can manage without me, is he? I've seen him, don't you worry. He was always sniffing around. Reckons he's got a chance now.'

The tough-guy act is suddenly gone, and his face is swimming with genuine feeling again. It comes and goes. Nothing is fixed with him. It never was. One thing washing over another. Why did she ever put her faith in him? She is exhausted. She has lost count of the number of times he has been back since he first reappeared, but he has ramped the pressure up recently. He's been coming here late every night for the past week. Making her stand on the doorstep, barricading her home and her child against him. He doesn't come when Carl's here. Only when he knows she's alone. And she has been alone all this week, because Carl's had to go and look after his gran. She knows that if she asked him to move in with her, he would. But she doesn't want to have to ask him. She wants to want it for its own sake, not because she's scared of being on her own. That was how it was with Benny, and it didn't do her any good at all. With Carl, she wants everything to be different. And she isn't scared of Benny, anyway. He's pathetic. But she is tired. She wants this to stop.

When he has gone, she slides the bolt gratefully

across the door, making sure it is fully engaged, then pushing the little knob flat against the paintwork. She leans her face against the cold wood and closes her eyes. In the throbbing silence, she can still hear his words, her words, spinning around inside her head. The sound of his voice. She had once loved to listen to him speak. His educated articulacy, the way his ideas flowed, one into the other, so persuasive and nuanced, whilst individual words and syllables stood out, carefully clipped and trimmed. Now his voice sounds strange to her, and Carl's is the one – so much more like her own – that makes her feel held and wanted.

Jake is stirring in his sleep. She can hear the flump of little limbs against the mattress as he turns over in his cot. She creeps down the hall and sidles in through the half-open bedroom door. He has settled back into sleep, the sound of his small moth breaths, like little sips of air. She gives a deep sigh. She needs to sleep.

It is almost one o'clock. Even pushed under the duvet, her feet are still cold from standing on the doorstep, and her mind churning with the past hour. Please, she thinks. Please don't come back tomorrow. She lies down and pulls the covers up to her chin. Please give me an evening off. She lies very still in the bed, listening to the silence again. She needs to sleep. She has to be up early to take Jake to her mum's place before going to Hope and Robert's in time to get Robert up and dressed. She stares at the ceiling. It must be terrible to be old. To want to care for someone and not be able to. She can understand the feeling of not being able to cope, well enough. And Hope isn't coping. Even with the extra help.

She stretches out her arm and turns off the light, exhausted. The orange glow from the streetlight outside resolves itself into a fuzzy rectangle around the edges of the curtains as her eyes adjust to the darkness. She closes her eyes.

At first, she isn't sure whether the sound has woken her, or whether she was already there, breaking the surface tension of sleep, when she heard it. She lies absolutely still. It was the letterbox. Nothing else would make a sound like that. And now, her heart is thumping so powerfully that, as she reaches her hand out to see what time it is, her whole arm seems to dip and rise with each pulse. She looks at her phone, winces at the sudden brightness, straining to make out the numerals – 3:42.

It comes again, and she is certain. She feels her body tighten. Her fear now is fortified by a rush of anger that someone could be doing this in the middle of the night. Someone being Benny. As quietly as she can, holding her breath, she swings her legs out of bed and puts them on the ground.

She strains forwards into the silence, listening. The bedroom door is half open, and the front door only a little way down the hall. It wasn't the sound of the letterbox being used as a knocker. Neither was it the sudden snap of something being posted through. It was the sound of the flap being pushed and then held open. She stands up, glancing at Jake humped under his blanket. Still sleeping. The narrow hallway turns a corner and she can't see without going out of the room. She eases herself through the doorway and stands in the hall, daring herself to take another step nearer, but she can't. She pictures him crouching outside with his face at the letterbox. His eyes peering in. He is only a few feet away from her. Does he know, then, that she is awake? Did he hear her getting out of bed and creeping to the door? Is he listening?

All her attention is focused on the effort of not moving, not giving herself away. Her breathing is too loud. Can he hear it? She daren't even blink. And then, suddenly, there is a smooth, withdrawing sound, like metal against metal, and the letterbox flap is eased down and only let go at the very last moment so that the snap is muted.

Hope is struggling to understand what has woken her. And then she understands all too well, and flaps her arm frantically at her side, patting at the mattress, trying to find him, but he isn't there. She sits up, gasping, and puts the light on. His dressing gown is still hanging on the back of the door, but he is up. She glances at the alarm clock and sighs. It was after midnight when she got him settled enough to fall asleep, and she could do with a few more hours. Still. She pushes her feet into her slippers and stands up.

He isn't in the kitchen, where she had expected to find him. She has been getting worried, recently, about leaving the knives in the drawers. What if he tries to use one and has an accident? They keep the carving knife in its little silk-lined box – always have done – and she has already put this out of harm's way, at the very back of the top shelf in her own wardrobe. He won't look there. He has never, in their entire married life, opened her wardrobe. But there are other sharp knives they keep in the kitchen drawer, and she wonders whether she ought to move these too.

She knots the belt of her dressing gown and looks in the living room. He isn't there either. Then she sees him, out on the balcony. With a pang of horror, she remembers that she didn't take the key out of the door and hide it before she went to bed. He is standing there in his pyjamas. He is alone, but she can see from the way he is moving his arms about and wagging his head that he is talking to someone. She walks a little way into the room.

'You're right,' he is saying. 'It's not the same, is it, looking at them in books? The colours aren't true … I'll take you out some time again soon, shall I, and we'll see how many we can… D'you remember the time we found that nest in the apple tree? Four little sky-blue eggs, all gone cold? We tried to warm them in the airing cupboard, but it wasn't any good. Do you remember?'

He listens carefully to the reply, his face grave, his head lowered and cocked slightly to one side. Such a familiar gesture, she feels she cannot bear it. There is nobody there. He is talking to his father.

It feels wrong to eavesdrop. She walks as far as the open door. 'Here,' she says, holding his dressing gown out, and he comes to her and slides his arms in obediently, first one then the other, as she imagines a child would do.

She lifts one of his hands and clasps it in her own. It is cold. She squeezes, trying to get some warmth into it, but he won't let her for long. She feels his gentle tugging, the need for release, and she lets it go. He is withdrawing further and further from her. Half drifting, half pulling away, winding himself in. More and more, at the moment, she finds him talking to his father, drifting back into the past. She wishes he would talk to her, too. She feels, at the same time, absolutely necessary, and entirely superfluous.

Perhaps it is because of the home carers. He is getting more used to having other people look after him, settling into the routine of being got up and dressed, or washed and undressed, by someone other than Hope, and it almost gives him permission to withdraw. As if he is relieved to be receding further from her life. She tries not to be unhappy about it. She doesn't want to end up resenting the help. It is going so well. All of the women are lovely, but there is something about Louise in particular that he really responds to. Hope can't deny that she is growing fond of her as well. She never makes Hope feel that she sees Robert as just another frail old thing somewhere near the end. There's a vulnerability about her, too, though she can't say quite what it is. She doesn't want to be nosy, so hasn't asked too many questions, though she is curious about her.

The balcony is strewn with spilt soil and there is a line of plant pots along the top of the wall. He has been potting up. Not that they have anything to pot. It was always Robert who did the gardening at the old house and last summer she bought him some little trays of bright annuals for the balcony. She has forgotten all about it this year. Perhaps this is his way of reminding her. He must be missing them. Maybe she can pop out when Louise is here later, and get him some.

'Come on in,' she says. 'You'll catch cold out here dressed like that. I'll make us some tea.' She touches him lightly on the elbow.

He jerks his arm away from her and turns back to his pots. He doesn't want to come in. She goes back inside, leaving the door open. He hasn't anything to put in the pots, so he diddles a bit more with the soil, but then he just stands, looking out at the street, and over towards the park, listening to the birds. The trees seem particularly green and vital in the dawn light, like they sometimes do after rain. She can't quite bring herself to relax and let him be. They are only on the first floor, she tries to reason with herself. And he is over eighty – he isn't likely to start climbing over the balustrade. He won't come to any harm. She forces herself to turn away and go and put the kettle on.

She doesn't want to admit to herself how hurt she feels because of the way he wrenched his arm away from her. As if he hated her. She knows that isn't true.

And yet, she isn't sure she knows at all. He is always so difficult now, it's hard to believe anything else. He is different with the carers. As soon as Louise or Grace is in charge, he becomes much calmer. As if he knows he can let his guard down. Hope wonders whether there is enough of the old Robert still intact for him to be trying to protect her, even now, from his illness. Like he did over the move. Not telling her about his diagnosis until he couldn't leave it any longer. Making her think he was being selfish, moving her away from their beloved house for no reason. It's unlikely, but it's a more consoling possibility than hatred.

She glances through the hatch into the living room. He is coming in. She watches as he steps carefully over the little ledge at the threshold, and pulls the door gently closed behind him. He didn't come to any harm. She worries too much about what might happen.

He sits himself calmly at the table. So he has remembered that tea is coming. Suddenly, she wants to rush over to him and kiss the top of his head. Feel his warmth, and breathe in the pillow-and-fresh-air smell of his hair, just for a moment, like she used to. But she doesn't do it. When the kettle reaches its frenzied peak of bubbling she switches it off to save herself the few seconds' delay whilst it simmers down and turns itself off, and she makes the tea.

She doesn't go out for bedding plants. When Louise arrives Hope can see, straight away, that something is wrong.

'Has something happened?' She feels worried Louise will think she is being nosy, but she looks so grey and troubled that she can't not ask. Louise shakes her head, but her mouth starts to tremble and she puts her face in her hands.

Hope sits down beside her and puts her hand lightly on her arm. 'What is it?' she asks. 'What's happened?'

Louise tells her. About how Benny has been coming round late at night. Trying to get back into her life. Wearing her down. And then last night. She has been imagining all sorts. She didn't see anything, but when she went back to bed there were so many things racing around her mind. He had a hunting knife, somewhere. He showed it to her once. Told her he'd skinned a rabbit with it when he was a kid. She has no idea whether it was true or not – he liked to brag, and wasn't always careful about telling the truth – but she has been imagining him jabbing the blade of it through the letterbox opening. She'd heard the rasp of something, like a breath being sucked in, and the letterbox snapping shut. She thinks she might be going mad. Hope listens in silence. Even before Louise sobs out that she thinks it was a knife, that he is trying to terrify her into doing what he wants, Hope is picturing her own carving knife, unclipped from its silk-lined box and on the loose, waving and glinting in the moonlight. Robert's pale, veiny hand, discoloured with age spots, clutching the handle. The pyjama sleeve neatly buttoned at the wrist.

She shakes the image away.

Louise shrugs. Her face is ghastly. 'I can't stop thinking about it.' She wipes more tears away angrily. 'It's stupid. I know he won't do anything. When none of it works, he'll get bored and disappear again. Convince himself he never wanted us back. I just have to sit it out.' She gives a grim laugh and looks at Hope. 'But I'm scared. It's really getting to me.'

Hope feels a wave of intense anger flare suddenly on Louise's behalf, and then subside until it is like a pilot light, flickering low and alive. She would like to offer her something. 'Would it help if you stayed here? Where he won't find you? You'd be very welcome to.'

Louise shakes her head, smiling but determined. 'It's lovely of you. But it's too much like giving in to him if I let him know I'm scared. He's a step closer to getting what he wants, that way, isn't he? '

'But if you don't feel safe...'

'My boyfriend's away this week. That's what this is about, I'm sure of it.' She gives another laugh. 'He's been watching me, Benny has. I thought I was imagining it, but... He's been hanging around, off and on, for weeks. And now Carl's away, he's making his move.' She looks up at Hope. 'He's too much of a coward to do it when he's around. It's pathetic, really.'

'When will Carl be back?'

'Not till Friday,' she says. She gives a heavy sigh and looks up at the ceiling. 'Last time, when Benny came back, I just let it happen. It's like you stop being a person. You're just a thing that stuff happens to, and you think you don't have any choice. I don't want to have to live like that any more. Why should I give him the satisfaction of knowing he's scared the shit out of me?'

Robert has woken up. Hope stays where she is, at the table, whilst Louise helps him out of bed and goes with him into the bathroom to change his incontinence pad. As he shambles slowly past the doorway, concentrating on each step, Hope is reminded briefly of her father at the end of his life. She pushes the thought away, automatically. She doesn't want to be reminded of her father, but her memory pushes back and, without meaning to, she is remembering how, when he died, she had felt such a profound sense of loss, and couldn't account for it. She is starting to experience similar pangs – a kind of awful, yearning hollowness – when she watches Robert. Yet she has loved Robert for more than fifty years. The feeling makes sense; she knows that losing him will be unbearable.

She can hear him murmuring in the bathroom. Louise is gently coaxing him into a clean pair of underpants while he sits on the closed toilet lid. He likes talking to her while she works. It is good to hear his voice. Hope goes to the hallway and stands, listening. He is talking about a book he once read. Only he hasn't mentioned this, so it sounds as if what he is talking about actually happened. She isn't sure whether Louise realises, but then it doesn't matter He doesn't read any more. She thinks he has already reached the point where he can't. He certainly can't follow the meaning any more, even if he can still decode the individual words. It has come so far, she thinks sadly. He is being pulled backwards past the same mileposts he dashed headlong towards at the age of four or five. Letters into words. Words into sentences. Everything that he once drank in so easily, leaking out and draining away.

She misses him. Such a gentle, patient man. She remembers how he was with his dad. Theirs had been a relationship so very different from the troubled one she had with her own father. They had always been close and after his father's head injury the affection seemed to grow stronger still. Robert had tried so hard, with such patience, to find him a route back into the language of things and experiences.

Yes, it is good to hear his voice. It still sounds calming, authoritative, even now. With the reassuring vowels and precise consonants of someone well-educated who knows what they are talking about. Whilst he sits with his bare, wasting buttocks on the toilet lid and rambles on about Ford Madox Ford. She smiles.

No, they never talk any more, and she misses that most of all. It would be better if he could chatter his nonsense with her, too, instead of leaving her with this drift into silence. It must be because he knows she knows the game is up. He has protected her from what is happening to him for as long as he can, and now he has nothing left, he is having to let go, and it's like he is ashamed. With the carers, it doesn't matter. They have never known him any other way, but with Hope, it is different. Maybe that's what is making him cut off and impatient with her, she thinks. The shame of letting go. Although, deep down, she still worries it really is because he hates her.

'How are you managing?' Louise asks.

'Oh, don't worry. I've done him some toast and he can choose what he wants on top.' She hands Louise a packet of ham slices and some cheese.

'No, I didn't mean with breakfast. I mean – well, how are you managing with Robert? I was so wrapped up in my own stuff when I got here, I didn't ask. You look tired.'

'Oh,' she says. 'I'm alright.' She had been meaning to tell her about Robert's balcony episode, but she doesn't say anything. Louise is going through enough. And anyway, nothing happened. 'He was up a bit in the night, but... I'm fine.'

Louise doesn't say anything but she doesn't look like she believes her. She takes the ham and cheese into the living room and puts the two packets on the table in front of Robert.

'Now,' she says. 'Can I give you a slice of this ham for your toast? Or would you rather have cheese?'

Hope smooths her hands across her hair and draws up her shoulders, as if she feels a quick spruce up and sprightly posture will be enough to show that she is managing. She isn't. She's not sure how she will get through the long hours between Louise leaving and Grace arriving for the bedtime shift. But she mustn't let it show. If she does, she knows they will want her to think about a home for him, and she can't face that.

Chapter Eleven – 1941

'STAY in the house,' he hissed.

Mary looked up at the sky. It was silent, now that the sirens had stopped wailing, but she knew what was coming. In a few minutes she would hear the low, far-off rumble, and it would get louder and louder and then everything would begin all over again. She didn't know whether she could stand it for another night. The moon was bright again. Last night it had been bad. Crouching together under the kitchen table, she and Hope could feel the throbbing of the engines reverberating through the floorboards, the planes were so close overhead. The house had felt as if it were made of paper. Hope sobbing in her arms, 'Why can't we go to the shelter, Mummy?'

St Michael's was gone now – they had walked in a stupor through the rubble-strewn streets this morning and seen the wreckage. Such a tall, slender spire it had sent up to the heavens. Nothing left now but broken bricks and glass and charred wooden beams, steaming in the sunlight. The damp, acrid smell had been in her nostrils all day.

He was pulling his coat on as he ran down the front steps to the street. He was going back to the cathedral again. He would get himself killed. He would get them all killed. Perhaps that was what he hoped for.

'Stay in the house,' he said again, and his voice was grey like ash. 'The old woman can do as she likes. But you and Hope, you stay.' He turned and walked away from her, back to where his heart was kept. She looked up at the sky again. Still nothing. The moon, just a shade off being full, drenched the whole unlit street in a brittle, watery light. Everything – every tile and finial and attic window latch would be visible from above. It would be impossible to hide. The cathedral will be the next to go, she thought vaguely, with William locked in his work inside. He won't even get up from his desk. He will die bending over his books, as the roof falls in on top of him. We, too, will be hit, and there will be nothing we can do to stop it, trapped in the glare of this huge moon.

It was because of Daniel Riley. When he asked, she had stood her ground. Yes, she had been to the hospital again to see him. And yes, Thomas Shaw had been there. And then the plunging sensation she had felt when he told her Thomas had denied it. He had said he wouldn't tell on her, and he had been true to his word.

Her honesty had cost her dearly. Gradually, her husband was wearing her down. Already, she could feel the pull of an unresisting life. She had not been back to the hospital again. It was almost a week. But obeying him frightened her, too. Letting loose the strings of her own wishes, her own beliefs and watching them rise up out of reach. She knew their loss would be permanent.

Will was closing in on her. Whether he believed she and Hope would be any more or less safe in the house or the shelter was immaterial. The point was to make her do as he said.

She went back inside and closed the door, pausing only a moment before shooting the bolt across. Let him hammer if he came back before morning. She felt the need of as much protection as she could muster, and the bolt made her feel safer. He wouldn't come back anyway.

The black-out curtains were already drawn. Pointlessly, she knew. As if the planes needed anything other than the moon. Their only hope lay in the fact that the moon was not partisan. It would pick out the planes as brilliantly as it lit the city, wouldn't it? Perhaps, then, the guns might get more of them tonight. She placed her hope there, squarely, using it as a barricade against the other things – the horror of what was coming; the fear of the house collapsing on top of them; the guilt of letting Mrs Hayes lie alone in the shelter, curled around her fear.

She could feel it now – just a faint, low vibration. But even as she strained to pick it up, she knew it was growing stronger. In a few minutes, she would be able to hear nothing else.

'Mummy?' Hope was standing at the bottom of the stairs, with her blanket wrapped around her shoulders. Her face was expectant, but Mary could see the deadness of resignation there, too. She already knew the answer to her question.

She sank onto the bottom step and Hope sat down beside her. 'Are we staying indoors again?' Her voice was tiny. She would do whatever her mother asked of her. Mary wrapped her arms around her child. Why did she not disobey Will? Why could she not take Hope to the shelter? He would never know. Why do as he ordered, when she knew it went against all sense? And even if he did find out, shouldn't she do what was right? Why could she not defy him any more?

The planes were close. A minute away. Maybe less. Hope clung to her. And then Mary shook herself out of her indecision, picked her daughter up and carried her into the kitchen. It was too late to do anything else, even if she dared. And, she knew, now, that she did not dare. He had won. They would stay in the house. A feather eiderdown was spread on the floor underneath the table, and she had put cushions there too, and the flask of hot chocolate they usually took into the shelter. She tried to push Mrs Hayes from her mind. She had done the best she could for her. She had aired the mattresses that morning, topped up the paraffin and refreshed the matches. And she had made her a flask of chocolate too, and carried it down to the shelter an hour ago.

She crouched down and pushed Hope under the

table. The sound of the planes was ever so much louder than even half a minute ago. They were here. Any moment, they would start to feel the ground shake as the planes rained their loads down on top of them.

She crawled underneath the table beside Hope and lay down on her side. The little girl turned to face her. For a moment they pressed their foreheads together and she felt the child's breath on her closed eyelids. And then Hope buried her face in her mother's chest, tunnelling her arms inside her cardigan and around her, and lay still.

Mary clung to her. At the last minute, Hope had stuffed rags into her ears and pulled a knitted hat on. It would be better, in some ways, she thought, to have done the same herself, and dulled the agony. But she wanted to hear. If death was coming for her, she preferred to have that half-second's foreknowledge. It felt important not to be extinguished without it, as if it gave her some control over her own ending. Ridiculous, really. Because what did it matter, that split second of knowing? Would it be enough time to give herself and Hope to God willingly, instead of being wrenched unready? And in any case, the raid at its height was so deafening, so all-consuming, that it was impossible to hear the individual sounds that made up the whole. The single droning engine, the one tiny whoosh that might spell the end – would be lost inside the rest of the noise. She pulled the blanket over their heads and put her hands over Hope's hat-covered ears. The child was shaking. In her mind, she placed two votive candles, one for each of them, in an alcove of the church in the village where she grew up. When she was Hope's age, that was the only church she knew. She watched the flames blur and flicker, dancing silently inside the cacophony.

She woke suddenly. A huge, low, window-juddering explosion. One so powerful it seemed momentarily to change the density of the air around her. She was in bed, and daylight was filtering weakly around the edges of the heavy blackout curtains. Hope, beside her in the bed, had sprung awake, too, and was sitting up already, her wide eyes written over with fresh worry.

'What was that?'

She hadn't dreamed it, then. It was a real sound.

She had no coherent memory of the end of the raid. She must have brought Hope upstairs after the all-clear. Half carrying, half steering her in a sleepwalking daze. Ears buzzing. She couldn't remember, not clearly, anyway, although she had a trailing half-impression of tripping on the blanket as they came up the stairs. She glanced at the clock. It was still early – not long past seven. They couldn't have been asleep for more than a couple of hours.

'What was it?' Hope said again. She slid out of bed and went to the window, pulling the curtain to one side. Peering out.

'Anything?'

Hope shook her head and climbed back into the bed, pulling her knees up to her chin inside her nightdress.

'The tower's still there,' she said, as if that were all that mattered.

Without the explosion, they might have slept for another hour. Still, she was awake now, and Mary knew she wouldn't be able to fall asleep again. 'You stay there,' she said. 'I'll make breakfast.' Hope probably wouldn't get any more sleep, either, but it was worth trying.

Will hadn't come home. In the mornings after a raid, when she didn't yet know how the world stood, or indeed if it stood, beyond the front door, she sometimes felt a sort of all-pervading calm. It was enough to know that she and Hope had made it into the next day. Anything more than that seemed superfluous. She would find out soon enough. But, today, she drew back the bolt, smiling to herself at the fact that it had protected them, after all. She opened the door and peered out into the street. It looked no different. The immediate neighbourhood, at least, had escaped damage. She glanced up at the half-finished tower showing above the rooftops. There was a strong smell of smoke, and she could see it hanging thickly, moving in a slow drift past the chimney stacks across the street. On a few doorsteps, other people were standing, looking. 'Did you hear it?' a man called across to her. He was still wearing his air raid warden's tabard, only just coming home after the night's exertions. He was covered in dust and grime. Perhaps he had been helping the firemen dig people out. She nodded. 'What on earth do you think it was?'

he called. 'Something big's gone up, that's for sure.'

Mary shrugged and pushed the door closed again.

She had already looked out into the garden and seen that the shelter was still intact, but she didn't go to check on Mrs Hayes until after breakfast. The door at the top of the stairs that led down to the basement flat was always left unbolted, but when she tried to open it, she couldn't. She twisted the handle and juddered the door, thinking it had somehow got stuck. Maybe the house had been affected by the bombing – gone skewed with all the vibrations – and the doorframes had slipped out of true. She called out to her. 'Mrs Hayes? Are you alright? The door seems to be jammed.' She rattled the handle again. 'I'm coming round to the front.' She had a spare key. She paused. No, Mrs Hayes would let her in. She wouldn't take it. But then, just in case, she took it out of the pot on the kitchen windowsill and put it in her pocket.

The door opened straight away, as if Mrs Hayes had been standing there, waiting. 'Oh,' Mary said, 'I'm sorry. I was worried. The door inside has got stuck.'

'It's locked,' said Mrs Hayes.

Mary looked at her. Something wasn't right. The face looking into hers was grim and grey. 'What's happened?' she asked. 'Was it last night?' The image of Mrs Hayes curled up on her mattress alone in the shelter which she had tried to banish from her thoughts through the night, returned, and she took the old woman's hand in her own, her eyes filling with tears.

'I'm so sorry,' she whispered. 'Leaving you alone. It

isn't fair…' Her voice tailed off. She couldn't speak.

Mrs Hayes shook her head, muttering. 'Sorry! She's sorry!'

'I… Mrs Hayes?'

The old woman looked her in the eye. 'Yes, you should be sorry. You should be.' She was shaking her head again, and Mary could see that her hands were shaking, too. 'Not on my account, but on the child's. How any mother could put her child's safety at risk…' She gave one last shake of her head and turned her back on Mary.

Mary started to follow her into the hall. 'I…' But there was nothing to say. She couldn't tell her why. She wouldn't believe her. She stood watching Mrs Hayes shuffle down the hall and disappear into her kitchen. Both of her boys had been lost in the Great War. Young men barely out of childhood. She had been powerless to stop them dying. Who could blame her? She saw what she saw: a mother needlessly risking her child's precious life.

Quietly, she pulled the front door closed and went back up the steps. She knew Hope would want to go down to Mrs Hayes, as she did every Sunday before they left for the morning service at the cathedral, and she feared her reaction when she found the door in the hall had been bolted against her. But the old woman had made her point. She knew Mary wouldn't come down. When Hope tried the door an hour later she found it unlocked and went down to the basement as usual. Mary sat alone in the kitchen, listening to their voices coming muffled through the floor. There was no sign of Will yet. Perhaps he wouldn't come home at all any more, but just stay at the cathedral all day and all night. She and Hope and Mrs Hayes would be left to manage alone.

A loud knocking at the door pulled her back to herself. It couldn't be Will: the bolt was unlocked now. Maybe something had happened to him after all. Maybe they had only now thought to send someone with news. Resigned, entirely calm, she stood and walked down the passage into the hall. The knocking came again, insistent, harried.

She opened the door. It was Thomas. She was surprised, momentarily, that he was the one bringing her the news. But then she came to herself. It wasn't Will he had come about.

'Is it Dan? ' she gasped. 'Has something–?'

Thomas nodded. 'He's dead,' he said. 'This morning. Exact same moment as the *Malakand* went up, they said.'

She shook her head. She didn't understand.

'He's dead?'

'Yeah,' he said. He paused. 'Is your husband here?'

She shook her head.

Thomas stepped into the hall and gently, deliberately, pushed the front door closed behind him. He looked at her. 'Are you alright? Let me get you a cup of tea or something. Here.' He put his hands on her shoulders and turned her round, so that she could lead the way to the kitchen. She allowed herself to be steered. She stood and watched as he turned the tap on full and filled the kettle, splashing the water up the tiles.

He set it on the gas and lit it. 'Sit down, for heaven's sake,' he said, turning to her. And then, more softly. 'You knew it was coming. Remember? I told you, didn't I? I warned you of it.'

He pulled a chair out and waited for her to sit. Slowly, in a kind of daze, she sank obediently onto the seat.

'What is the "Malakand"?'

He looked at her strangely. 'It's a ship,' he said. 'Or was,' he corrected himself. 'It's nothing any more. Bloody great ship, packed full of explosives. Went up about seven this morning. Took the whole bloody dock with it. You must have heard it…'

She nodded slowly. 'I didn't know what it was,' she whispered.

She looked at him, and for a moment he felt he could see exactly what she was thinking. It was the most peculiar sensation. To understand another person's thoughts as if they were your own. He shivered. A mystical look, half of wonder, half of terror, had crept into her eyes. 'Oh, no you don't,' he said, and he took her by the arms and tried to shake her free of it. 'It had nothing to do with Dan. Or with you.'

'But I haven't been. For nearly a week. If I…'

'No,' he said. 'No. For Christ's sake, woman. He would have died anyway. Whether or not you came.'

Tears were spilling down her cheeks. He knew he shouldn't be so hard with her, but she had to understand. She couldn't have changed anything. He wasn't going to shield her from it. He felt himself swimming with the kind of frustration that nudged into anger, and wondered whether this was how Jenner felt when he was with her. Perhaps she provoked him. Her mind refused to see sense. Here it was now, running away with itself, seeing connection where there was none. Finding meaning at the bottom of every cup she drank from. It wouldn't do. He stood up and turned his back on her, ashamed, fearful that she might be able to see his thoughts playing out on his face, as he had seen hers. Maybe the transparency ran both ways. Hell, it was difficult. He had tried to avoid getting involved, but, try as he might, she had a hold on him – a furious muddle of concern and fascination and something he couldn't put his finger on – that he hadn't seen coming. But she was enough to try the patience of a saint.

The kettle was whistling. He turned off the gas and fumbled for a spoon. His hands shaking, he tipped tea into the teapot and scalded the leaves with the boiling water, then clattered the lid into place and took down a cup from the shelf.

When he turned back to her, he was calmer, his rebellious thoughts reined in and stabled. He pulled out another chair from the table so that he could sit right in front of her. Their knees were almost touching. He took a thin wrist in each of his hands and held one on each knee. She might have some crackpot ideas, but it didn't give Jenner the right. It didn't give anyone the right.

'Listen,' he said. 'None of this is your fault. You have to understand that. Dan was always going to die. Always. You couldn't save him. Neither could I. Neither could all the doctors in the country, even if they had been able to spare the time to have a look at him. He was too badly hurt.' He paused. Her marble face was blank, disbelieving. Pushing his words away. He felt the flush of anger rising again. Why did she think she had any influence, any power over such things? It seemed self-flagellating, but surely it was arrogance, too, wasn't it, to think she held such sway? And yet she was so self-effacing – not a fraction of an inch of self-love in her. Which left him only naivety. But surely, even allowing for that, she must know she wasn't to blame. He couldn't puzzle her out, and trying turned him in on himself, in a sort of broil of agitation. Mostly, he let such things alone.

She was looking at him, waiting for him to speak again. He shook his head. And spoke wearily, wanting, now, only to be away from her. For a flicker of a moment, he wished she'd never appeared at Riley's bedside that day, months ago. 'You not coming isn't why he died,' he said quietly. 'He just died.'

She opened her mouth, as if to speak, but he silenced her with his own voice. He knew what she was going to say. 'The explosion? No,' he said. 'You know as well as I do. Stop torturing yourself. That was coincidence, nothing more. No God. No punishment. Just things happening. As they do.'

He let go of her wrists and took hold of her hands. She let her fingertips rest in his palms. 'Look at me,' he said. 'What can I do?'

She shook her head.

He gave up. He released her hands and leaned heavily against the chair back, making it creak. He wanted, more than anything, to lie down and sleep. 'I'm your friend,' he said. He stood up. 'Now he's gone, I won't see you at the hospital.' He paused, weighing up whether to say anything more, or to take the opportunity of severing the fragile bond that had grown between them. It might be for the best. 'I'm at Albion Gardens,' he said eventually. 'Number 25. If you need...' He saw her small nod of acknowledgement, though the gesture might just as much have been meant to stay his words. He didn't know what he was offering her. He had never had a woman at the flat. 'Through the arch with the worker,' he muttered, though such details seemed suddenly too intimate, too presumptuous, even spoken quietly. 'The other entrance, with the architect over the top, gets you on the wrong side.' He left her abruptly. As he walked through the passage back to the hallway, he noticed the child, standing at the top of the steps leading down to the basement. He wondered how long she'd been there.

Outside, even with the smell of the previous night still heavy in the air, he felt free, released, after being with Mary, after the awkward, unresolved way things had come to an end. He shook his head, trying to throw off his tiredness. He hadn't been on firewatch duty, but he'd barely slept anyway. There couldn't be a soul alive in the city who had managed to. At some point, he had given up trying, and stood at the bedroom window, watching. From his fourth-floor vantage point he could see the whole sky alight. The cathedral tower silhouetted against a red glare. It had managed to look both impregnable and pathetically vulnerable. Up there on the Mount, impossible to ignore. How the hell it was still standing, he couldn't account for. Maybe there was a God, after all. Mary certainly believed it. With so little sleep, it was possible to believe in anything. Here he was, after all, being drawn towards the place on a Sunday morning when he didn't need to be there. Crunching his way through streets littered with broken glass. The high, acrid smell of fires still burning, and a greyish pall hanging over an otherwise bright spring morning. He stopped for a moment and looked at it. He had to admit it was magnificent, standing there, huge and unblemished, in the smouldering city. But an end would come to its luck. He didn't believe it was anything more than blind chance that had protected it up to now. Its moment would come, and he would be sorry when it did, after all that had gone into it. There were masons who had spent their whole working lives there. All that labour and care. And the lives that had been lost to it, too. How many other Dan Rileys had there been? He stared up at the scaffolding-shrouded tower: yes, this kind of magnificence came at a price. And it might yet be for nothing. They certainly seemed to have it in for the city, those faceless pilots who came each night, and the shadowy figures who issued their orders. He sighed, turning away from the huge building. He needed to sleep.

'Why were you not there?' he demanded.

She looked up, startled. Her eyes seemed wrong. They looked too distracted, with a wildness in them that Will hadn't seen before.

'Why were you not there,' he asked again. 'You always go. Why not today?'

He stood in front of her, waiting for her answer. Mary always went to mass on a Sunday morning. Since he had been at the cathedral all night, he had stolen a few uncomfortable hours lying along a bench in the contractors' office, and had woken just as the congregation was coming in. He had bent himself upright, still half-asleep, and staggered out into the central space, finding that he wanted the comfort of seeing people filing in and seating themselves in ordered silence. The low-key decorum of strangers congregating suddenly appealed to him. And Mary would be there. He had looked around for her, expecting to see her, with Hope in tow, edging her way through the rows of carefully laid-out chairs. Taking up a meek, straight-backed position as she gazed towards the altar.

But she hadn't come. He stood and waited, knowing

she would come. Slowly, the space filled up; the low murmur of voices built into a respectful hum. He watched the people coming. Men, women, young, old. With children and without them. He recognised some of the masons with their families. He thought he saw Daniel Riley amongst them, his hair slicked back and his Sunday suit on, before remembering that that could not possibly be. The service had actually begun when his heart began to pound and he worked out what was staring him in the face. She wasn't coming. She would never come again.

From the roof, the previous night, he had looked out on something other-worldly and oddly beautiful. Fires had been burning all around, and he had felt remote from it all. Remote, too, from the usual dread that besieged him before his twice-weekly climb to inspect the works. Last night, up there with the men, he had felt the familiar paper version of the tower he carried round in his head subside. It was useless; it had no currency, no earthly use. Instead, he started to feel something of the building itself, and it surprised him. As the bombs rained down, he had felt their deep reverberations. The stones, the bricks, the wooden platform all echoed with them and he, too, felt them travelling through his body. The city was burning around him. Up on the tower, vulnerable, yet clanging at the same pitch as the fabric of the building, he had felt untouchable, almost mighty. And all the time, below, the city had burned, and she was there, in the burning city. Below him. Burning.

He ran in a kind of soundless mist. People moved out of his way instinctively. A door seemed to open of its own accord and he was out in the street, running towards home. Not allowing himself to picture what he would find there, but knowing it, and feeling the knowledge thicken his blood. Moving his limbs, breathing, had him gasping with pain. He pushed himself on. There was rubble everywhere. Bits of burnt paper littered the road, and black fragments of ash were still falling, like snow, to the ground. He passed a house whose bowels had been spilled out into the street. He could see right into an upstairs bedroom, where a double bed stood empty, crisscrossed with collapsed roofbeams, and a wardrobe lurched sideways, doors flung wide, towards the ragged edge of torn-away floorboards and plaster. An oval mirror in one of the doors caught the sun and winked a forlorn Morse telegraph as it flapped there, helplessly, on the brink of falling.

The nextdoor house was nothing but a pile of rubble. An ambulance pulled slowly away from the kerb. A gaggle of onlookers, grey-faced, watched it go.

He rounded the last corner, keeping his mind blank, not allowing himself to think. When he reached the street, he couldn't look up. He was bent double, as if he had taken the full force of a punch in the belly. Great heaving breaths. If the house was gone. It was the last thing he had spoken to her. 'Stay in the house.'

He clenched his jaw and looked up.

There was the house.

He sank down onto the kerbstone and let his head fall between his knees.

Inside, all was quiet. Was she not there? Where had she gone? And then, in the kitchen, he found her, slumped in a chair, her arms hanging loose by her sides. For a moment, she looked like someone beyond hope. Her eyes were febrile and anxious, but they had a hardness, too, as she turned them on him, polished and impenetrable. He shook the impression away. Saw, again, his wife, restored to him.

'My love,' he choked out, his voice cracking and failing him as he tried to speak. He had known, with absolute certainty, that she was gone. And he had been wrong. He gathered her dangling arms and pressed them around his own body. He took her face in his hands and kissed it. He dropped to his knees and wept in her lap.

'I thought you were dead,' he sobbed. 'When you didn't come. I thought you were dead.'

He felt her hands stroking him, smoothing his hair. It soothed him a little. It was a long time since she had touched him like this. A long time since he had needed it, perhaps. He needed it now. He clung around her waist, his damp face buried in her lap, breathing her warmth, her clothes, the comforting, familiar smell of her, and the hot, muffled sound of his own breathing. He would never again let her go.

He wished he could merge himself with her, and really keep her safe. He knew of no other way. They had kept close before they came here – but it was this city, his ambition, which had pushed them away from each other. He must keep her close.

Something from deeper beneath the surface nagged at him. He tried to shove it back down but it pushed against the pressure, then outsmarted him, slipping from his grasp, and floating up unimpeded a few moments later.

He had been out in the fields. It was summer, and his mother had encouraged him to go and so he had left her. He had spent all afternoon in the sun and the smell of earth and drying grass, filling his sketchbook with drifts of watercolour cornflowers on gangly stems, minutely detailed drawings of blown poppies and browning seedheads, and an abandoned lark's nest hidden in the long, wheatlike grasses. As the height of the day passed and looked towards evening, he had run back home to show her. He wanted her to see the drawings he had made, hear his account of where he had been, how he had passed his day. He enjoyed her questions, the smile she sometimes wore as she listened to him. The house was in silence. He had run everywhere looking for her, and she wasn't in the kitchen, nor was she upstairs making the beds, or out in the yard unpegging the washing, which hung, stiff and dry, on the line. He had thrashed his way through it, as panic rose in his throat, and found only her absence and the smell of fresh air in the weave of the bedsheets. Again and again he returned to each room, thinking perhaps she was there after all and he hadn't seen. When eventually someone came back to the house and found him, he was huddled in a corner of the yard, his search abandoned, one of the clean white sheets wrapped tightly around him. Washing it was one of the last things she had done. In the weeks and months that followed, he wondered where, and how, she had finished herself. He was never told.

Perhaps he should give it all up. They could go back home, leave this city, and rekindle the closeness there had once been between them. Repair the damage. He looked up at her. His face felt swollen and ugly. Was it even possible to go back? They had a child, now, whose whole life had been spent here. And had it really made him happy, that other life? He had striven so hard to get away from it. To make something of himself. To prove his mother's faith in him, perhaps. Well, now here he was. Mary's eyes roved over him, seeing and not seeing. Flint and inviolable.

'Why were you not at mass?' he asked. 'You always go. Why not today?'

'He's dead.' Her voice was barely audible, but it was enough for him to hear the surface flatness not quite camouflaging her feelings. He put his hands to her face, cupping her chin, forcing her to be still. He could see now – it wasn't hardness in her eyes, it was sorrow, and she was fighting to control it. He felt she was moving away from him, withdrawing as surely as an outgoing tide.

'What do you mean?' He lowered his hands from her face. 'Who's dead?'

'Mr Riley.'

'I told you not to go to the hospital.'

'I didn't go.'

'Then how…' He leaned towards her. 'How do you know?'

'Mr Shaw,' she said, in an empty voice. 'He came to tell me.'

'Shaw?' Will stood up and went to the window. Out in the garden he could see the door of that cursed tin can of an air raid shelter, with its door propped open, and thin, grubby little mattresses sagging against the wall. For all he knew, she might have spent the night out there, against his orders. He could no longer count on her doing as he asked. For a flicker, he couldn't quite remember why he had told her not to use the shelter. It didn't matter. He pushed it away.

He turned back to her. 'Shaw's been here?'

She nodded.

So. That was it, was it? He wasn't even bothering to keep it hidden, now. Coming up to the house, bold as brass, letting everyone see how he did as he wanted with other men's wives. He had warned her about him and yet it had come to this. A thought struck him. 'Did you ask him to come?'

She shook her head, a blank, stupid look on her face. 'I didn't know he was going to die. Why would I…?'

He sighed. 'Mary. Even you can't be that naïve. Do you think that was the only reason he came?'

'Yes. I–'

'You know what he wants. You must –'

'– He wants nothing. Nothing. He came to tell me...' A huge sob erupted from her, stoppering her words. She put her face in her hands. He watched her shoulders shaking.

'You know what he wants!' He realised he was shouting. Will knew how men like Shaw looked at women. As if they could smell the sex in them. Lifting up their noses like dogs scenting a trail. Nostrils flaring. 'You know exactly what he wants. Don't play the innocent.' She was crying. Usually her tears provoked his pity, but now they stoked his rage. He could feel it mounting as he glowered down at her. Did Mary really think a man like Shaw, with the reputation he had, would come here just to tell her about the fallen lad? Of course not. She knew alright. Maybe she even encouraged him.

He stopped, appalled at his lack of control, wanting to hide himself from her as he forced the anger down. He stared hard at the floor. He felt terribly wounded; that was at the root of it. The miracle of her restoration to him seemed barely to have registered with her. She cared more about the loss of a boy she had never known. He wanted to shake her, to hammer into her the horror of what had just happened to him.

It took several shuddering breaths before he felt able to lift his head and speak. 'I thought you were dead,' he said again.

She looked up at him, and he could see the strangeness was there in her eyes still, but whether it held sorrow or stone, he couldn't tell any more.

It seemed to reach him with difficulty, as if there were a great distance between them. 'You,' she said bitterly. 'It's your fault he's dead.'

He felt a stabbing sensation on the left side of his forehead and his hand flew up to his face as if he had been struck there. 'My fault?' he whispered, his fingers pressing hard against his eye socket. And then it fell into place and he nodded. 'Yes. It is my fault.' But already she was weeping, withdrawing, hating herself again. Saying over and over that she hadn't been to see him, she was to blame, she could have helped him, she had failed him.

The pain subsided as suddenly as it had arisen, leaving a suggestion of itself behind, like a scorchmark in grass where burning debris has fallen. He felt himself collapsing inwards. Down at her feet again, on his knees. He was to blame. He was to blame.

His head was heavy in her lap. He was suffering, in full confessional agony. And yet she could feel nothing about it. It made no difference. What he had told her could not disturb the foundation of her belief. It didn't alter the two key facts: that she had obeyed his orders and stayed away, and that the boy was dead.

'Don't you see?' he begged her again, lifting his head heavily, as if he were drunk. 'If I hadn't listened to Shaw, if I had stuck to my decision and not been swayed...'

She shook her head, but he persisted. She couldn't shut his voice out. '...perhaps it wouldn't have happened at all. It was I who took bad advice, I who allowed myself to be influenced because it suited me to hear it. For Christ's sake – I advised Mathieson that the masons should go up that day. I. Do you hear me? And then Mathieson gave the go-ahead. We can all of us find ourselves guilty if we try hard enough. But I... I am guilty.'

She felt sorry for him in a distant way. He was ashamed of what he had done, or failed to do. But he didn't understand. His confession had no bearing. Did he really believe that his own prior guilt cancelled out her own? Her involvement with the dead boy had begun after the fall. She had failed to visit him, as she had promised, and he had died. The reason why he fell in the first place had absolutely nothing to do with it.

'And I thought you were dead,' he began again. He kept coming back to this, as if it mattered. 'All this...' he lifted his arm heavily and swiped it across the air as if batting away a fly, '...this nonsense.' He took both of her hands in his. 'Forget Riley. Riley isn't important. I thought I had lost you. I ran back here, knowing that you were gone...' He stopped, overcome with emotion. She tried to speak. She didn't want him to go over it all again, but he flapped his hand to silence her, kept ploughing on with his words. 'Knowing that I had stopped you from leaving the house. And then, by some... some miracle, you are here, unharmed, alive. I have a second chance. And all I hear from you is Thomas Shaw and Daniel Riley. I don't want to hear about them. Shaw's no good, I've told you. And Riley's dead. But you're not. You're not, my love. You're here. That is what matters.'

She felt herself shrinking away. She didn't want his miracles, his confessions. His version of what mattered was just that. His version. Not hers. She concentrated on shutting him out. He was clutching her hands. She remembered how Thomas had held her hands before he left. He had also tried to persuade her out of her guilt. Had offered her… what? She didn't know. He had told her where she could find him. She remembered the touch of his wide, work-roughened hands where now she felt the pressure of her husband's fingers. Thomas had said nothing, in all the times they had met, about why the accident had happened. Only that it had.

'He… he cared,' she muttered, more to herself than to Will. But he heard her.

'Cared? You think so?' He stood up and straightened his cuffs. Bent down to pick up his crumpled jacket from the floor and put it back on. 'Well, you won't be seeing him again.'

Chapter Twelve – 2014

IT happens while she is having a quick wash before bed. She daren't have a proper bath these days, or even a shower, unless Louise is there. Louise understands. She knows what it is like having to be on constant watch.

She seizes her chance once he's in bed. Grace has just left and he seems to have dozed off. She is a couple of minutes, no more than that. Enough time to run a basin of warm water and give her face and neck a quick going over with the flannel. She is just squeezing toothpaste onto her brush when she notices the smell. She calls out to him, but he doesn't reply. And then he shrieks and there is the crash of something hitting the floor. She drops the brush and paste into the basin and opens the bathroom door. The hallway is tinged with grey. Something is burning.

He cries out again and she rushes into the kitchen to find him holding one hand out in front of him, its wrist clasped tightly in his other hand. It is a strange, oddly pleading gesture, full of forlorn hope. He stares at the hand, at her, then back again, his wide eyes un-comprehending and savagely wounded. The blackened, misshapen electric kettle is on the floor, its contents spilt across the lino and dripping from the bottoms of the cupboard doors. One of the gas rings is blazing.

It's a very nasty burn, the ambulance driver tells her. Because he is elderly, they might decide to keep him in. She feels half apologetic for calling them. She knows they are rushed off their feet, but she panicked when she saw what had happened. The skin has gone a livid pink. Whilst they dress the wound and settle him into the wheelchair they've brought with them, she cleans up the mess. The kettle is beige and the bottom of it looks now like half-chewed toffee. There are knobbles of burnt plastic stuck fast on the hob. Here and there, a fine, brittle strand where it has been drawn out in a thread as he pulled the kettle out of the flame.

She goes with him in the ambulance. It is very late when she gets home, and, thrown off-kilter by what has happened, she oversleeps. When the intercom buzzes, it takes her a moment to realise what it is, and only when she sees Louise's face, distorted on the little screen, does it occur to her that she should have let her know.

'It's alright,' Louise says, and she puts her arms round Hope, who is standing waiting for her at the flat door, sobbing out her apologies for the wasted journey. 'Anyway, who says you don't still need the help? It looks like you need someone to make you a cup of tea.'

Hope smiles, and lets Louise release her. It feels so wonderful, even just for a few moments, to be held.

She watches Louise fill a pan with water and set it on the side of the hob that isn't covered in melted plastic. She picks experimentally at the blackened stuff on the other side. 'I'm going to have a go at getting this clean before I go,' she says, and when the tea is made she carefully lifts the cast iron bit of hob into the sink.

Hope sits at the tiny kitchen table, watching, as she scrubs at it.

'He's getting worse, isn't he?' Louise says, over her shoulder.

He is. She admits it. She blurts out what happened with him getting out onto the balcony a few nights ago, and how he's been getting up every night since and roaming around the flat. If he's not opening drawers and looking for things in the kitchen, he's rattling at the balcony door, and the front door, trying to get out. She lies awake in bed, listening to him. It seems as if he is so desperate to escape from her. She knows he must hate her, if he is trying so hard to be free.

'But why should he hate you? Surely it's his illness.'

Hope shakes her head. 'I don't know that it is, you see. I think he does hate me.'

Louise turns round, wiping her rubber gloves down the front of her apron.

'Why would he hate you?'

When she and Robert met, he was beginning to get himself known as a sculptor. She, fresh from teacher

training college, was new to London, and they had somehow found each other and recognised that they fitted together.

When they got married, she had moved into his bedsit with him. It was meant to be temporary. But it wasn't pleasant. The kitchen was all corners and hard chairs, with a bare lightbulb and everything caked in grease and old cooking smells. She remembers spending more time back at the flat she had shared with some other girls than she spent at the bedsit, until, eventually, she had moved back into her old room with a girl called Sue, and brought Robert along with her. Robert slept on the sitting room sofa, and the newly-weds stole what moments they could when Sue was out. For a few months, it suited them well enough. It was a time when all the wheels of the future had been set turning at once. She had found the love of her life. She had her first teaching post, and Robert had been given his first commission, for the garden of a primary school. And it was during that period, tucked together under the bedspread in her single bed one afternoon, that they had talked about the future. The distant future. She can remember it as if it happened last week. What they would do when they were old. For they were neither of them in any doubt that they would grow old together.

How would they manage the end of things, when it came? That was where their conversation had led them, and was the question they had asked themselves, and each other. They were both young. Neither had any experience of old age and illness. Although Hope had already known death, it was not that sort of death. She had only been a child when her mother died and had quickly perfected the art of never thinking about it. There was still almost a decade until Robert's father would have his accident. These things were to be faced in the future. And, that bright, cold afternoon, lying together in the single bed, they had talked with an openness that was possible perhaps only because of the great distance between themselves and their topic.

He had made her promise. For herself, she hadn't asked what he asked. She hadn't been sure why, at the time, but perhaps it was a feeling that in the continuation of life itself, no matter how spare it seemed, there nevertheless lay some value. Or perhaps she hadn't fully entered into the contemplation of the life to come, as he had. For him, it was clear-cut and serious. He feared the loss of control over his own body and mind. Couldn't face the prospect of something so baldly catastrophic to his own person. And she had made the promise he asked of her. She had agreed to do it, if he became incapable of doing it for himself. And then, because they were young, and because they were alone in the flat, they had made love and fallen asleep tangled together in the blankets and counterpane, and woken up later, hungry, in the dark. Nobody came home all evening, and they made toast in front of the fire and switched the lamps on and made everything cosy, and she had let the earnestness of their earlier conversation fade. They hadn't ever really spoken of it again. Not directly – maybe a slanting reference once or twice over the years – enough for her to know he still took the promise as sound.

And now? He was enduring the existence she had promised he would never have to face. She was failing him. Wasn't that why he got so angry? Because of what she had promised and failed to do?

'He's been getting angry again?'

Hope nods. She looks so defeated. 'He frightens me,' she says. 'Such rage. It isn't him.' She pauses. 'At least, it's not the Robert I know.' She looks at Louise. 'I'm sorry. I haven't even asked. Last night… did you have any more… visits?'

Louise takes a deep breath, trying to summon the sense of calm she is determined to maintain. 'No,' she says. 'No, he stayed away last night. I kept on checking, but he wasn't there.' She turns back to the sink and the section of the hob she has been working on. 'This looks a bit better.' She can feel the tremor in her voice, and she doesn't want Hope to ask her any more about it. The poor thing has troubles enough at the moment, without having her home help to worry about. And she can't account for the feeling she has, anyway. She wouldn't be able to explain it. Last night, nothing happened, so why is she so unsettled? She lifts the section of hob onto the drainer and watches the soap suds drip from it and slide down the draining board back into the sink.

She left Jake with her mum last night. Maybe that's

what is getting to her. Last night was the first night she has spent alone since he was born. She isn't used to it. Every hour or so, she had woken up, listening out for his cry, or the murmurings he makes in his sleep, and he wasn't there. She felt a kind of hollowness and it made her want to get up and phone her mum to check he was alright. First thing this morning she had called, and of course he was fine. Having a bowl of Rice Krispies on the sofa, in front of a Thomas the Tank-Engine DVD. Barely able to tear himself away long enough for her to say hello and hear his little piping voice, so tiny over the phone, without his boisterous presence to give it substance.

He will stay there tonight, too, she has decided. Not because she is expecting anything to happen, but because it eases her anxiety. Carl will be back from Ireland tomorrow, and she'll tell him she wants him to stay at hers for a few nights. Just until Benny gets the message and backs off. It is the thought of spending another night so alone that brings the tears to her eyes and before she has time to check them, she is standing there in the old lady's kitchen crying, and Hope is there, holding her hand in both of hers and patting at the back of it. Wanting to help, to make it better.

'I'm sorry,' she sniffs. 'I didn't mean to. I didn't get much sleep last night.' She tells Hope about leaving Jake with her mum. 'I know he's safe with her,' she says. 'But it's so awful not to have him with me.'

'Why not stay with your mum, too?' Hope urges, but Louise shakes her head. Her mind is unchanged.

'No,' she says. 'I don't want him to have the satisfaction. I know it seems pointless, but I've got to stick it out.' She gives a grim laugh. 'I think I need to prove it. That I'm stronger now.'

'Oh, you're strong, alright,' Hope says. 'You don't need to prove it.'

'I do,' she says. 'To myself, I do.'

They drink their tea in silence. Louise watches the spinning mechanism inside the clock on the shelf above the television. It would fascinate Jake, she thinks. The whole of the workings, and the clock face itself, are all contained inside a miniature glass dome, and the bit that spins goes first one way, then the other, back and forth, back and forth, over and over again. It's like a kid's windmill on a stick, or one of those silver chimney pot caps that glints in the sunlight as it whirrs.

'So,' she says eventually. 'We'll both be on our own tonight. Would you like me to pop back later? I mean – I don't need to get home for Jake, so…'

Hope smiles, shaking her head. 'It's nice of you,' she says. 'But I'll be fine, don't worry.' She straightens her shoulders and looks directly at Louise. 'It will be a little taste of what's to come, won't it?'

Louise nods uncertainly, not fully sure whether she is talking about the more distant future, after Robert has died, or something more immediate. At any rate, for the next day or two, Hope will manage better without Robert. Physically, at least. She is worn out, and with any luck she'll have a bit of a rest while he is in hospital, if she doesn't exhaust herself running there and back twice a day. She thinks she can understand her reluctance to accept help. It would be conceding the same kind of defeat she herself doesn't want to admit to Benny. Neither of them wants to relinquish their hold over the life they have. Hope's opponent isn't a person, but it's not so different – the fear of what will happen if she gives in.

It's clear, though, that she won't be able to manage for much longer. Louise feels she should talk to her about it, but she doesn't know how to broach the subject.

Hope shoots her an abrupt glance, as if she has just spoken her thoughts aloud without realising. She feels guilty, caught out. She hopes it doesn't show.

'I was just thinking,' Hope says. 'Well, wondering, really…' She stops, then starts again. 'Maybe you don't know, of course, but…'

Louise sits forward on the sofa, watches as Hope selects her words. Always so careful and precise.

'…when he is ready to come out of hospital,' Hope says. '– I don't know how long they intend to keep him there, but…' She pauses and looks across the room, blinking slowly. 'Do you think… I mean, should I ready myself for questions about what's best? For Robert? Coming home and such?'

'You mean are they going to ask you about residential care?'

Hope nods. Her gaze is still fixed somewhere across the room. Maybe on the spinning clock's hypnotic movement.

'I think they might, yes.' She tries to choose her words as scrupulously as Hope does. 'I think they have to. When... you know... someone is elderly... and...'

'...and when their elderly wife is clearly not coping?'

She nods. 'I think they'll probably ask you to consider it. Not that you have to...'

'...No... but do you think...?'

She shakes her head. 'I don't know what I think, Hope.' She takes a breath. 'I know you're struggling.' She shrugs. 'I can't make a decision like that any easier.' She turns to Hope, and she can feel the prickle of tears again as she speaks. 'He's such a lovely man, and I love looking after him and coming here. But I can see how hard it is...'

'I can't bear the thought...' Hope says, spacing out her words like glass ornaments on a mantelpiece, that could fall and shatter if mishandled, '...the thought of abandoning him. The thought that something might happen to him and I wouldn't be there to stop it.'

'Yes,' Louise says, her voice scarcely above a whisper. 'Yes, there is that. Although, nothing might happen. Or, if it did, you might not be able to stop it, even if you were there.'

She drops into Lewisham Hospital before she goes home. They don't let her see him, of course, not being family. But they tell her he's doing ok, that he's sleeping, and that makes her feel a little better. She is tempted to ring Hope, just to let her know, but she doesn't want to alarm her with an unexpected phonecall, so she doesn't bother. She will go and see her tomorrow, instead. When she gets home, she pulls all the blinds down without looking outside. If Benny is there, she doesn't want him to see that she cares.

After Louise has gone, Hope makes herself a poached egg on toast and eats it quickly, standing up to clear the plate away immediately she has finished. She isn't used to having her meals alone. She wonders whether they will have been able to persuade Robert to eat anything. It is a warm evening and, since he isn't there, she has opened the balcony door. The blackbird is singing, as usual, and she eats to his accompaniment, the skein of notes seeming to unravel as they tumble down from the bird's chimneytop perch and into the empty flat.

She carries her plate into the kitchen and rinses it. The hob is still on the drainer, taking up all the space, so she lifts it back into place over the gas rings and puts her plate to dry. So pathetic – just one small plate and a knife and fork. She refills the pan with water and gets the teapot ready. She will go into the shopping centre after she has been to see Robert, and buy a new kettle. And then, when Louise comes round tomorrow, they can have a proper cup of tea, with water boiled the way it should be. And after that, Louise will get her little boy back, and she will have her boyfriend back, too. She smiles to herself. Louise, at least, won't be alone for much longer. She carries her tea across to the living room before changing her mind and going out to the balcony.

She takes a sip and leans back in the garden chair, balancing her saucer in her lap. She feels so tired. She closes her eyes, and lets the blackbird's superfluity of notes wash over her. Then something shakes her, jolts her out of the moment. It is such a sudden, sharp memory of her mother she pulls herself upright in the chair and some of the tea spills into her saucer and onto her skirt. 'Damn it,' she says, feeling the brief scald as it soaks through to her leg and begins, immediately, to cool. She lifts the cup out of the saucer and carefully tips the slopped tea into the soil in one of Robert's plant pots. Just a flicker of a memory. Her mother kneeling, praying. But it was difficult to see her. And then it snapped shut and she was left with the afterimage of the kind of decorative gravestones they have at the old Victorian cemeteries. Those monumental carved angels in postures of reflection and prayer. She tries to reach again through the curtaining birdsong of the present, back inside the memory, but it won't come. She hasn't thought about either of her parents for years, has skilfully avoided them both for longer than she cares to remember. How strange that they seem to be circling her now, cautiously moving into sight at the same time after so long away.

Chapter Thirteen – 1941

AFTER Hope had left for school, she went straight up to Will's study. He kept maps of all the towns he had lived and worked in, and some of places he had never even visited. She would be able to find the address Thomas had given her, half-unwilling, before he left. She scanned the shelves for what she needed. Carefully, she pulled the maps out one by one, working along the row. A dog-eared one of Derby caught her eye and she felt briefly homesick. Perhaps it was there that she ought to be running. But, for all that she missed her distant home, she knew the limits of what she had left behind. She would find no understanding there. Her life was here now.

She found a map of the city and spread it out on the floor. She remembered Thomas saying he walked everywhere, so she guessed his home must not be far. She made the cathedral her starting point and leaned over the network of streets, moving gradually outwards, square by square, until she found it.

She tore open an envelope and marked out a hurried sketch in shaky pencil, then refolded the map and slipped it back onto the shelf, taking care to leave it exactly as she had found it. She didn't want Will to know. She felt guilty even for having thought about Albion Gardens, let alone intending to go there. Thomas was her goal, and he was forbidden. But she was going there to speak to him, nothing more. She pulled the study door closed behind her.

He lived past the museum and the big central library. She had never been so far north in the city before. It was a warm morning so she took off her coat as she walked and carried it over her arm. As she turned into Hunter Street and approached Albion Gardens her courage began to ebb. The huge block of flats looked forbidding and ugly. She searched for the archway, the sculpture above it. What was it he had said? That the architect would lead her the wrong way; she should find the worker. Or was it the other way round? She looked up at the figure, trying to make out which one it was. It wasn't easy to tell. It was so high above the entrance she could barely make anything out. It seemed as unappealing as the rest of the building – a relief rather than a sculpture, flat and expressionless.

She walked through the entrance and found herself in a large courtyard that was curved all around one side and overlooked by tier upon tier of encircling walkways. The strong morning sun was already high and a steep diagonal line slanted down across the yard, leaving one half in deep shadow, whilst she stood blinking in too much brightness. She felt she had entered some ancient arena, imagined lions, bulls, dragons even, advancing down dark corridors ready to burst towards her into the light. She shaded her eyes and tried peering around into the various crannies at ground level that might let onto a stairwell, but everything seemed bleached away and out of reach. A child with a piece of chalk, or maybe it was a stone, stopped scratching at the concrete and watched her through narrowed eyes. On the second floor walkway, she could see an elderly man in a battered trilby leaning on the wall as he smoked, looking down at her. There were perhaps others too, that she couldn't see. Watching. Waiting to see what she would do.

She turned slowly on the spot, scanning the blank rows of windows and closed doors. She didn't know where to go, what to do next. She turned a full circle and then stopped. The old man was coming towards her. She glanced back up at where he had been standing, to make sure. The walkway was empty.

He stopped a few steps away from her. He didn't speak but his eyes seemed to be waiting so she asked him directions. He pointed across the courtyard, at a staircase that stood half in shadow, half in sun, the oblique demarcation line running straight up the middle of the entrance and picking out the concrete steps beyond in a sequence of bright zigzags that rose into the darkness.

The stairwell was cold and smelled of soup and disinfectant. She found the door at last, up on the top floor. It was clear that Thomas wasn't expecting her, but his eyes filled with gentleness when he saw her. He was bare-chested, the straps of his braces hanging loose at his sides. He glanced behind him into the flat – she couldn't see in; he kept the door half-closed at his back – then smiled and said why didn't she wait on the landing. He'd only be a minute or two.

She sat on the kitchen chair he brought out for her. If anybody came along and needed to get past, she would have to stand up, it was so narrow. She waited. She could hear the tick tick of a stone being thrown, and then the rhythmic scuffing of shoes in the courtyard below, followed by silence, and then the stone again. The child was playing hopscotch.

She closed her eyes and swallowed. She had never seen so much of him before. He was so much paler than she had imagined. The tops of his arms, his shoulders, his chest. A fly buzzed past her head. Why had she come? She had interrupted him dressing. He didn't want her here – she had intruded. She had seen too much. She wasn't even sure she wanted to ask him about Riley's fall any more. Let it be. The boy was dead.

She stood up to leave just as he reappeared, his familiar, fully-dressed self again. 'I'm sorry,' he said, swinging the chair expertly back inside the flat with one hand before pulling the door closed. He flicked his eyes at the door, indicating what lay behind it. 'A mess, I'm afraid. I'm not used to visitors.' He looked at her. 'Do you mind walking?'

She shook her head and followed him to the stair-well.

Outside, they crossed the courtyard and passed through the archway in silence. He seemed to be in a hurry. She felt again that she oughtn't to have come. He was angry with her. Perhaps his flat really was a mess. Or maybe there was something else. She hurried after him down the street and, drawing level with him, caught hold of his arm to make him stop.

'I'm sorry,' she said. 'I didn't mean to… I can leave, let you get on with things, I mean. I don't want…'

'What's happened, Mary? Why have you come?'

'Nothing,' she said. 'Nothing's happened.'

'Then why? Because if…'

'No,' she said, shaking it away before he said any more. 'I wanted to talk to you. But it doesn't matter now.'

He frowned, not understanding or fully believing her.

'What did you want to talk to me about?'

She stared down at his boots. They were brown and scuffed and bigger than Will's shoes.

'Well?'

She watched his boots shift on the ground. One of them lifted up and came down closer to her. She could hear the crunch of grit beneath his tread. He put his hands on her shoulders, turned her so that she faced towards him.

'Did you tell him I came to see you?'

She nodded. She heard his marked intake of breath, as if steeling himself for whatever was coming next.

'What has he said to you, then? Why don't you tell me?' His voice was steady. He let his hands drop from her shoulders. 'Mary? Will you look at me?'

She wouldn't. The second boot had joined the first. There was a scuff above the big toe that was almost a hole. He would have to get it patched. She closed her eyes. She didn't want to know, any more. If Will was right – about any of the things he had said about Thomas – she didn't want to know.

'Right,' he said. 'So you're not saying, is that it? Well, I can have a pretty good guess. He thinks I've been working on you, that's what he thinks. He thinks you and me are going behind his back, doesn't he? And now he reckons I've got what I wanted and I've the nerve to come to his house and rub his nose in it.' He pushed his hands into his pockets. 'So, what's he said he'll do about it, then?'

She turned and started walking away from him up the street. Anywhere, just to get away. He caught up with her and tried to catch hold of her arm, but she wrenched it back. She wasn't going to listen to him. Not here, like this, in the street. 'Has he got it in for me?' he cajoled. He gave a humourless chuckle. 'Well, he wouldn't be the first.'

She turned round then. 'Don't,' she said, her voice loud and uncounterable. 'Don't tell me.'

'Sure, you know it already, eh,' he said, his voice going lewd and smudgy-low. 'I'm sure he has delighted in telling you about my, er… reputation.'

She stayed ahead of him. There was a church up ahead. She would go in there. He wouldn't follow her. She could get away from him.

'Let's see,' his voice went on behind her. 'How does it go? When a man finds out his wife's gone behind his back? Of course. He'll kick you out. No? Not it? Well then, he'll take the child from you. Wrong again? Ah well. It must be that he's going to go the full mile and kill you, then. Is that it? If you ever see me again? Isn't that right? He'll kill you. And me too, of course. And probably himself for good measure. Am I right?'

She hated him. She turned and looked at him. And she saw his expression fall in on itself the moment he saw her face. He followed her mutely, then, until they reached the church, and he went up the wide steps and into the dusky interior behind her without a murmur. She didn't try to stop him.

She walked up the aisle and ducked into a pew about halfway to the altar, giving the shallowest of genuflections as she did so, self-consciously angry that she had to do it in front of Thomas, but compelled to do it anyway. She could hear his coat sweeping along the seat, buttons rattling against the polished wood, as he sidled in after her.

They sat down.

'Do we have to be here?' he asked, his voice chastened, but still gruff. 'It's so… churchy.'

'You don't have to be here,' she said. 'You can leave.'

'I'm sorry,' he said at last, his voice unsteady with

the effort of keeping it low. She could see very clearly now how different they were from each other: he was so much more himself in the open, whereas she felt she had come into the ascendancy, here, in this dark, close, muttering interior. Indoors, he seemed altogether too big – his voice; his ungainly, dusty clothes. She glanced at his knees – they were almost touching the back of the pew in front.

'I shouldn't have spoken to you like that,' he said. 'I am sorry. It was unforgiveable. It's just... well, it bothers me. I mean – it all bothers me: how you're being made to live, for one. Doing as you're ordered. And it bothers me how you are, how you take things into yourself. And it bothers me how people talk. Letting their tongues run away with themselves. Most of what they say about me's not true, you know.' He gave her a pleading look.

It was Mary's turn to stay silent. She didn't know what to say.

'I'm serious,' he said, sitting forward in the pew and taking hold of her hand, as he had done in the kitchen the day Riley died. 'If I'm speaking out of turn, well... I've no right, and you must say so and I'll stop. But I don't think it does you any good, seeing things linked up, one thing with another, the way you did about Dan. As if there's some great pattern or plan. There isn't.' He shrugged. 'Least, I don't think there is.' He stopped and looked up at the distant beams and dark, slanting underside of the church's roof, as if he were searching there for the right words.

He lowered his eyes again, and looked at her. 'I think you let yourself be ruled too much. I don't mean it's your fault. But you pen yourself in, with how one thing has to be because of something else, and as if you deserve everything bad that happens. That's no way to live. You shouldn't be looking over your shoulder the whole time. Life's in your hands, if you want it to be. Not your husband's. Not God's. That's all I've got to say, and I'm sorry if I've spoken when I shouldn't.' He stopped. His words had left him a little breathless. She had never heard him say so much in one go.

She slowly withdrew her hand from his. Despite her resolve to confront him, now that he was here beside her, she could feel herself flowing out towards him, out from the harbour of her view of the world, and her life with Will. She was frightened. It was all very well for him to talk like this. He who saw no link between one thing and another. She would be left on the open sea if she followed the current he was pulling her into.

She bowed her head low over her lap, laced her fingers tightly together, trying to shut him out, but even with her eyes closed, she could see his face. She shook her head, trying to rid herself of him. She would not see him again.

She felt his arm come around her, and she bent even lower into her lap, as if by pulling away into herself she might be able to erase herself altogether. She could feel the weight of his arm on her back. She let it rest there.

He was speaking again. She tried to shut it out, but his voice was low and warm and he drew her out to him again. She lifted her head and looked at him, feeling his gaze take in her ugly, swollen eyes and wet cheeks. If she didn't say something now, she would never say it. 'My husband hates you, you know.'

Thomas nodded. 'I figured as much this morning.'

'Why?'

'I've had my marching orders,' he said. 'Got the sack.'

She felt her breath catch. 'How? He has no say over–'

'–Ach, not officially, maybe. But they listen to him.'

They sat in silence.

'It's because of Riley he hates you,' she said at last. 'Because you told him to send them up the tower.'

'What?'

'The day he fell. It was you who convinced him to say they should go up.'

'But it wasn't his decision to make. It was Mr Mathieson's…'

'You said yourself. He has influence.'

'I didn't mean…'

'No.'

There was a pause.

'So he blames me?'

'He blames himself more.'

'Then why…?' He gave a mirthless laugh and leaned his head right back on the pew, blinking up at the rafters. 'And you,' he said after a pause. 'Do you blame me, too?'

He didn't wait for her answer, but sat up straight again and took hold of the pew in front. 'He hated me before then,' he muttered. 'Riley made no difference.' He was gripping the pew tightly. She could see the tension in his arms. 'Christ,' he said at last, and he brought his fist down hard against the top of the pew. 'That's not why he fell! For Christ's sake. He just fell. It could have been any one of us, and it was him. It happened then, but it could have been any other day.' He looked at her. 'Who exactly does well out of thinking like this? What good does it do to anyone? That boy, lying there in the hospital for weeks and all of us powerless to do anything at all to help him. Just watching him die.' He shrugged, made a pathetic gesture of surrender with his hands and let them fall into his lap. 'I just don't see the point.'

So, he had wriggled out of it. She didn't have the energy or the wish to pursue it any further. But Will was right: she wouldn't see Thomas again.

'What will you do?' she asked, pulling on her gloves.

'He wants me gone. But I'm not going to…' He was muttering the words almost to himself, as if he were speaking his thoughts out loud as he shaped them.

'Why? Where will you go?'

'Nowhere,' he said. 'I'm going nowhere.' He was back on solid ground. 'I've lived here all my life. I've about as much right as anyone to stay.' He suddenly laughed again. 'If it carries on like last night for much longer, the whole bloody lot of us will be out of work, not just me.' He looked at her. 'If any of us is left alive.'

'What do you mean?'

He shrugged. 'I dunno.' He seemed to wish the

comment unsaid, but it was too late. 'Tell me.'

He shook his head slowly. 'If you'd been up there...' He was on the verge of saying something, and then he stopped.

She waited.

'You don't give up, do you? I meant nothing.' He stretched both arms over the back of the pew in front and let his head hang between them. He flexed his neck first one way and then the other. She watched him, saw the slight wince as the movement aggravated some ache, some tender spot. He lifted his head again. 'Last night,' he said carefully, 'it felt like they were moving in on us. That was all I meant. They were circling, dropping incendiaries so there were fires all around us.' He paused. 'I don't know. It was bad.'

'Do you think they'll come back?'

He nodded, staring straight ahead, along his outstretched arms, towards the altar.

She got up to leave. He made no sign of moving out of her way, so she edged out of the pew on the other side and crossed through the row in front. As she passed him, he grasped her wrist and made her stop.

'It's not all linked up, you know. Like you say it is. It's not.'

She pulled herself free. 'It is, more than you think,' she said.

She stood for a moment at the window with Hope. It was still light, but the life was beginning to drain from the day and a violet tinge was creeping in. Hope had given up measuring the tower. It never grew any taller, now. The last mark she had made on the side of the window frame was weeks old. She had lost her faith in it.

Down in the garden, the mound of the half-buried shelter rose from the centre of the lawn. The door was closed, and Mary remembered she had forgotten to drag out the mattresses in the morning and leave the door propped open. Mrs Hayes would perhaps suffer with the damp in there tonight. She felt she had wronged Mrs Hayes. It sat badly that someone so old should have to lie there alone, frozen with a fear she could not express. After Hope was in bed, she would go down with dry blankets and fresh matches and top up the paraffin in the lamp. There was nothing more she could do. And, she supposed, she and Hope would spend another night underneath the kitchen table.

Unless. She felt a strange stirring low in her stomach. She and Hope might keep her company there tonight, if there was another raid. Why shouldn't they? It really was that simple. Thomas might have been wrong about some things, but he was at least right about that. Taking control of her own life was possible. She had shown it to be possible this morning, choosing for herself to sever her link with her new friend. It saddened her, but she wouldn't think about that now. She would tell Hope the good news instead. She was quieter than ever, these days. As every evening moved towards night, she grew a little more inward.

'We'll go to the shelter, tonight, my darling. If there's

a raid. We'll keep Mrs Hayes company.'

The child looked up at her quickly. Mary had noticed this recently – the intensity of focus, the hunger with which any new piece of information was absorbed. Hope was growing up much more suddenly because of the war, she thought. There seemed little of childhood left in her.

'Will Father come?'

'I don't think so.'

'Will he know we're there?'

'If he comes home.'

'Will we go to the shelter even then?'

'Yes, my love.'

Hope kissed her mother and climbed into bed. Her reaction was instant, like moving from a cold corner to the fireside. Her body uncurled itself in response, and seemed to lose the hunched-up woodenness which had been stiffening inside it for months. She wriggled herself down underneath the covers like she used to when she was much younger, pushing her legs between the tight, tucked in sheets, pulling the plump, cushiony eiderdown up to her chin.

'Will we really go with Mrs Hayes?'

Mary nodded, smiling. She leant over and kissed her daughter lightly on the forehead. And then she pulled her into a sitting position, hugging her roughly, breathing the child's hair, the warmth of her neck, not wanting to let her go.

The sirens started just before midnight. She was lying awake in the dark, waiting, imagining people lying in bed in coastal towns – in East Anglia, Lincolnshire, Humberside – wherever it was that the planes met the contours of land again after the blackness of the sea. And in midland towns. Hearing them grow louder and then fainter, and breathing a guilty sigh of relief that it wasn't for them they were coming. She imagined, too, what it must be like, up there. Looking down at the darkness below. Trying to make out the terrain. Over the sea there would be nothing at all. Was it possible to see through such deep black? And, when they found land again, it was to face great barrages from the defences stretched along the coast. Any moment the fall might begin and the end would come. From so high, how long would it take to fall, she wondered. In darkness. Or perhaps in flames. Conscious? Or not? She thought again of poor Dan Riley, his motionless face the colour of bread. His broken body. His terribly damaged head – still whole and warm as it lay there, denting the pillow, but all the connections severed inside. Like an egg scrambled in its shell.

And if the end didn't come, as they crossed back from water to land, what then? How long did it take, that slow throb east to west? How much could they see of the places they passed over? The towns heavy with blackout. Factories disguised, buried under great mounds of earth. And yet – they must still see the rows and rows of terraces below. And the river. And the church spires. The cathedral. It wasn't possible to hide such things, even if there was no moon.

The bedroom door opened and Hope appeared in the gap.

'Mother? They're coming.'

She sat up and pulled back the covers, pushing her feet into her waiting shoes. They moved wordlessly down the stairs together, the siren-sound emptying them of all impulses except the need to reach the shelter. They pulled on their coats in the hall and wrapped their quilts around their shoulders. Mary picked up the bag she had set ready by the back door. In it was a flask of Ovaltine and a tin of oat biscuits. Mrs Hayes would be there already. She always went out the moment the sirens started.

By the time Mary came down the ladder into the close, paraffin-smelling space, Hope was sitting beside the old woman on her bunk, embracing her. Mary busied herself with the bag of provisions, tucking it onto the shelf securely so that it wouldn't fall off with the vibrations. She avoided the old woman's eyes. They were there. That was enough.

This time there were no preliminaries. No droning engines faded in and out as the planes circled. It started almost as soon as the door was pulled closed and hooked in place. With trembling hands, Mary unrolled the curtain she had made to cover the door. A few ends of material from the blackout curtains which she'd stitched together and backed with a double thickness of hessian sacking. It wasn't much, but it just covered the doorway and might deflect some of the debris if a blast blew the door in. It kept the draught out, at least. She had resisted the idea of using sandbags against the inside of the door. It would feel too much like burying themselves alive.

She climbed up beside Hope in the top bunk and tried to prepare herself for the hours ahead. She needed to still her mind and shrink down until all she could see were the two tiny votive flames in the alcove at St Joseph's back in Derbyshire. She tried now, but she couldn't do it. She wrapped herself as closely as she could around Hope. Just a spark was all she needed. She could kindle it into something stronger. But the flames wouldn't come alive.

At one time, she thought, there had been three flames. At what point had Will's been allowed to die? She couldn't remember. But the thought jerked her eyes open. Something was going to happen tonight. What was it Thomas had said? That the planes had circled and ringed the cathedral in fire. That was the warning. Tonight, they would finish it. She loosened her grip around Hope and sat up.

It came to her fully formed and yet not fully seen. She didn't know what it was, but she knew it was monstrous. She groped her way towards it. Tonight was to be the end. Hope didn't want her to go, she cried for her to stay, but she heard her own voice saying William was in danger. She had to make him come away from the cathedral. The words seemed to fit, though the impulse seemed to come from the cathedral itself. The old woman was sitting up too and Mary handed her daughter over into her care. She said nothing, but she seemed to understand even as Mary struggled to make sense of what was happening. The words came out of her mouth the right way, but she didn't know how they married up with what she was doing. Mrs Hayes took hold of her wrist and stayed her for a moment, forcing her to be still. It might have offered her something, if she had known what to look for, but then again, it mightn't. She held her tight until Mary was forced to meet her eyes. Not a word. A note of query in the look, certainly. But she didn't try to stop her, and Mary knew that she would look after Hope.

In the house, she found herself at Hope's empty bedside, her shaking hands pressed hard against her forehead. She tried to shut out the noise. It was impossible. She screwed up her face and felt a kind of thundering in her head. Everything was racing in her mind. If only it could be still. She stood up and twitched the blackout curtain aside. She could see the planes. She had never seen one before. Had never seen a raid in progress – only the after-effects. This was something altogether different. It seemed almost forbidden, seeing those grim silhouettes, as if to look at them, exposed in the very act of devilry they had come to perform, might bring a hex down on the looker. Something that wasn't meant for seeing. She stood there in a sort of wonder, just watching.

The sky was glowing with a warm, hazy light. She could see the cathedral tower – square and solid and utterly present, as always. But something must be ablaze, surely, for it to be so ruddily lit. Had it been hit already? Was she too late? She craned her neck, looking up urgently at the planes, as if they could give her an answer. It was difficult to see how many there were. They seemed to sweep and turn, but they were like the starlings that massed over the city every evening at dusk, clustering together, moving apart, going first one way then the other, irregular. Impossible to follow. They were so much like living machines, it was hard to believe there were people inside them. Perhaps there weren't. She pushed up the window and leaned out. They were everywhere in the sky. Right overhead. She felt a brief pang, looking out at the tiny shelter in the middle of the garden. Such a paltry covering of earth. It would do nothing. But then the planes dragged her thoughts away, back to themselves again. The noise they made had got inside her head. It was all over her; she felt she was crawling with its infection. She closed the window but it made no difference. If anything, it was worse. She fumbled the curtains across and hurried onto the landing, and then it was pure noise that drove her, lifting her from her feet and sending her crashing down the stairs towards the front door.

She was outside, everything coming louder still, but through the cacophony she could see flashes of stillness, now. She saw Will. When had she seen Will? She hadn't seen him for days, had she? She wasn't sure she could remember the colour of his eyes, though she knew the texture of his skin. How little they touched each other. And Riley's fallen-in face. So young and yet so finished with. If his chin hadn't been sunken into his chest, lying there in that hospital bed, he'd have had a fine profile, a good, strong jawline. So soon his life had been over. She had never seen him in living life, only in dying life. Only ever a figure in a bed. And Thomas, with his unruly, out-of-doors manner, and his gentleness, too. Would he be up there, on the tower, now? No because he had lost his job; he wasn't wanted any more. But he belonged up there, where he could truly live, in sight of the river, the wind roughening his face.

And Hope? She turned in the middle of the deserted street and looked back. So much noise, she couldn't even see where the house was, in the midst of it all. Hope. She closed her eyes and tried to conjure the tiny candle flames she needed, but still they wouldn't come. There was too much noise; too many things were alight and blazing in her head. She needed silence and space to conjure the tame little yellow buds. Their two pilot lights. Once there had been three. She turned back into the street. A fire engine there, right in front of her, its roaring undetectable inside the rest of the noise, so that it came towards her like something in a silent film. A fraction of a second stretching into hours, but still not enough time for her to stop or change direction. She felt the air turn solid, her loosened hair whipping across her face. The driver hadn't seen her.

Chapter Fourteen – 2014

LOUISE sits up, instantly awake. Something is wrong. The noise is in the hallway. A continuous rasping inhalation, breathing in and in and in. Like the open fire at her grandparents' place before they had a gas one put in. A shovel propped over the grate and a sheet of newspaper sucking inwards as the flames drew, eating the air.

Fire. She is out of bed and at the bedroom door, her whole body shaking. Too late, she understands that this time she has been wrong about Benny. He hasn't gone away to lick his wounds. His grandiose ideas, for once in his life, have actually come to something because, surely, he is behind what is happening now.

Fire. It is there, unmistakeable, on the other side of the door. She is trapped in the bedroom. Automatically, her mind switches to Jake, the need to get him to safety. And then she remembers. He is already safe. So, she had been wise to take him away from here. She has at least got that right.

She never thought Benny would do something like

this, though. Would he really go so far? She doesn't believe he would. Threats – that's what he's good at. Not action. Not real violence. He's a fucking coward. She screws her eyes shut, tries to locate the memory of how she left the kitchen before she went to bed. Pulling the blind, checking there was milk for the morning. Did she check the gas rings were all turned off? Did she? She does it so often, these days, now that Jake has taken to fiddling with the knobs when she's not looking. She can't remember. She punches herself in the arm as hard as she can. She needs to stop thinking like this. Of course she did. For fuck's sake: Jake's not even here. She hasn't left anything switched on. This is not her doing. Benny is a coward, but then starting fires when people are sleeping – only a coward would do that. And did he think Jake was here, too? Does he want to punish both of them? No, he has been watching her. He knows she is alone tonight. This might be his only chance.

Smoke is wisping in around the edges of the door. She fumbles for her mobile on the bedside table and dials 999, speaks, in barely coherent gasps, to a voice that is calm and firm. Her head is swimming with fury that he has done this. He will not separate her from her son. She will not give him the satisfaction. She forces herself to focus on the voice that is speaking to her, telling her what to do. She pins everything on doing as it says. She drags the covers from the bed and pushes them up against the bottom of the door. Fumbles the key for the window locks out of the corner of her underwear drawer and opens the window wide. Calls for help, her voice tiny and trembling in the still air. She must get out of here, for Jake. She won't leave him motherless. They are coming, the voice on her mobile says. They are on their way. She mustn't open the door. Mustn't go near the door. Stay by the window. Shout for help. There is more smoke, now; the room feels grey and cloudy.

'Are you still there?' the voice asks. 'Tell me what's happening now.' It is difficult to speak. The smoke is getting everywhere, making her cough. They are coming, the voice says. They are only minutes away. They are coming.

She looks out of the open window. There is grass where she would land, but it is much too far to jump. She imagines doing it, though. She has spent the past year worrying about how low these sills are, frightened that Jake will climb up and somehow manage to pull a window open and fall out, even though she keeps them locked, always. Now she sees how easy it would be to sit on the sill and slowly lift one leg and then the other so that they hang down on the outside. She finds herself sitting and pulling up one leg in readiness. How long will it be until they come? 'They're on their way,' the voice says. Still strong and calm. 'It won't be long now.' It's getting difficult to see anything in the room, and the roaring at the door is filling her head so she can barely hear the voice. A woman's voice. Wonder what her name is. Where she is. Here but not here. She looks down again. The ground is not so far away after all.

Sitting there, like a bird poised for flight. Both heels kicking against the bricks. Ready. So easy. What does it feel like, the moment of letting go? That breath-held instant of no going back.

How long now? They are almost here, the voice says. Can you hear them? The sirens. You should be able to hear them. And the lights. Look out for the lights, the blue lights, but be careful not to fall. Knowing she is addled with the smoke and could so easily topple out. They will be here soon. They are here. Can you see them?

And how does it feel. The falling? Once the decisive moment is history and you're on the way down. No wings to spread and lift you up into the waiting branches of a tree. The clean, sharp air rushing past. The sound of it filling your head. Roaring. It's through into the room. Not a fire door. Just a normal door. One of the first questions the voice had asked. Keep it closed, though. Closed, but the fire's getting through anyway – the middle completely gone and great orange flames going up the walls and bending round the ceiling. Meeting at the top, like a moving archway. Sort of beautiful and alive. But the noise. And the smoke so thick you can't breathe or see any more.

The rushing of air maybe a better option. Grass is soft. Even from up here. Soft and green, tickles your fingers. Can't see the lights. Maybe someone in the trees. Is there? Dropped the phone. Rush of air. Roaring smoke. Which way is better?

Hope has unpacked the new kettle. She didn't have the energy when she got home yesterday, what with two visits to the hospital and going to Argos in between. In place on the kitchen worktop it looks so shiny it makes everything else seem a bit shabby. She smiles. Louise will understand that, she thinks. It's not a plastic one, this time, but stainless steel. Very modern looking. Yet at the same time a bit more like the old-fashioned stove-top kettle she remembers from when she was a child. The handle is plastic, though. So it could still melt in parts, given the opportunity.

She fills it up for its inaugural boiling and sets it on its base. It's quiet in the flat without Robert. She isn't sure why that should be. It isn't as if he makes very much noise. It's his presence that somehow absorbs some of the stillness and silence she can feel so strongly now. She has lost her buffer against loneliness, she thinks, as the whispery stirrings of the kettle begin to round out into a comforting purl.

At the hospital, he had looked so frail and – how can she put it – close to the end – sitting there in an institutional chair, pulled out of his own context. As if the strangeness of the surroundings had shrunk him. At home, he is so much more of a piece with everything else, that she hasn't really noticed how thin he is, or how lank and colourless his face has become. It could be the fluorescent lights, of course. They always emphasise the worst of things. But she knows it's more than that.

He was different in himself, too. More distant than

ever. She wonders – and it saddens her that it has come to this point – whether he actually recognised her at all. Without the context of home to remind him how she fitted in, perhaps she was just another person coming to have a look at him.

On the bus home, she had scarcely noticed the journey. She balanced the new kettle in its box on her knee and kept her unblinking eyes fixed on the view outside the window. She didn't want to start crying. Not on the bus. An old lady crying on the bus with a new kettle in a box that she had to carry back home to her empty flat. No, she didn't want to be that.

She unlocks the balcony door and opens it, hoping to hear the blackbird, but he won't come out singing until later. There is an electric saw going, the sound drifting across from a front garden somewhere along the street. And there's a woman with a toddler. The two of them making the slowest of progress along the road, because of the child stopping every few steps to climb up on the park railings and peer through them. The mother is so patient, standing there with her hands on the handles of the empty buggy. Watching him with such attentiveness, such care. She thinks of Louise and her little boy. He must be about the same age. Louise has shown her a photograph on her phone. A serious-faced little child in bright pyjamas. Perhaps one day she will meet him. She isn't accustomed to children, particularly, but she thinks she would like to meet him. It has occurred to her before, the fact that, when Robert is gone, she will be alone. No other living relatives. If she had children, there might be a grown-up son or daughter staying with her right now, keeping her company whilst their father is in hospital. She turns to look back inside the room, for a moment imagining someone there, leaning back into the sofa cushions. Casually crossed ankles at the ends of legs so long they reach right underneath the coffee table. Car keys jangled onto the kitchen worktop when he arrived. Her son. Or a daughter's handbag propped against the side of the armchair. Items of makeup left on the bathroom shelf, and the smell of someone else's perfume hanging in the hallway. And of course, there might have been the grandchildren, too. That woman out there could be her daughter. The little boy her grandson.

She glances down at the two of them again. They have barely moved. The child's shoe has fallen through the railings and he is pointing down at it. His mother bends down and tries, but it is too far to reach. Now they must retrace their steps up to the gate at the corner and go inside the park to retrieve it. The woman picks the child up and carries him on one hip, her free hand steering the empty buggy.

Hope goes back inside, glancing at the clock on the shelf. Where is Louise? Of course she may have decided not to come after all. Perhaps Carl has come home early, or her mother has brought her little boy back already. She wouldn't expect her to come, in that case. But she'd said she would. It strikes an odd note, that's all.

The new kettle has boiled and switched itself off. She pours the water down the sink, and the stainless steel warps and thunks in protest at the sudden heat as steam take off in curls and arcs from around the plughole. It seems a waste, but the instructions said to do it. To get rid of any factory residue around the heating element. She wouldn't want that in her tea. She fills it up again and puts it back on the base. She won't boil it yet. She'll hang on a bit longer for Louise.

She thinks, again, of the sudden memory she had yesterday. Her mother, kneeling and praying. Hope was only eight years old when she died. Such a slender store of memories to carry into life with her, and she'd as good as smothered what few she had. But, in wartime, so many people went like that: suddenly – unexpectedness a daily occurrence – and everyone just got on with it. She wasn't alone in having lost a part of herself back then.

Just kneeling, praying. She is perhaps remembering how they used to say bedtime prayers together, before she climbed into bed. But her mother is alone. Hope isn't praying with her; she is watching her.

She sighs and sits down on the sofa, keeping to her usual side. She glances at the place where Robert usually sits. He has spent so much time there that the piping around the edge of the arm has become worn and frayed. And with his endless picking of thread ends, he has made quite a mess of it in a few places. She needs to have a go with the nail scissors.

After her mother was gone, her father's sister came

to live with them and did the best she could. The person she'd spent most of her time with, though, was the old woman who lived downstairs. After the house was destroyed, she came along with them to their new home. Hope has far more memories of her than she does of her mother. Sitting together by the fire in her airless sitting room with its permanently half-drawn curtains and bare walls, in the house they lived in after the war. She would talk and talk and Hope would just listen, and the memory of any life other than the one they were living slowly sank and was gradually covered by the life that settled into place on top of it, inevitable as dust.

Once she had been to teacher training college and armed herself with a profession, Hope had left her home town behind. She had come here, to London. So much more of her life has been spent here that it is almost as if she has always lived here. Almost.

She hasn't been back since her father died. Nearly thirty years ago, now. Nothing else to tie her to the place. She'll probably never go there again, she thinks. The gravestone she had her father's name added to, beneath her mother's, she has never actually seen. She has always half meant to go back and at least visit the grave, but she never has. She was too angry at first, and then, somehow, the necessity faded.

For the few months around her father's death she'd had to take time off work, and Robert had been terribly worried about her. So much grief came pouring out. She hated her father for it. That he could take all her sorrow like that and yet he wouldn't let her feel any for her mother when she died.

She glances at her watch. Louise is more than an hour later than she said she would be. She wonders whether she should give her a ring. Just a quick one. She could maybe leave a message if there's no answer. She might be busy with something, and not have time to come. She could leave a message saying please don't feel you have to. I'm fine. And I've seen Robert. He's doing ok.

What she would really like to talk to her about is Robert coming home. They are going to discharge him later this afternoon, and she has to go back to the hospital to collect him. Of course she will manage, but she will have to get a taxi. She would feel so much better if she knew Louise could be there, too. She is so good with him. Hope knows he would be much calmer than if it is just the two of them.

She sighs. It is lunchtime. Often, before she leaves, Louise will make Robert a sandwich, and she makes one for Hope as well. To save her the bother, as she puts it. She doesn't have to, but if there's time, she always does. Robert is even different with food when it comes to Louise. He will eat anything she has prepared – even if it is exactly the same as Hope would have made. Same bread, same slices of ham and tomato. And yet. She knows she is silly to think he is even capable, now, of bearing a coherent grudge against her. But she can't shake the conviction away. Apart from Louise, she has told nobody about it. She doesn't think she could. She pictures herself sitting in the consultant's office, in one of those slightly too-low chairs that it is so difficult to get out of without someone's arm to pull on. She imagines herself speaking, and the consultant with her head slightly on one side, at an understanding angle, listening to her saying that fifty years ago she promised to kill her husband if he lost his marbles, and now he hates her because she hasn't done it yet. Maybe even Louise thinks she's crazy. She had seemed to understand, yesterday, but maybe she was just being nice. She's probably used to old women with wandering thoughts and funny ideas.

She is feeling hungry. This morning, she didn't really have anything to eat at breakfast time – only a bite or two of the toast she'd made herself. She can feel, now, a low down feeling in her stomach that could become a growl if she doesn't eat something soon. She glances at her watch again. With a sudden empty feeling, she realises that Louise is not going to come.

She makes a sandwich. As she goes through the familiar motions, she tries not to give way to the sense of abandonment. Louise probably hasn't had any choice about it. If she has let her employers know that Robert is in hospital, she might even have been assigned to someone else. Hope feels a flutter of panic at this thought. If that has happened, will she be able to get her back when Robert comes home? She so looks forward to seeing her. Grace, who comes in the evenings, is nice, too, of course, but another person replacing Louise wouldn't be the same. There is something special about her.

She takes the sharp knife from where she now keeps it hidden from Robert, behind the breadbin, and presses it into her sandwich from corner to corner. Then she rinses the salad cream and tomato juice off the blade, wipes it and is sliding it back into its hiding place when she remembers what Louise told her about Benny outside the door in the middle of the night. Opening the letterbox and looking in. Sliding something in through the opening. When was it: two nights, three nights ago? A knife. Had she actually mentioned a knife, or did Hope imagine it?

She sits down quickly on the kitchen chair. What if something has happened? Louise was alone last night. She looks at her watch again. It is past the time she would normally have left. She wonders whether she has turned up at her next person's house. What if she hasn't? What if something really has happened? What can she do?

She telephones. There is no answer, just a message in Louise's voice saying to leave your name and number and she will get back to you. Hope says who it is but forgets to leave her number. She wonders whether to call back and leave it, but Louise has her number anyway, and she doesn't want her to think she is making a fuss.

Once she has left the message, she feels slightly better and takes her sandwich through to the living room. She eats mechanically, barely tasting it. She doesn't want it any more but she makes herself eat, because she doesn't want to start having problems this afternoon when she goes for Robert. If she's going to be on her own, she'll need to have her wits about her.

She leaves another message before she leaves for the hospital. This time she remembers to include her number, and she says she is going to collect Robert and will be home later. Call me when you get this message, she finishes. Just so that I know things are ok.

He is dressed and waiting for her in a little day room at the end of the ward. There's a TV on low and one or two of the other patients are sitting in front of it. One of them in a wheelchair with a blanket over his knees. And a woman in slippers and a faded candlewick dressing gown, who keeps shuffling back and forth between the window and the television. She doesn't do anything once she gets where she's going. She stands and stares at the TV, or stands and stares at the window, and then turns round and shuffles back again.

The taxi rank is next to the hospital entrance. She ushers her discharged husband to the end of the queue – there is a young couple with a baby in front of them, but nobody else. Still, she can't help feeling conspicuous. As if she has just bought an exotic pet from the pet shop without knowing anything about how to look after and feed it, and is now hoping nobody will notice she doesn't know what she's doing.

He is quiet in the taxi. Again, she is shocked by how vulnerable he looks out of context. The huge interior seems to swallow him up when he climbs in. Almost weightless, he slides about on the seat as the driver turns into the street. She points out the handle to him, says why not hold on like she is, but he won't do it. He picks at the cut end of the bandage around his hand and wrist and looks out of the window. There's a bit of traffic, and, although they never come to a dead stop for long, the journey is slow and sedate. It makes it feel solemn, as if they are on their way to a funeral. It's rare for them to be in a car together like this. They haven't had one of their own for years. And this too – the unusualness – lends the journey a peculiar sense of occasion.

The driver is kind. He carries Robert's bag up the stairs for them and leaves it outside the flat door. She thanks him profusely. She could almost cry with relief, now that the journey is over and has passed without incident.

He won't be helped up the stairs, or even waited for. She has to go into the flat and pretend she isn't just inside the door, listening for him. Now that they are alone she is dreading the return of his difficult behaviour.

He peers around and she is reminded of an animal – a cat – exploring a new home. She can't be sure he recognises where he is.

Once he's safely inside, and the door shut and locked, she glances at the answering machine. There is no flashing light. Louise hasn't phoned. She settles Robert and then rings her again, not even pausing, this time, to compose a message in her head before she dials. The voicemail clicks in and she listens to Louise's voice then puts the phone down.

When Grace arrives, Robert has been shouting, and has barely touched his dinner. He won't let her clear the plate away, and so the food is still there, cold, on the table when the entry phone goes. Apart from that, she has cleared everything else and done the washing up, but it doesn't look very good.

Grace seems pregnant with something important when she bustles in. Like a balloon that's desperate to burst. 'Has Louise been to you today?' she asks, once she's put her bag down and hung up her jacket.

Hope feels herself swaying slightly on her feet as she stands in the hall. 'No,' she says. 'No. I was going to ask you if –'

'– She has not been to any of her home calls today,' Grace cuts in. 'I have done a few of them, but...' She shrugs and gives Hope a meaningful look.

'Has anyone spoken to her?'

Grace shrugs again. 'I don't know. I think she is in trouble, maybe, when she returns.'

Something is wrong. Something has happened. Hope allows Grace to take control of getting Robert his hot bedtime drink and the couple of Rich Tea he always has on a plate. She needs to concentrate. She goes into the spare bedroom and gently pushes the door closed. She doesn't want to be followed in. She lowers herself onto the single bed. This is the room Louise might have stayed in, if she hadn't insisted on holding out against the intimidation. The curtains are undrawn and, with no light switched on, the dusky onset of evening gives everything a slightly violet tinge.

She tries to clear her mind and concentrate on the things Louise has told her over the past couple of weeks. How her son's father has been hanging around, watching. Waiting for his chance. And then, with Carl gone, coming to the flat and threatening her. Coming in the middle of the night with a knife. Christ. Hope swallows hard. Has she told anyone else about it? Carl? Her mother? Even as she wonders this, she knows Louise has told no-one. If she had, they would have insisted she do something. No, she wanted to deal with it in her own way. Wanted to show that she wasn't frightened of him, and she hasn't told a soul. Hope realises with a sudden stab of certainty, that she is probably the only person, other than Louise herself, who knows what has been happening. She feels, suddenly, very sick. What has he done?

Chapter Fifteen – 1941

HOPE waited for five minutes. Mrs Hayes was trying to calm her, to sit her down and comfort her. 'Hush, my darling. Hush now. It will all be over soon.' They were words that should have been murmured, but she had to shout them for Hope to hear above the noise. 'Come, my darling. Sit with me. We can wait together.'

Her mother had gone out there, into the noise. Just pulled open the door and let it close behind her, and Mrs Hayes had hooked it shut and pulled the curtain back across. How had she let her go? Why hadn't they stopped her? How could she just walk out like that and leave Hope behind? 'I need to find her,' she screamed. The old woman was clinging onto her arm, terrified, and didn't hear. Hope pulled herself free. She needed to find her mother. Mrs Hayes half-rose from the edge of the bunk and grasped hold of the back of her cardigan. She wasn't to let her go, she screamed. She had promised to look after her.

Hope dragged herself away and pulled the flimsy door open, ducking under the curtain and out into the dark garden before Mrs Hayes could get hold of her again.

The sky was glowing orange. It was dark in the garden, though. With difficulty, she stumbled across the hummocky grass towards the dark shape of the house. Her eyes needed time to adjust, and she met the old privy wall with a jolt, not seeing it, and grazed her cheek against the bricks. She felt her way around the corner and up the steps to the back door. It was standing open.

The light in the hall was switched on and a little wedge of its yellow was showing through the half-open kitchen door. She moved quickly through the darkness, trying not to notice the familiar shapes that had grown suddenly monstrous. The dresser loomed on one side. The black mouth of the oven that had flames in its throat when her mother was cooking. She rushed past them, into the hall. He mother would have had to unbolt the front door and go out. She pulled the blackout curtain to one side: the bolt was still across. Had she not gone after all? Or had she come back already with her father? She stood in the hall, uncertain. Her legs were trembling. Fear was seeping in, no matter how hard she fought against it. Where was her mother? Where was she? She glanced at the stairs. The hall light made the idea of going up them less frightening, but the noise of the raid seemed to be getting louder, and upstairs it would be worse, because it was closer to the planes. She pictured herself climbing upwards, the staircase going on and on into the terrible sky.

But her mother must be up there. If she could find her, then everything would be alright. They would go back to the shelter and Mrs Hayes wouldn't be frightened any more. She made up her mind to follow her.

Everything was different in the night-time, and the most customary actions were strange when you did them alone. She had grown used to being out of bed and coming down the stairs in the dark, because of the raids, but now, climbing the stairs in the deserted house, with the roaring outside, she was more afraid than she could ever remember being. The stairs, with the same, familiar carpet, the same creaky one halfway up, seemed changed and malevolent, as if they had turned against her in the night. Yet up she climbed. To the first floor landing. Perhaps her mother was back in her bedroom. For a breath-held moment she thought she might simply have gone back to bed. If she had, she would climb in with her and they would both lie there under the blankets until it was over. But she wasn't there. The blankets were still turned back from her hasty departure.

She glanced inside her father's empty study. He never used it any more because he spent all his time at the cathedral. There was only her own room left, now, on the top landing. She grasped the banister and started upwards. The light hadn't been turned on and she climbed into growing darkness, fearful of touching the light switch herself. She couldn't hear her own breathing, but she could feel it juddering in her chest, her whole body now caught by the shaking that had started in her knees. Up the stairs towards the darkness of her own bedroom.

The door was slightly open. Her mother was there.

Afterwards she wouldn't understand what stopped her from rushing into the room, and would bury the question deep in the rubble of it all and try never to remember it. Her mother was on her knees at the side of the bed. It was just like when they said prayers together at bedtime. Even in the middle of the worst air raid ever, it was a wonderful, comforting sight. She trembled at the door, aching for her mother's arms. But she held back. Her mother was praying. She was absolutely still, head bowed, eyes closed. Like one of the angels standing watch over the graves in old churchyards. She had seen them, weathered, patched with lichen, their impassive features held calm through everything, even the loss of arms and nosetips. Perhaps at that moment her mother was steering her father back to them, in her prayer, away from the danger coming near him. If Hope were to interrupt, the prayer might not work. If that was her reason, it held fast. It was good enough. She didn't disturb her mother. She watched her through the gap. The noise of the planes was constant, and every few moments she could feel low, juddering vibrations. Her mother surely would not be long. If Hope stayed, she might break the prayer and ruin everything. She must creep away and her mother would follow. But she stood and watched her hungrily. She looked so still that her absorption seemed to have stopped time inside her. But only inside her. Outside, the planes still circled, dropped their loads. Hope wanted to run to her and hide inside the protection she seemed to have found in the midst of it all. Instead, she screwed her eyes shut and muttered her own short prayer, before she turned away and retraced her steps, down the stairs and through the kitchen. At the back door she paused. Her mother wasn't coming yet. Should she go back up and make her come? Perhaps she should. She half-turned, then changed her mind again and went through the open door.

She stumbled across the garden and slipped back inside the shelter. She had imagined Mrs Hayes would be sitting where she had left her, upright at the edge of the lower bunk, her feet pressed nervously together. But the old woman was underneath her blanket, with her knees drawn as far into her chest as she could manage to pull them, and her face turned to the corrugated wall. She didn't stir, even as Hope sat on the bunk beside her and shook her shoulder, trying to rouse her. Her mother was coming back soon, she said, over and over. She had found her. She was praying and she was coming back soon.

The blast shook the ground so hard the lamp fell off its crate and went out. The darkness that followed felt eviscerated, as if there was nothing left in it.

Hope didn't know whether she and Mrs Hayes were still really there. She wondered if she was floating through the air, or if this was what it felt like to be dead. Everything seemed to have been quenched in an instant. The noise of the planes, the bombardment, the lamp smashing onto the earth floor. Everything was gone.

And then she noticed Mrs Hayes' ragged breathing. So they weren't dead. At least, Mrs Hayes wasn't. Sound was returning – the whining burr of engines above, and the rumbling chaos of whatever was happening just outside. She was clinging to the old woman's back, which curved away from her, resolute and frozen. Just enough of life and will left in her to endure it.

Hope started to shake her out of her rapture of misery and fear. 'Mrs Hayes! Mrs Hayes! Mrs Hayes!' Finally, the old woman moved onto her back and then turned to face Hope. She put her arms around her and pulled her in close. Hope concentrated on breathing: one breath following another following another. Her ears still weren't right, but the planes did seem further off. Her mother hadn't come back yet, though. Where was her mother?

It was the very worst. The contractors' offices were up in flames and the timber in the yard had caught. Will had come down from the roof to help fight it off, but it was no use. They would lose the lot. Then another load of incendiaries had rained down and caught the setting-out shed. If they lost the machinery in there,

there was no knowing how long it would put them back. They would have to wait for this damned war to be over, and begin all over again. He glanced up at the tower. There it stood, even in the midst of all of this. How was it possible? Did something repel the bombs from the building? Even now, in the depths of this hell, he could find some sanctuary for his mind if he knew the building would be safe.

He shook his head. He had to keep his mind clear. It kept clouding over. It was the noise. At its worst, it filled his head until it reached a kind of plateau which was almost indistinguishable from silence. And, like silence, it obscured his judgement, his good sense and clarity. It let demons in. He had never been able to work in total silence, had always to banish it by positioning himself with his papers where there was some background noise to pull against, as if his own mental labours were balanced against the masons' or the joiners' physical exertions. At home in his study, he would have to switch on the wireless or set a record spinning, in order to have the opposite force of distraction he needed. Otherwise, he would feel himself drifting away, becoming lost. After his mother died, his home had been swallowed by silence and he couldn't settle to anything. He needed the clatter of saucepans, the sound of her singing, or else the rasp of brush bristles in the yard and the mournful clanging as she tipped shovelfuls of ashes into the dustbin. He began to stay in at school breaktime to do his homework, because he could no longer concentrate at home. The background noise of children playing made it easier.

'Jenner! Jenner! Shape yourself, Dolly! Just take it from him.' He opened his eyes as wide as he could, blinking himself back into focus. He needed to stop wandering in his mind like this. He wasn't the only one who needed sleep. He was pumping the stirrup pump in a dry bucket, and the lad at the end of the hose was gesticulating at him, mouthing words he couldn't hear. Another bucket, full to the brim, was already in position, and a young woman was standing there, frozen, waiting. He wrenched the pump out and plunged it angrily into the water. Why had she just stood there? What was wrong with her? But already she had grabbed the empty and was running back with it to the line of volunteers. He started pumping again. His arms were like separate entities, working under their own command. He couldn't feel them. And then, suddenly, everything shifted again. The firewatchers on the roof started waving and pointing. There seemed to be a new blaze on the other side of the building and everyone moved towards it, leaving the timber yard to the fire engines. Will stumbled after them with his bucket, water sloshing over his feet. The chain of volunteers reconfigured itself and the whole process began again.

At some point, one of the fire engines left. He heard someone bellowing that Saint Luke's had gone up. He sensed a ripple of unease pass through everyone and there was a moment's pause. The lad who had taken over the pump from him stopped pumping, put his hands on his knees and stood there, bent over, shaking his head and breathing heavily. The line of moving buckets stopped. The pale wrists and bared forearms of the shadowy people passing them down the chain froze briefly. If St Luke's could go, then... For a moment, their efforts seemed pointless. The fires were too far gone.

He looked up at the tower again. Another plane went over and he saw the thing briefly glint before it hit. He cried out. It had missed the tower but he saw it hit the roof, and he felt himself cry out and hurl himself forwards, but there was no sound, and as he ran towards it there were others who had seen it, too, and were running, and they all saw it burst out again, as if flung away by the building, and explode in the air above them. They covered their heads then, as the debris pattered onto the ground. Turning and running, with their arms covering their heads. They had all seen it. The roof of the cathedral had been hit. And yet the bomb had not been allowed to enter. It had been repelled and had exploded, magnificently, in the air. He could feel his heart pounding. He was laughing. If only it were possible! If only it were possible that there was a God after all! A God who could bestow his protection as easily as throwing out a blanket and letting it fall over them. That would be their salvation! He gazed up at the sky. Held his arms out, palms upraised. The bomb had been turned into a harmless, miraculous firework in a moment! Had his Mary been right, after all? Had he just been blind to it? If she was right, then how, how could he make amends? If he was wrong about this, how much else had he got wrong? He looked at the assembled crowd of workers. All of them staring up at the point in the sky where it had happened. 'A miracle!' someone shouted. 'That was a bloody miracle!' and a great cheer went up. With a surge of emotion, he cheered too, his voice thrown out in thanks and lost in the hubbub.

He turned away reluctantly. The gaggle of rejoicers was dispersing already, getting back to work. Some went off to their stations beside the Lady Chapel at the east end; Jenner wandered back towards the fire that was still raging in the timber yard. The fight against it had been given up now. He stood and watched it burn. His mind was worn so thin he couldn't remember what machinery was in the shed that had been abandoned. But it didn't matter! It was peripheral, and perhaps that was the price they would have to pay for their greater protection. A voice he recognised spoke in his ear: 'Your cathedral will be alright – look, the wind's blowing the other way.' The man beside him pointed. It was true – he could see the flames reaching out across the street. There were houses opposite, but the road was wide enough to preserve them. The important thing was that the fire was not being blown towards the huge wooden wall that covered the raw edges of the building where the cavernous, half-built interior came to a dead stop. He turned to thank the man, to shake his hand, but he was already striding away.

When the cry went up about an unexploded bomb lying on the steps of the main porch, he knew there was nothing to worry about. The warmth of his new-found sense of the miraculous had left him feeling calm and confident. They would get through this night. He went round to the porch with everyone else to have a look at it. The bomb lay there, blind and impotent in the moonlight, like an unearthed mole. Nevertheless, it was chilling to see the dull metal, the blunt rounding of its nose. It was a bomb, after all: it didn't need to brag about what it could do. It was lying slightly at an angle, on the bottom step, its nose and a fair amount of its body protruding over the edge. By the looks of it, there was more of it off the step than on. Someone else seemed to have noticed this too:

'It could roll off,' they shouted. 'Stand back!' And the assembled gaggle of onlookers shuffled backwards a hasty couple of paces. But it wouldn't harm them. Will was certain about that. There was no danger now. Even as he thought this, someone came to rope the area off. It would lie there on the step until the sappers came to dismantle it. He turned away.

Another wave of planes was coming over. His head was swimming. He couldn't see straight – everything in his vision was moving independently, like a set of cogs turning against each other. And his ears were still blinded by the explosion – the miracle – he had witnessed. He ran where he was directed, but no sooner had he started one way, then some other fire warden seemed to direct him somewhere different.

A burly man in a grey tin helmet took him by the elbow and seemed to be steering him away altogether, but he broke free.

The fire at the west end was still feeding on the outbuildings, and, as he looked around, he could see that the sky in all directions was heavy with the fog of orange-lit smoke. The planes were dropping more incendiaries. Up on the tower he caught a glimpse of something dark moving upwards, but when he looked at it directly it was gone. Maybe one of the firewatchers on the lower roof had spotted something on the scaffolding and was climbing up to investigate.

He was beginning to feel dizzy. He tried to keep his eyes on the ground, focusing on something steady, but they kept being drawn upwards to the tower. Again, the flicker of movement at the periphery of his vision, yet he could see nothing distinctly. And then someone was jabbing roughly at his shoulder. 'Oi, if you're helping, help. If you're not, then bugger off!' He swung round to see who it was, and stumbled to his knees. The fellow who had been rough with him pulled him to his feet and led him to one side. 'You're dead beat, mate. Sit this one out, for all our sakes, won't you?'

He sat on the damp ground and put his head between his knees. Everything was sound, now, even the darkness and the fire. Orange noise and black noise and great tearing flashes of white and the cogs in front of his eyes spinning wildly. He shook his head, trying to throw off the disorientation, but it just made it worse.

He glanced up at the tower again. Definitely something there. A figure moving up the ladders, he could see now. With a plunge of horror, he thought of the boy who had fallen. Still, the figure kept evading him. Every time he tried to see, it was one step ahead of him.

He stood up and went closer. There was no incendiary up there. It wasn't a firewatcher. Yet it was someone. He caught the movement again. Whoever it was had climbed past the first platform now, and was moving up the ladders towards the higher platform at the foot of the huge aperture that would house the sound vents on the south side of the bell chamber. He shouted out. A couple of lads he recognised as apprentice bricklayers turned their heads and followed the direction of his pointing arm. They looked back at him briefly, then at each other. One shrugged his shoulders, and they turned away.

He screwed up his eyes and strained to see through the disorder that was filling his head and fragmenting his vision. Why had they not seen?

The figure was on the platform now, moving first one way then the other, as if looking for a way up. It wasn't the dead boy, he realised, his understanding now unfolding calmly until it was spread like a map in front of him. It was Mary. He shouted again, half to her, half to anyone who would listen, but his voice, his gestures, were swallowed up in the confusion. No-one was taking any notice. He would have to go after her himself. He ran around to the main porch, forgetting that it was now roped off because of the unexploded bomb. He cursed, then skirted the perimeter of the building round to the Lady Chapel, bumping into people, stumbling over rubbled earth and hummocky grass. He craned up at the tower again. He couldn't see her. He ran backwards, trying to catch a glimpse, tripped and fell. Still he scoured the side of the tower. Where the hell had she gone?

He picked himself up. His elbow was throbbing where it had caught against a chunk of stone. He had twisted his ankle. He staggered forwards.

Then he could see her. She was almost at the next level. Jesus Christ – surely she wasn't going to climb to the very top. Why hadn't one of the watchers on the roof stopped her? Why were they not making her come down? She reached the level platform and paused, looking up at the planes. He was near the entrance to the chapel. He needed to go inside and get up onto the roof so that he could follow her. Yet he couldn't take his eyes off her. Still she gazed up at the planes, as if hypnotised.

And then she stepped forwards and looked down. There was a regal lift to her head. She wasn't looking at him, but over the top of him, out across the whole of what lay beneath her. As he watched, she grasped one of the uprights and used it to steady herself as she stepped up onto the horizontal pole that served as a rail around the platform. She wavered there a moment. Jenner couldn't move.

When she let go, nothing happened. For a blink, she

was perfectly balanced, motionless, as if, finally, she had found her element and was relishing the moment. Air and fire and stone. She seemed part of the building and yet part of the air around her, too, a living statue made of nothing but lightness, and grown out of stone. She stood on the rail, her proud head lifted, as if to do so were nothing out of the ordinary. Slowly, her arms lifted, and only when they were exactly at right angles to her body did she tilt forwards. She was like one of the planes she had just been watching. The dark shape of her moving against the stone and sky. As she dropped, her coat billowed out for a moment, and then she disappeared.

When they crawled from the shelter, they saw straight away that the house was gone. From the bottom of the garden Hope could look right into the road, where, over the top of the rubble, she could see part of a fire engine skewed at an odd angle across the street, and she could see the row of houses opposite which ought only to be visible from the front door or through the window in the best room. The long, unwavering tone of the all-clear siren died away as she and Mrs Hayes stood there together in the fuzzy grey light. It felt funny being in the garden and seeing the road, with no house in between. It was like being caught at the window in your underclothes, or having the blankets pulled suddenly off the bed while you were still lying underneath them. It wasn't a nice feeling. She wondered how she was going to get dressed and how she could possibly go to school if all her clothes were in a house that wasn't there.

And then it struck her that her mother, too, was in the house that wasn't there. She ran towards it, trying to find a way inside, but the inside was outside and there was no outside left to go in through and Mrs Hayes had caught up with her as she stumbled over broken pieces of brick and roof tiles and was dragging on her arm, pulling her back, saying something she couldn't understand. She had to use all her strength to break away from her. She was crying out, now, that her mother was inside, that they needed to find where the door had gone so that they could fetch her out. Mrs Hayes had let go of her arm, was just standing there, open-mouthed. Hope, making towards part of a green-painted lintel she could see, thought she had found the way in, when a pair of strong, veiny hands with bloody scratches and brick dust all over them caught her by the waist and lifted her away.

Chapter Sixteen – 2014

'So,' the police constable says. 'After telephoning Miss Erskine for a third time, I proceeded to the hospital unaccompanied to collect my husband." Does that sound right?'

Hope would much rather write the thing herself, so that she could dispense with all the proceeding and traversing. But apparently that's not how it's done. They have to write your statement for you, and then you agree that what they have written is what you said. She nods wearily. 'Yes, that sounds fine.'

Constable Webster has the same kind of round-bodied, flat-bottomed handwriting as the replacement carer who has been coming to see to Robert in the mornings instead of Louise since the day before yesterday. She wonders how they both manage to get it so straight underneath without having a ruler there. It is very neat. Uniformly legible. Her own handwriting, although easy to decipher, is a much looser, more looping affair. She watches the police constable's sedulous progress across the page.

Robert is in bed. He has slept a lot since coming out of hospital. He seems to have picked up a nasty cough, and it's tired him out. She sighs. She's tired too. She has been all of a jitter since she found out what happened. She wishes, now, that she had phoned the police sooner. When she mentioned this to Constable Webster, she was kind. She said that it was natural to feel that way after something like this, and to wonder if you could have done more. 'You did everything you could,' that's what she said, 'and you phoned us when you suspected she was in danger. I don't think she could find fault with that, do you?' She's probably right. But Hope keeps going over and over it. How scared Louise was, how she was determined not to show it. Last night she had woken up with a gasp and realised she was dreaming about the fire. She hadn't been able to get back to sleep.

The constable looks up and smiles sympathetically. 'I'm sorry this all takes such a long time,' she says. 'But it is important we get the full picture.'

'Will you get him, do you think?'

Constable Webster smiles again. 'We'll certainly try to find whoever's responsible, if the fire was started deliberately, yes.'

'Is there any doubt about that?'

'Well, as I say, the investigation is ongoing. I can't tell you any more, at the moment, I'm afraid.'

Hope has a sudden thought. 'Do you think,' she says, leaning forwards in her chair. 'Do you think they would mind – her family – if I visited her?' She takes a breath. She can feel the wobble coming back into her voice. It's the same every time she thinks about Louise lying there covered in bandages in a hospital bed. 'I don't mean now. I know she's...' She has to stop.

Constable Webster leans forward, her well-polished shoes creaking against each other, and puts her hand gently on Hope's back. 'I know,' she says quietly. 'It's a terrible shock.' She takes her hand away and the shoes squeak again. 'I think, once things settle down... if things go well... I'm sure they would have no objection. I'll make some enquiries, shall I?'

Hope nods. She can't trust herself to speak. It's the statement that's set her off. Having to go over everything again and again. Hearing it being read back to her in such wretchedly formal language.

The constable shuffles the loose handwritten pages together and passes them to Hope with the biro and clipboard she has been using, so that she can sign them all individually.

'And that's it,' she says. She is trying to be kind. 'We shouldn't need to put you through any more of this just yet.'

She takes the clipboard back, folding over the rigid front cover to protect the pages, and pushes it into her bag. She stands up and holds out her hand. 'I'm so sorry,' she says. 'I can see how worried you are about Ms Erskine. I realise it probably doesn't help much, but I know she's in the best possible hands, now.'

Hope nods and manages a weak smile as she walks the policewoman to the door. When she's gone, she just wants to lie down and sleep. She daren't disturb Robert, so she goes into the guest room again, pushing the door almost closed behind her, and sits down on the side of the bed, easing off her shoes. Then she pulls up her feet and stretches out on top of the covers. She lets her eyes close and her weight sink into the mattress.

She has been mulling something over. She supposes she started thinking about it even before what happened to Louise, but it's since two days ago that the thoughts have grown stronger. She has been so determined to keep Robert with her. Always by her side, where she can keep him safe. Except she can't, any more. It isn't possible to keep him safe twenty-four hours a day with just the little bit of help she has been getting.

Keeping him with her isn't going to change anything, either. She can't bring him back from the distance he has already travelled away from her. And she acknowledges, now, that she isn't going to keep her promise to him – she isn't going to help him on his way. She has known it for a long time, of course, but since she spoke about it to Louise, something about putting it into words has helped her admit it. She can't do what she promised him, all those years ago. She thinks the Robert he was when she made the promise would accept this: a decision not to go against her own code. It had been a promise made in youth, when neither of them knew the preciousness, the fragility of life. Now that Louise's life has been so threatened, she can't escape this. She thinks the Robert she once knew would understand and forgive her. And if he wouldn't – well – she has made her decision.

So, if she can't change anything or stop anything happening, maybe a home wouldn't be such a bad thing, after all. She wouldn't be abandoning him. She could see him every day, and he would be safe. Safer than he is here. She can at least look into it. She sighs and closes her eyes. She feels cold, lying on top of the covers, but is too weary to move. Everything is still and silent.

There is something about this room that helps her to think. It's almost a room outside her own life. Everything in it – the bed, the linen, the chest of drawers, the bedside table – is new and unused. Nobody has ever stayed here. The pot plant on the bedside table is an orchid from Marks and Spencer's that she bought fully potted up and in flower. The only reason to go into the room at all is to water it.

She opens her eyes and blinks up at the ceiling. There is only so much hold anyone can have over life, she thinks. Nothing can really be contained or predicted. Things, and people, change constantly, incrementally, without your noticing. And then there are the big one-offs, the heavyweight catastrophes that come hurtling in from nowhere, to throw you off your course.

In the months before he died, her father had started saying the most peculiar things about her mother's death. He had sent her badly off track. She ended up being away from work for weeks, unable to face going into the school where she taught and seeing all those little faces gazing up at her, waiting for her to tell them what to do, and give them the facts, the dates. This happened in such and such a year, and it was followed by this, then this. As if she knew anything about things that had happened hundreds of years before she was born, when she was no longer sure what had happened in her own life. And then he had died and left her to scrabble through the grit of words he had left scratching away inside her head. Robert had tried to help, of course, but he was outside it. His sense of reality wasn't the one that had been called into question.

Nevertheless, Robert had taken a laudably practical approach, undertaking the small amount of research that was necessary to find things out, and then presenting her with a choice. If she didn't want to know, he wouldn't tell her, but if she did, he had it all there, in black and white. The evidence. What had really happened. Had she been wrong to react the way she did? She has always thought she should have been braver, should have allowed herself to know what was knowable. After all, Robert knew, and he was still able to look at her, to speak to her in the same way he always had. It hadn't altered how he saw her or felt about her. But she had forbidden him from retaining even a slip of paper that might reveal anything. Destroy it all, she had said. I don't want to know.

However she looks at it, the picture is the same. Her father hadn't been a good father. He hadn't looked after her. He had closed her out completely after her mother died, and Hope always accepted that this was because he blamed her. She had left her mother alone in the house. Left alone, she had died and Hope had not. Just like that, the house was gone, and her mother with it. And it was she who had left her there. She who had just walked away.

She sighs. She doesn't know why she has been thinking so much about all of this. It was all so very long ago. She was just a child. Yet her memory feels ploughed up at the moment, with the stuff from way down suddenly turned over and dumped, in all its cool and wormy dampness, face up to the sun, and it feels unsettlingly familiar. How strange it is, to be flung so far back, when what is really filling her mind is what is happening now.

Robert coughs in the next room, and starts muttering in his sleep. She sits up and lets her legs dangle over the side of the bed, feeling for her shoes. He is due another dose of antibiotics soon, but she doesn't want to wake him. If she does, she may as well forget the tablets. He won't take them from her anyway, but particularly when he's groggy from sleep. They will have to keep until Grace gets here.

Chapter Seventeen – 1978

THERE was a sudden lull. The anticipatory murmurings had been rising in a continuous low sibilance, like gradually released steam, from the packed rows of chairs flanking each side of the nave. But now there was a hush, a cough, a chair leg scraped the flags, and then the fanfare began. Her father leaned a little forwards in his chair. Here comes the Queen, she thought, resisting the urge to lean forwards too, and peer at the tiny figure towards which every head had now turned.

She allowed herself to look while the congregation chewed their way through the national anthem. Bright blue, she noticed. And a matching hat. Well, it would stand out for the TV cameras, at least. Maybe that was why she had chosen it – or her ladies-in-waiting, or whoever it was that helped the Queen pick out her wardrobe. She wondered whether Robert would bother to watch at home and try to pick her and her father out in the crowd. Probably not.

She hadn't wanted to come. In fact, Robert had persuaded her. He's old, he had said. It's important to him. If you don't go, you'll end up wishing you had. She hadn't really understood how that could ever be the case, but she softened enough to go. She even bought herself a new skirt and blouse.

She couldn't help her lack of enthusiasm. Even after her father retired, he had followed the cathedral's slow growth almost as closely as he had when it had been his livelihood. He threw his arms up in impotent despair at every delay he heard about. When there was a problem with the stone quality he cried out that the building was cursed, as if he really believed such nonsense. It irritated Robert, got him all wound up the wrong way. 'William,' he would say, his voice a model of calm control. 'Surely it's better to be delayed, if the result is a stronger building. Would you rather they went ahead with the inferior stone to get it built sooner? After a few years' weather it would start to crumble away, but no matter...' Hope knew it made her husband angry to think about it. A cathedral, on which countless thousands had already been spent, and in which nobody was intended to live, had the luxury of waiting. Not so the future residents of the cardboard-coloured blocks he tried to humanise with his sculptures. Those people needed homes. And here was this great edifice going up to the glory of God. Why waste time fretting over delays caused by a seam of bad sandstone at the quarry? God had waited this long; surely he could wait a little longer.

And yet, Robert wasn't opposed to the place, any more than she was. She knew that he, too, recognised it had a kind of magnificence. When they went to the city together, to visit her father, he told her it made a lump in his throat, seeing the tower, first from the train, dwarfing everything around it, and then implacably there, huge and unapologetic, in the gaps between buildings and at the end of every street. It was undeniably a good thing.

The singing finished and everyone sat down again. She felt her father shifting in his seat as the first speech started. She wondered whether his joints were seizing up already; the chairs were not very comfortable. They would be stuck there for more than an hour. And he had said he wanted to go up the tower before she left again for London. He was nearly eighty-three. She didn't think he could manage it.

She wondered why he wanted to do it now. Since the tower's completion, he hadn't once gone up there. He hadn't let her go up, either. She was invited once – some official do with the architect placing the last stone on the last of the pinnacles that crowned the tower. It was to be the highest point in the whole cathedral – but he refused to give his permission. She had never forgiven him for that. She had so very much wanted to go. Her mother had died only the spring before and, in her child's mind, she had thought she might feel closer to her, up there. She had always told her that church towers were high because they were reaching up to God. And the two of them had talked, often, of what the view from the very top would be like when it was finished. It was the middle of winter and she'd sat at her desk at school with an extra jumper on underneath her school blouse, imagining the icy wind blowing in off the river. The sound of it roaring in her ears. Numbing her face. But he wouldn't let her go, and she had sulked. They rarely spoke about her mother.

Her father's breathing was audible beside her. She couldn't tell whether it was because he was falling asleep, or because he was concentrating hard on listening.

She nudged him gently with her elbow, but he wasn't asleep. He looked at her. His gaze characteristically clear yet unrevealing. She had never really known him.

They stood up for a hymn. Without thinking, she held out her arm for him. He took it and pulled himself upright. He had been younger than she was now, Hope thought, when her mother died. She found her place on the hymn sheet, and pointed it out to him. He was fiddling with his reading glasses. Not that he would sing, of course, but he liked to know where he was. All people that on earth do dwell. She tried to imagine what it would be like if Robert were to die, suddenly, without warning, as her mother had done. They didn't have any children, of course. It was different. But how might such a death affect her? Would it close her off from the world? Would it lock her away like her father was locked away?

The scaffolding had been taken away from the

tower, bit by bit, during an even colder winter several years later. Even then, he had fussed. It was all taking too long, and when it wasn't the war and shortages of this and that it was the weather causing problems. If she had thought that, once the tower was completed, the grip the cathedral had on him might loosen a little, and he might have some space in his life for his teenage daughter, it wasn't to be. He took little pleasure in anything, seemed to experience none of the thrill of achievement that everyone else felt when the last of the scaffolding came away and the tower could be seen clearly for the first time in all its solid squareness. He moved on without a backwards look, his attention turned already to the next phase of building, and he left home every morning when Hope was just getting out of bed, in order to prepare plans for the digging out of the nave. Hope breakfasted alone with Mrs Hayes. It was as if nothing of what had come before was of any further importance to him. He could dismiss things with such perfunctory ease. Did he forget her mother as easily? He behaved as if he did, but Hope wasn't convinced. Part of her always knew that in choosing to shut out the past he was punishing her. She had hated him for it, and herself for being the cause of it.

Living with the constant reminder of her guilt wasn't easy. She had stayed with her father only as long as was needed to build the means for permanent escape. The day she gained her teaching certificate was the day she started writing off for jobs in other cities, and once she had moved to London and found Robert, her life was elsewhere and she began dismantling the bridge that connected her to her past.

The hymn came to an end and her father sank gratefully into his seat, again holding her arm as he lowered himself. He felt as light as a bird. There was more fabric in the empty, hanging folds of his old suit than there was flesh on his thinning bones. He had been there, in a manner of speaking, all her life, she thought grimly. He wasn't going to live much longer, and she scarcely knew him at all.

They went up the tower a couple of days later. He wore his overcoat because in late October it could get chilly, and there had been a lot of rain. His joints were always more painful in damp weather and they had been keeping him awake for the past week with their constant, low throbbing. He wouldn't take painkillers. It was old age. The price of getting so old was in feeling it. Being able to feel it was the proof that you still went on living. He knew most people despaired of him, and he was alright with that. He wasn't about to start doing as he was told just to make people like him more. He couldn't care less about being liked. Still, he wore his overcoat, and he could see that his daughter approved. Underneath, he wore his suit. Surely you'll be better in something a bit more comfortable, Dad, she'd said. What did she know?

They stood in silence in the lift. He felt a slightly odd sensation at the pit of his stomach and then the doors slid open and they stepped out, his daughter offering her arm. He wished she wouldn't. They crossed over to the second lift, which would take them up to the base of the tower proper. From there they would have to climb the stairs. She would fuss, in all probability, and ask him, for the hundredth time, whether he thought it was a good idea. She didn't want him to go up. He had been able to tell from the way her closed mouth seemed to get smaller when he first mentioned wanting to make the climb, the day before the ceremony.

'But, Dad, there are hundreds of steps. You know that. You know what it's like. Why go up there now, at your age? Isn't it all a bit… unnecessary?'

'Not hundreds. One hundred and eight. And I can take it slowly. I am perfectly able.'

'But why do it at all?' She was persistent.

'Because I want to.' He couldn't tell her why. Couldn't tell her that for thirty-seven years he had been too afraid to. Was still afraid, even now. She would have to accept it – that was all.

The last time he had been up there was the night he lost Mary. That night, as with every other time he'd joined the firewatchers during a raid, he had forgotten his usual fear of heights, a constant, low-burning ache which dogged him each time he performed his inspection rounds. Snapping at his heels as he climbed the ladders, snarling and curling its lip if he dared to look down, always threatening to burst into sudden, bright, agonising flame. Those nights had been different: as he watched the city being destroyed around him, he had mastered his weakness. But he had never been up the tower again.

They stepped into the second lift.

Of course, that bloody mason had been able to sense his fear, whenever he did his rounds. As the lift doors slid open he allowed himself to think, briefly, about the man. Thomas Shaw. Mostly, it was as if he had never existed. Mary's death had eclipsed everything which came before. The face he pictured now wore an insolent expression that seemed to be suppressing a nod, a conspiratorial wink in his direction, as if to say, 'Don't worry. I won't tell anyone you're scared witless every time you come up here. I won't let your secret out. It's safe with me.' How he knew it, Will hadn't a clue – nobody else had figured it out – but he knew it alright, and silently taunted him. Used it to his advantage. Will had felt the man's power over him. Damn it, hadn't he used it to get the men up the tower the day that young lad fell? No, he couldn't be trusted. Not one inch.

Still, it didn't matter now. He was long gone. He'd hopped it when the company laid him off.

After Mary died, Will was urged to take time off work, but had refused. He was better working, he said, and the child was well enough, given the circumstances. His being at home wouldn't help her. He couldn't bring her mother back. He had taken the time necessary to find another place to live, and settle the child and the old woman into their new, half-empty home. And then he had returned to work.

They reached the bell chamber. The air felt cool on his face and his nostrils picked up the mineral smell of stone and weather which he had not known for a long time. Now he remembered it. He recognised, too, the odd timbre which so much solid material gave to the sound that carried across the vast, empty space which was enclosed, yet open. The air up here was living – he had forgotten that – it came in freely through oak louvres that filtered the light as through a half-closed Venetian blind. If he listened hard, he could hear the sounds of the city far below. And an aeroplane, flying overhead.

The steps zigzagged up one side of the tower to the roof. He stared at them. If he took it slowly, he could do it. Apart from his age and his arthritis, he was in very good health. He had a sound heart, and his weight, although a little less than ideal, was at least steady. He grasped the handrail.

He remembered how, that first day back at work, he had checked his tie in the wardrobe mirror before setting off. The wardrobe was from the Salvation Army, like most of the furniture they'd had to make do with in the months after they were bombed out. It had a door that kept swinging open so that the first thing you saw when you walked into the room was a reflection of yourself. Like seeing a ghost. He kept it wedged shut with a bit of cardboard. He had checked his tie, as he did every morning. As if to challenge anyone to say that this morning was any different from those that had come before. And then he had gone to work. Avoiding the street where they used to live. He hadn't been there since. He tried never to think about the gap in the terrace, the pile of rubble, the absence.

He hadn't needed to go up the tower immediately, of course, but he knew he would have to sooner or later. Nobody said anything about what had happened. He stepped back into his role and went on as before. When the time came to make an ascent, he did so. Mentally, he equipped himself with a contraption for his mind that was something like the cardboard collars you sometimes saw on dogs, to stop them licking at a wound. He strapped it on and looked straight ahead. Slowly, methodically, he made his inspection round, as he had done before. Nothing had changed. He could feel his heart thumping in his chest, yet could sense the drawing back of his blood, away from the extremities.

His hands were cold and sweaty. He became a little light-headed. And yet, he made his inspection, and nobody said a thing.

Only, of course, he was misremembering. He shook his mind back into focus. He hadn't been back to work for a long time afterwards. Just as the clerk of works returned, he, who had worked so hard in the older man's absence, began his own long period of leave. He never went up the tower again. Though he was right about the tie. Every morning, he had left home the same as usual, and every evening come home again. How he had filled the intervening hours he had no recollection at all.

He paused a few moments at the end of each short flight. First one way, then the other. She was very patient; he would allow her that. She wasn't hurrying him on. Each time he stopped, she simply stopped too, and waited with him. If not exactly companionable, it was good enough, and was what he needed. He wouldn't have been able to manage chit-chat. Perhaps she knew that. She was leaning on the low concrete wall, waiting for him, looking out into the space. He joined her, looking down at the circle of bells, all standing on end, upside down, like sculpted campanulas with their stamens resting wearily against the inside rim. They surrounded the huge, round shoulders of the massive central bourdon bell, hanging in its iron cage, so heavy it couldn't be swung.

She turned to him. 'The other day,' she said. 'After the ceremony. When we were going out. That vicar fellow. He seemed to know you.'

He nodded. 'Yes,' he said. He shifted his walking stick to his other hand and grasped hold of the concrete ledge. 'I see him sometimes,' he said. 'I know him to say hello to.'

She frowned. 'See him? Where? Here?'

He nodded.

'I thought you never came here.'

'Oh, I come here, sometimes.'

'When?'

'Sundays, usually. For the evensong, you know.'

'You don't like singing.'

'No.' He sighed. 'But I like to listen.'

'Really?' She was looking at him with such a penetrating look, he felt he couldn't meet her gaze.

'Yes. Really.'

Mary had enjoyed singing. She had enjoyed the services here, when the place was just half-built. She had joined in, of course. Knew the words to all the hymns. She would sing them at home, too. While she was cooking, or making up the beds. Sitting in his study at the top of the stairs, he would hear her. He could remember some things so clearly.

'Every Sunday?'

'Most, yes.'

He looked at her then. He had collected himself sufficiently. He was surprised to feel the need to collect himself. As if he had been found out. She was shaking her head, half, it seemed, in irritated disbelief, half in a kind of superior amusement.

He couldn't remember when it started. His memory was full of holes. Simple things, usually. People's names. The things he needed to buy when he went to the Co-op. And dates. Time could be such a tricky thing to keep hold of. He looked at her, no longer a silent little girl, but a middle-aged woman, older, much older, than the woman who was once his wife. Her mother. She had her likeness about the eyes, although Hope's had a penetration he had never seen in Mary's. And more crows' feet. He looked away from her, down at the silent bells again. No, he couldn't be sure when he had first set foot in the cathedral as a member of the congregation.

When the bells were rung, the louvres in each wall of the chamber channelled the sound downwards, towards the city below. Mary would have preferred the sound to go upwards, of course, to God. For her, bells were always meant for God. He had told her it was foolish, naïve of her to think so, but occasionally during the past year he had heard them ringing out and for a moment it had seemed to be sound for the pure joy of it, and it made him wonder whether Mary was right after all. He closed his eyes. The fact was, if they had been angled so as to channel the sound upwards, the rain would come in. He smiled. She never would have liked that answer. Would have thought he was mocking her. And she would have been right.

'What's so funny?'

How long had she been watching him? He had

forgotten she was there at all. He shook his head.

'Nothing.'

He could tell she was annoyed with him. Cross that, in coming to the cathedral on Sundays, he had been doing something that didn't square with her idea of him. He knew she wanted to ask him more about it. She wasn't satisfied.

'Shall we go on?' he said.

She nodded. A short, curt nod. Her face shuttered. He felt sorry, then, for not trying harder. Always, this closed up face. Even before, when Mary was still alive. She was his child, too, and for most of her life she had had only him. But she had always belonged more to her mother.

He was beginning to feel light-headed, but there wasn't far to go. He couldn't see how many flights there were left to climb, but he focused on reaching the top of each one in turn. Hope was making him rest on every half-landing now. She told him he was looking tired. She muttered something about a wheelchair to carry him down. 'I'm alright,' he growled.

At the top, he was surprised by the intensity of the light after the double-enclosure of the staircase and bell-chamber. So much brightness and sky after the heavy, grey concrete, and the pull of gravity.

There were some folding stools leaning against a wall. She took one, unfolding it as she walked back to him, and gestured for him to sit down. He shook his head. 'I don't need it.' His voice came out in the same phlegmy growl as before. He didn't seem able to get rid of it.

'Sit down.'

It was a little too low to sit on easily, but he tried. She held his elbow and put a steadying hand on his back as he relinquished control for the last few inches and allowed himself to be steered onto the seat. He was breathing heavily. His hearing had been overtaken by a kind of thumping that, now he was sitting, seemed to be getting louder, filling his head. She said nothing. She walked a few paces from him and looked out at the view through one of the glassless windows in the surrounding wall, peering through the tracery. He rested his forearms on his knees and leant forwards, closing his eyes, although that seemed to make things worse. A shifting mass of blue and purple, and the silhouetted shapes of the ornamental finials rising from each corner of the tower, cut out against a livid yellow sky, started sliding sideways in a way that sickened him. He opened his eyes again and stared hard at the ground beneath his feet. It wasn't ground, of course. It was over three-hundred feet in the air. Below him hung the huge belfry chamber he had just climbed up.

Mary hadn't come this high, of course. The night she died, the tower wasn't finished. But it was high enough. He lifted his head experimentally and took a couple of steadying breaths before attempting to stand. Hope turned instantly and came to his aid. He realised her scrutiny of the horizon was simply to give him space to collect himself. She wasn't interested in the view. She didn't want to be here at all. She was doing it for him.

'Thank you,' he said.

He went first to where she had been standing. There were hills in the far distance. Wales? The Pennines? He couldn't quite remember which was where. He followed the wall around, staggering slightly, peering through each of the window-spaces in the stonework until he could orient himself. The river was south. He found it, wide and black, and followed it as far as he could see, widening towards the estuary. The hills must be Wales. Further away would be the Pennines. He peered at the horizon, trying to see beyond it. At some point, the Pennines became the Peak District. And beyond them, somewhere, the village near Matlock where he had been born.

He realised he had been standing, staring, for some time. She must have walked the complete circuit, and was coming towards him looking expectant. She was ready to go down again. For her, he thought sadly, this had been nothing more than a logistical exercise. Get him up in one piece. Get him down again. The sooner it was over with, the better.

He sighed. He wasn't ready, yet. He wasn't sure what he had been hoping for, coming up here. Certainly not the seasick horror of looking down and seeing how far it was to the ground. He had seen her fall so many times in his mind, the memory had been worn out long ago. Absolution, then? Forgiveness from her God?

He was no longer sure he even wanted that any more. What was it? Confirmation? He had seen it happen; surely that was enough. Looking up at the tower, he had seen her standing there in her dark coat, poised for flight, like a bird. And the slow, deliberate control with which she leaned out into the thinnest of thin air, filled with the noise of war, and disappeared from view as the building came between them. The chaos of that night had been so all-engulfing that no-one else saw her. She had been an insignificant side-show to the main event. No-one but he had run into the deserted cathedral and panicked his way up to the roof as if he were trapped underwater and searching, frantic, for a way up to the surface. Trying to figure out where on the roof she would have landed. But he... he had seen.

Hope stopped in front of him. 'Are you ready to go down?'

He nodded. He didn't know why he had come, after all. He was shivering slightly. He had been right to bring his coat.

Chapter Eighteen – 2014

CARL has come to collect her. It is generous of him. He has more than enough on his plate, but when she telephoned him on the number Constable Webster had given her, he was quietly insistent. In another life, she thinks briefly – as she catches herself doing more and more these days – it might have been her son collecting her. Coming to take his mother out for the day.

She notices how tired he looks. He is wearing saggy grey tracksuit trousers and a T-shirt that has seen better days. His face is round and boyish, but already overcast with the fallen-away look of somebody older. His eyes seem troubled, as if they have already seen too much of life. The young don't have it easy, she thinks.

Carl stands awkwardly in the middle of the living room as she collects her cardigan and bag, and the flowers she has bought for Louise. She has also bought something for the little boy. A book with pictures and flaps that you lift up. She isn't sure whether it is the sort of thing a child his age will like, but she has wrapped it up and put it ready with the flowers.

In the car, once she has asked after Louise and the little boy and Carl has asked after her husband, there is a lull. He has the radio on, but it is turned down low, and, she realises, is playing Schubert. She wonders whether he has retuned it for her benefit.

She looks out of the window. They are passing what is left of the Blackbird Estate. The long, grey blocks, with their graffiti and grime and rows of metal-shuttered flats, have gone now. Where the nearest one stood is a huge pile of rubble, with, here and there, water jets playing out over its surface. It looks as if they are hoping something might grow out of the ruins.

It gives her a shiver of mortality. This place where so many lives have been and gone. So many births and deaths. She thinks of Robert's parents, moving in after his father's accident. That photograph of them – one on either side of Robert, standing beside his sculpture. How proud they both were. Even his father, lacking the words to say it, had worn his pride, beaming in the photograph, patting the head of the little bronze boy as he peeped round the wall of their flat. She thinks of Louise, playing with her friends on the grass between the blocks, running amongst the trees, laughing and chattering. Their mothers keeping an eye on them from kitchen windows and walkways. Louise becoming a teenager there, smoking, holding hands with Carl. Kissing. And more.

How sad that things always seem to end up going bad, she thinks. The estate has been a good home to a lot of people. That has been forgotten. And now, after just forty years, it is a pile of rubble. Such a long stretch of it, like a huge burial mound. And even with the water jets, she can see the thin gruel of dust lifting up from the surface, refusing to accept defeat and stay put. All those homes and memories buried.

She looks away. When she was a child, there were so many ruined homes piled up like this. Her own home, too. The utter sense of dislocation and horror when she and Mrs Hayes had emerged from the shelter and the house wasn't there any more, and neither was her mother. She shakes the memory away. Makes a deliberate effort to think about something else as the traffic lights go green again and Carl eases the car forwards. The demolition site recedes from view.

Robert seems to be settling in well at the nursing home. She is glad. It has been a fortnight, now. He has put on a little weight, and is getting angry less often. In the meantime, she is learning how to be alone. She has found, for instance, that she likes having a nap every day after her lunch. She does it properly – removing most of her clothes and getting into bed. Sometimes she reads for twenty minutes. Sometimes she puts the radio on. Other times, she simply lies, in a light doze, until forty-five minutes have passed, and then she gets up again. It is a simple luxury that gives her pleasure. And it brings a little structure to her day, to replace the tasks she no longer has to perform. She has so much more time available which has to be filled. It's quite thrilling, in a way, to know that she could spend the whole day in bed reading if she wished, but it is also unnerving. Frightening, even. She isn't sure why.

The loneliness is taking a little longer to come to terms with. She has lived with Robert for more than fifty years. The depth of silence in a home inhabited by only one person is different from all other kinds of silence. More a quality of stillness, really, because there is always sound, coming from somewhere, elsewhere. Lawnmowers, aeroplanes, cars going down the street. The pull of buses straining up the hill. Recently, an ice-cream van, and at certain times of day, the sticky swarm of children gathering round it with their mothers standing at the periphery. As evening approaches, the blackbird starts singing, or fussing and startling under the rhododendron bushes, foraging for worms. At night there are more cars, and foxes patrol the park, standing and looking, just inside the railings, with their sharp, expressionless faces. Closer to hand, there's the gurgle of water in the pipes, the boiler firing up and flaring briefly. The inexplicable creaks and cracks the building makes as its various parts expand or contract against each other. Like creaking joints. Cracking knuckles. No, it isn't silence that bothers her. But she does feel the press of the stillness. She had been feeling it yesterday, lying in bed for her nap. She hadn't been able to read or to switch on the radio, but neither had she been disposed to sleep. After fifteen minutes she had given up, and it was this sudden burst of irritation with her inability to be alone with herself that had made up her mind.

She had got out of bed, put her clothes back on, found the slip of paper with the number Constable Webster had taken the trouble to get for her, and typed it into the telephone. She had spoken, on a very unclear line, to Carl. He had sounded friendly. Said Louise had talked about her a lot and was fond of her. He was sure she would appreciate a visit. She had come out of hospital the previous day and was staying at her mother's house. Her own home, of course, was no longer an option. She was doing well, he said. Not up and about, of course. Her breathing was still difficult, because of the smoke. And the burns would take time to heal. They gave her a lot of pain. It was the pain relief, mainly, that made her so woozy, he said. She was sleeping a lot.

They stop at a zebra crossing and watch as an elderly man carefully crosses, his arm linked with that of a middle-aged woman who patiently keeps pace with him. A father and daughter? They watch the pair cross in silence. Hope wonders where they are going together. They are both smartly-dressed.

The last time she went anywhere with her own father was when he insisted she take him up the cathedral tower. She had known it was too much for him, but he had been so determined she hadn't the will to refuse it. He always did as he wished. But he had gone into a decline almost immediately afterwards. As if suddenly he had no more use for his life. A few months later, he was dead.

He had managed to embed a barb in the most

vulnerable place he could, before he went, though. In the months following his death, she had come somehow unhinged from herself, and the mending was slow and painful. She had grieved so much she felt she might never retrieve herself. She had never been close to him, never felt very much love for him. So why grieve this way? Of course, it all seems so obvious now. But at the time, she hadn't been able to understand what she was mourning for.

So much sorrow. He unleashed it all. She had been living with a lie was the gist of what he told her. Robert had pleaded with her to see sense. It was old age, confusion, dementia – call it what you will – taking hold of her father's tongue, he said. None of it was real. But she wasn't so sure. Her father was rigid in his belief.

Her mother hadn't been killed in the raid, he told her. She had killed herself. He had seen her jump. Over and over again, with his eyes intent on Hope's face. It's what happened, I tell you. Willing his words to hit home. She didn't die in the house. I didn't know what to tell you.

He had left her in a mess. It was like falling down a mineshaft, right back into her own childhood and the rawness of a loss which had never been acknowledged. She tried to remember what she had actually been told at the time, but, try as she might, she couldn't remember anyone telling her anything.

Don't be so hard on yourself, Robert had said. It

was nearly forty years ago. No-one can remember everything.

I'd remember that, she'd said. Nobody told me.

If her mother really had died the way her father insisted, perhaps everyone had thought it would be easier for her not to know. They hadn't reckoned on the conclusions she would come to by herself, of course. Or the guilt. Because it was Hope who had left her mother praying in the house. Hope who hadn't roused her from the bedside and said come to the shelter now. For God's sake, come. Hope who had gone back through the dark house and out to the shelter alone. It was Hope's fault.

And then forever afterwards, her mother wasn't spoken of. She simply disappeared – as if she had been taken from memory as well as from life. As if she had never been there. So Hope had drawn it all into herself. Her memories of her mother and her guilt. Only to be told, forty years later, that it wasn't true.

But people didn't fall from the tops of cathedral towers or get buried beneath houses without there being a record of it made, somewhere; that was Robert's view. And he had set about finding what records he could so that his wife could know the truth and come back to herself. He had done it quietly and thoroughly, the way he went about all his work. And he had done it without telling her. Then he had given her the choice. To know, or not to know: it was up to her.

Louise is sitting slightly forwards in a high-backed wicker chair. Beside her is a cannister of oxygen, the face mask hanging from it on a length of thin rubber tubing. Carl stays with them for a few minutes, arranging a chair for Hope and settling her down, and then offers to fetch her a cup of tea.

She would like to hug Louise, but she is fearful of hurting her. She is changed. Her eyes are over-bright, her colour different. It is maybe the painkillers. She reaches out and takes the young woman's bandaged hand gently in hers. Feels the strength of the grip that is given in return. She pulls her chair nearer, as close as she can get. With her other hand, she touches the side of Louise's face. 'I'm so glad to see you,' she says.

Jake has gone out with his grandma, Louise tells her. Her voice is scratchy, and not much more than a whisper. She says it's frustrating not being able to talk so much, but Jake is loving it. He never gets told off, because she can't do it, and her mum's too soft with him. She smiles. Looks into Hope's eyes. 'I thought I was a goner,' she whispers. 'I really did.'

She came close. Very close. But she is still here. She hasn't been destroyed. She isn't going to make it easy. She refuses to disappear. Hope rummages in her handbag for a hanky. Her thoughts are suddenly whirring, clicking back, again, to the past. She can't stop it happening at the moment. Every little thing seems to set her off. Her mother. In her father's version of what happened, her mother had chosen to disappear. Not an accident, but a choice. It absolves

Hope of her guilt, but at what cost? Would her mother really have given up on life? Abandoned her child? Her father hadn't known what he was saying. She didn't kill herself. She was killed when a bomb hit the house. She had no choice but to die. She never stood a chance. Sometimes, it is still better to believe that.

Well, Louise is still here. She does have a chance. That is a wonderful thing. Carl has come back with the tea. She extricates her hand from Louise's, quickly blows her nose and stuffs the tissue back in her bag. He pulls over a little side table, finds a coaster and puts the tea on it. 'Careful,' he says. 'It's a bit hot.' He puts a plate of custard creams next to the mug and goes out again.

'I'd like to go into the garden,' Louise says. 'Mum's got it really nice out there. I'd like you to see.'

'Are you sure you should...' Louise is already gripping the wicker arms, gritting her teeth against the pain in her back. Carl comes running in again to help.

She walks down the garden on his arm. Hope follows a few steps behind. Louise is right; the garden is lovely. Past the neatly paved patio, the lawn gradually narrows as the flower beds on each side gradually encroach, until they meet and join hands in the form of climbing roses and clematis flowing over a rustic arch.

'Through here,' Louise says, and she and Carl go one after the other, Carl still supporting her elbow as she walks in front of him. They duck their heads to avoid a low-hanging swag of clematis in full bloom, so that they appear to genuflect as they enter.

On the other side of the archway is a sort of outdoor haven. Two benches face each other beneath a roof of wisteria, its long, light-seeking tendrils carefully woven around the supporting framework of wooden beams. The heavy, blue flowers hang down in great, fragrant clusters. For a moment, there is nothing but birdsong.

'Lovely, isn't it?' Louise says.

It is. The house is hidden from view and so, too, are all the surrounding houses. They could be anywhere at all.

Carl leaves them to it, but says to call him when they want to come back in. 'We'll manage,' Louise says, smiling, but Hope can see how she is holding herself bolt upright on the bench. She is clearly in a lot of pain, but she won't let it show.

She sits down beside her. She is glad she has come. It has done her the power of good to see Louise.

'Will you stay for a bit? Have something to eat with us?' Louise asks, suddenly. 'Mum and Jake went out to give us a bit of space. Jake can be … a handful… But I'd love you to meet him. If you'd like to.'

Hope nods, smiling. 'I'd love to,' she says.

'Also…' Louise pauses, adjusting her position slightly, and winces, her breath catching between her teeth. Hope straightens, her hands lifting without warning from her lap, ready to help. 'It's ok,' Louise says. 'It just takes me by surprise sometimes.' She smiles. 'Anyway, Carl has something he would like to show you. It's near here. About five minutes in the car.'

Hope turns to look at her friend. 'What is it?'

'I've been sworn to secrecy,' she says. 'He wants to be the one to show you.'

Hope must look worried, because she says, 'Don't worry. It's nothing bad. At least I hope it isn't.'

When it is time to go back into the house, Louise takes Hope's arm. Slowly, the two of them emerge through the archway, back onto the lawn. The sunlight is brilliant.

He takes her to a pub outside the new development of housing – an older building. Thirties, perhaps. A dark, reddish brick in a style that is a little institutional and sombre. It's well-kept, though. There are window boxes on all the windowsills, spilling over with petunias and lobelia. Every picnic table at the front is occupied. It seems a friendly, family kind of place. There are one or two groups of young people, a couple with a baby sleeping in a pushchair, and an elderly couple with two little girls – presumably their grandchildren – kneeling up on the bench to drink their cola through straws.

Inside, she waits at a table whilst he orders something to drink, then carries the tray over. A tiny pot of tea with a bright orange cup and saucer for her, and a pint of fizzy cola for himself. The thing he wants to show her is in the garden, so she stands up and follows him out.

She doesn't see them immediately. They are arranged tastefully around the beer garden and there are so many actual children running about, playing and hiding, crouching down, huddling into groups and then dispersing, that the little bronze figures are lost amongst them. But then she sees the first one, the seeker, leaning into the trunk of a large oak tree which shades the garden. His tarnished forearms press into the bark, his hands tightly cupped around his eyes. His feet, precisely placed, side-by-side, slightly tiptoed. And his back, held so very straight as he counts. She remembers how many drawings Robert made of that figure, trying to get the posture exactly right. Standing up himself and shielding his eyes against the wall, to feel how the rest of his body positioned itself, and trying to translate that feeling into the little plaster maquettes he used to make.

She looks around. There's another one, under a bench. A toddler is squatting next to it, poking her finger at its face. Trying to see if it will move, perhaps. There is a third one sitting on a windowsill, one knee pulled up under its chin, the other leg dangling, both socks wrinkled down to the shoe.

And then she sees him, the little boy who used to peep around the corner of Robert's parents' flat. The garden is slightly L-shaped, and he is in the crook of the L, looking straight at her. There is an empty table next to him.

'Let's sit over there,' she says.

They sit for a long time. They finish their drinks and at some point one of the young bar tenders comes and takes their empty cups.

He had been worried about how she would react. Louise has told him a lot about her over the months, and had mentioned that her husband was the artist who made the bronze figures that were stolen a few years back. He remembered them from when he lived on the estate, but only dimly – they hadn't been near his block and he never had much cause to go past them. So he'd been to the pub a few times before he put two and two together. He didn't say anything to Louise or to anyone. He wasn't even a hundred percent sure they were the same figures, and he didn't want to get anyone in trouble about it if they were. Then there was the fire, and it had gone completely out of his head. Until today.

She smiles. 'It's alright,' she says. 'I think my husband would be quite happy if he could see them here. I think they have adapted to their new home remarkably well, don't you?'

He nods. He is clearly relieved she has taken it so well. It is all so simple, really. Let them stay lost and where is the harm? She feels a curious dropping sensation. A letting go, as something unsettled gently comes to rest.

When Robert had found out what happened the night her mother died, and presented her with a choice, she had chosen not to know. And that had been that. He had done as she asked, taken away the evidence he had accumulated, and nothing more was said of it. And, she can see now, there really was no harm in it. She had lived with her guilt for most of her life. If her father's version of events – however far-fetched – offered her an alternative, what was so wrong with accepting what he held out to her? Not a certainty – no, she had never taken it as that. A definite uncertainty. But for all of that, it did give her some relief. She had been able to see that there was another way of reading things where the responsibility for what had happened was lifted away from her.

'Are you ok?' Carl asks.

She nods. 'Yes,' she says. 'I'm ok.'

There is something else. Something, now, that she must be prepared for. She unfolds a clean tissue from the pack in her handbag and dabs at the corners of her eyes. Now that Robert is as he is. He says so many random, unconnected things. She has to be ready for it. It might never come – and even if it does, who's to know what's true and what isn't? Coming from Robert's jumbled-up mind, it's just as likely to be as muddled as everything else. Still, it's wise to be ready, just in case. She doesn't want herself getting all stirred up over it again. Not now, when it was all so long ago. If it happened again, she wouldn't have Robert there to help her through.

She blows her nose and looks up at Carl. He has been so patient. 'Thank you,' she says, 'for putting up with an old lady's sniffling.'

'That's ok,' he says. He shrugs. 'I guess it must be

pretty weird, all this.'

'It is,' she says. 'But things are going to work out alright, aren't they?'

He nods, picking up his mobile phone from the table. 'We should get going,' he says. 'Jean and Jake will be back by now.' He scoots round to her side of the table and hovers anxiously while she extricates herself from the chair. He offers her his arm, and, although she doesn't need it, she is touched by the gesture and allows him to take some of her weight. He glances at the mobile phone again and slips it into his pocket. They are about to leave when she has a thought.

'Is your telephone the sort that can take pictures?' she asks.

'It is,' he says. And then, understanding her meaning, 'Shall I?'

She stands beside the little bronze boy. Gently, she touches the top of his head. It is shiny and worn smooth. There must be a great many more people than her father-in-law who have been tousling his hair over the years. She looks up and smiles at Carl. Funny how these days the camera isn't held up to the face. He holds it out towards her, frowning down at the tiny screen. And then he looks up and smiles at her.

'Job done,' he says, holding out the phone with the tiny picture on its lit-up screen. 'I took a few. We can go through them when we get back and you can pick the ones you like. I'll get some printed up for you.'

'That would be lovely,' she says. 'I'd like that very much.' She takes his arm again and lets him lead the way. She can take the picture in to the home and show it to Robert. It will please her to do that, even if he doesn't recognise it. She will have done the best she can.

She might put one up at home, too. On the shelf next to the old photograph. Times have changed. That old photograph is a relic now, a memento from the past. It will be good for her to have something to balance it out. Something that shows the present and her place in it, whatever is to come.

Author's Note

ALL characters in *The Blackbird* are fictional. A number of the locations and events mentioned, however, are real, or are based on real places and incidents, and I enjoyed the challenge of interweaving fictional characters and lives with actual events. Two local history books – *The Building of Liverpool Cathedral* by Peter Kennerley, and *The Great Liverpool Blitz* by Richard Whittington-Egan – helped me get to grips with the timeline of bombs falling and the cathedral tower rising in Liverpool in 1941.

A visit to Historic England's exhibition – *Out There: our post-war public art* – at Somerset House in London in 2016, influenced my thinking about the character Robert, and his former career as a civic sculptor.

The Blackbird Estate is (very loosely) based on the Heygate Estate at Elephant and Castle in London, completed in 1974 and demolished between 2011 and 2014. Thomas Shaw's home in Albion Gardens is based on the 1930s Gerard Gardens housing estate in Liverpool, which had relief sculptures of a builder and architect by George Henry Tyson Smith above two of the entrances. Gerard Gardens was demolished in 1987, although the sculptures were rescued and are now on display in Liverpool Museum. There is a replica of the builder sculpture near the site of Gerard Gardens as a memorial to those who have lost their lives in the construction industry.

Acknowledgements

CLAIRE ALLEN would like to thank Christian Hansen for his close reading of early drafts, and Joyce Allen, Kate Goldenberg and Viv Pegram for reading the manuscript and giving valuable suggestions and encouragement. Also David and Ping Henningham for adding an extra dimension to the book with their illustrations. These developed from the character Robert's work as a civic sculptor in the 1960's and '70's, exploring some of the preparatory drawings of children playing which he would have made for his sculptures.

David and Ping Henningham would like to thank Sophie O'Neill, Jane Pike and everyone at Inpress. Arts Council England literature team. John Mitchinson and everyone at Unbound. Megan Simpkins, Matt Ford and G. F Smith.
 Virginia and Leonard Woolf bought papers from G. F Smith for their Hogarth Press books. G. F Smith's sponsorship of our 2020 *Historiographic Fictions* is our tribute to a pioneering independent press.

Foundation Stones

THE publication of this book was made possible by the following supporters on Unbound:

CORNERSTONES

Paul Griffiths • Viv Pegram • Joyce & Philip Allen
Sumitra Lahiri • Wendy Whidden • Bernie Corbett

FLYING BUTTRESSES

John Mitchinson • Emma Warnock • Amy McCauley
Oscar Mardell • Ronan Hession • Carmel Elwell • Alice
Renouf • Bella Budasz • Justin Gau • Paul Mccombs • Steve
Lambert • Jane Tinkler • Sarah Dickinson • Susan Carberry
Francesca Wolf • Nadine Clarkson • Helene Kreysa
Chris Fenwick • Linda Quinn • Mark Malcomson • Anne
Hartree • Jane Hutcheon • Ole Hansen • Nina Hansen
Niels Hansen • Lars Hansen • Pamela Hansen • Alan Teder
Patricia Shaw • Jacobo Borrero • Sophie Oxenham
Patricia Rose Sweeney • Robert Cox • Christopher Madden
Linda Taylor • Justin Pollard • Dan Kieran • Lulu Allison
Niall Craig • Anne Sawbridge • Richard Hughes
E R Andrew Davis • Rhona Rowland • Paul Jeorrett • Una
Gordon • Liam Riley • Julian Birch • Maya Dancey • Jason
Ballinger • Sa Du

Thank you also to our anonymous supporters.

Henningham Family Press

Since 2006, we have been a microbrewery for books.

Our ingenious handmade editions can be found in the V&A, Tate, National Galleries Scotland, National Poetry Library and Stanford University.

Our Performance Publishing shows compress the creation of printed matter into hectic live events.

Now our Fiction brings you authors who are reinventing the conventions of Modern writing.

Paul Griffiths
Mr. Beethoven

Chris McCabe
Mud
Dedalus

Sophie Herxheimer
60 Lovers To Make and Do
Your Candle Accompanies The Sun
The Listening Forest

Pascal O'Loughlin
Now Legwarmers

 HENNINGHAM
FAMILY
PRESS

About the Author

CLAIRE ALLEN spent her childhood in Liverpool and lives in London. She teaches English literature and creative writing at City Lit.

Her first two novels, *The Mountain of Light* (2004) and *Protection* (2006) were published by Headline Review.

Her books have been translated into French and Greek.

I ♥ CURRY

The best Indian curries
you'll ever cook

Anjum Anand

photography by Jonathan Gregson

Quadrille
PUBLISHING

To my daughter Mahi whose smile, laughter and presence bring pure joy to my life

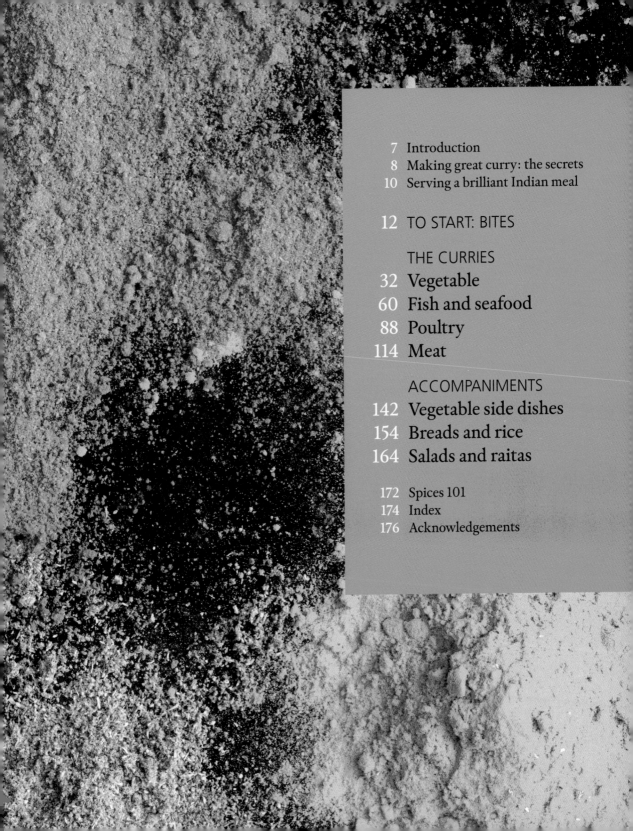

introduction

During the week I wrote this page, I taught a class of 10-year-old boys how to make a chickpea curry. They had no fear, they trusted me and were excited to try their hands at something new. They all listened as I explained what to look for and how to tell when the base of the curry – the 'masala' – was cooked. And then came the moment when I suggested they try the dish; it was so lovely to see their faces light up as they tasted their own cooking. They had no idea how it would turn out, all these unfamiliar ingredients added one after the other and the dish ready to eat in less than half an hour. Surely Indian food isn't so easy to cook? But it is, you just need to get stuck in and watch as the complex flavours add up to more than the sum of their parts. When you are finished and you try the sauce, you will feel just as proud and elated as those boys.

I used to wince when I heard someone call any Indian dish 'a curry'. 'Going for a curry' simply meant eating at an Indian restaurant, and I wondered how such a majestic, broad cuisine could be shrunk down to just one word. To me – and to most Indian people – a 'curry' is simply a dish with lots of sauce or gravy, and might be a term introduced by the British Raj. The spices will change from region to region. So when mum said that our Punjabi family were having chicken curry for dinner, I knew what to expect. For us it meant succulent chicken in a light tomato and onion-based sauce with a north Indian mix of spices: green and black cardamom, cinnamon, bay, cloves and green chillies, finished with garam masala. But a child in Andhra would know her chicken curry was going to be more fiery, with red chillies and a more aromatic spice mix containing fennel and white poppy seeds, while in Mangalore the spices would be toasted before grinding and the dish finished with rich coconut and tangy tamarind.

So when my publishers and I started talking about a book of Britain's favourite curries, as well as a few of my own creations, I got really excited. Curry, in the real sense of the word, is the ultimate comfort food. We then got down to the thorny question of what a curry really is. Our conclusion – and the premise of this book – is that a curry is a stand-alone main course dish, with or without lots of sauce and with or without a dominant spice, that you only need some rice or bread to enjoy.

I've thought a lot about what curries people want to eat. The result is 54 curry recipes, both easy everyday dishes and restaurant classics, plus loads of ideas for starters and accompaniments. Here are all our favourites: chicken tikka masala, lamb do piaza, balti, vindaloo and many, many more. The more adventurous cook will also find lots of exciting new flavours, such as lamb chops with dried pomegranate, or Bengali mustard fish. This is the whole world of curries in all their glory.

It was great fun making up these recipes and I hope you'll find just as much joy in cooking them. Involve friends and/or children – or just put on some great music – and watch and taste the magic come to life... just as it did for those 10-year-old boys.

making great curry: the secrets

The best way to learn a country's cuisine is to cook with a native, because you pick up so many tips that will make the difference between a good dish and a fabulous one. Because not all of us can cook beside an Indian, I want to be a stand-in here for you. I hope to give you a deeper understanding of how to cook a curry and maximise its flavours. So, when you get to the stove, remember these five distinct and vital building blocks…

STAGE 1: whole spices

Always the first ingredient to go into the hot oil. They add a greater depth of flavour than ground spices.

cumin seeds should be fried until they release a nutty aroma and have reddened a couple of shades. It should only take five seconds sizzling in hot oil.
fenugreek seeds should darken to medium brown.
mustard seeds start popping straight away in hot oil. As they pop, reduce the heat and, once the popping dies down, move on to the next stage.
nigella and carom seeds need only about 10 seconds in hot oil to release their full aroma.
other whole spices (cinnamon, cloves, cardamom pods, black pepper etc) should be cooked in hot oil for 20–30 seconds, to release their aromatic oils.

STAGE 2: onions

The base of most curries, so getting them right is crucial. Always make sure they are cooked through until soft and turning golden at the edges. After that, the further you cook them the deeper the flavours of the curry. For a lamb or chicken curry, cook onions until the edges are well-browned. In curries containing more delicate ingredients - such as vegetables or some seafood - onions only need to be golden, or their resonant taste could overpower the rest of the dish.

STAGE 3: garlic and ginger

I often make a paste of ginger and garlic for a smoother sauce. For small amounts, I grate both on a Microplane. For larger quantities, chop them coarsely, use a small stick blender and add a little water to help break them down. Cooking garlic fully is essential. You can tell when it's cooked by the fragrance, which changes from raw and strong to mellow. In a paste, garlic will start to look grainy and turn a pale gold colour.

STAGE 4: ground spices

grinding Whether you use a mortar and pestle, a spice grinder or a clean coffee grinder, make sure spices are really well ground so they melt into the sauce. Any gritty spices added will remain so in the finished dish.
cooking These burn easily so keep the heat down and stir often. Many people add a little water with their spices to ensure they don't scorch. They will cook in 40 seconds, or two minutes if you add water.

STAGE 5: tomatoes and/or yogurt

tomatoes Once these have been added, the ingredients in the pot are thought of as a 'masala', which simply means the mixed and spiced base of a sauce. The masala lets you know when it is cooked by releasing some oil back into the pan, so look for droplets of oil on the base as you stir. If you're not sure if a masala is ready, try a little. It should taste smooth. If it's still too strong, add some water and cook it for a little longer. Once the masala is cooked, you can *bhuno* it (see right).

yogurt This adds sourness and creaminess. You have to be careful, as it can split in the pan; this isn't a disaster but will mean the dish isn't as creamy as it could be. To avoid curdling, use full-fat yogurt at room temperature, as the fat stabilises the yogurt and a cold product added to a hot pan is more likely to split. Add yogurt in batches if it is a large quantity, stir constantly until it comes to a boil and continue to do so for a further few minutes. It should now be fine with only an occasional stir.

slow-cooking

In the early days of Indian restaurants in Britain, a curry was left on very low heat for hours with a chef stirring it every time he passed. This helped the flavours fully develop and, with every stir, the ingredients broke down into a more homogenous sauce. When you have time, try cooking your curry more slowly than the recipe suggests, stirring often, to help the ingredients melt together.

the bhuno-ing process

In Indian cookery dishes are often 'bhunoed', or browned, towards the end, to intensify the flavours, while constant stirring improves the consistency of the sauce. To bhuno a recipe, increase the heat and stir constantly for four to six minutes as the sauce reduces. If your pan seems dry, add a splash of water and bhuno until reduced again.

the role of water

When you start to cook, put the kettle on. You'll need to add water while cooking a curry and, if it's cold, you'll bring the temperature down in the pan, prolonging the cooking time and - some say - affecting the taste. Add a little at any time if you think an ingredient's about to burn before it's properly cooked, then cook off excess before moving to the next stage. Though I indicate specific quantities, be aware of how much liquid is in the pan; your heat may be higher than mine, or your pot wider with more chance for water to evaporate off.

a bony issue

I keep bones in fish, poultry and meat; it adds so much flavour. Indians cook fish steaks, heads and tails in a curry for maximum taste, while poultry and meat are cut into small bone-in pieces. But many people hate bones. If you want to use fish fillets, ask your fishmonger for a firm white fish that won't flake too easily. Halibut is great. And if you really hate eating meat off the bone, ask your butcher for some bones to add to the pot while cooking, which can easily be removed before serving.

balancing the final dish

Just as a chef should never let a single dish leave his kitchen without tasting it, you must taste your curry at the end of cooking and before serving. A curry is a delicate balance of sweet, sour, spicy and salty and you need to correct all these flavours to achieve the most delicious dish. Here are your most important tools.

a note about chillies In all my recipes, I suggest a variable amount of chillies (such as 1-3) you could add. I want to leave it up to you to balance the heat of a dish to suit yourself. But, when using dried chillies, you should usually shake out and discard the seeds before preparing them, or your dish will be too hot.

add heat... Sprinkle in chilli flakes or halve a green chilli lengthways, add to the pot and simmer for few minutes.

...or tame the flame Add a little cream, coconut cream or sugar, depending on the other ingredients in the curry.

to add sweetness Use a little sugar, cream or coconut cream, depending on the dish. Restaurants add caramelised onion paste: to do the same, fry onions until golden or brown, depending on the dish (remembering delicate curries will be overwhelmed by over-brown onions), then blend with a little water until smooth.

for more acidity Try lemon juice, tamarind paste, dried mango or pomegranate powder, even sour cream. Be guided by the other ingredients in the curry as to which souring agent is most suitable.

to perk things up Add garam masala for warming spices, cumin powder (raw or roasted, see page 55) for earthy depth and black pepper for aromatic heat.

sleep on it Many curries improve overnight, as the flavours mature and permeate the main ingredients. You can cook chicken, meat, potato and lentil curries a day earlier, they will taste even better tomorrow.

serving a brilliant Indian meal

You can relax; there are no 'rules' about how to serve curry. Even traditional Indian dining mores were as fragmented as the country itself and every region - even every family - had its own customs.

In our Punjabi home we ate one-course meals with either rice or flatbreads, not both. Pickles were only brought out when the meal was very simple, and chutneys only served with snacks. At the other end of the spectrum, Bengali meals had a succession of courses, each dish eaten only with rice. Yet again, my husband's Marwari family ate three courses, the first something sweet, then flatbreads with vegetables and raita, then rice with lentils or a yogurt curry. They finished with poppadoms, used to cleanse the palate.

As India has evolved, all such dining norms have been further diluted. The modern generation have their own rules, based loosely on how they grew up, but tailored to suit their lifestyles. As is the case all around the world, time is now at a premium, so dishes will be simplified, though the meal will remain well balanced, containing protein, carbohydrates and - if possible - fresh seasonal vegetables, even in the poorest families. These days we cook to the beat of our own drum, even if that drum has on it a faded (in my case), Made in Punjab stamp.

entertaining the indian way

When Indian people entertain, it is with huge generosity of spirit. Guests are always served the best food their hosts can afford. Punjabis are known for their love of food and people, and my childhood had an abundance of both. My parents entertained large groups of people regularly and my mother always made enough to feed her guests twice over!

The evening would start with drinks and appetisers which were bite-sized pieces of heaven: kebabs, mini samosas, crisp little potato cakes and more, all served with our family's spicy Tangy Herb Chutney (see page 27). As a girl I would have helped my mother in the kitchen earlier in

the day, carefully filling samosas or shaping tiny potato cakes. These wonderful appetisers were the inspiration for my exciting and tempting 'bites', and the recipes for them start overleaf!

When we got to the table, there would be three or four curries, two of them always vegetarian, containing lentils or paneer. There would follow an array of vegetable sides, all carefully chosen for their different colours and textures, breads, rice and raita. There was always an Indian dessert, but also fresh or cooked fruits.

entertaining my way...

I have inherited my mother's entertaining style but have adapted it to be a little simpler and more practical for a modern way of life. My parties are smaller - and I have less time than my mother did - but my menu will still have a wonderful variety of vibrant colours, textures and flavours. There will always be rice and warm breads (some bought in, to achieve a good broad selection) and pickles... if I remember! I make only one appetiser, but often also provide a dip with crunchy crudités and some spiced nuts (see page 26). I like fruity desserts after Indian meals, to refresh the palate.

... and your way

Everyone has their own style and you must be true to your own. Don't overextend yourself with a complicated menu; it will just cause stress, which is not the point of having people over. Serve just one great curry, a vegetable or two, a raita and some rice or naan. That's more than enough to make your guests feel special and enjoy a great evening. The good news is that most curries improve overnight (though I would advise making those with vegetables, fish and seafood on the day of serving). Even a pilaf reheats really well in the microwave, covered with damp kitchen paper, while breads and dessert can be bought in. Entertaining should be a pleasure. It is about showing love for your friends, having a good time and living life according to your own rules.

1 BITES

chicken kathi rolls

One of my favourite starters: delicious chicken, a tangle of onions, tomatoes and herb chutney all wrapped in lovely pastry. I have been eating variations of this dish since childhood. You can substitute the chicken for lamb or even Fresh Paneer (see page 25) or stir-fried chickpeas. It does have a few stages, but is really easy to do and all the components can be prepared earlier in the day. I use puff pastry here, as it has the same character as the traditional paratha and is easily available, but make it with Paratha (see page 157) if you prefer.

Whizz together all the ingredients for the marinade with 2 tbsp water until smooth. Place the chicken in the marinade and leave for as long as possible (a minimum of one hour, or up to overnight in the fridge).

Using a 10cm bowl or saucer as a guide, cut out five circles from the pastry. Take one at a time and roll each out into thinner 15cm circles, using a little flour to help. Heat a non-stick frying pan, place in a pastry round, and cook until golden spots appear on the base (around 20 seconds), then turn over and cook the other side until golden. Meanwhile, spread a good layer of the egg over the upper surface, using a small spoon. Then flip and cook the egg side for 10 seconds. Take out and place on a plate. Repeat with the others.

Heat a saucepan, add the chicken and marinade and stir-fry for two or three minutes, or until you can see droplets of oil on the base of the pan. Add a splash of water (to deglaze the base) and the onion and cook for another minute or so until the chicken is done. Add the tomato, stir for 20 seconds, then remove from the heat. Taste and adjust the seasoning.

Taking one 'bread' at a time, egg side up, spoon a line of the chicken mixture down the centre, then add a rounded tablespoon of the chutney. Roll into a log and slice in half.

You can make these ahead, wrap the finished rolls in foil and reheat in the oven when you are ready to serve, but they will be a little softer.

makes 10 pieces

for the marinade
15g fresh root ginger, peeled weight
4 fat garlic cloves
2½ tbsp lemon juice
1½ tsp ground cumin
2 tbsp vegetable oil
¾–1 tsp chilli powder
¾ tsp garam masala
salt, to taste
¼ tsp freshly ground black pepper

for the rolls
2 chicken breasts (around 160g each), cut into small cubes
400g packet ready-rolled puff pastry
plain flour, to dust
2 small eggs, beaten
1 onion, sliced
1 large vine tomato, sliced into strips
1 x recipe Tangy Herb Chutney (see page 27)

mixed vegetable pakoras

These delicious north Indian snacks are loved by everyone. They are really quick to make, so are great when you have unexpected guests. In India they love to eat hot pakoras in the monsoon season, when it is wet and rainy and they are stuck indoors. You can use any vegetable you like as long as it is not watery. We generally use a selection, but you can use just one type. Serve with Tangy Herb Chutney (see page 27).

Whisk together all the ingredients for the batter with 150ml water. Taste and adjust the seasoning; it should be slightly overseasoned. If using onions among your vegetables, salt them now and leave for a short while until they start to wilt, then rinse and pat dry.

Heat 7.5cm of oil in a large, wide saucepan, karahi or wok. It should be around 180°C or, if you don't have a thermometer, a drop of batter should start sizzling immediately.

Cook one type of vegetable at a time, finishing with the onions. Dip the pieces of potato, cauliflower or aubergine in the batter, then drop them into the pan in batches, making sure not to crowd the pan.

Reduce the heat so the vegetables cook as the batter browns. Once they are done, remove from the pan with a slotted spoon and place on a plate lined with kitchen paper.

Throw the wilted onions in the remaining batter, then take a small walnut-sized ball of them at a time and add it to the pan. Once they are golden brown, remove with a slotted spoon and drain on kitchen paper.

Serve each batch hot as you cook the next.

serves 4–6

for the batter
100g gram flour
2 tsp ground rice (optional, but it makes them crispy)
1 good tsp salt, or to taste
⅔ tsp carom seeds (if you have them)
½–¾ tsp chilli powder
½ tsp turmeric
2 tsp ground coriander
1½ tsp ground cumin
⅔ tsp garam masala
1½ tsp dried mango powder
2 garlic cloves, grated into a paste

for the vegetables
1 small onion, sliced
vegetable oil, to deep-fry
100g potato, peeled and sliced 1cm thick
150g cauliflower or broccoli, cut into small-medium florets
100g aubergines, cut into 1cm slices or half moons

spicy prawn cakes

These Goan-inspired cakes are delicious and moreish; perfect as canapés. You can buy finely grated frozen coconut in many Asian supermarkets; keep it in the freezer and defrost the amount you need. If you can't find any, use unsweetened desiccated coconut. These prawn cakes are delicious simply with a squeeze of lime or lemon, or with Tangy Herb Chutney (see page 27). If you choose the chutney, try adding a couple of spoons of coconut to the recipe, then adjust the tartness.

Using a sturdy mortar and pestle, pound the whole spices to a powder.

Heat half the oil in a small non-stick saucepan and fry the onion until softened and turning golden at the edges. Add the ginger and garlic and cook on a gentle flame for a couple of minutes, or until the garlic is cooked. Add the salt and all the spices and cook, stirring, for another 20 seconds. Add the prawns and stir-fry until cooked (around two minutes).

Tip everything from the pan into a blender with the crumbs and coconut and roughly blend to a coarse paste; a few larger pieces of prawn left in the mix is ideal. Taste and adjust the seasoning and chilli, then stir in the egg and the chopped coriander. Set aside and allow to rest for 10 minutes.

Heat the remaining oil in a large non-stick frying pan. Make small balls from the mixture and pat into 5cm cakes. Shallow-fry gently for two or three minutes each side, until golden, crisp and heated through to the centre. You will need to do this in two batches.

Serve with lime or lemon wedges or Tangy Herb Chutney (see page 27).

makes 20 small cakes

4 cloves
2.5cm cinnamon stick
10 black peppercorns
5 tbsp vegetable oil
1 onion, finely chopped
16g fresh root ginger, peeled weight, chopped
4 fat garlic cloves, chopped
salt, to taste
1½ tsp ground cumin
¾-1¼ tsp chilli powder, or to taste
400g small-to-medium raw prawns, shelled, deveined and rinsed
4 large slices white bread, crusts removed, made into crumbs
80g finely grated frozen coconut, or 4 tbsp unsweetened desiccated coconut
2 eggs, beaten
large handful of chopped fresh coriander

salmon tikka lettuce wraps

I think salmon works really well in tandoori-style dishes and this 'fusion food' starter is as stunning in colour as it is in taste. The earthy tandoori salmon is lifted by the creamy herb dressing and tart capers. The red cabbage has a lovely mustardy flavour but is mostly there for a colour contrast, so I leave it to you to decide whether to add it or not.

Mix together the ingredients for the marinade until smooth. Season well and taste; it should be slightly overseasoned at this point. Add the salmon, turn to coat and marinate for one hour.

Meanwhile, mix together the ingredients for the topping and season with salt and lots of freshly ground pepper.

When you are ready to serve, preheat your grill to high (I use the grill setting in my oven and place the baking tray on the top shelf). Place the fish on a baking tray lined with greaseproof paper or foil and grill for seven to nine minutes, turning once, or until the fish is just done and charring in places.

Meanwhile, lay out the lettuce leaves. When the fish is done, cut each fillet lengthwise into four or five pieces, then break up into large chunks. Place each broken-up piece into a lettuce leaf. Add a teaspoon of the topping and scatter with a few capers. Sprinkle with the cabbage (if using) and serve immediately.

makes 8–10, can be doubled

for the tandoori marinade
50g plain yogurt
6g fresh root ginger, peeled weight, grated into a paste
2 garlic cloves, grated into a paste
2 tsp gram flour
1 tsp paprika
¾ tsp chilli powder
1½ tbsp vegetable oil
¾ tsp ground cumin
¼ tsp freshly ground black pepper
1 tbsp lemon juice
1 tbsp light crème fraîche

for the wraps
2 small, skinless salmon fillets
8–10 even-sized Baby Gem lettuce leaves, washed and dried
2 tbsp capers
a little finely shredded red cabbage (optional)

for the topping
30g Greek yogurt
30g light crème fraîche
10g finely chopped onion
10g finely chopped fresh coriander
1–2 green chillies, deseeded and finely chopped (optional)
salt, to taste
freshly ground black pepper, to taste

crispy chilli squid

I love this way of cooking squid, perhaps because I have so many fond memories of eating calamari under the Mediterranean sun, or maybe it's the texture of the soft squid against the crisp coating. The marinade adds a kick while the lovely mayonnaise finishes it off and is especially good at flattering squid which hasn't had enough time in the marinade. But you can forget the mayonnaise and serve the squid simply with lemon wedges, if you prefer.

Whizz together all the ingredients for the marinade with 2 tbsp water to make a fine paste. Mix into the squid and leave to marinate for an hour or more, or for several hours in the fridge.

Stir together the ingredients for the mayonnaise and season to taste.

Heat around 7.5cm of vegetable oil in a wok, karahi or saucepan until a small piece of bread dropped in sizzles immediately.

Mix together the semolina and flour. Remove the squid from its marinade and dredge it in the flour mixture. Pat off any excess, then add the squid to the deep-frying pan in two or three batches (make sure not to overcrowd the pan). Fry for two to three minutes, or until golden and crisp.

Remove with a slotted spoon, place on kitchen paper and keep warm while you fry the remaining squid. Serve hot, with the mayonnaise on the side.

serves 4

for the marinade
2 fresh large fat red chillies, deseeded
10g fresh root ginger, peeled weight
3 large garlic cloves
1½ tbsp white wine vinegar
1½ tbsp vegetable oil
¾ tsp ground cumin
salt, to taste

for the squid
300g prepared squid, rings, tentacles and flaps
vegetable oil, for deep-frying
3 tbsp semolina
5 tbsp plain flour

for the chilli, lemon and garlic mayonnaise
150g mayonnaise (the better the quality, the less sweet)
3 tsp lemon juice
freshly ground black pepper, to taste
1 tsp chilli powder, or to taste
1 fat garlic clove, grated into a paste, or to taste

lamb kebabs with mint and cucumber dip

I like to serve these kebabs piled on a platter with a bowl of the dip and some soft flatbreads (flour tortillas or Indian breads) and toothpicks on the side. Then some people can tear off some bread and use it to scoop up a piece of lamb and yogurt, while others can skewer the lamb with a toothpick and dip it in the thick, luscious dip; others still will just eat the bread with the dip. You can also serve the lamb with Tangy Herb Chutney (see page 27) for a more traditional take.

Blend together the ingredients for the marinade until smooth. Taste and make sure it is over-seasoned, as the lamb will need it. Add the lamb and leave for as long as possible (overnight in the fridge is best). Bring back to room temperature before continuing.

Grate the cucumber coarsely, then squeeze out all the excess water, using your fists or a tea towel to help. Add to the yogurt along with the remaining dip ingredients.

Heat the grill to a high setting. Place the lamb on a baking tray lined with foil and grill for six to eight minutes, turning halfway, or until done to your liking. Sprinkle with the chaat masala (if using).

Serve hot with the cool cucumber and mint dip and flatbreads (see recipe introduction).

serves 6

for the marinade
15g fresh root ginger, peeled weight, grated into a paste
5 fat garlic cloves, grated into a paste
4 tbsp Greek yogurt
3 tbsp vegetable oil
2 tsp garam masala
2 tsp ground cumin
2/3 tsp black pepper
1 tsp chilli powder
2½ tbsp lemon juice
salt, to taste

for the lamb
400-450g leg of lamb, in 2.5cm cubes
1 tsp chaat masala (optional)

for the mint and cucumber dip
150g cucumber
200g Greek yogurt
1 tbsp tahini paste
15 large mint leaves, shredded
1 green chilli, deseeded and finely chopped (optional)
1½ tbsp olive oil
1/3 tsp freshly ground black pepper

quick steamed pea cakes

These light, fluffy cakes are a fantastic starter or teatime snack. I serve them with Tangy Herb Chutney (see page 27) but they taste lovely just as they are. There are special deep-sided steel plates or tins which are used in India for this type of steamed cake, but I use two small 15cm baking tins in a double steamer. If you don't have a steamer, boil water in a wide pan, place a pudding bowl filled with water inside and place the tin on top. (If you do this, don't use a springform tin, or the water will rise up into the batter.) If you don't have a double steamer and need to make the recipe in two batches, make the batter up to the point of adding the baking powder and bicarbonate of soda, then halve it. Then add half the raising agents to half the batter, cook, and repeat with the remaining batter.

Oil two 15cm steel plates with deep sides, or baking tins. Pour about 7.5cm water into the base of a double steamer or a wide and deep saucepan (see recipe introduction). Cover and bring to a boil.

Meanwhile, blend the peas, lemon juice, oil, ginger and chillies to a smooth paste with 120ml water. Stir in the gram flour and salt. Taste to check the seasoning. Stir in the baking powder and bicarbonate of soda and divide between the oiled tins. Carefully place them in the steamer, cover and steam on a moderate to high heat for 18 minutes, or until a toothpick inserted into the centre comes out clean.

Remove from the steamer and leave to cool for 10 minutes, then run a knife around the edge of the tins and turn the pea cakes out on to a plate.

Heat the oil for the tarka in a small pan and add the mustard seeds. When they are popping well, add the sesame seeds and, once they start to colour, the curry leaves. Stir for five seconds, then spoon evenly over the cakes. Cut the cakes into diamonds, squares or wedges. Serve hot or at room temperature.

serves 4–6, can be halved

for the pea cakes
2 tbsp vegetable oil, plus more for the tins
170g frozen peas, defrosted
5 tbsp lemon juice
16g fresh root ginger, peeled weight, roughly quartered
2-4 green chillies (ideally Indian finger), stalk removed
140g gram flour
salt, to taste
⅔ tsp baking powder
⅔ tsp bicarbonate of soda

for the tarka
4 tsp vegetable oil
1 tsp mustard seeds
2 tsp sesame seeds
16 fresh curry leaves

paneer bruschetta

I love bruschetta in the summer and make my Indian version with fresh paneer, which has the creaminess of mozzarella but a different texture. It is easy to make, fresh, vibrant and lovely for a light lunch with salad, or as a pre-dinner appetiser. Do not use store-bought paneer; it can be rubbery and would ruin the freshness of this bruschetta. Paneer is really easy to make and with very few ingredients; you can also make it a day ahead and keep it in the fridge, covered with damp muslin or kitchen paper. Normally, paneer is set into a hard block, but here I only press it for 15–20 minutes for a softer texture. I use ciabatta, but you can use any good-quality bread.

1 x recipe Fresh Paneer (see below)
3 tbsp finely chopped onion, or to taste
2 green chillies (ideally Indian green finger), finely sliced
large handful of finely chopped fresh coriander, leaves and stalks
150g baby plum tomatoes, chopped
2 big tbsp good-quality olive oil
¼ tsp coarsely ground black pepper
salt, to taste
1 ciabatta or other good-quality loaf, sliced into 1½cm slices on the diagonal

Crumble the paneer into a bowl in smallish chunks. Add the onion, chillies, coriander, tomatoes, olive oil and black pepper and season to taste with salt. Stir well and allow to sit until you are ready to eat.

Just before eating, toast or griddle the bread, spoon the mixture on top and serve.

makes 8–9 pieces, can be doubled

fresh paneer

Bring the milk to a boil in a heavy-based saucepan. Once the milk starts to rise up in the pan, stir in the lemon juice. Keep stirring until the milk splits, adding more lemon if it doesn't; the curds will eventually separate from the watery whey. Remove from the heat and pour into a muslin-lined sieve to drain off the water. Rinse the paneer in cold water. Make a little bundle of the paneer in the muslin, twist the open ends of the muslin together to form a round cheese, place on a work top and top with a heavy weight (I use a saucepan filled with water). Leave for 15 minutes (I put it in or near my sink, so the curds can drain away down the plug hole), then remove the weight. Use immediately, or cover with damp muslin or kitchen paper and keep in the fridge for a day.

1 litre whole milk
3 tbsp lemon juice, plus more if needed

makes 160g

quick spiced cashew nuts

You can buy lots of spiced nuts in the shops these days, but making them at home is really quick and easy and you can spice them to taste.

1 rounded tsp butter
200g raw, unsalted cashew nuts
½ tsp salt
½ tsp freshly ground black pepper
¼–½ tsp chilli powder
1 tsp ground cumin
½ tsp dried mango powder

Melt the butter in a frying pan. Add the cashew nuts and sauté until lightly roasted. Turn off the heat and stir in all the remaining ingredients. Pour into a bowl and leave to cool.

makes enough for 5–6

creamy mint chutney

This is that lovely, refreshing dip that is often on the table as you start your curry house meal. I always find that I pick at it to start with, then keep it to eat with tandoori food. It is a lovely, sweet, spicy and lightly sour chutney that goes really well with all grills, barbecues and many snacks. I prefer to use measurements such as 'a small handful' for tiny amounts of herbs; however mint can be very strong, so it's best to measure it out for this recipe, so as not to overpower the dish.

7g mint leaves, washed
20g fresh coriander leaves and stalks, washed
1–2 green chillies (preferably Indian green finger), stalk removed
2 tsp sugar
½ tsp tamarind paste, or to taste
1 tsp lemon juice, or to taste
150g plain yogurt
⅓ tsp roasted cumin powder (see page 55)

Blend all the ingredients together until smooth. Taste, adjust the seasoning, adding more tamarind paste or lemon if you want more tang, then serve.

serves 4–6

tangy herb chutney

An incredibly versatile recipe, this is the cornerstone of all north Indian snacks. We love it with our samosas, bhajis, pakoras, kebabs... and most other things! There are many variations, some people will add a little sugar, some raw garlic and others yogurt. This is how we like it in my family and it is a perfect base from which to experiment.

Blend together all the ingredients with 4 tbsp water until smooth; it might take a few minutes. Taste and adjust the seasoning. Keep in a glass jar in the fridge for up to a week, or freeze until ready to use.

makes around 200ml

60g fresh coriander, leaves and stalks
2½ tbsp lemon juice
2 green chillies, deseeded if you
    prefer
12g mint leaves
20g raw or roasted unsalted
    pistachios
salt, to taste

fresh mango chutney

The typical mango chutneys you find in Indian restaurants are made from unripe green mangoes but, as these are hard to find, I decided to come up with my own recipe for a fresh mango chutney. It is delicious, spicy and fruity.

Heat the oil in a saucepan and add the whole chillies, cumin and fennel seeds. Once the cumin is aromatic (a matter of seconds) and the chillies are darker, add the vinegar, sugar, 160ml water and a little salt and pepper. Simmer for six or seven minutes. Add the mango and cook for six or seven minutes more, or until the mango is soft and easy to mash.

Mash half the mango pieces into the chutney and mix well. It should be thick, but not jammy. Serve hot or cold.

makes one largish bowl

2 tsp vegetable oil
2–5 dried red chillies, or to taste
1 tsp cumin seeds
1 tsp fennel seeds
180ml white wine vinegar
40–50g sugar (depends on the
    sweetness of the mangoes)
salt and a little black pepper, to taste
2 large ripe mangoes, peeled, stoned
    and cut into pieces (see page 169)

puchkas

These are little taste bombs and I don't know anyone who doesn't love them. Small, crisp, hollow balls of semolina pastry are filled with potatoes, chickpeas, yogurt, then both a sweet-and-sour and a herb chutney. They are topped with sev, which look like fine yellow pieces of thread. You place the puchkas in your mouth whole and bite into an explosion of tastes and textures. Buy the tamarind chutney if you don't want to make the quick recipe here, and pani puris and sev are available in Indian shops (look for the handmade variety). This looks complicated, but is really easy and indescribably delicious.

For the tamarind chutney, place the tamarind, sugar and 6 tbsp water in a small saucepan. Bring to a boil and simmer for three minutes. Add the salt, pepper and ¾ tsp of roasted cumin powder (reserve the rest) and cook until the chutney is syrupy (another minute or two). You should have around 4 tbsp of chutney. If it becomes hard as it sits, loosen it with 1 tbsp boiling water.

Whisk the yogurt with a little salt, the chilli powder and reserved roasted cumin powder until smooth. Set aside.

Boil the potato in salted water until tender, then peel and cut into 1cm cubes.

Assemble the puchkas when you are ready to eat. You will find that the puris have a thicker, harder side and a thinner side… it might not be so obvious at first, but when you tap both convex sides with your fingernail you will easily spot the thinner side. Break a 2.5cm hole in the thinner side with your finger. Fill each puri with a couple of chickpeas and a piece of potato. Spoon 1 tsp yogurt into each and top with ⅓ tsp each of tamarind chutney and Tangy Herb Chutney. Sprinkle generously with the sev (if using) and serve immediately.

makes 20, enough for 4–5 people

for the quick sweet-and-sour
   tamarind chutney
2 good tsp tamarind paste
35–40g jaggery, chopped up, or
   3¾ tbsp sugar
¼ tsp salt
¼-⅓ tsp freshly ground black pepper
1 rounded tsp roasted cumin powder
   (see page 55)

for the puchkas
200g plain yogurt, not too sour
salt, to taste
scant ¼ tsp chilli powder
100g potato
20 ready-made puris (sold as pani
   puris)
50g cooked chickpeas, rinsed
½ x recipe Tangy Herb Chutney,
   (see page 27)
handful of sev (optional)

2 THE CURRIES

vegetable

velvety black lentil curry

This is essentially the restaurant-style lentil dish that we all love. A professional kitchen would leave these cooking really gently overnight on top of the warm tandoor oven so they turn into an even, creamy mass. Don't worry, you don't have to do the same! This curry is in fact very simple to make, though it takes a while to cook, and the flavour of earthy lentils, tart tomatoes, spices, rich cream and butter is divine. Serve with Naan (see page 155) or Paratha (see page 157).

Wash the black gram and pick out and discard any discoloured lentils you can see. Place them in a large bowl, cover with fresh water and leave to soak for at least two hours, or preferably overnight.

Rinse the lentils and tip them, with 1½ litres of fresh water, into a large saucepan. Bring to a boil, then reduce the heat, cover and simmer gently for 1–1½ hours, or until soft; stir occasionally and top up with water, if necessary.

Meanwhile, blend together the 20g ginger, garlic and tomatoes until smooth (I use my trusty stick blender). Pour this mixture into the soft lentils along with some salt, cover and cook for a further hour. Stir occasionally and add extra hot water, if necessary.

By now the lentils should be very soft and a little creamy. Lightly mash some of them against the side of the pan with your spoon. Add the cream, butter, spices, crushed fenugreek leaves and a little more salt, to taste, along with the red kidney beans. Cook for another 10 minutes, mashing a few more of the lentils if necessary until you have a creamy, homogenous curry. Taste, adjust the seasoning and sprinkle with the ginger julienne.

serves 4

80g whole black gram
20g fresh root ginger, peeled weight, plus a little in julienne to serve
5 large garlic cloves
4 largish tomatoes
salt, to taste
80–100ml double cream
2–4 tbsp butter, or to taste
¼–½ tsp chilli powder, or to taste
¾ tsp ground cumin
1 tsp garam masala, or to taste
¾ tsp dried fenugreek leaves, crushed
100g cooked red kidney beans

spinach with black-eyed peas

A simple, everyday main course that shows how most Indians eat: a no-fuss dish with fresh vegetables and some sort of protein. This is only lightly spiced, so as not to overpower the spinach, and goes well with rice, breads and a little yogurt.

Heat the oil in a non-stick saucepan. Add the mustard and fenugreek seeds and whole dried chillies. Once the mustard seeds have spluttered, add the garlic and curry leaves and cook them gently until the garlic is just starting to turn golden.

Add the spinach, seasoning and a splash of water; mix well and cover. Cook for five to seven minutes, until well wilted, stirring occasionally. Add the ground coriander and cumin, half the black-eyed peas and a splash of water. Cover and cook for five or six minutes. Take out one-third of the mix and blend to a fine puree. Return to the pan with the remaining beans.

Stir in the tamarind paste and peanuts. Boil off any excess water: you should be left with a slightly thick, creamy mass. Taste and adjust the seasoning and tartness, adding more tamarind if you would like more tang, and serve.

serves 4

3 tbsp vegetable oil
rounded ½ tsp mustard seeds
½ tsp fenugreek seeds
2–4 dried red chillies
5 garlic cloves, finely chopped or
  grated into a paste
14 fresh curry leaves
250g whole leaf spinach, shredded,
  or baby spinach, washed well
salt, to taste
lots of freshly ground black pepper
1 tsp ground coriander
1 rounded tsp ground cumin
400g can of black-eyed peas, drained
  well and rinsed
1½–2 tsp tamarind paste, or to taste
good handful of roasted and salted
  peanuts

creamy almond vegetable curry

The yogurt and toasted almonds give this a wonderful nutty flavour, while the vegetables remain vibrant. I blanch and toast my own almonds, but you can buy them blanched and ready-toasted if this is a step too far. Use whatever non-watery vegetables you like, or different nuts. I blanch my vegetables and finish them in the gravy so they don't lose their character, but you can add them straight into the bubbling curry if you prefer, or even sauté them in butter first. Serve with Naan (see page 155), Paratha (see page 157), or a pilaf (see pages 160-163).

Heat 1 tsp oil in a small pan and fry the almonds until well and evenly golden. Pour them straight into a mortar and crush to a powder with the pestle.

Heat the remaining oil in a large non-stick saucepan and add the cloves, cardamom and caraway seeds. Follow after 20 seconds with the onion and cook until golden on the edges. Scrape in the ginger and garlic pastes and sauté gently for one or two minutes, or until the garlic is just golden.

Add the ground spices and yogurt and bring to a boil, stirring constantly. Continue to cook until the oil leaves the masala. It should take five to eight minutes. Add 250ml water and bring to a boil, then simmer gently for 10–12 minutes more.

Cook your vegetables as you like them (see recipe introduction). To blanch mine, I bring a pot of salted water to a boil as the sauce is cooking and add my potatoes. After five minutes I add the carrots. Once they are cooked, I fish them out and add my broccoli and, three minutes later, the mangetout and peas. I drain them after another minute or so.

Now add the vegetables, salt, cream, tomatoes and crushed almonds, then cook for another two or three minutes for everything to come together. The sauce should be thick, creamy and slightly granular from the nuts. Add a small splash of water, if necessary. Check the seasoning and serve.

serves 3–4

to blanch almonds Place whole almonds in a small bowl, cover with boiling water and leave for 30 minutes or so. The skins will loosen and wrinkle. Peel them off the nuts to reveal creamy, blanched almonds.

for the curry
4 tbsp vegetable oil, plus 1 tsp
60g blanched almonds
6 cloves
6 green cardamom pods
1 tsp caraway seeds
1 smallish onion, finely chopped
15g fresh root ginger, peeled weight, grated into a paste
4 fat garlic cloves, grated into a paste
1⅓ tsp ground cumin
2 tsp ground coriander
¼ tsp turmeric
⅛–¼ tsp chilli powder, or to taste
4 tbsp plain yogurt
salt, to taste
6 tbsp single cream
8 cherry tomatoes, halved

for the vegetables
125g potatoes, peeled and cut into 2cm cubes
60g carrots, peeled and cut into half moons
70g broccoli, cut into small florets
60g mangetout, trimmed
large handful of peas

everyday lentil and vegetable curry

A staple for many people on the west coast of India. There are many variations; some are hotter, others add ginger or garlic. I like to make it with the added vegetables here, so I don't need to cook another dish. You can adapt this nearly endlessly to your tastes, with or without the sugar, coconut and vegetables. Choose any vegetables you like, though starchy varieties aren't traditional. I have listed those I often use, but I vary them depending on the season and what I have in the fridge.

Put the lentils in a big pan with 1 litre of water and bring to a boil. If any scum forms on top, skim it off. Add the turmeric. Reduce the heat and simmer until the lentils are really soft and starting to break down; it should take around 20 minutes. Add the aubergines (if using) and continue cooking gently.

Meanwhile, make the tarka. Heat the oil in a small saucepan. Add the mustard, cumin and sesame seeds, split black lentils (if using), cloves and whole dried chillies. Once the mustard seeds have stopped popping, add the curry leaves and, a beat later, the onions. Cook gently until the onions are soft and starting to colour. Add the tomatoes, okra (if using), ground coriander and salt. Stir-fry for four minutes and, once the tomatoes start to soften, pour everything into the lentil curry. Add the tamarind, coconut and sugar (if using). Add the green beans (if using) and simmer for five minutes, or until your vegetables are done. Taste, adjust the salt, sugar and tamarind, then serve.

serves 4–5

for the curry
200g split pigeon pea lentils (*tovar dal*), well washed
⅓ tsp turmeric
1 tsp tamarind paste, or to taste
2 tbsp unsweetened desiccated coconut (optional)
1½–2½ tsp sugar, or to taste (optional)

for the tarka
2 tbsp vegetable oil
1 tsp mustard seeds
1 tsp cumin seeds
1 tsp sesame seeds (optional)
2 tsp split and husked black gram (*urad dal*), if you have it
2 cloves
2–3 dried red chillies
12 fresh curry leaves
2 small onions, finely sliced
2 tomatoes, each cut into 6 wedges
1½ tsp ground coriander
salt, to taste

for the vegetables (optional)
3 Japanese or small aubergines, halved lengthwise then cut across into 3
8 okra, topped, tailed and halved widthways
handful of green beans

karahi mushrooms with peppers and peas

A lovely vegetarian dish that manages to be both hearty and delicate at the same time. It can serve two as a main dish, or up to four if it is to accompany other things. I like to use a selection of mushrooms, as they all add their own flavour and texture to the dish. Don't use portabella mushrooms, though, as they make the whole thing turn black. I use equal quantities of oyster, shiitake and chestnut mushrooms. Leave the oyster mushrooms whole, or tear them in half if they are large.

Heat half the oil in a large non-stick sauté pan or karahi. Add the mushrooms and a little salt and sauté over a moderate flame for four to five minutes, until they have a lovely golden tinge. Remove from the pan and set aside.

Heat the remaining oil, add the coriander seeds and, once they have darkened a little, the onion. Cook until golden. Add the ginger and garlic pastes and cook, stirring, over a low flame for one to two minutes, or until you can smell that the garlic is cooked. Pour in the tomatoes and add the remaining spices. Season and cook, stirring occasionally, for eight to 10 minutes, or until the paste releases some oil back into the pan.

Stir in the pepper dice, peas and a good splash of water, cover and cook for four minutes, or until the peppers are softening. Add the mushrooms, cover and allow the flavours to come together for a few minutes. Stir in the cream (if using) and about 50ml water, or enough to form a light sauce. Bring to a boil, taste, adjust the seasoning and sprinkle with the chopped coriander.

serves 4

4 tbsp vegetable oil
250g mushrooms, cleaned, in 2cm slices (see recipe introduction)
salt, to taste
½ tsp coriander seeds, lightly crushed
1 small onion, finely chopped
6g fresh root ginger, peeled weight, grated into a paste
3 garlic cloves, grated into a paste
3 tomatoes, blended to a puree with a stick blender
1 tsp ground coriander
¾ tsp ground cumin
¾–1 tsp garam masala
⅛ tsp chilli powder, or to taste
¾ large red pepper, in coarse dice
generous handful of green peas
2 tbsp double cream (optional)
small handful of chopped fresh coriander leaves, to serve

tarka dhal

This is a classic, it is absolutely wonderful and easy to make. Tarka simply means a few ingredients fried up and stirred in at the end; most Indian lentil dishes are made this way. Many restaurant tarka dhals often have two tarkas; the first prepared as in this recipe and the second as fried cumin seeds and sliced garlic poured over the top. I haven't done the latter as I didn't want to add another step and all the flavour you need is already here. But feel free to fry two or three finely sliced garlic cloves or a small onion in lots of oil until golden (garlic) or well-browned and slightly crisp (onions), then pile them on top.

Wash both types of lentils together in several changes of water. Place the lentils and 1 litre of water in a large saucepan. Bring to a boil, skimming off any scum that forms. Add the turmeric, garlic, ginger and a little salt. Simmer, covered, for 40 minutes, giving the pot an occasional stir.

After the lentils have been cooking for about 30 minutes, heat the oil and butter for the tarka. Add the whole dried chillies and cumin seeds and, once they have browned, add the onion; sauté until well-browned. Add the tomatoes, garam masala and a little more salt and sauté until the masala releases oil, around 10 minutes. Pour some of the lentils into this pan, swirl and scrape the base to extract all the flavours, then pour everything back into the lentils.

Cook for another 10 minutes, mashing some of the lentils on the side of the pan to make a homogenous dhal. Add a little water if the lentils are too thick (remember it will thicken further as it cools). Taste, adjust the seasoning and serve scattered with the chopped coriander.

serves 4

for the dhal
100g Bengal gram (*chana dal*)
50g red lentils (*masur dal*)
½ tsp turmeric
3 fat garlic cloves, grated into a paste
10g fresh root ginger, peeled weight, grated into a paste
salt, to taste
handful of chopped fresh coriander leaves

for the tarka
3 tbsp vegetable oil
1 rounded tbsp butter
2–4 dried red chillies
1 rounded tsp cumin seeds
1 small onion, finely chopped
2 small tomatoes, chopped
½–¾ tsp garam masala, or to taste

punjabi yogurt and dumpling kadhi

This type of yogurt curry seems to exist in most northern, dairy-producing regions of India. Everyone has their own version, which might be sweeter, tangier, thinner, thicker or even contain coconut. This is the Punjabi version I grew up with and I do - objectively, of course! - think it is the best. It is full of flavour, the dumplings are earthy and give a toothsome, protein-filled bite to the smooth curry. Serve with rice.

Using your hands, mix together all the ingredients for the dumplings, adding 2½–3 tbsp water, or enough to make a thick, clinging paste. Set aside; the onions will soften as they stand. For the curry, stir the gram flour and yogurt until it is lump-free. Gradually add 700ml water to make a smooth paste.

Heat the 2 tbsp oil in a large non-stick saucepan. Add the whole spices and, once the light seeds have browned well, the onion, ginger, garlic, curry leaves and whole dried chillies or chilli powder. Sauté gently until the onions have softened. Add the yogurt mix and bring to a boil, stirring constantly to ensure it doesn't split. Add the powdered spices and tomato, stir well for another three or four minutes, then simmer for 30 minutes, stirring occasionally.

Meanwhile, pour enough oil into a small-medium saucepan to come 5–7.5cm up the sides, and heat until it is a moderate temperature for deep-frying: a drop of dumpling batter dropped in should sizzle immediately. Make small walnut-sized balls out of the dumpling mixture and add each to the oil. Do not overcrowd the pan (if your pan is small, do it in two batches). Keep the heat low so they fry evenly for seven or eight minutes and become a lovely golden brown, turning them in the oil. Drain on kitchen paper.

Once the curry is cooked, add the dumplings. The curry should have a consistency between single and double cream (add a splash of water if it's too thick, or cook some off if it seems watery). Season well, taste and add lemon juice; the kadhi should be tangy. Cook for another five minutes and serve, scattered with chopped fresh coriander and sliced green chillies, if you like.

serves 4

variations Add a handful of shredded spinach or any other green vegetable to the dumplings, as well as green chillies and fresh coriander leaves. Or omit the dumplings and add more vegetables - such as spinach, carrots, peas and cauliflower - to the curry instead.

for the dumplings
80g gram flour
½ tsp baking powder
½ onion, halved and finely sliced
¼ tsp salt
⅓ tsp carom seeds
⅓ tsp garam masala
⅓ tsp cumin seeds

for the curry
35g gram flour
200g plain yogurt (ideally a bit sour)
2 tbsp vegetable oil, plus more to deep-fry
2 cloves
½ tsp fenugreek seeds
¾ tsp mustard seeds
¾ tsp cumin seeds
½ onion, finely sliced
7g fresh root ginger, peeled weight, chopped
2 small garlic cloves, chopped
8 fresh curry leaves
1–2 dried red chillies, or a little chilli powder
⅓ tsp turmeric
1 tsp garam masala
1 tomato, cut into 8 pieces
salt, to taste
1–2 tbsp lemon juice, or to taste (depending on the tartness of the yogurt)
a little chopped fresh coriander and sliced green chilli, to serve (optional)

bengali-style mixed vegetables

Inspired by a Bengali staple called *shukto*, this is a mild dish with a mix of sweet, starchy vegetables as well as an essential bitter one, which was originally added to whet the appetite for future courses. I have used autumnal vegetables here, but this is not a heavy dish and is often eaten in the summer in Bengal. You can substitute any other vegetables, as long as you include some sweet and some bitter. I've used western vegetables here instead of the traditional Indian green bananas and bitter gourd, but the dish still works beautifully. Serve with rice.

Using a spice grinder, grind the poppy and both types of mustard seeds to a fine powder. Set aside.

Heat the oil, add the panch phoran and, once it splutters, tip in the parsnips and sweet potatoes and sauté over a moderate flame for five to six minutes, or until softening. Add the ginger paste, aubergines, beans and salt and sauté for another three minutes. Add the bitter leaves, ground seeds, cumin and 200ml water. Bring to a boil, cover, reduce the heat and cook for three or four minutes, until all the ingredients are tender.

Uncover, add the chickpeas, then reduce most of liquid in the pan over high heat, stirring so nothing catches on the base. Add the milk and sugar, bring to a boil, taste, adjust the seasoning and serve.

serves 4

3 tbsp white poppy seeds
1½ tbsp yellow mustard seeds
½ tsp brown mustard seeds
5 tbsp vegetable oil
1 tsp panch phoran
225g parsnips, peeled, cored and cut into 1.5cm half moons
225g sweet potato, peeled and cut into 1.5cm half moons
15g fresh root ginger, peeled weight, grated into a paste
3 long, thin aubergines (around 150g), or round aubergines, halved lengthways and cut into 2–3 pieces
15–20 green beans, topped, tailed and halved
salt, to taste
50g radicchio, endive or other bitter vegetable, diced
½–¾ tsp ground cumin
2 handfuls of cooked chickpeas
150ml full-fat milk
½ tsp sugar, or to taste

southern potato curry, two ways

This is a really delicious curry that you can tailor to your own tastes. If you like north Indian flavours, you can leave out the curry leaves and coconut milk and just add water. If you prefer the flavours of the south west coast, leave them in. The dish is wonderful either way. We would eat this with Indian fried breads (puris or Bhaturas, see page 158) for lunch, to give us plenty of time to digest the meal, but any flatbreads will do, or even some buttered toast. The sauce should have a light and creamy consistency, not too thin and not too thick.

Halve the potatoes and boil until just tender, (they will break up in the sauce if overcooked now). I prefer to boil them in their skins, to minimise the amount of water they absorb, then peel them before continuing.

Meanwhile, heat the oil in a large saucepan and add the mustard and cumin seeds, the lentils and cinnamon stick. Once the popping of the mustard seeds has died down, add the curry leaves (if using). Follow immediately with the onions and cook until soft and lightly golden.

Add the ginger, tomatoes, chilli, coriander, fennel, turmeric and salt and stir-fry over a high heat for three minutes. Add 200ml water, bring to a boil and simmer gently for 10 minutes. Add the cooked potatoes to the sauce to absorb the flavours for five minutes, or until the liquid in the pan has dried up.

Add the coconut milk (if using) and enough water to get a medium consistency sauce. Taste, adjust the seasoning and stir in the chopped coriander. Serve.

serves 4

500g potatoes
4 tbsp vegetable oil
$\frac{2}{3}$ tsp brown mustard seeds
$\frac{2}{3}$ tsp cumin seeds
1½ tsp Bengal gram (*chana dal*), washed and dried
5cm cinnamon stick
12 fresh curry leaves (optional, see recipe introduction)
2 small onions, finely chopped
10g fresh root ginger, peeled weight, finely chopped
2 large tomatoes, chopped
¼–½ tsp chilli powder
2 rounded tsp ground coriander
½ tsp fennel seeds, ground
$\frac{1}{3}$ tsp turmeric
salt, to taste
150ml coconut milk (optional, see recipe introduction)
large handful of chopped fresh coriander, to serve

paneer and pepper karahi

Paneer is a homemade white cheese, similar to ricotta and mozzarella in taste but firm enough to cut into cubes. It's really easy, can be prepared in advance and very satisfying to create (see page 25). You can buy ready-made blocks of paneer in many well-stocked supermarkets and Indian stores, but it won't be as good as homemade. This dish is full of flavours and textures and makes a fantastic vegetarian main course. Serve with Naan (see page 155) or Paratha (see page 157).

Heat the oil in a large non-stick saucepan or karahi. Add the cumin seeds and cook until they have darkened and released their aromas. Add the ginger and garlic pastes and gently sauté for a minute, or until the garlic smells cooked. Add the onion and green chillies and sauté for another minute.

Add the tomatoes and all the spices and season. Cook over a high heat, stirring often, for 10-15 minutes, until the mixture is cooked and releases some oil back into the pan. Taste; the flavours should be harmonious.

Stir in the paneer, peppers and a good splash of water from the kettle. Cook for three or four minutes, or until the peppers are crisp but tender and the sauce is thick and clinging to the vegetables. Add the cream, taste and adjust the seasoning, and serve.

serves 4–6

6 tbsp vegetable oil
1½ tsp cumin seeds
12g fresh root ginger, peeled weight, grated into a paste
2 garlic cloves, grated into a paste
1 smallish onion, roughly diced
3–4 green chillies, whole but pierced
3 small tomatoes, blended until smooth or chopped
⅓ tsp turmeric
¼–½ tsp chilli powder
3 tsp ground coriander
¾ tsp ground cumin
1 tsp garam masala
salt, to taste
2 x recipe Fresh Paneer (see page 25), or 300g shop-bought paneer, cut into 2.5cm dice
½ each small green and red pepper, cut into 2.5cm dice
2–3 tbsp single cream

aubergine in a creamy peanut sauce

This is such a delicious dish that it is renowned across India. It is an orchestra of flavours; sweet, tangy, nutty, spicy and salty, one of those meals that even meat-eaters crave. It is rich so, though it takes less than 20 minutes to make, it is one to serve as a treat to friends. As aubergines collapse when cooked, Indians use small whole vegetables and make a deep cross from the base to just under the stalk – without cutting the aubergine into pieces – so you can see the whole vegetable and the insides get flavoured too. Serve with Indian breads or a pilaf.

In a small pan, gently dry roast the coriander seeds until they turn a light brown. Pour straight into a spice grinder or mortar. Add the sesame seeds and coconut to the pan and dry roast these until the coconut is golden. Add to the coriander seeds. Toast the peanuts (if raw) in the same way. Add the peanuts to the seeds and coconut and whizz or pestle to a fine powder.

Heat half the oil in a large saucepan. Add the onion and, once it is soft and colouring on the edges, the ginger. Once the onions are a lovely golden brown, spoon the whole lot into a blender, leaving behind the oil, and add the ground nut powder and 150ml water. Blend until smooth.

Pour the remaining oil into the pan and add the remaining whole spices. Once the fenugreek seeds have browned, add the aubergines, give them a good stir in the oil and pour in the onion paste with 350ml water, the salt, turmeric, chilli powder and sugar. Bring to a boil, cover and cook gently for 10–15 minutes, or until the aubergine is soft. The sauce should be like double cream and thickens as it sits so, if necessary, add a splash of water from the kettle.

Add the tamarind and adjust the seasoning and sugar to taste, and serve sprinkled with chopped coriander.

serves 4

traditionally…the aubergine would be lightly shallow-fried before being added to the sauce. I have left out this step to cut down on the oil, but the crispy texture is nice. I'll leave it up to you.

1 tbsp coriander seeds
1½ tbsp sesame seeds
4 tbsp unsweetened desiccated coconut
7 tbsp lightly roasted or raw peanuts
5 tbsp vegetable oil
1 largish onion, sliced
10g fresh root ginger, peeled weight, roughly chopped
¾ tsp mustard seeds
¾ tsp cumin seeds
½ tsp nigella seeds
pinch of fenugreek seeds
450g Japanese aubergines (around 8), or small round aubergines, quartered but left attached at the stalk end (see recipe introduction)
salt, to taste
½ tsp turmeric
⅓–⅔ tsp chilli powder
1 tbsp sugar or jaggery, or to taste
1¼–1¾ tsp tamarind paste
a little chopped fresh coriander, to serve

tangy chickpea curry

Whenever I translate the Indian name of this dish literally into English it comes out as 'bean curry', which is misleadingly and depressingly reminiscent of the sandal-wearing hippies of the 1960s and 1970s and detracts from its Indian roots and utter deliciousness. A lovely, flavourful dish, it's great with Bhatura (see page 158) for a fabulous weekend lunch. But I often eat it with buttered wholemeal bread for a divine, simple meal.

Blend together the ginger, garlic and tomatoes with a little water until smooth (I use a stick blender). Set aside.

Heat the oil in a large saucepan. Add the cloves, cardamom pods, cinnamon and half the cumin seeds and cook until they release their aroma and start to crackle. Add the green chillies and onion and cook until the onion is well browned. Add the tomato paste with the turmeric, ground coriander, chilli powder and salt and cook over a moderate to high heat until the oil comes out at the sides (around 15 minutes), stirring often.

Meanwhile, use the remaining cumin seeds to make roasted cumin powder (see below). Add it to the pot.

Add the chickpeas and 500ml water. Bring to a boil then simmer over a medium heat for seven or eight minutes. Stir in the garam masala and tamarind paste. Mash a few of the chickpeas on the side of the pan to thicken the sauce a little. Taste for seasoning and tartness, adjusting if necessary, then sprinkle with the chopped coriander and serve.

serves 4–5

to make roasted cumin powder roast cumin seeds in a small dry pan for about 40 seconds, stirring constantly, until they have darkened quite a bit. Grind to a fine powder.

12g fresh root ginger, peeled weight
4 fat garlic cloves
2 largish tomatoes, quartered
5–6 tbsp vegetable oil
4 cloves
4 green cardamom pods
1 black cardamom pod
2 large shards of cinnamon
2 tsp cumin seeds
2–3 green chillies, whole but pierced
1 onion, finely chopped
½ tsp turmeric
1 tbsp ground coriander
¼–½ tsp chilli powder
salt, to taste
2 x 400g cans of chickpeas, drained
   and rinsed
1¼ tsp garam masala
½–⅔ tsp tamarind paste, or dried
   pomegranate powder, or to taste
handful of finely chopped fresh
   coriander

light tofu and pea curry

This is a dish I eat regularly as it tastes good and is healthy. It is based on the classic *mattar paneer* (paneer with peas) but, as paneer can be heavy, I've substituted tofu for years. Though it has a completely different taste, it is still a vegetarian protein and absorbs other flavours in the same way, so works well here. You can, of course, use paneer instead if you prefer. I eat this with brown rice.

Make a smooth paste of the ginger, garlic and tomatoes, using a little water to help (I use a stick blender).

Heat the vegetable oil in a non-stick saucepan. Add the whole spices and bay leaf and, once the cumin seeds have darkened, tip in the onion and cook until golden brown. Add the tomato paste, turmeric, chilli, coriander and salt. Bring to a boil and cook over a moderate flame until the paste releases oil droplets on the base of the pan, around 10 minutes, then gently sauté the paste for a further five or six minutes; it will deepen in colour and flavour.

Add the peas and tofu and stir for two or three minutes. Add the milk with 350ml water and bring to a boil. Simmer for five or six minutes, or until the curry has a light, creamy consistency. Taste, adjust the seasoning and serve, scattered with chopped coriander.

serves 3–4 moderately

12g fresh root ginger, peeled weight
3 garlic cloves
2 tomatoes, quartered
2 tbsp vegetable oil
¾ tsp cumin seeds
8 black peppercorns
3 cloves
5cm cinnamon stick
1 large bay leaf
1 onion, finely chopped
½ tsp turmeric
⅛–¼ tsp chilli powder, or to taste
2 level tsp ground coriander
salt, to taste
200g peas
200g firm tofu, cut into cubes
100ml whole milk
small handful of chopped fresh
   coriander leaves

fluffy spinach koftas in a creamy tomato curry

A kofta was traditionally a meatball, but the vegetarian masses of India (perhaps the most inventive cooks I've ever come across) soon started to make their own versions. These would have been made with paneer but I didn't want to add the extra work, so I tried it with ricotta instead. The resulting koftas are light, fluffy and absolutely delicious with this full-bodied, lightly spiced sauce. Serve with pilaf (see pages 160-163) or Naan (see page 155).

Blend together the tomatoes, garlic and ginger to a fine paste, using a little water to help; I use a stick blender. Heat the 5 tbsp of oil in a large non-stick saucepan. Add the onion and cook until lightly browned. Add the tomato paste, cashew nuts, spices and salt. Cook over a moderate heat for around 15 minutes, stirring occasionally, until the paste releases oil. Blend until smooth with a stick blender, adding a little water, if necessary, to help. Pour back into the pan, add 500ml water, bring to a boil and simmer for eight to 10 minutes, until the curry is the consistency of single cream.

While the curry is cooking, make the dumplings. Wilt the spinach in a pan with a little water and a good pinch of salt. Once cool enough to handle, squeeze out the excess water and blend to a coarse puree with a stick blender. Add the cornflour and ricotta and stir well.

Heat the oil for deep-frying in a wide sauté pan or a karahi. There should be enough to come 5cm up the sides of the sauté pan, or 10cm up the sides of a small karahi. Test the oil temperature by dropping in a small amount of the spinach mixture; it should sizzle immediately but not colour straight away. Drop heaped teaspoonfuls of the mixture straight into the oil. You may need to do this in batches, so as not to crowd the pan. You should be able to make about 20. Carefully cook them, turning to ensure even cooking; they take about seven or eight minutes and will (unfortunately) turn brown, losing their vivid green colour. Remove and blot off excess oil on kitchen paper.

Once the dumplings are all cooked, place them in the curry and cook for five minutes. Stir in the cream or butter (if using) and serve.

serves 4-5

for the curry
2 large tomatoes, quartered and deseeded
3 garlic cloves
10g fresh root ginger, peeled weight
5 tbsp vegetable oil, plus more to deep-fry
1 onion, sliced
40g cashew nuts
½ tsp turmeric
¼–½ tsp chilli powder for heat, or ½ tsp paprika for colour
1¼ tsp ground coriander
1 tsp ground cumin
1 tsp garam masala
salt, to taste
2–3 tbsp double cream, or a knob of butter (optional)

for the koftas
200g spinach, I use whole leaf (not baby leaf) for more flavour, well washed
2 tbsp cornflour
200g ricotta cheese

fish and
seafood

green sindhi fish curry

A lovely dish that is everyday fare for the Sindhi community. It is quick and easy and the flavour is herby, deep and rich, but doesn't overpower the fish. This same sauce is also used to cook leftover rotis and pieces of bread, so I would serve this with Indian flatbreads or even lightly buttered bread.

4 tbsp vegetable oil
1 smallish onion, sliced
20g fresh coriander leaves and stalks
4 garlic cloves
10g fresh root ginger, peeled weight
1 tomato, chopped
salt, to taste
1 rounded tsp ground coriander
2–4 green chillies, whole but pierced
3 fillets of firm white fish, left whole
    or cut into large cubes

Heat the oil in a non-stick saucepan. Add the onion and cook until well browned. Remove from the heat.

Blend together the coriander leaves and stalks, garlic, ginger and cooked onion with a little water until smooth. Pour back into the saucepan along with the tomato, salt, ground coriander and chillies. Add 150ml water, bring to a boil, cover and cook for 20 minutes, stirring occasionally.

Uncover, reduce any remaining water by boiling hard, then sauté until the oil leaves the masala. Add 250ml water and the fish, bring to a boil, then reduce the heat and simmer gently for three or four minutes, or until the fish is cooked through. Taste, adjust the seasoning and serve.

serves 3–4

bengali mustard fish

A classic, this is absolutely terrific and so different from other fish curries. It has very few ingredients, so they all play an important part. The fish should be in steaks so that they do not break up when you fry them, and the bones will ensure extra flavour. You can also use sea bass, bream or tilapia. The dish will not taste as good without the green chillies, so try it with them: you might find it spicy, but I bet you can't stop eating! Mustard seeds can be bitter if overworked, so grind them only briefly in a spice grinder. Measure this powder, not the seeds, before adding it to the curry. Serve with plain boiled rice.

450g halibut steaks, left whole
   or quartered
¾ tsp turmeric
salt, to taste
1½ small tomatoes (around 150g)
3 fat garlic cloves
4–5 green chillies (preferably Indian
   finger)
1½ tbsp powdered brown mustard
   seeds (see recipe introduction)
4 tbsp mustard or vegetable oil
1¼ tsp nigella seeds
handful of fresh coriander leaves

Marinate the fish in ¼ tsp of the turmeric and a good pinch of salt, tossing with your hands to coat.

Meanwhile, blend the tomatoes, garlic and two or three of the green chillies (deseeded if you are worried about their heat), a little more salt, the powdered mustard seeds, remaining turmeric and 150ml water to a smooth paste.

If using mustard oil, heat 3 tbsp in a non-stick pan until smoking, then remove from the heat and wait for 30 seconds before proceeding with the recipe. If using vegetable oil, simply heat 3 tbsp of the oil. Add the nigella seeds and, once they have sizzled for 10 seconds, put in the tomato-chilli-mustard paste.

Cook over a moderate flame until all the excess moisture has evaporated and the paste releases oil, stirring occasionally. Then reduce the heat and continue cooking for four minutes or so until it darkens a little. Add 400ml water and the remaining chillies; bring to a boil and simmer for seven or eight minutes. It should not be too watery, so cook until it has a medium consistency. Check the seasoning and keep it on a low heat.

Heat the remaining oil in a frying pan until smoking. Add the fish and fry well on all sides for about six minutes, until golden brown. Now put the fish in the mustard sauce, bring back to a boil and cook for two minutes. Gently shake in the coriander leaves and serve.

serves 3–4

crab curry

My brother-in-law has been telling me about his mother's crab curry for years so, when I started to work on this recipe, I invited him over and we cooked together as we reminisced about our mothers' food. This lovely curry is the product of that fun, disjointed Saturday afternoon. If the whole peppercorns and cloves bother you, strain the sauce to remove them before pouring it over the crab. This curry improves after sitting for a few hours, as the sauce seeps into the crab. I buy my crab fresh from my fishmonger who kindly cleans and cuts it up for me. I add about 4–5 tbsp of the brown meat for extra flavour, but you can add more or less, as you prefer.

2 x 750g whole raw crabs, cleaned
    and cut into pieces
7 tbsp vegetable oil
20 fenugreek seeds
8 cloves
20 black peppercorns
15 fresh curry leaves
2–4 green chillies, whole but pierced
2 largish onions, chopped
10 large garlic cloves
4 small tomatoes, quartered
15g fresh root ginger, peeled weight
salt, to taste
¼–½ tsp chilli powder
2 tsp ground coriander
2 level tsp ground cumin
½ tsp turmeric
1–1½ tsp tamarind paste, or to taste
200ml coconut milk (optional)

Ask your fishmonger to clean the crabs, smash the claws slightly so you can get at the meat later, and to halve or quarter the bodies. He will also give you the brown meat separately, if you ask nicely.

Heat the oil in a large non-stick saucepan or karahi. Add the fenugreek, cloves and peppercorns and, once the fenugreek has browned, the curry leaves.

Tip in the green chillies and onions and cook until golden. Meanwhile, blend together the garlic, tomatoes, ginger and a good splash of water until smooth. Add to the pot with the salt, chilli, coriander, cumin and turmeric. Bring to a boil and simmer until the masala releases oil into the pan, then gently stir-fry for a further five to seven minutes to intensify the flavours.

Add 800ml water and bring to a boil. Stir in the tamarind paste. Add the crab pieces and brown meat, bring back to a boil, cover and simmer over a moderate heat for about 15 minutes, until the crab is cooked. There should only be a little liquid left. Stir in the coconut milk (if using) and add a little boiled water if you think the dish needs more sauce. Taste and adjust the seasoning, adding more tamarind to taste, then serve.

serves 4

prawn patia

This is a great fruity, sweet, sour and spicy curry, served on special occasions in Parsi homes with a simple yellow lentil curry and white rice. But it needn't be saved for best, as it's not hard to make. Kashmiri chillies are known for their deep red colour and mild heat. I found mine in a well-stocked local supermarket - which was lucky - but you can also buy them in Indian stores or on the internet, and they last really well in the larder. If you can't find any, use 1–2 normal dried red chillies. Sambhar powder is a spice blend usually used in this dish to add an extra punch of flavour, though I have to admit that I don't generally have any, so it's not essential.

4–7 dried Kashmiri chillies, stalks and seeds removed
6 tbsp vegetable oil
2 onions, finely sliced
3 largish tomatoes, quartered
5 large garlic cloves
1 rounded tsp ground coriander
1½ tsp ground cumin
⅓ tsp turmeric
½ good tsp garam masala
½ tsp sambhar powder (optional)
salt, to taste
2–2½ tsp grated jaggery, or sugar, to taste
1¼–1¾ tsp tamarind paste, or to taste
400g raw prawns, shelled, deveined and rinsed
handful of chopped fresh coriander leaves

Soak the dried chillies in hot water for 30 minutes.

Heat the oil in a deep saute pan. Add the onions and cook for 10–12 minutes, until really quite brown.

Meanwhile, blend together the tomatoes, garlic and soaked chillies until you have a fine paste. Add to the pan with 350ml water, the spices and salt. Bring to a boil and cook, stirring occasionally, for 20 minutes. It will get really thick and darken considerably; stir more often as it thickens.

Stir in the jaggery or sugar, most of the tamarind and a good splash of water. Bring to a boil; the sauce should still be quite thick. Add the prawns and cook for two or three minutes until done. Taste and adjust the seasoning, adding more sweet jaggery or sour tamarind to taste. Sprinkle over the chopped coriander and serve.

serves 4

creamy tomato fish curry

This is a lovely, mild dish whose star ingredients are sweet-sour tomatoes and, of course, the fish. It is easy to cook for a delicious midweek meal, but also elegant enough to impress your friends. You can choose any fish you like; I like to use fish steaks in most of my curries, but monkfish also works well (though if you use monkfish, don't fry it before adding to the curry; just tip it straight in). This is lovely with a pilaf or Indian flatbreads (see Breads and Rice, page 154).

Rub half the turmeric and a good pinch of salt into the fish and leave to marinate as you cook the sauce.

Heat 5 tbsp of the oil in a non-stick saucepan. Add the whole spices and bay leaves and, once they have sizzled for 10 seconds, the onion. Cook until golden brown.

Meanwhile, blend the tomatoes, ginger and garlic until smooth, adding a splash of water to help, if needed. Add this paste to the pan with all the spices (except the garam masala) and salt, to taste. Cook over a medium-high flame, stirring often, for 10–12 minutes, until the spice mix (masala) releases oil droplets. Reduce the heat and brown the paste for a further six minutes to intensify the flavours. Add 500ml water and bring to a boil, reduce the heat and simmer for six or seven minutes. Taste and adjust the seasoning.

Meanwhile fry the fish. Heat the remaining oil in a frying pan until very hot. Add the marinated pieces of fish and cook, undisturbed, for two minutes. Turn and cook for another two minutes or so, until golden brown. Add the fried fish, garam masala and cream to the curry. Simmer for another three minutes so the fish finishes cooking and starts to absorb the sauce. Taste, adjust the seasoning and serve scattered with chopped coriander.

serves 4

1 tsp turmeric
salt, to taste
500–550g firm white fish steaks, such as halibut, halved
7 tbsp vegetable oil
6 cloves
6 green cardamom pods
12 black peppercorns
2 bay leaves
1 small onion, finely chopped
4 tomatoes, quartered and deseeded
10g fresh root ginger, peeled weight
6 fat garlic cloves
¼–½ tsp chilli powder
1 tbsp ground coriander
freshly ground black pepper, to taste
¾ tsp garam masala
2 tbsp single cream
handful of fresh coriander leaves, chopped

mild prawn curry with cashew nuts

A lovely, delicate curry inspired by the Christian dishes and ingredients of Kerala. It is easy, quick and great for family (without the chilli) or friends. The cashew nuts are lightly roasted, then added to the prawns, but you can leave them out. The Keralans would use a thin extract of coconut milk to cook the prawns, then add thicker coconut milk at the end. Canned coconut milk should have its cream accumulated at the top, so spoon this off and stir it in at the end; it adds a lovely aroma and richness.

Blend the ginger and garlic to a fine paste, adding a little water to help. Heat 1 tsp of the oil in a non-stick saucepan; add the cashew nuts and stir-fry until golden. Remove with a slotted spoon, toss in a little salt and set aside.

Add the rest of the oil to the pan. Once hot, add the fenugreek and mustard seeds; they will start popping. Once the noise dies down a little, add the onion and cook gently until soft. Add the ginger and garlic paste and cook until any excess moisture dries up, then reduce the heat and stir over a low flame for two minutes or so, until the garlic smells cooked.

Add the spices and chillies, salt and a splash of water. Once the water has dried up, add 250ml of the thinner part of the coconut milk (see recipe introduction), 100ml water and the vinegar.

Bring to a boil, then simmer for 10 minutes. Taste, adjust the seasoning and tartness (if the garlic was still raw, you will be able to taste it here. If it is, cook for another five minutes, then check again). The sauce should have the consistency of single cream.

Add the prawns and cook until done; in around three minutes they will have curled up and become opaque. Stir in the remaining, thicker coconut milk and the cashews. Serve with rice.

serves 4, can be halved

30g fresh root ginger, peeled weight, roughly chopped
6 fat garlic cloves, halved
5 tbsp vegetable oil
60g raw cashew nuts
salt, to taste
scant ½ tsp fenugreek seeds
scant 1 tsp mustard seeds
1 onion, sliced
1 rounded tbsp ground coriander
¾ tsp turmeric
generous ¾–1 tsp ground black pepper
1 tsp ground cumin
4–6 red or green chillies, or to taste, left whole or slit for more heat
400ml creamy coconut milk
2 tbsp white wine vinegar, or to taste
350g large raw prawns, shelled, deveined and rinsed

authentic goan fish curry

This is delicious. Many coconut curries are mild – there are several in this book – so here I give a spicy example. Use a firm white fish such as halibut, tilapia or monkfish. You can use boneless pieces, but bear in mind they must stand up to cooking in a curry without breaking up. Serve with rice.

Using a spice grinder, grind the cumin seeds, dried chillies and coriander seeds to a fine powder.

Heat the oil in a large non-stick saucepan. Add the onion and cook over a medium flame until golden.

Meanwhile, blend together the ginger, garlic and tomatoes until smooth, adding a little water to help. Add to the onions and cook over a medium flame for eight to 10 minutes, until the paste releases oil droplets on the base of the pan. Add the ground whole spices, turmeric and salt along with a small splash of water and cook for two minutes. Add the coconut milk and 300ml water, bring to a boil and simmer for a few minutes.

Add the tamarind paste, green chillies and fish, bring back to a boil and simmer gently until the fish is just done; it will take three to six minutes, depending on the cut and type of fish. Add the coconut cream and shake the pan to incorporate. Taste, adjust the salt and tamarind until the balance is perfect for you, then serve.

serves 4

2 scant tsp cumin seeds
4–7 Kashmiri (mild) dried red chillies, seeds shaken out
4 tsp coriander seeds
3 tbsp vegetable oil
1 small onion, finely chopped
30g fresh root ginger, peeled weight, cut into large chunks
6 fat garlic cloves
1 small tomato, quartered
¾ tsp turmeric
salt, to taste
100ml coconut milk
1 tsp tamarind paste, or to taste
2–4 green chillies (preferably Indian finger), whole but pierced
600g firm white fish steaks or fillets (see recipe introduction)
4 good tbsp coconut cream (I find mine in cartons)

north indian-spiced prawn curry

This is one of my favourite ways to eat prawns. The tomato- and garlic-based sauce is lightly spiced and there is a lot of flavour, but not so much that it dominates the sweet prawns. This is lovely with rice or Indian breads, or even a piece of buttered, crusty bread to dip into the sauce. Mustard oil adds a further layer of flavour; if you use it, bring it to smoking point then take off the heat for 30 seconds to cool before continuing.

Blend the tomatoes, garlic and 5g of the ginger to a fine puree. Finely slice the remaining ginger into julienne.

Heat the oil in a large, non-stick saucepan, add the panch phoran and let it sizzle for 10–15 seconds, or until the lighter seeds have become a warm brown colour. Add the onion, chillies and ginger julienne and cook until the onions are lightly golden.

Add the tomato paste, remaining spices and salt. Cook over a moderate heat for around 15 minutes until the spice paste releases oil, stirring often as it thickens. Taste, it should be well-balanced and harmonious. Add the prawns and enough water to cover them by half. Bring to a boil, then simmer gently for three or four minutes, until the prawns are done. The sauce should be light but not watery. Stir in the cream, taste and adjust the seasoning, adding lemon juice if you like, and serve with the chopped coriander.

serves 4–5

2 tomatoes
5 fat garlic cloves
12g ginger, peeled weight
5 tbsp mustard or vegetable oil
1 rounded tsp panch phoran
1 small onion, finely chopped
1–3 green chillies (preferably Indian finger), whole but pierced
1½ tsp ground coriander
⅓ tsp turmeric
¼ tsp chilli powder
1 tsp garam masala
¾ tsp ground cumin
salt, to taste
400g large raw prawns, shelled, deveined and rinsed
1 tbsp double cream
1–2 tsp lemon juice, or to taste (depends on the tartness of your tomatoes)
handful of chopped fresh coriander leaves, to serve

creamy keralan seafood curry

This lovely, harmonious coconut sauce goes perfectly with seafood. I use an assortment here as I like the different textures and flavours that a good variety of seafood offers. Or you can also use the same amount of firm white-fleshed fish instead. This is a wonderful dish; serve it with rice.

Heat the oil in a large sauté pan. Add the mustard seeds and peppercorns and, once they have popped, the curry leaves, onion and chillies. Cook until the onions are just soft and turning golden. Add the ginger and garlic and sauté for a couple of minutes on a gentle heat.

Add the tomatoes, spices and salt and cook for seven or eight minutes until the paste releases oil. Add the coconut milk and 250ml water. Bring to a boil and simmer for five minutes.

The sauce should have a consistency just thicker than single cream (if necessary reduce it a little more to thicken, or add a splash of water to loosen). Add the tamarind and follow with the seafood. Cook gently until done, around three minutes (if using crab claws, they may need to be added first to cook a little longer), then stir in the reserved coconut cream. Taste and adjust the seasoning, chilli heat and tamarind, to taste, then serve.

serves 4

5 tbsp coconut or vegetable oil
1 rounded tsp mustard seeds
10 black peppercorns
15 fresh curry leaves
1 onion, finely chopped
2–4 green chillies, whole but pierced
20g fresh root ginger, peeled weight, grated into a paste
5 fat garlic cloves, grated into a paste
2 tomatoes, blended to a paste or chopped
½ tsp chilli powder, or to taste
¾ tsp turmeric
1 good tbsp ground coriander
1 tsp ground cumin
salt, to taste
400ml creamy coconut milk (reserve 2 tbsp of the cream that accumulates on top)
¾–1 tsp tamarind paste, or to taste
500g assorted raw seafood (prawns, mussels, squid rings, crab claws), or white fish

fish caldine

This is a mild and creamy fish curry from Goa in spite of the long list of spices. If you do like the heat, add more than a couple of the dried chillies; I break them open and shake out the seeds before using. Or you can add a couple of red chillies to the oil before the onion to get some heat, then taste the sauce at any time and, if you find it has the right amount of heat, you can fish them out. Serve with rice.

Heat the oil in a non-stick saucepan. Add the onion and fry until golden. At the same time, using a spice grinder, make a fine powder of the chillies, all the whole spices and the poppy seeds or almonds. You can do this in a mortar and pestle, but remember it must be a fine powder.

Add the garlic and ginger to the onions and gently cook for a couple of minutes, until the raw smell of the garlic has disappeared. Add the spice powder, turmeric and salt and cook, stirring, for 40–50 seconds.

Add the coconut milk, 350ml water and the tamarind paste. Bring to a gentle boil and simmer for five minutes. Taste and adjust the seasoning. Add the fish and cook until done, anything from four to eight minutes depending on whether they are fillets or steaks. The sauce should be light and creamy; add a little boiling water if it is too thick. Serve scattered with chopped coriander.

serves 4

3 tbsp vegetable oil
1 smallish onion, sliced
1–3 dried red chillies, seeds shaken out (optional, see recipe introduction)
1 tsp cumin seeds
2 tsp coriander seeds
16 black peppercorns
2 cloves
2cm cinnamon stick
2 heaped tbsp white poppy seeds or ground almonds
6 fat garlic cloves, grated into a paste
10g ginger, peeled weight, grated into a paste
½ tsp turmeric
salt, to taste
320ml coconut milk, or more for a creamier curry
1 tsp tamarind paste, or to taste
450g fish steaks, or firm white fillets
handful of chopped fresh coriander leaves

prawn, mango and coconut curry

An unusual curry that came to life after a chat with my publisher who wanted to include mangoes in the book, particularly in a savoury curry. It was not something I had tried, but I gave it some thought and this slightly sweet, slightly hot curry is the delicious result of that conversation. It works really well, cooks in less than 10 minutes and is lovely with rice in late spring when mangoes come into season.

Blend the powdered mustard seeds with 100ml water. This helps the powder to become more of a paste and incorporates more easily with the sauce.

Heat the oil in a large non-stick saucepan and add the whole mustard seeds. Once they have popped, add the curry leaves, black peppercorns and whole chillies. Follow five seconds later with the coconut milk, mustard seed paste, salt, sugar, rice powder and 300ml water. Bring to a boil and simmer for five minutes. Add the prawns and simmer for two minutes more. Add the mango and cook for another minute. Taste, adjust the seasoning and sugar to taste and serve sprinkled with chopped coriander.

… or a vegetarian version Instead of prawns, you can add two handfuls of raw cashew nuts. I know it sounds odd, but on the west coast of India they cook a similar dish with pineapples or mangoes and nuts. It is eaten instead of lentils; the cashews provide the protein and it makes a delicious side dish.

serves 4

1 tsp powdered brown mustard seeds (see page 62)
3 tbsp vegetable oil
1 tsp brown mustard seeds
15 fresh curry leaves
10 black peppercorns
5–7 dried red chillies
350–375ml coconut milk
salt, to taste
1½–2 tsp sugar, or to taste
1 rounded tsp rice powder
350g medium or large raw prawns, peeled, deveined and rinsed
2 ripe (but not mushy) mangoes, peeled and cut into squares
handful of chopped fresh coriander

bengali yogurt fish

One of Bengal's most popular dishes, and deservedly so. It is absolutely delicious: creamy, but not heavy, and delicately spiced. I have added tomatoes as I think it tastes better. Fresh water fish would be perfect in this dish, but I have cooked it many ways and most firm-fleshed white fish work well. It goes brilliantly with both rice and Indian breads.

5 tbsp vegetable oil
1 small onion, finely chopped
10g fresh root ginger, peeled weight,
   grated into a paste
2 fat garlic cloves, grated into a paste
¼–½ tsp chilli powder, or to taste
2 tsp ground coriander
salt, to taste
1–3 green chillies, stalks removed,
   left whole
2 small tomatoes, blended to a puree
2 heaped tbsp good Greek yogurt
500-600g firm white fish fillets, cut
   into fairly large pieces
a few fresh coriander leaves,
   chopped, to serve

Heat the oil in a saucepan. Add the onion and cook until soft and lightly golden. Add the ginger and garlic pastes and cook over a gentle flame for around two minutes, stirring often; the garlic should smell cooked.
Stir in the spices, salt and green chillies. Pour in the pureed tomatoes and 150ml water and cook over a moderate flame until the liquid has evaporated, then continue stirring until the tomato takes on the rich colour of tomato puree. Stir in the yogurt until really well blended.

Pour in 200ml water, bring to a gentle boil, stirring constantly, then simmer for five to eight minutes, or until the sauce has the consistency of single cream. Taste; you may want more salt or chilli powder.

Add your fish and shake the pan to coat the fillets with the sauce. Cover and cook gently for three to five minutes, or until the fish is cooked through. Serve sprinkled with a little fresh coriander.

Serves 4, can be halved

mussels with saffron

This curry is a reflection of my childhood, as we spent many holidays in France and I have fond memories of eating light saffron-flavoured seafood dishes under the sun. I wanted to evoke those meals, but to give them a new life and zest with Indian flavours, particularly ginger and chillies. There is plenty of sauce to mop up with rice or a hunk of bread. Make sure the mussels are as fresh as can be and buy extra; even if you cook them the day you buy them, there are often a few that are unuseable. Any raw mussels that are open and do not close when firmly tapped on the counter should be thrown away, as should any that remain closed once cooked.

4 tbsp vegetable oil
25 black peppercorns
2½ small onions, chopped
4–6 green chillies, whole but pierced
35g ginger, peeled weight, grated into a paste
5 garlic cloves, grated into a paste
2½ tomatoes, chopped
1 tsp fennel seeds, ground, or to taste
½ tsp turmeric
2 tsp ground coriander
good pinch of saffron (around 20-25 strands), slightly crumbled, or to taste
salt, to taste
1kg mussels, scrubbed and debearded
150ml double cream
a little chopped fresh coriander, to serve

Heat the oil in a saucepan large enough to hold all the mussels. Add the peppercorns and follow with the onions, cooking them until lightly golden. Add the green chillies, ginger and garlic pastes and gently sauté until the garlic smells cooked; it should take about two minutes.

Add the tomatoes, spices and salt and cook, stirring often and lightly mashing the tomatoes with a spoon, for 10–12 minutes, or until you have a thick masala that has released oil back into the pan. Taste it; there should be no harsh flavours.

Add 500ml water and bring to a boil. Simmer for five minutes. Add the mussels, cover, shake, then simmer for three minutes or until the mussels have opened. Add the cream, taste and adjust the seasoning, saffron and ground fennel seed to taste. The sauce should be lightly creamy. If it is too watery, put your mussels in a warmed serving bowl while you boil the sauce to reduce it, then pour this back over the mussels. Stir in the chopped coriander and serve.

serves 4

karahi prawns

A karahi is a concave pan similar to a wok and, like wok cooking, a 'karahi' dish conjures up images of ingredients being tossed into the pan in quick succession and cooked over high heat. The resulting dish should be slightly caramelised in places but also retain lots of fresh flavours with a warm, rich sauce. Dried fenugreek leaves have a wonderful flavour and it is worth buying a packet as they keep really well for a year and can be used to enhance most north Indian dishes. Carom seeds are also known as *ajwain* and have a wonderful thyme-like taste that adds a special note. Serve with Indian breads.

Heat 4 tbsp of the ghee or oil in a karahi or sauté pan. Add the onion and cook over a high heat until browned. Add the ginger and garlic pastes and chillies. Sauté gently for a minute or two, until the garlic smells cooked. Add the tomatoes, ground coriander and cumin, carom seeds, crumbled fenugreek leaves and chilli powder. Cook, stirring occasionally, for about 15 minutes, or until the oil comes out of the paste, then stir for three or four minutes more, or until the tomatoes have darkened a little. Set this masala aside.

Heat the remaining ghee or oil in the pan, add the prawns and sauté for a minute. Add the masala paste, garam masala, cream and 50ml water; cook for another two minutes. The sauce should be fairly thick and clinging to the prawns. Taste and adjust the seasoning. Stir in the coriander leaves and add lemon, to taste.

serves 4

5 tbsp ghee or vegetable oil
1 small onion, finely chopped
20g fresh root ginger, peeled weight, grated into a paste
7 fat garlic cloves, grated into a paste
2–4 fresh green chillies, whole but pierced
6 small tomatoes, chopped
1½ tsp ground coriander
1½ tsp ground cumin
¾ tsp carom seeds
2 tsp dried fenugreek leaves, crumbled
¼–½ tsp chilli powder, or to taste
400g large or medium raw prawns, peeled, deveined and rinsed
1½ tsp garam masala
1–2 tbsp single cream
salt and freshly ground pepper, to taste
handful of fresh coriander leaves
1 tsp lemon juice, or to taste

poultry

punjabi chicken curry

I grew up eating this. It has a thin liquor rather than a thick sauce but is full of flavour. This recipe appears in *Anjum's New Indian* but I wanted to give it here too, as this is the curry I am most asked about and my book on curries wouldn't be complete without it. Please do use chicken on the bone as it really makes a difference, giving that lovely rounded flavour. If you have a friendly butcher, ask him to joint and skin the chicken for you. I use small chickens as I find them more succulent. Eat with Chapati (see page 156), or a pilaf.

Using a little water, make a fine paste of the ginger and garlic. Set aside.

Heat the oil in a large non-stick frying pan. Add the whole spices and bay leaves and, once they have sizzled for 10 seconds, add the onion and cook until golden brown. Add the chillies and the ginger-garlic paste and sauté until the moisture has evaporated and the garlic has had a chance to cook. Add the tomatoes, salt and powdered spices and sauté for six or seven minutes more.

Add the chicken and stir it in the masala (spice paste) for four to five minutes. Pour in enough water to come halfway up the chicken, bring to a boil, then cover and cook over a low heat for 20–30 minutes, or until the chicken is nearly cooked through.

Uncover the pan, increase the flame to high and reduce the liquid in the pan until thick and creamy, stirring often. This will help the sauce become homogenous and deepen its flavours.

Add enough hot water to give a sauce with the consistency of light cream. Taste and adjust the seasoning, stir in the chopped coriander and serve.

serves 6

15g fresh root ginger, peeled weight, cut into large pieces
10 fat garlic cloves
5 tbsp vegetable oil
5cm cinnamon stick
3 large black cardamom pods
4 green cardamom pods
4 cloves
2 bay leaves
1 onion, chopped
2–4 green chillies, whole but pierced
3 tomatoes (not too ripe), cut into thin wedges
salt, to taste
2 tbsp ground coriander
2 tsp ground cumin
½ tsp turmeric
¼–½ tsp chilli powder
1½ tsp garam masala
750g skinless chicken joints
large handful of chopped fresh coriander

herby chicken curry

There are many recipes for cooking meats with green herbs in India, this is from the north. Other cooks would add tomatoes and, in the south, they would add fresh coconut or coconut milk as well, so you can change this recipe to reflect your food mood. I find I have started thinking about dishes as being masculine or feminine in nature. This dish has a soft edge, with a perfume of fresh herbs and a delicacy of flavour I feel is rounded and feminine. Men, do not be put off! It might not be robust but is still delicious when you want a light curry. Serve with Chapati or Paratha (see pages 156 and 157), or rice.

Heat 4 tbsp of the oil in a large, non-stick saucepan. Add the onion and cook until well browned. Place all the ingredients for the spice paste into a blender, add the onions and their oil and blend to a fine paste.

Heat the remaining oil in the pan, add the bay leaf and follow after five seconds with the spice paste and chicken joints. Cook, stirring, over a moderate flame for eight to 10 minutes, making sure the paste does not stick to the base of the pan. If it does, add a splash of hot water from the kettle.

Now pour in enough water to cover the chicken by half. Bring to a boil, then cover and place over a low heat until the chicken is cooked through. It should take 20–25 minutes, depending on the size of the chicken joints, and there should be plenty of gorgeous creamy green gravy. If it seems watery, uncover and cook off some of the extra liquid over a high heat, stirring often.

Stir in the garam masala, ground cumin and sour cream; taste. This is when you can balance the dish to perfection by adjusting the salt, lemon juice, garam masala, chilli, or sour cream, as you prefer.

serves 4–6

for the chicken curry
5 tbsp vegetable oil
1 onion, sliced
1 bay leaf
700g small chicken, skinned and jointed
1 good tsp garam masala, or to taste
1 tsp ground cumin
1 tbsp sour cream, or to taste

for the spice paste
100g fresh coriander leaves and stems, washed
1–2 green chillies, stalk removed, or to taste
40g mint leaves, washed
5 large garlic cloves
10g fresh root ginger, peeled weight
2 tsp ground coriander
3 tbsp cashew nuts
3 tbsp lemon juice, or to taste
1 good tsp salt, or to taste

chicken tikka masala

Though everybody 'knows' this dish was invented in Britain, when a diner supposedly wanted sauce with his chicken tikka, its roots are firmly entrenched in one of India's favourite dishes: butter chicken. It is velvety and unapologetically rich. You will need to taste carefully while you cook, as the sweet-sour balance of tomatoes changes with the season and variety. Balance tartness with sugar or cream or, if it is already sweet, omit the sugar. Do not use plum tomatoes; they are too sweet. Serve with Naan or Paratha (see pages 155 and 157).

Mix together all the marinade ingredients with 1 tsp salt. Add the chicken and marinate for as long as possible (overnight, covered, in the fridge is best).

Blend together the ginger and garlic for the curry, using a little water to help. Heat the oil and half the butter in a large non-stick saucepan and add the whole spices. Once they have sizzled for 15 seconds, add the ginger and garlic paste; cook until all the moisture has evaporated and the garlic smells mellow and looks grainy. Add the tomatoes and tomato puree and cook down until the resulting paste releases oil; it should take around 20 minutes. Now brown this paste over gentle heat, stirring often, for six to eight minutes, or until it darkens considerably. Pour in 250ml water, bring to a boil, then pass through a sieve, pressing down to extract as much liquid and flavour as possible from the tomatoes and spices. Discard the solids. Set the sauce aside.

Heat the oven to 240°C, ideally with the grill on too, if your oven can do that. Remove the chicken from the fridge. Place it on a foil-lined baking tray on the uppermost shelf of the oven and cook for eight minutes, or until slightly charred. Remove from the oven. The chicken will finish cooking in the sauce. Cut or pull the meat into large chunks.

Heat the remaining butter and add the green chillies. Add the sauce, salt and a good splash of water and simmer for three or four minutes. Add the chicken, cream, sugar, chilli powder and enough paprika to get a colour you like, then add the powdered fenugreek leaves and garam masala. Simmer, stirring often, for four or five minutes, or until the chicken is done and the sauce is lovely and creamy. You may need to add a little more water. Taste and adjust the balance to your palate by adding more salt, sugar or cream. Sprinkle over the coriander leaves and serve.

serves 4

for the tikka marinade
3–4 tsp lemon juice, depending on the tartness of the yogurt
110g Greek yogurt
2 fat garlic cloves, grated into a paste
10g fresh root ginger, peeled weight, grated into a paste
¼–½ tsp chilli powder
1½ tsp paprika powder, for colour (optional)
1½ tsp ground cumin
2 tbsp vegetable oil

for the curry
6 boneless chicken thighs
20g fresh root ginger, peeled weight
8 garlic cloves
2 tbsp vegetable oil
80g butter
1 black cardamom pod
6 green cardamom pods
2cm cinnamon stick
4 cloves
500g vine tomatoes, blended to a fine puree
1 tbsp tomato puree
2–4 small green chillies, whole but pierced
salt, to taste
80–100ml single cream, or to taste
1 tsp sugar, or to taste
¼–½ tsp chilli powder
1 tsp paprika powder, or to taste
1 rounded tsp dried fenugreek leaves, crushed to a powder
1 tsp garam masala
small handful of fresh coriander leaves, to serve

chicken and vegetables in an aromatic coconut sauce

This is a beautiful, full-flavoured, creamy dish that hails from the Christians of Kerala. It is known as *ishtu*, a word that is a derivation of 'stew', because this is a naturally-fused dish of east and west. Chicken and vegetables are all cooked together with the local flavours of the south western coast of India. There are lots of spices, but the flavours have been mellowed by coconut. Don't worry, you can still taste lovely bits of ginger and the flavours of star anise and fennel seeds. You can make this without vegetables, or add whatever vegetables you have in the fridge; it's that kind of dish. Lovely with rice, Naan or Paratha (see pages 155 and 157), or even the rice noodles which are often eaten in Kerala.

Heat the oil in a wide pan (a karahi or wok is ideal). Add the whole spices and, once the seeds have stopped popping, the curry leaves. Follow immediately with the onion and cook over a moderate heat until translucent. Add the ginger, garlic and green chillies and sauté gently for one or two minutes, or until the garlic is cooked.

Add the turmeric, chilli, ground coriander, fennel seeds and salt with a splash of water and cook for two minutes. Put in the chicken and cook in the spice paste for two minutes more. Pour in water to come one-third of the way up the chicken, bring to a boil, then lower the flame and cook, covered, for 20 minutes, stirring occasionally. The liquid in the pot should have reduced quite a bit by now. Add most of the coconut milk (try and add only the thin milk that collects at the bottom of the can at this point), cover and cook for another five minutes. Uncover and cook off most of the excess liquid, giving the pan occasional stirs. Check the chicken is cooked all the way through, with no trace of pink.

Stir in the remaining thick coconut milk, coconut cream (if using), tamarind, beans and peas; the dish should be creamy. Taste and adjust the seasoning. Simmer for three to four minutes, then serve with the coriander leaves.

serves 4-6

6 tbsp coconut or vegetable oil
1 tsp mustard seeds
5cm cinnamon stick
6 green cardamom pods
4 cloves
10 black peppercorns
2 star anise
15 curry leaves
1 onion, finely sliced
20g fresh root ginger, peeled weight, finely chopped
6 garlic cloves, finely chopped
2–4 green chillies, whole but pierced
½ tsp turmeric
¼–½ tsp chilli powder
1 tbsp ground coriander
2 tsp fennel seeds, roughly powdered
salt, to taste
500g skinless chicken joints
400ml can coconut milk
1 tbsp coconut cream (optional)
¾–1 tsp tamarind paste, or to taste
handful of green beans, topped and tailed, halved on the diagonal
2 handfuls of green peas, fresh or frozen and defrosted
small fistful of fresh coriander leaves

spicy andhra chicken curry

Andhra is a region known for its great hot food and this dish is just that, bold and absolutely wonderful. Although it might look complicated, it's actually quite easy to cook and, as it uses boneless chicken, all comes together quite quickly. The chicken would normally be deep-fried before being added to the sauce, but I don't do that. It's up to you. If the dish seems too spicy, add a little milk, single cream or coconut milk to tame the flavours. White poppy seeds have a lovely taste and creaminess, you can make it without them but I recommend you seek them out as they are a fantastic store cupboard ingredient. This is great with rice and Indian breads.

Using a mortar and pestle, or a spice grinder, grind together the whole spices and chillies to a fine powder. Separately blend together the ginger and garlic to a fine paste, adding a little water to help. Take around one-third of this paste and mix it with the marinade ingredients, adding ¼ tsp of salt. Add to the chicken, mix well and marinate for as long as possible, up to overnight in the refrigerator, though even 30 minutes will help.

Heat the oil in a non-stick saucepan. Add the onion and sauté until golden brown. Add the remaining ginger-garlic paste and cook until the water has evaporated, then continute to cook gently until the garlic is colouring. Add the tomatoes and curry leaves and cook for six to eight minutes over high heat until the oil is released on the sides of the pan; stir more as it thickens.

Add the ground whole spices, cumin, coriander, salt and a good splash of water. Cook until the pan dries out, stirring often. Add another splash of water and repeat. By now the sauce should be cooked and homogenous.

Add the chicken and its marinade. Continue cooking over a high heat, stirring constantly until the yogurt has been incorporated. Add 150ml water, bring to a boil and cook until the chicken is done (around five minutes for breast and eight for thighs). Stir often, as it will help bring the sauce to a lovely creamy consistency. Taste and adjust the seasoning to your taste; you may want more chilli powder or lemon juice.

serves 4

for the curry
1 tbsp white poppy seeds
6 cloves
1cm cinnamon stick
½ tsp black peppercorns or ground black pepper
2 tsp fennel seeds
3–6 dried red chillies, seeds shaken out if you prefer
20g fresh root ginger, peeled weight
6 fat garlic cloves
salt, to taste
400g boneless, skinless chicken thighs or breast, in 5cm pieces
5–6 tbsp vegetable oil
1 onion, finely chopped
2 smallish tomatoes, blended to a smooth puree
14 fresh curry leaves
½ tsp ground cumin
2 tsp ground coriander

for the marinade
½ tsp turmeric
½ tsp chilli powder, or to taste
2 heaped tbsp yogurt
2 tsp lemon juice, or to taste

chilli chicken balti

Many curryphiles have argued over the roots of balti, but I don't think there has been a general consensus. What I do know is that Birmingham is known for its baltis, rich tomato- and yogurt-based curries that can contain almost anything. This is my chicken balti, with lots of green chillies as much for their flavour as heat. They really add to the dish and I do recommend you leave them in. I'm not sure it will taste quite the same as the balti in your favourite curry house, but it is delicious nonetheless.

15g fresh root ginger, peeled weight
6 fat garlic cloves
2 largish tomatoes, quartered
1½ tsp garam masala
1½ tsp ground cumin
1 tbsp ground coriander
½ tsp turmeric
1 tsp paprika, for colour
1 rounded tbsp full-fat yogurt
salt, to taste
6 tbsp vegetable oil
¾ tsp brown mustard seeds
1 bay leaf
1 onion, finely chopped
6–10 green chillies, whole but
  pierced
500g boneless chicken thighs, cut
  into 2.5–5cm pieces
lots of freshly ground black pepper
1 tbsp lemon juice, or to taste
large handful of finely chopped fresh
  coriander leaves and stems

Blend together the ginger, garlic and tomatoes until smooth. Stir in the ground spices, yogurt and ¾ tsp salt.

Heat the oil in a non-stick saucepan. Add the mustard seeds and cook until they have popped. Add the bay leaf, onion and green chillies and cook over a moderate flame, stirring often, for six to eight minutes, until the onions are well browned.

Add the blended ingredients and cook on a high flame, stirring constantly, until the mixture comes to a boil and most of the excess liquid in the pan has evaporated. Continue cooking, stirring often, until the paste releases oil.

Add the chicken and stir it in the thick masala for a few minutes. Add enough water to come halfway up the chicken. Bring back to a boil and cook for seven minutes.

Increase the heat and toss the chicken in the sauce for another five minutes; the sauce will reduce to a lovely creamy consistency. Check a piece of chicken by cutting through; there should be no pink in the middle. Adjust the consistency of the sauce by adding a little water or reducing it a little further, as you prefer.

Taste and adjust the seasoning to your liking, adding lots of black pepper and a little lemon juice if your sauce is not tart enough. Stir in the chopped coriander and serve.

serves 4–5, can be halved

creamy almond chicken curry

A fabulous creamy, nutty dish that is great for the family and for friends. I like to use small chickens as I find them more succulent, and keep the bones in for that delicious flavour. If you don't like the bones you can just cook thigh fillets, the dish will still work. If your yogurt is particularly sour, add only 160-180g. I like to top the dish with lightly fried and halved almonds, or fried brown, crisp onions.

Marinate the chicken in the yogurt, ginger and garlic with 1 tsp salt for as long as possible; even 20 minutes if that is all you have, though you can leave it overnight in the fridge.

Heat 4 tbsp of the ghee or oil in a non-stick saucepan. Add the bay leaves and onion and gently fry until translucent and really soft. Add the chicken and cook over a highish flame, stirring and turning the chicken in the yogurt constantly, until it comes to a boil. Continue to cook and stir for five minutes further. Now cook, stirring often but not constantly, until the yogurt has reduced considerably and you can see the fat being released at the base of the pan. It should take another 10 minutes or so. Taste, it should be well-balanced and the garlic should be cooked.

Pour in enough water to cover the chicken by half, bring to a boil, cover and simmer over a gentle flame for 10–20 minutes, or until the chicken is ready. The time it takes will depend on the size of the chicken joints and how long it took to reduce the yogurt. Give the pot an occasional stir and make sure it does not run dry. Check the chicken is done by cutting into a thick piece; there should be no trace of pink.

Meanwhile, heat the remaining 1 tbsp ghee or oil in a small saucepan. Add the almonds and fry over a medium-low heat until lightly toasted and golden. Drain on kitchen paper, split in half where the natural crease is, and set aside.

Stir the remaining ingredients into the chicken, then pour in enough water to get a sauce the consistency of double cream. Taste; this is the time to balance the flavours by adding a little more cumin, black pepper or garam masala, as you prefer. Sprinkle over the almonds and serve.

serves 4–5

600g small skinless chicken joints
 (see recipe introduction)
200g plain, full-fat yogurt
25g fresh root ginger, peeled weight,
 grated into a paste
5 fat garlic cloves, grated into a paste
salt, to taste
5 tbsp ghee or vegetable oil
2 bay leaves
1 onion, finely chopped
25g blanched almonds (see page 36)
2–4 green chillies, whole but pierced,
 or to taste
5 rounded tbsp ground almonds
½ tsp ground, sifted green
 cardamom seeds
1 tsp ground cumin, or to taste
1 tsp garam masala, or to taste
¾ tsp finely ground black pepper,
 or to taste
80–100ml single cream
handful of chopped fresh coriander

cardamom-scented chicken curry

This is a really light, almost broth-like curry from the Sindhi community. It is like chicken soup: soul food, comfort food, home food and what you want to eat when you feel poorly. You can eat it like a soup with buttered crusty bread, or with plain boiled rice. Cardamom can differ in strength, so I leave it to you to decide how much to add; you can always put in more at the end of cooking, if you want.

Heat the oil in a non-stick saucepan. Add the onion and sauté until well browned. Add the ginger and garlic pastes and cook, stirring, for a minute or two, until the garlic is cooked and starting to colour.

Add the tomato, chillies, powdered spices and salt. Sauté for a few minutes, then add a splash of water and cook for six or seven minutes more, until the oil begins to come out of the masala, stirring more as the mixture dries up.

Add the chicken and sauté and brown in the masala for a few minutes; it will start to stick to the base of the pan. Add 400ml water, bring to a boil, cover and simmer until the chicken is cooked. It will take 25–35 minutes, depending on the size of the joints.

Stir a little water into the cornflour so that it dissolves, stir this into the chicken and cook for another few minutes. Add extra water to the pan if necessary; the sauce should be light and thin. Stir in the chopped coriander, taste and adjust with more black pepper or cardamom, to taste, then serve.

serves 4

4 tbsp vegetable oil
1 onion, finely chopped
15g fresh root ginger, peeled weight, grated into a paste
4 fat garlic cloves, grated into a paste
1 tomato, chopped
2–3 green chillies, whole but pierced
⅔–¾ tsp ground cardamom seeds, or to taste
1 rounded tsp ground coriander
¾ tsp ground cumin
⅓–½ tsp freshly ground black pepper, or to taste
salt, to taste
450g skinless chicken joints
1 rounded tsp cornflour
handful of chopped fresh coriander

chicken coconut masala

This is a spicy, full-bodied curry from the region of Andhra, known for its hot food and red chillies, with both tomatoes and tamarind adding a tang. The sweet flecks of fresh coconut hidden inside both soften the spices and add a lovely texture. If you don't have fresh coconut, add a little coconut cream; you will not have the same texture but it will still taste delicious. Serve with wholewheat Indian breads, such as Chapati or Paratha (see pages 156 and 157).

Place the whole spices in a small saucepan and dry roast until the coriander seeds are lightly coloured. Grind to a fine powder.

Heat the oil in a pan and fry the onion until brown. Add the ginger and garlic pastes and fry gently for a couple of minutes, until the garlic smells cooked. Add all the spices and salt, stir for 20 seconds, add a small splash of water and cook for two minutes more. Now tip in the tomatoes and chicken and sauté over a medium-high flame for seven or eight minutes, or until the sauce has been absorbed by the chicken. Add enough water to come halfway up the chicken, bring to a boil, then cover and simmer gently for 25–35 minutes, or until done, depending on the size of the joints. Stir occasionally and make sure there is enough water in the pan.

Once the chicken is cooked, add the tamarind paste and coconut and cook for a further three or four minutes. The sauce should be quite thick; if it isn't, cook for a little longer on a high flame. Taste and adjust the seasoning and tamarind to taste, and serve sprinkled with chopped coriander.

serves 4–5

1½ tsp fennel seeds
4–6 dried red chillies, seeds shaken out
⅔ tsp black peppercorns
2.5cm cinnamon stick
4 cloves
4 green cardamom pods, whole
1½ tsp coriander seeds
6 tbsp vegetable oil
1 onion, finely chopped
15g ginger, peeled weight, grated into a paste
4 fat garlic cloves, grated into a paste
salt, to taste
2½ tomatoes (not sweet), quartered and blended or chopped
600g skinless chicken joints
½–⅔ tsp tamarind paste, or to taste
50–60g grated fresh coconut, or 30g creamed coconut (the latter will be sweeter)
handful of fresh coriander leaves, chopped

golden chicken korma

A lovely dish, creamy and nutty with the clear flavours of whole spices. Korma was not always a Friday night special. It started life in palaces and was eaten by kings, so while I've added turmeric here, I prefer to give this dish the respect it deserves and use a good pinch of saffron (infuse it in 2 tbsp hot milk as you cook, and add it at the end), though the budget can't always stretch to that! If you're feeling flush, finish with a little edible gold leaf on top. The white poppy seeds are one of those secret ingredients that will make your korma special.

Blend the ginger and garlic with a little water to help make a smooth paste. Separately blend the cashew nuts with enough water to cover, to make another smooth paste. Set both aside.

Heat the oil in a large, wide non-stick saucepan. Add the whole spices and bay leaves and allow to sizzle for 10–20 seconds. Add the onion and cook gently until really soft but not coloured. Add the ginger-garlic paste and continue to cook until the liquid has dried up and the garlic smells cooked and is lightly golden.

Add the chicken, yogurt, coriander, turmeric and salt. Cook, stirring and folding the chicken in the yogurt constantly, until it comes to a boil. Then continue cooking until the yogurt has been absorbed by the chicken. Add enough water to come halfway up the chicken, bring back to a boil, then reduce the heat to low, cover and cook gently for 20–30 minutes, giving the pot an occasional stir. The chicken should be nearly done.

Check the pot after 20 minutes and, if there is a lot of liquid, finish cooking the chicken over a high heat, uncovered so the excess cooks off. The sauce should be creamy.

Once the chicken is done, add the ground almonds, cashew nut paste, cream, poppy seeds and coconut. Simmer for five minutes, or until the sauce has the right creamy consistency. Add lemon juice to taste and adjust the seasonings. Serve topped with any one - or even several - of the options given, to finish the dish.

serves 4–5

for the korma
25g fresh root ginger, peeled weight
5 fat garlic cloves
40g cashew nuts
4 tbsp vegetable oil
1 tsp caraway seeds
7.5cm cinnamon stick
6 cloves
2 blades mace
10 green cardamom pods
10 black peppercorns
2 bay leaves
1 onion, finely chopped
600g chicken, skinned and jointed
   (I prefer small chickens)
160g plain yogurt
1 rounded tsp ground coriander
⅓ tsp turmeric
salt, to taste
3 tbsp ground almonds
4 tbsp double cream
1 tbsp white poppy seeds (optional
   but special)
30–40g block creamed coconut, or
   2–3 tbsp coconut cream
1–2 tsp lemon juice

to finish
Choose from quartered dried figs, raisins, toasted flaked almonds, roasted cashews, hazelnuts or pistachios, saffron, fried fresh root ginger julienne, edible gold leaf

light cumin-flavoured chicken curry

A simple, delicious curry that's one of my favourites, and a lovely platform for the humble cumin seed to shine. The flavours are simple, so the chicken should be on the bone for maximum taste. Ideally, serve with Chapati (see page 156).

150g plain yogurt
20g fresh root ginger, peeled weight
6 fat garlic cloves
2 tsp ground cumin
2 tsp ground coriander
salt, to taste
¼ tsp freshly ground black pepper
600g small skinless chicken joints
4–5 tbsp vegetable oil
1 rounded tsp cumin seeds
2 small onions, finely chopped
2–5 green chillies, whole but pierced
1 tsp garam masala
handful of chopped fresh coriander

Blend together the yogurt, ginger and garlic until smooth. Stir in the ground cumin and coriander, ¾ tsp salt and the black pepper. Pour this marinade over the chicken and leave for as long as you can, even 20 minutes will help, or up to one day, covered, in the refrigerator.

Heat the oil in a non-stick saucepan. Add the cumin seeds and, once they have darkened, add the onions and fry until golden brown. Add the chicken, its marinade, the chillies and garam masala and cook over a medium-high flame, stirring often, until the yogurt comes to a boil and then gets absorbed by the chicken. Pour in enough water to come halfway up the chicken and bring back to a boil.

Cover and simmer over a gentle flame for 20–30 minutes, until the chicken is nearly done (20 minutes for a small chicken, 30 minutes for a medium chicken). Check occasionally and give the pot a stir.

Uncover the pan and reduce the liquid until it is quite thick and creamy; this will deepen the flavour. Add a splash of water if you need to, you want to achieve a thick, creamy sauce. Taste and adjust the seasoning, stir in the chopped coriander and serve.

serves 4–5

parsi-style duck with apricots

Inspired by a chicken dish, but I love these sweet, sour and fruity flavours with duck. The Parsis were originally from Persia, but their food is a fascinating story of their Indian journey. They adopted the sweet flavours of Gujarat, where many of them first lived, but also of the Raj, as they considered themselves quite western. They employed some of India's best chefs who were – at the time – from Goa. This recipe combines all these influences. It's always served with a tangle of fine, straw-like fried potatoes, which add a lovely crunch.

Make a paste of the ginger and garlic, using a little water to help. Using a spice blender or mortar and pestle, make a fine powder of the dried chillies, cumin and coriander seeds, peppercorns, cloves and cardamom.

Heat the oil in a large non-stick saucepan. Add the cinnamon and onions and fry until well browned. Add the ginger and garlic pastes and cook for a couple of minutes, until golden and the garlic smells cooked. Tip in the powdered spices and salt with a good splash of water and cook for two minutes. Add the duck and tomatoes and stir for a few minutes, then pour in enough water to just cover, bring to a boil, cover and cook gently for 40 minutes, stirring occasionally. You shouldn't need more water, but add a little if the pan is dry.

Add the apricots, jaggery or sugar, vinegar and a splash of water if the pan looks a little too dry; cover and cook for another 10 minutes. The sauce should now be quite thick and the duck will be tender. Taste and adjust the balance of sour and sweet flavours, adding vinegar or sugar to your taste. Serve with the potato straws below.

serves 4

15g fresh root ginger, peeled weight
5 garlic cloves
4–6 dried Kashmiri chillies, seeds shaken out
1½ tsp cumin seeds
1½ tsp coriander seeds
14 black peppercorns
6 cloves
seeds from 6 green cardamom pods
5 tbsp vegetable oil
4cm cinnamon stick
2 onions, chopped
salt, to taste
500g duck legs and thighs, skinned and jointed
4 largish tomatoes, finely chopped
14 dried, ready-to-eat apricots
1½-2 tsp grated jaggery, or sugar, or to taste
2 tsp white wine vinegar, or to taste

for the potato straws (*salli*)

Toss the potato straws in the salt in a bowl. Gently heat 4cm oil in a saucepan (the wider the pan the more you can cook at once). Once the oil is medium hot, squeeze out as much water as you can from the potatoes and add a couple of large handfuls to the oil. (Do not overcrowd the pan.)

Fry for five to six minutes, breaking up any tangles as much as you can with a spoon, until lightly golden and crisp. Remove with a slotted spoon and drain on kitchen paper. Repeat until you have cooked all the straws.

400g potatoes, finely shredded (I use the slicer part of my box grater, then finely slice the paper-thin potato rounds into long, fine julienne, it works beautifully)
½ tsp salt
vegetable oil, to deep-fry

tamarind duck curry

This is a lovely, deep, tangy dish that is great with or without coconut milk. Without the coconut, the flavours are clear and deep. The coconut adds sweetness to this Keralan recipe and is authentic. I leave it to you; taste before adding the coconut and decide. Balance the tamarind accordingly, the coconut version requires more tartness, as well as salt. I have tried this with duck breasts but it doesn't work nearly as well. If you hate bones, I still urge you to keep them in and take a few minutes at the end to pick the meat from the bones and stir it back in.

Using a good mortar and pestle, pound the green cardamom, cloves and black peppercorns together to a fine powder, removing the green cardamom skin. Separately blend together the ginger and garlic with a little water until smooth.

Heat the oil in a non-stick saucepan. Add the cinnamon and onions and cook until well browned. Add the ginger-garlic paste and cook until the excess water has dried up and the garlic has had a chance to fry and smells cooked. Add all the powdered spices and salt along with a small splash of water and cook for two minutes.

Add the duck and stir well in the masala; start to brown the duck, then add the chillies (if using). Pour in enough water to just cover, bring to a boil, cover the pan, reduce the heat and simmer gently for 50–60 minutes, until the duck is tender; stir occasionally and check there is some liquid in the pan. After 45 minutes, check to see how much liquid remains; if it is more than halfway up the duck, finish cooking the duck uncovered so the excess water cooks off.

At this time, heat the oil for the tarka in a small pan. Add the mustard seeds and, once they have popped, the curry leaves. Follow with the onion and cook until well browned. Add to the duck with the coconut milk (if using) and tamarind, then simmer for five minutes. Taste, adjust the seasoning, adding more tamarind if you would prefer a tangier dish, then serve.

serves 4

for the curry
12 green cardamom pods
6 cloves
12 black peppercorns
30g fresh root ginger, peeled weight
9 garlic cloves
6 tbsp vegetable oil
5cm cinnamon stick
3 small onions, sliced
1 rounded tbsp ground coriander
¾ tsp turmeric
½ tsp chilli powder
salt, to taste
600g duck joints (I buy 3 whole duck legs and joint them into thighs and drumsticks, leave the skin on or not, as you prefer)
3–6 green chillies, whole but pierced (optional)
150–200ml coconut milk (optional, see recipe introduction)
1–1½ tsp tamarind paste, or to taste

for the tarka
1 tbsp vegetable oil
¾ tsp mustard seeds
15 fresh curry leaves
1 small onion, chopped

meat

lamb and spinach curry

This is delicious and so much better than the sum of its parts, another of the dishes from my childhood. When I wanted to write this recipe, I only had a vague memory of what went in it, so I spent days in my kitchen getting the balance right until it was good enough to remind me of home. I finally got there and it is as sublime as I remember. It does take a while to cook, but involves minimal preparation and is not difficult to make. Serve with Chapati (see page 156) and nothing else. Whole leaf spinach has more flavour and I use the roots too, if there are any. Baby spinach tastes lighter and more velvety so, if you choose that, increase the quantity to 400g.

30g fresh root ginger, peeled weight
3 tomatoes, quartered
6 large garlic cloves
6 tbsp vegetable oil
2 black cardamom pods
4 cloves
5cm cinnamon stick
2 bay leaves
1 onion, finely chopped
salt, to taste
2 tbsp ground coriander
¾ tsp turmeric
¾ tsp ground cumin
¼–½ tsp chilli powder, or to taste
600g leg of lamb, with bones, cubed by the butcher, or 500g boneless lamb, cubed
1–3 green chillies, whole but pierced (optional)
300–350g spinach, well washed
1 rounded tsp garam masala

Finely slice 20g of the ginger into matchsticks and set aside. Blend the rest of the ginger with the tomatoes, garlic and a splash of water until smooth.

Heat 5½ tbsp oil in a large non-stick saucepan, add the whole spices and bay leaves and follow 15 seconds later with the onion. Cook the onion until deep golden. Add the tomato paste, salt, coriander, turmeric, cumin and chilli powder and cook over a moderate flame until it becomes a paste and releases droplets of oil on the base of a pan; it should take 15-20 minutes. Reduce the heat and sauté the paste for another five to seven minutes, stirring.

Add the lamb and a splash of water, then sauté the meat and paste over a moderate flame for five or six minutes, until the paste has been completely absorbed by the lamb. Pour in enough water to cover, bring to a boil, then reduce the heat to low, cover and simmer gently for 50–60 minutes, or until the lamb is tender. The sauce should only come one-quarter of the way up the lamb. If necessary, reduce some of the liquid over a high heat.

Heat the remaining oil in a saucepan, add the ginger julienne and green chillies (if using); cook for a minute, then remove both with a slotted spoon. Add the spinach and a splash of water to the empty saucepan and cook until completely wilted. At this stage, you can blend the spinach to a smooth paste or leave it whole. Add to the lamb with the garam masala, ginger julienne and chillies, cover and simmer for another four minutes. Taste, adjust the seasoning and serve.

serves 4–5

authentic pork vindaloo

I have tried the vindaloo served in some British curry houses and I'm sorry to say it is mostly an amalgamation of those restaurants' different curry sauces with lots of chillies, with no real Goan flavour. Those curries have little to do with real vindaloo... except that they are hot. An authentic vindaloo does use a fair amount of chillies, but that's not its defining feature. It has wonderful spices, vinegar, ginger and garlic to bring the best out of the rich pork, and doesn't have the thick sauce of curry house versions. This is a true vindaloo, with a light liquor. For the best flavour, cook the pork in minimal water so it stews, as much as possible, in its own juices. I quite like it with sautéed potatoes to soak up the lovely sauce. This is my version, learnt from a Goan, but I have lightened up on the number of chillies he would use.

Using a spice grinder, grind the whole spices and chillies to a fine powder.

Make a paste of the ginger, garlic and vinegar. Add this to the pork along with the spices and salt, cover and marinate in the fridge for a couple of hours, if you have time.

Heat the oil in a non-stick saucepan. Add the onion and fry until golden brown. Add the pork and marinade and brown gently over a moderate heat for six or seven minutes. Reduce the heat to low, cover and cook for 40–50 minutes, or until the pork is tender, checking every so often and adding a splash of water from the kettle if the pot looks like it is running dry.

Once the pork is tender, taste, adjust the seasoning and serve. Some people like to add a little sugar. I don't, but I leave it to you to decide.

serves 4

1 tsp cumin seeds
1 tsp coriander seeds
6 black peppercorns
3 green cardamom pods
4 cloves
2cm cinnamon stick
5–10 dried red Kashmiri chillies (or 3–6 hotter dried red chillies), halved, seeds shaken out
13g ginger, peeled weight, roughly chopped
7 fat garlic cloves
3 tbsp good-quality white wine vinegar, or to taste
400g pork shoulder with some fat, in 2.5cm cubes
50g belly of pork, in 2.5cm pieces
salt, to taste
4 tbsp vegetable oil
1 small onion, finely chopped
sugar, to taste

tangy lamb chops with dried pomegranate

I love this dish and cook it when I have people over and want to wow them, as it's delicious and different but also really easy. The main flavour is the dried pomegranate powder, which you can buy in Asian stores or on the internet. It comes from the seeds of a very different variety of fruit from that we are used to eating; the flavours are really distinctive and tangy rather than sweet. The sauce clings to the meat with a little extra left to mop up with flatbread. For the best flavour, make this recipe with spring lamb chops. Serve with a vegetable dish or simply a raita (see pages 169-171) and Indian flatbread.

6 tbsp vegetable oil
2 small onions, finely chopped
20g fresh root ginger, peeled weight
6 fat garlic cloves
650g (around 8) lamb chops, trimmed of excess fat
1 tsp garam masala
1½ tsp ground coriander
3 tsp dried pomegranate powder (*anardana*), or to taste
2–4 green chillies, whole but pierced, or to taste
salt, to taste
handful of chopped fresh coriander leaves
handful of fresh pomegranate seeds

Heat the oil in a large non-stick saucepan. Add the onions and fry for six to eight minutes, until well browned.

Meanwhile, make a fine paste of the ginger and garlic with the help of a little water. Add to the cooked onions, cook off the excess moisture, then gently fry the paste for another minute.

Add the lamb and brown well. Add the spices, chillies, salt and a splash of water. Cook over a moderate flame, stirring often until the pan is dry again. Add 200ml water, bring to a boil, then cover the pan and cook gently until the lamb is done; it should take 30–35 minutes. Stir occasionally and check to see there is enough water in the pan.

Once the lamb is cooked, reduce any leftover sauce until it is quite thick. Taste and adjust the seasoning, adding a little more dried pomegranate powder if you feel it needs more of that lovely, fruity tartness. Stir in the chopped coriander and pomegranate seeds and serve.

serves 4

beef madras

A firm British favourite, this is rich in flavour, spicy and comforting. A madras is normally a hot curry; for a medium heat I add four dried Kashmiri chillies and two green chillies, so bear this in mind and add as many as you think you will like. Kashmiri chillies are mild with an amazing deep red colour and can be found in well-stocked supermarkets. If you can't find them, add chilli powder to taste instead. Serve with pilaf, Naan (see page 155) or Indian flatbreads.

Using a spice grinder, grind all the whole spices and chillies to a fine powder.

Heat the oil in a large non-stick saucepan. Add the onion and cook until well browned. Stir in all the spices, salt and a splash of water and cook for one minute.

Add the beef and brown in the spice paste for a good six to eight minutes over a moderate heat. I often add a splash of water when it starts to stick.

Meanwhile, blend the ginger, garlic and tomatoes until smooth, using a little water to help. Add to the pan with the green chillies, bring to a boil, then cover and simmer gently until the liquid has reduced. Check after 10 minutes, give the pot a stir and come back in another five minutes.

Now increase the heat and brown the beef and sauce together until it has been absorbed by the beef. Pour in enough water to cover, bring back to a boil, cover and cook until the meat is tender; it will take around 1¼ hours.

Uncover the lid and reduce the sauce in the pan until it is creamy. Add the cream and chopped coriander, taste, adjust the seasoning and serve.

serves 4

2.5cm cinnamon stick
10 green cardamom pods
8 cloves
10 black peppercorns
2 tsp cumin seeds
1 tbsp coriander seeds
3–6 dried Kashmiri red chillies, seeds shaken out
5 tbsp vegetable oil
1 onion, sliced
½ tsp turmeric
1–1¼ tsp garam masala, or to taste
salt, to taste
500g diced beef
20g fresh root ginger, peeled weight
7 garlic cloves
2 tomatoes
2–5 green chillies, whole but pierced (optional)
4 tbsp single cream
handful of chopped fresh coriander

rich lamb shank curry

An absolutely delicious, meaty feast that is the perfect dish for a dinner party. The lamb shanks look so dramatic on the plate and people know you have made an effort. It is not difficult to make and, though it takes a little patience, it's worth it. The sauce is rich and deep in flavour and works with Indian breads or with rice.

Blend the tomatoes, ginger and garlic until smooth.

Heat the oil in a large saucepan. Brown the lamb shanks in the oil for two or three minutes, getting a little colour on all sides. Remove and set aside.

Reheat the oil, add the whole spices and bay leaves and, after 20 seconds, the onion; cook until the onion is well browned. Add the lamb, blended tomatoes, cumin, chilli powder, ground coriander, green chillies and salt; bring to a boil. Cover and cook over a low heat, stirring occasionally, until you have a little less than half the liquid you started with; it should take 15–20 minutes.

Now increase the heat and brown the meat and sauce, stirring very often, until the oil comes out of the sauce and it has reduced considerably. This really intensifies the flavours.

Add enough water to just cover the lamb shanks, bring to a boil, cover and cook over a gentle flame for 1–1¼ hours, or until the lamb is tender and done to your liking. Stir every 10–15 minutes and turn the meat in the sauce. Add a splash of hot water if the pan looks like it is running dry.

When the lamb is tender and coming off the bone, reduce any excess liquid in the pan over a high heat until you have a creamy sauce. Taste and adjust the seasoning, stir in the garam masala and herbs and serve.

serves 4

2 large tomatoes, quartered
15g fresh root ginger, peeled weight
6 fat garlic cloves
6 tbsp vegetable oil
4 x 400–500g lamb shanks
20 black peppercorns
5 cloves
2.5cm cinnamon stick
4 green cardamom pods
2 black cardamom pods
2 bay leaves
1 largish onion, chopped
1 good tsp ground cumin
¼–½ tsp chilli powder for heat, or paprika powder for colour (optional)
2 tsp ground coriander
2–4 green chillies (preferably Indian green finger), whole but pierced
salt, to taste
1 tsp garam masala
handful of fresh coriander and/or a few shredded mint leaves

hearty meatball and pea curry

Meatballs in the west are known as hearty home-style food. But in India, meatballs - or koftas as they are known - are so loved that they have been refined to restaurant fare, stuffed with nuts or raisins and finished with cream. This sauce has a light, creamy consistency that coats all the grains of fluffy white basmati rice with which it should be served. The fresh coriander is more than a decoration here, it really lifts the deep, earthy flavours of the meat.

Mix together all the ingredients for the meatballs until really well combined - your hands are the best tool for this - and set aside. Start the sauce by blending together the tomatoes, ginger and garlic until smooth.

Heat the oil in a large saucepan. Add the whole spices and bay leaves and cook for 20 seconds. Now add the onion and cook until golden brown. Add the blended tomatoes, powdered spices and salt and cook down until it is a thick paste that starts to release oil on the sides of the pan. Cook further, stirring constantly, for a few more minutes to deepen the flavours.

Add 700ml water and bring to a boil. Check the seasoning. Make walnut-sized meatballs from the minced meat mixture and pop each into the simmering curry (I get 20 meatballs). Simmer, covered, for 10 minutes, then add the peas, bring back to a simmer and cook for another five minutes.

Uncover; the sauce should have reduced to a light creamy consistency. If not, take out the meatballs and boil over a high heat until it is. Check the seasoning, shake in the chopped coriander and serve.

serves 4-6

for the meatballs
400g minced beef or lamb
2 large slices of white bread, crusts removed, made into breadcrumbs
1 egg, beaten
¾ tsp salt
½ tsp garam masala
5g fresh root ginger, peeled weight, grated into a paste
1 fat garlic clove, grated into a paste

for the sauce
3 tomatoes
20g fresh root ginger, peeled weight
5 fat garlic cloves
6 tbsp vegetable oil
6 green cardamom pods
6 cloves
2.5cm cinnamon stick
1 blade mace
2 bay leaves
1 onion, finely chopped
2 tsp ground coriander
¼–¾ tsp chilli powder, to taste
1 rounded tsp garam masala
½ tsp ground cumin
salt, to taste
2 handfuls of peas
large handful of chopped fresh coriander

lamb do piaza

A much-loved British dish that's also a favourite in India. It is, at heart, a richly flavoured mutton or goat curry with double the amount of onions normally used. This is a great recipe to prepare a day in advance of serving, as the beautiful tangle of flavours continue to soften and marry. If you can add some lamb bones (ask your butcher), you'll get an added depth of flavour. For a wow factor, deep-fry some more finely sliced onions until crispy and pile a dramatic mound of them on top.

Heat the oil in a non-stick saucepan. Add the whole spices and, once they have sizzled a bit, add the chopped onions and cook until browned; the darker the onion, the deeper the flavour.

Meanwhile, make a fine paste of the tomatoes, ginger and garlic using a hand blender. Stir in the powdered spices, salt and yogurt until smooth.

Add the lamb to the pan and seal the outsides. Add the tomato-yogurt paste and bring to a boil while stirring very often. Then reduce the heat, cover and cook for 45–50 minutes, or until the lamb is tender. Add the sliced onions 30 minutes into the cooking process and give the pot a stir every 10–15 minutes, making sure it does not dry out. Ideally, the dish should cook in its own sauce but, if necessary, add a splash of water.

By the time the lamb is tender, the sauce should have reduced to a creamy consistency with a tangle of sweet, sliced onions. If it is too dry, add a splash of water. Taste and add more salt, chilli powder or lemon juice, as you prefer, until it is perfect for you. Stir in the chopped coriander and serve with Paratha, Chapati or Naan (see pages 155–157).

serves 4–6

4–5 tbsp vegetable oil (use 5 tbsp if your lamb is quite lean)
3 green cardamom pods
2.5cm cinnamon stick
4 cloves
8 black peppercorns
2 smallish onions, 1½ chopped and ½ sliced
2 large tomatoes, quartered
10g fresh root ginger, peeled weight
5 large garlic cloves
½ tsp turmeric
1 tsp ground cumin
1½ tsp ground coriander
1 tsp garam masala
¼–½ tsp chilli powder, or to taste (add some paprika for colour if you don't use much)
salt, to taste
4 tbsp Greek yogurt
500g leg of lamb, cubed
lemon juice, to taste
good handful of chopped fresh coriander leaves

keralan pork curry

This delicious recipe must come from the Christians of Kerala. It is not too spicy and has a lovely blend of flavours, with a hint of fruitiness from the raisins that really complements pork. I like to sprinkle the finished dish with grated coconut, which you fold in when you serve yourself, but if you don't have any the curry is just as good without it. You can find frozen grated coconut in Asian stores; it's a great freezer staple. Serve with rice or Paratha (see page 157).

⅔ tsp mustard seeds
1.5cm cinnamon stick, broken up
4 cloves
4 fat garlic cloves
15g ginger, peeled weight
1 rounded tbsp raisins
5 tbsp vegetable oil
10 fresh curry leaves
1 onion, finely chopped
1–3 green chillies, whole but pierced
1 largish tomato, blended or
   chopped
½ tsp turmeric
1½ tsp ground coriander
½ tsp ground cumin
½ tsp black pepper
400g shoulder of pork, diced into
   2.5–4cm cubes
salt, to taste
½–⅔ tsp tamarind paste, or to taste
a large handful of grated coconut,
   to serve (optional, see recipe
   introduction)

Using a good mortar and pestle, pound the mustard seeds, cinnamon and cloves until fine. Separately blend together the garlic, ginger and raisins with a small splash of water until smooth.

Heat the oil in a large non-stick saucepan. Add the curry leaves and onion and fry until these are golden. Add the ginger paste and chillies and fry for two or three minutes. Add the tomato, all the ground spices, pork and salt.

Cook over a moderate to high flame, stirring and folding the meat in the sauce quite often, until all the paste has been absorbed; it will take 10–15 minutes. If it is absorbed sooner than this, you might need to add a splash of water and continue until you can see the masala release some oil.

Add enough water to the pan to cover the pork by 1cm; bring to a boil. Cover, reduce the heat and simmer gently for 45–55 minutes, or until the pork is tender; give the pan an occasional stir and add some water if it is getting dry. Uncover and cook off any excess water over a high heat, the sauce should be creamy. Stir in the tamarind, taste and adjust the seasoning. Serve sprinkled with fresh coconut (if using).

serves 4

creamy, nutty lamb curry with dried figs

This fabulous dish has a wonderful warmth and flavour of whole spices. I have lightened it a little by replacing some of the cream that would normally be used with milk. I like the figs and pistachios for a burst of sublime, complementary flavours, but it doesn't really need the embellishment. I leave it to you; you can leave them out or choose to top off the dish with toasted flaked almonds, cashews or pine nuts instead. You can also stir in a little coconut cream at the end. Serve with rice or Naan (see page 155).

Soak the cashew nuts in the milk for 10 minutes, then blend them together until smooth and set aside.

Heat 4 tbsp of the oil in a non-stick saucepan. Add the onions and fry gently for 10–12 minutes, until soft and translucent. Remove two-thirds of the onions, set aside, and continue to fry the rest until well browned. Remove and set these aside separately. Put any residual oil into a small bowl. Give the pan a wipe with kitchen paper.

Blend the soft, pale onions with the garlic, ginger and yogurt to a smooth paste; season. If you have time, marinate the lamb in this mixture for at least one hour; ideally, cover the dish and refrigerate overnight.

Heat the remaining oil and any residual oil (from cooking the onion), add the whole spices and bay leaves and allow them to sizzle for 10 seconds. Add the lamb, marinade, green chillies and ground coriander. Bring to a boil over a moderate flame, stirring very often. Continue to cook, stirring frequently, until all the yogurt has been absorbed and the paste releases oil; the meat will start to stick to the pan.

Add enough water to cover the lamb. Bring to a boil, cover and simmer gently for 45–60 minutes, or until the lamb is tender. Stir the pot every 10–15 minutes or so, and make sure there is always some liquid in the pan. Uncover the pot and reduce the sauce in the pan until it comes just one-third of the way up the meat. Add the cashew nut paste, cream, garam masala and dried figs (if using). Bring back to a boil and simmer for three or four minutes, the sauce should be creamy. Stir in the reserved onions and sprinkle with the nuts.

serves 6

60g cashew nuts
200ml whole milk
5 tbsp vegetable oil
3 small onions, sliced
6 large garlic cloves
20g ginger, peeled weight
160g plain full-fat yogurt (not too sour, if it is add a little less)
salt, to taste
500g diced leg or shoulder of lamb
7.5cm cinnamon stick
6 cloves
7 green cardamom pods
2 blades mace
2 bay leaves
1–3 green chillies, whole but pierced (optional)
1½ tsp ground coriander
4 tbsp double cream, or to taste
1–1¼ tsp garam masala, or to taste
6 large dried ready-to-eat figs, halved or quartered (optional)
handful of pistachios, shelled and blanched (see page 36), or flaked almonds

my roganjosh

Rojanjosh as we know it is a deep, rich lamb curry which doesn't bear much resemblance to the real Indian dish. I have given a recipe for roganjosh with tomatoes, as we have come to expect it to taste, in *Anjum's New Indian*, but wanted to write this more authentic version. With its yogurt and almond base, it is equally delicious and quite different. In India they use mutton or leg of baby lamb with the bone in (try spring lamb and ask the butcher to cut into large bone-in pieces). Serve with a lovely pilaf, Naan or Chapati (see pages 155 and 156).

Using a spice grinder or a good mortar and pestle, grind the whole spices to a fine powder with the dried bay leaves. Separately blend together the garlic and ginger with a good splash of water until fine.

Heat the oil in a large non-stick saucepan. Add the lamb or mutton and brown well over a high flame; this will take a good eight to 10 minutes. Add the ginger-garlic paste and cook over a moderate flame, stirring constantly as the water starts to dry. Once the paste is cooked, all you will see is clear oil in the pan and the garlic will smell cooked.

Add half the yogurt and cook over a moderate to high flame, stirring constantly and quite briskly, almost folding the yogurt into the lamb until it has been fully absorbed by the meat; it will take another eight to 10 minutes. Repeat with the remaining yogurt, stirring constantly as before. Once it is boiling, simmer, stirring every now and again, until the liquid in the pan has reduced by around one-third. Now add the ground whole spices, ground coriander and salt and cook, stirring, for a few minutes more.

Cover and cook over a low flame for 30–40 minutes, or until the meat is tender, remembering that mutton will take quite a bit longer to cook than lamb. Keep an eye on the pan and give it an occasional stir; add a good splash of water if the sauce looks dry.

Add the garam masala, black pepper, fennel seed powder and ground almonds. Taste, adjust the seasoning and add paprika (if using) for a rich red colour. Cook for another minute, add the chopped coriander and serve.

serves 4–6

2 black cardamom pods
8 green cardamom pods
6 cloves
5cm cinnamon stick
2 tsp cumin seeds
5–8 Kashmiri dried chillies, seeds shaken out, or chilli powder, to taste
2 dried bay leaves (if fresh, add to lamb only once it has browned)
8 large garlic cloves
25g ginger, peeled weight, cut into large pieces
7 tbsp vegetable oil
600g spring lamb or mutton, cut into large bone-in cubes
300g full-fat yogurt, stirred well
1 tbsp ground coriander
salt, to taste
¾–1 tsp garam masala
½ tsp freshly ground black pepper
1½ tsp fennel seeds, ground
2 tbsp ground almonds
1 tsp paprika, for colour (optional)
handful of chopped fresh coriander leaves

lamb dhansak

Dhansak is sweet, sour and always contains lentils, though you can use whichever vegetables and meat you like. Traditionally, the vegetables are cooked in the lentils and then all is pureed together, although leaving the pieces of butternut squash intact in this recipe adds texture and little morsels of sweet earthiness. The Parsi serve this with lightly sweetened pilaf: they caramelise sugar in a small pan, add water and simmer while frying whole spices in ghee. The rice is added to the spices, then the syrup, covering with enough water to cook the rice. Plain rice or any other pilaf work just as well.

Using a sturdy mortar and pestle, grind together the whole spices to a fine powder. Add the remaining powdered spices (except the garam masala) and set aside.

Heat the oil in a large saucepan. Add the onion and sauté until golden brown. Add the ginger and garlic and sauté for a minute. Now tip in the lamb and brown for three or four minutes, or until lightly seared. Stir in the spices and a splash of water and cook for two minutes more.

Add the pigeon peas and lentils, tomato, vegetables, a handful of fresh coriander and salt, stir well and add enough water to cover. Bring to a boil, cover and simmer gently for 45–55 minutes, or until the lamb is tender. Now you can decide if you want to leave the vegetables whole in a more rustic sauce, or to blend them to a smooth result. If you would prefer the latter, remove the lamb with a slotted spoon and set aside. Blend the sauce until smooth (I stick in my hand blender), then return the meat.

Stir in the tamarind, sugar, garam masala and crushed fenugreek leaves. Taste and adjust the seasoning, balancing the levels of sweet (sugar) and sour (tamarind) to your taste. Chop the remaining fresh coriander, sprinkle it over, and serve.

serves 6, can be halved

1½ tsp fennel seeds
½ tsp fenugreek seeds
⅔ tsp mustard seeds
½ star anise
¼ tsp turmeric
¼ tsp grated nutmeg
1¾ tsp ground cumin
1½ tsp ground coriander
¼ tsp chilli powder
7 tbsp vegetable oil
1 onion, sliced
15g ginger, peeled weight, roughly chopped
4 fat garlic cloves, roughly chopped
500g lamb, in large cubes
70g split pigeon peas (*toor dal*), washed well
70g red lentils (*masur dal*), washed well
1 small tomato, roughly chopped
200g butternut squash or pumpkin, peeled and cut into 5cm cubes
1 Japanese aubergine (they are small and long), or normal aubergine, cut into 6 crossways
2 handfuls of fresh coriander
salt, to taste
1 tsp tamarind paste, or to taste
1 rounded tsp sugar, or to taste
2 tsp garam masala
1 rounded tsp fenugreek leaves, crushed between your fingers

mangalorean mutton curry

This is an absolutely delicious, robust curry and the flavours are deep and complex. I like to use mutton in this dish, but lamb also works well. Ideally try and find leg of mutton or lamb with the bone in (halal shops cut meat in this way, but ask your local butcher). This is not a quick and easy curry – it is one that you commit to with love – but it is so fabulous that you'll find it is one of those dishes you always turn to when you have friends coming around. Serve with rice or Paratha (see page 157).

Place the coconut in a small pan and dry roast for a minute or two, until golden. Grind with the cumin and poppy seeds until fine; I use a spice grinder.

Heat the oil in a non-stick saucepan and fry the onion until well browned, then tip into a blender along with the fresh coriander, chillies, ginger and garlic and a small splash of water. Whizz to a fine paste. Return to the pan and sauté for six to eight minutes. Add the tomato and all the powdered and ground spices except the garam masala, salt and around 100ml water. Sauté for seven or eight minutes, until the tomatoes have become pulpy.

Add the meat and sauté in the paste for four or five minutes. The paste should have completely reduced and be clinging to the meat, while the oil should be coming out of the masala. Add enough water to come three-quarters of the way up the lamb, bring to a boil, cover and simmer for around 45–55 minutes, or until done, stirring occasionally. Remember that mutton will take considerably longer; allow 90 minutes if using that, just in case.

Uncover, stir in the tamarind and garam masala. The sauce should be lovely, creamy and homogenous by now; if necessary boil off excess water or add a little extra from the kettle, until the consistency is as you prefer. Taste and adjust the seasoning and tamarind to your taste.

serves 6, can be halved

6 tbsp unsweetened desiccated coconut
1½ tsp cumin seeds
1 rounded tbsp white poppy seeds
6 tbsp vegetable oil
1 large onion, sliced
20g fresh coriander leaves and stalks
1–3 green chillies, or to taste, stalk removed
10g fresh root ginger, peeled weight
6 fat garlic cloves
1 tomato, chopped
½ tsp turmeric
1½ tsp ground coriander
salt, to taste
600g bone-in mutton or lamb, in large cubes
½–¾ tsp tamarind paste, or to taste
1 tsp garam masala

spicy lamb, tomato and coconut curry

A really easy-to-make dish that is rich and deep in flavours, from the coast of south west India. Nearly everything is thrown into a pot and cooked until done. Taste a little both before and after the browning or 'bhunoing' process, just for you to see how it changes a dish in flavour and texture. I use ghee here as a little adds so much flavour; if you don't have any then use half oil and half butter. Serve with Indian breads.

1 tbsp coriander seeds
1 tsp cumin seeds
15 black peppercorns
5cm cinnamon stick
4 cloves
500g boneless or 600g bone-in lamb
   leg or shoulder, cubed
3 small onions, finely chopped
3 tomatoes, chopped
15g ginger, peeled weight, grated
   into a paste
8 fat garlic cloves, grated into a paste
3–6 green chillies, whole but pierced
salt, to taste
2 tbsp ghee, or vegetable oil and
   butter
200–300ml coconut milk, or to taste
1½ tsp lemon juice, or to taste

Using a spice grinder or a good mortar and pestle, pound the whole spices to a fine powder.

Place the lamb, 2 of the chopped onions, tomatoes, ginger, garlic, chillies, spices and salt in a large saucepan. Add 500ml water, bring to a boil, then cover and cook gently for 45–60 minutes, or until the lamb is cooked and tender. Give the pot a stir every 10 minutes or so.

After about 45 minutes, melt the ghee in a small saucepan and fry the remaining onion until well browned.

There shouldn't be too much liquid left in the pan once the lamb is cooked. Cook off any excess moisture in the pan over a high flame for six or seven minutes, stirring quite often, until the sauce has mostly been absorbed by the lamb. This bhunoing process will help homogenise the sauce and deepen the flavours. Add the browned onion and ghee.

Pour in the coconut milk and lemon juice, bring to a boil and simmer for five minutes; the sauce should be thick and creamy. Taste and adjust the seasoning, adding lemon juice or coconut milk until the dish is perfect for you, then serve.

serves 4

3 ACCOMPANIMENTS

vegetable
side dishes

simple, lightly spiced vegetables

This is a really easy dish to make and a great way of getting your vegetables in, but it does require a little patience. The end result is that all the vegetables retain their own flavour and character. I have listed those I would typically use, but you can put in any you like as long as you add one sweet vegetable. The sweet potato is really nice in this.

Heat the oil in a non-stick sauté pan or saucepan. Add the chillies and panch phoran, reduce the flame and, once the seeds stop popping, add the vegetables, salt and turmeric. Stir well to mix, cover, reduce the heat right down and cook gently, stirring often to make sure the vegetables don't stick to the pan.

Once the vegetables are tender, after 25–30 minutes, stir in the sugar and serve immediately.

serves 2–3

2 tbsp vegetable oil
1–2 dried red chillies, seeds shaken out
scant 1½ tsp panch phoran
120g sweet potato, peeled and cut into small cubes or half- or quarter-moons
2 Japanese aubergines, or normal aubergines (around 100g), in 2.5cm half-moons
handful of small cauliflower florets
100g potato, peeled and cut into 1–1.5cm cubes
50g green beans or mangetout, topped and tailed or de-stringed
70g carrots, peeled and sliced into 1cm coins
salt, to taste
¼ tsp turmeric
¾ tsp sugar

opposite serving spicy peas with ginger, *see page 150*

sweet and sour squash

A lovely side dish from Rajasthan, with a fantastic flavour and heat to it. Serve with lentils, meat or chicken curries, or even to add a twist to your Sunday roast. I like to leave the skin on my squash as it keeps the vegetable together and adds texture.

Heat the oil in a non-stick saucepan. Add the asafoetida and cook for 20 seconds. Add the fenugreek seeds and cook until brown, then add the chillies and ginger and sauté for one or two minutes. Stir in the ground coriander and turmeric along with 1 tbsp water, and cook for a minute more.

Add the squash and sauté for two minutes. Pour in 150ml water, bring to a boil, then cover and cook for around 15 minutes, until just tender.

Add the jaggery or sugar, dried mango powder and ground fennel seeds. Make sure there is enough water in the pan; the squash should be breaking down at the edges, creamy and soft and will help form the sauce along with the water and spices. The sauce will be thick and will cling to the vegetable with a little extra to mop up with your bread. If necessary, add 3–4 tbsp more water. Taste and adjust the salt, then serve.

serves 4

2 tbsp vegetable oil
pinch of asafoetida
½ tsp fenugreek seeds
2 dried red chillies, seeds shaken out
13g fresh root ginger, peeled weight, grated into a paste
2 tsp ground coriander
½ tsp turmeric
500g butternut squash, skin on, cut into large chunks
1 tbsp jaggery or brown sugar
2–2½ tsp dried mango powder
¾ tsp ground fennel seeds
salt, to taste

quick sautéed spinach with dill

A delicious, easy accompaniment to any curry, the dill adds a lovely flavour but you can leave it out if you prefer.

Steam or boil the spinach until wilted. When cool enough to handle, squeeze out the excess water.

Heat the oil and butter in a sauté pan. Add the onion and cook for a few minutes, or until softened. Add the garlic and cook gently for another minute or so, until just cooked but not coloured. Add the spinach and tomatoes, spices and seasoning. Stir-fry for five minutes, without adding any water.

Finish with the dill and lemon juice, and serve.

serves 4

400g baby spinach, washed
1 tbsp vegetable oil
20g butter
½ small onion, chopped
4 fat garlic cloves, finely chopped
6 baby tomatoes, halved
good ½ tsp ground cumin
good ½ tsp ground coriander
generous pinch of freshly ground
    black pepper
⅛ tsp turmeric
salt, to taste
1 tbsp chopped dill
1 tsp lemon juice, or to taste

stir-fried cabbage, bengal gram and coconut

Cabbage often gets passed over for more 'interesting' greens, but whenever I make this it is loved by all, so give it another try. This is a great, light stir-fry with crisp tender cabbage enlivened by the flavours of south India. If you don't have time to cook the lentils, leave them out; the dish will still be fantastic, just not as nutritionally well-balanced.

Soak the lentils, if you have time, for as long as possible. Cook by boiling in plenty of lightly salted water until just soft; it should take 35–45 minutes, less if they have been soaked. Drain and reserve.

Heat the oil in a large frying pan. Add the mustard and nigella seeds and, once the popping dies down, the dried chillies, ginger and curry leaves; cook for a further 10 seconds. Add the cabbage, turmeric and salt and stir-fry for five to six minutes, or until the cabbage is crisp yet tender. Stir in the peanuts, lentils, coconut and a little lemon juice. Taste, adjust the seasoning and lemon juice, and serve.

serves 2

25g Bengal gram, washed well
1 tbsp vegetable oil
⅓ tsp mustard seeds
¼ tsp nigella seeds
1–3 dried red chillies, whole
8g fresh root ginger, peeled weight,
    grated into a paste
10 fresh curry leaves
¼ white cabbage head, finely
    shredded
¾ tsp turmeric
salt, to taste
40g roasted peanuts, halved or
    roughly chopped
50g fresh grated coconut, or
    3–4 tbsp unsweetened
    desiccated coconut
1½ tsp lemon juice, or to taste

creamy peas, sweetcorn and spinach

A mild, creamy curry where the spinach is a lovely, velvety foil to bursts of sweetness from the peas and crisp sweetcorn, simply flavoured with cumin and dried fenugreek leaves. This can be a main course or an accompaniment. I often serve it with Naan (see page 155) or rice to complement a robust curry. It is also lovely with roast chicken, lamb or simply cooked fish.

Heat the butter or oil in a non-stick saucepan. Add the cumin and, once it has sizzled for 10 seconds, add the onion and sauté gently until really soft. Tip in the ginger, garlic, fenugreek leaves and chillies; saute for a couple of minutes until the garlic starts to colour.

Meanwhile blend together the cashews and yogurt until smooth. Add to the pan and sauté for four or five minutes, or until it is a thick paste and releasing oil. Add 250ml water, bring back to a boil, stirring constantly, then simmer, covered, for 10 minutes.

Add the salt and pepper, spinach, peas, sweetcorn, cream and milk. Cover and cook until the spinach is soft; you may need to add another splash of water but bear in mind this should be a slightly thick, creamy curry. Taste, adjust the seasoning and serve.

serves 4

1 good tbsp butter or vegetable oil
½ tsp cumin seeds
¾ small onion, chopped
10g fresh root ginger, peeled weight, finely chopped
2 fat garlic cloves, finely chopped
1½ tsp dried fenugreek leaves, crumbled into a powder
1–2 green chillies, whole but pierced
25g cashew nuts
40g plain yogurt
salt, to taste
freshly ground black pepper, to taste
60g spinach, shredded (or left whole if baby spinach)
2 handfuls of frozen peas
3 tbsp canned sweetcorn kernels
4 tbsp single cream
4 tbsp milk

green spring vegetable thoran

A quick and easy, fresh dish that is simply spiced, this goes well with most south Indian curries or even a simple piece of grilled fish. You can use any vegetables you like; this is just one possible combination.

Heat the oil in a non-stick frying pan. Add the mustard seeds and, once they are spluttering, add the curry leaves and onion; cook until the onion is soft. Add the garlic and gently sauté for one or two minutes, until it smells cooked.

Add the vegetables, turmeric, salt, coconut and chilli and enough water to cover the base of the pan by 1–1.5cm. Cook over a moderate flame for three or four minutes, or until the vegetables are cooked to your liking (I like mine to have just a little bite). By now the water should have evaporated; if not increase the heat and quickly boil off the rest. The onions and coconut should cling to the vegetables.

Sprinkle with a little extra coconut and serve.

serves 4

3 tbsp vegetable oil
1 tsp brown mustard seeds
20 fresh curry leaves
1 onion, finely chopped
2 fat garlic cloves, finely chopped
12 large asparagus stalks, woody bit snapped off, sliced diagonally into 1cm pieces
120g green beans, topped and tailed, sliced into two or three
150g broccoli or purple-sprouting broccoli, cut into small florets
1/3 tsp turmeric
salt, to taste
2–3 tbsp unsweetened desiccated coconut, plus more to serve
1/3–1/2 tsp dried red chilli flakes, or to taste

stir-fried okra

As easy as pie, this quick recipe is delicious and one I cook regularly. You taste the okra, but the spices make for really flavourful mouthfuls of a truly healthy vegetable. I feel okra goes with everything - chicken, lamb, fish and lentils - so feel free to cook this with any main course.

Heat the oil in a frying pan. Add the cumin seeds and, once they have browned, the coriander, turmeric, chilli and salt. After they have cooked gently for 10 seconds, add the okra and stir-fry over a moderate flame until it is just cooked which, in my kitchen, takes five to seven minutes for young, fresh pods (older okra will take a little longer).

Stir in the dried mango powder, taste and adjust the flavours and seasoning to suit your palate and serve.

serves 2–3, can be doubled

2 tbsp vegetable oil
1 tsp cumin seeds
1½ tsp ground coriander
¼ tsp turmeric
⅛–¼ tsp chilli powder
salt, to taste
200g okra, wiped with damp kitchen paper, topped, tailed and sliced into 1cm pieces
⅛ tsp dried mango powder, or to taste

spicy peas with ginger

A lovely, easy dish that I often make when I have people around, both because everyone likes peas and because my mother made them for her dinner parties. We call this recipe *chat-patta*, a term which means spicy, salty and sour, all flavours that go really well with sweet peas.

Heat the oil in a saucepan, add the cumin seeds and, once they've sizzled for 10 seconds and darkened, the ginger and green chillies; sauté for a minute.

Add the coriander, cumin, salt and a splash of water and give the pot a stir. Once the water has evaporated, stir in the peas and, once they are well coated in the spices, cover and cook on a gentle flame for 10–12 minutes. I like them slightly wrinkled as I feel they have a little more flavour that way. Stir in the dried mango powder and garam masala, taste, adjust the seasoning and serve sprinkled with chopped coriander.

serves 4–6

2½ tbsp vegetable oil
2 tsp cumin seeds
20g fresh root ginger, peeled weight, finely chopped or cut into fine julienne
2 green chillies, whole but pierced
1¾ tsp ground coriander
1 good tsp ground cumin
salt, to taste
400g green peas, fresh or frozen and defrosted
⅔ tsp dried mango powder, or to taste
⅓ tsp garam masala
handful of fresh chopped coriander

cumin-crusted sautéed potatoes

I was thinking aloud with some friends about which quick potato dish I should give in this chapter and everyone pointed to these. This is really easy and quick, extremely moreish and very versatile. It could accompany a whole host of non-Indian dishes, even roast chicken. The dried mango powder is to add sourness, but if you don't have any you can add a little lemon juice or chopped tomato instead. The fresh coriander is quite important as it really lifts and enlivens the flavours.

Halve the potatoes and boil them in salted water until just tender. Drain.

Heat the oil in a large frying pan. Add the cumin seeds and, once they have browned, remove the pan from the heat and add all the remaining spices and the salt. Stir to mix, return to the heat and cook for 20 seconds.

Add the potatoes and coat well in the spices. Sauté gently for five or six minutes, or until you have some brown, crusty bits, then add the fresh coriander and toss once again. Taste and adjust the seasoning, chilli and dried mango powder until you are happy with the balance, then serve.

serves 4–6

450g potatoes, peeled
3½ tbsp vegetable oil
2 tsp cumin seeds
2 tsp ground coriander
⅓ tsp turmeric
1 rounded tsp ground cumin
¾ tsp garam masala
¼–½ tsp chilli powder, or to taste
1 tsp dried mango powder, or
   to taste
salt, to taste
large handful of fresh, chopped
   coriander

simply spiced lotus root

Most of us associate lotus root with the crisp yet flavourless spoke-like shapes found in Chinese stir-fries. But lotus root is much loved in India; the lotus is almost the national flower and is hugely symbolic. I have seen lotus root cooked in many ways, some fry it like crisps and others make it into koftas to go in a curry. This is my favourite way of eating it. The best place to find good-quality lotus roots is still in Chinese stores.

Place the lotus root in a large saucepan, cover with lots of water, season well and bring to a boil, then cover and cook until crisp but tender; it should take 12–15 minutes. Drain and leave in the colander.

Heat the oil in a wide, large non-stick pan. Add the gram flour and roast over a gentle flame for two or three minutes, stirring constantly, until it smells and tastes cooked. Add the powdered spices and salt and stir for a minute.

Add the lotus root and stir-fry gently for another four or five minutes, making sure the pieces are all well coated with the spices. Taste and adjust the seasoning, sprinkle over the chopped coriander and serve.

serves 4–5

500g lotus root, cleaned, peeled and
    sliced diagonally into 1cm pieces
salt, to taste
2½ tbsp vegetable oil
60g gram flour
1 rounded tsp garam masala
1 level tbsp dried mango powder
½–¾ tsp chilli powder
½ tsp turmeric
1¾ tbsp ground coriander
2 tsp ground cumin
large handful of chopped fresh
    coriander

breads
and rice

instant naan

Naan is our favourite restaurant bread, soft with a few dark, crisp spots that come from cooking in a super-hot tandoor oven. You can get really good results at home and, once you start making these, it is hard to stop! They are delicious and you can tailor them to your own tastes. Here is a very quick recipe with three of my favourite variations. Feel free to use the basic recipe and create your own toppings.

300g plain flour, plus more to dust
¾ tsp baking powder
½ tsp bicarbonate of soda
½ tsp salt
1½ tsp sugar
4 tbsp milk
4 tbsp plain yogurt
15g butter, melted, plus more for brushing

Preheat the oven to its highest setting (mine goes up to 275°C). Place a baking sheet on the uppermost shelf to heat through.

Mix together all the dry ingredients. Make a well in the middle and add your wet ingredients with 85–90ml of water. Bring together with your hands into a dough. Knead quickly until smooth.

Roll out into 0.75cm-thick naan breads - trying to achieve that characteristic teardrop shape - using a little more flour. Pat off any excess flour and place the breads on the hot baking sheet (you will need to do this in two batches). Cook for two to four minutes, or until there are brown spots on the upper surface. Brush with the extra melted butter, which helps to soften and brighten the surface, and serve hot.

makes 6 medium naan

caramelised onion Heat 2 tbsp vegetable oil and fry 1 sliced onion until soft. Scatter over the top of the naan before cooking.

garlic and coriander butter Crush 1 large garlic clove and add to a small saucepan with 2 tbsp butter. Melt the butter. Stir in 2 tbsp chopped fresh coriander and brush over the cooked naan.

seeded Press 1 rounded tsp of nigella or sesame seeds, or 1 rounded tbsp pumpkin seeds, or any other seeds you like (try black onion or poppy seeds) evenly into the upper surface of the breads before baking.

chapati/roti/phulka

These are all different names for the same basic, everyday wholewheat flatbreads. They are soft, puff up when cooked and, if you have a gas cooker, become a little crisp on the underside. Don't worry about not rolling a perfect circle, practice makes perfect, just keep giving the bread quarter turns for an even thickness. You can find chapati (*atta*) flour in most large supermarkets but, if you can't get hold of any, use equal quantities of wholewheat and plain flour instead. These can be made in advance and reheated, wrapped in foil, in a medium oven. I don't season this bread as it is used to mop up well-seasoned sauces, but you can add salt if you like.

300g chapati flour (or half
    wholewheat and half plain flour),
    plus more to dust
salt (optional)
200-240ml water

Sift the flour and salt (if using) into a bowl and make a well in the centre. Slowly drizzle in most of the water and, using your hand, draw the flour into the centre, mixing all the time. You may not need all the water. The dough should be slightly sticky and will firm up as you knead it. Knead for eight to 10 minutes, or until it is elastic. Place in a bowl, cover with a damp tea towel and leave for 30 minutes in a warm area, or at room temperature in the summer.

Divide the dough into 10 equal portions and roll into golf ball-sized pieces; cover again. Flour a work surface and rolling pin. Roll each ball into 12.5–15cm circles. The best way to do this is to keep rolling in one direction, regularly giving the dough a quarter turn to get a round shape.

Heat a tava or frying pan until hot. Toss the chapati from one hand to the other to remove excess flour, and place on the tava. Reduce the heat to moderate and cook until small bubbles appear on the underside, about 10–20 seconds, then flip. Cook this side until it has small dark beige spots.

Now, using tongs, place the bread directly on the gas flame. It will puff up immediately and, 10 seconds later, dark spots will appear. Turn the bread with tongs, leave for a few seconds more, then wrap in foil and keep warm in a low oven while you make the rest.

If you only have an electric cooker, press down gently on the cooked bread in the pan; as you press one area the rest should puff up. Then tackle the next bit. This way the bread should puff up all over.

makes 10, can be doubled

paratha, many ways

These flatbreads are absolutely delicious, flaky and slightly crisp. The minted type go really well with lamb curries. These are not as heavy as store-bought or restaurant varieties.

200–220ml water
300g chapati flour (*atta*), plus more to dust
a small bowl of vegetable oil, ghee or melted butter
salt, to taste

Mix the water into the flour, kneading until smooth. Divide into 10 balls. Heat a tava, flat griddle pan or frying pan. Take a ball of dough and roll it into a 15cm circle, using a little extra flour. Spread with ¾ tsp oil, ghee or butter, sprinkle evenly with a little salt and flour. Roll into a very tight log (Swiss-roll style). Then, with your palms, roll this log a bit longer, coil it tightly and pat down into a disc. Flour both sides and roll out again into a 15–17.5cm circle.

Pat off excess flour and place the paratha on the hot pan. Cook until light brown spots appear underneath, around 10–15 seconds. Turn over and spread with ¾ tsp more oil, butter or ghee (I use the back of the spoon I drizzled it over with). Once the underside has browned in spots, turn again and repeat with another ¾ tsp oil.

Now, cut small slashes over the bread to help it crisp up. Turn again and repeat the slashes. Cook the remaining breads and serve hot.

makes 10

my favourite variations

spicy Sprinkle a pinch of both carom seeds and chilli powder over the breads with the salt.

mint Sprinkle ¾ tsp dried mint over the breads with the salt.

onion, coriander and green chilli As you knead, add a handful of chopped fresh coriander, 1 small, finely chopped onion, 2 green chillies, deseeded and sliced, 1½ tsp nigella seeds and ½ tsp salt. Don't make the rolled layers, just cook in the pan with the oil, ghee or butter as above.

a quick and easy variation You don't need to make the layers, you can just add ½ tsp salt to the dough and cook using the oil as above.

really easy bhaturas

These are lovely, fluffy, flaky breads that have been fried but don't feel at all heavy. The authentic recipe takes a lot longer to make and requires four hours of fermenting time, so my family have been using this quick way for years. They take just seconds to make and everyone loves them. Try them with Southern Potato Curry (see page 49), Tangy Chickpea Curry (see page 55) or in fact any other dish! They are truly delicious.

200g plain flour, plus more to dust
2/3 tsp salt
1 tsp sugar
1/4 tsp fast-action yeast (optional)
140ml sparkling water
1 tsp vegetable oil, plus more to fry

Put the flour into a bowl and mix in the salt, sugar and yeast (if using), then pour in the sparkling water. Bring together with your hands until you have a dough, then knead until it is smooth and soft and doesn't have any cracks. Smear with the 1 tsp oil, put into a bowl and leave to rest for 30 minutes.

Divide the dough into 8 equal balls. Spoon 5 tbsp of the extra flour on to a small plate.

Flatten one ball and pat both sides in the flour. Roll out into thin 0.25–0.5cm-thick circles or ovals. Heat up about 20cm oil in a large open pan - a karahi or wok is ideal - until just smoking.

Place the bread straight into the hot oil and hold it down with a slotted spoon for five or six seconds, as it will try to rise and will puff up. Turn over; the underside should be golden. Cook this side for another few seconds, or until golden on both sides. Remove from the oil and blot off excess oil on kitchen paper. Serve, or keep them hot while you make the rest. Serve hot.

makes 8 medium breads

perfect boiled rice

Rice is one of the simplest and quickest grains to cook, yet so many people are afraid to tackle it, fearing stodgy or wet grains. The way to achieve great fluffy rice is actually really easy. This is how we have always made it in my family; it is foolproof. We are advised to discard leftover rice within a day of making it – as the bacteria in rice increases at a really fast rate – and to make sure it is always properly reheated.

50–60g good-quality basmati rice per person

Wash the rice really well in several changes of water, until the water runs clear, showing that all the starch has been removed. Place in a large, deep saucepan and cover with water to come at least 15-20cm above the level of the rice, depending on how much you are making. Bring to a boil and simmer fast (as you would for pasta) for seven to eight minutes. Taste a grain; it should be cooked through, if not wait a minute then check again.

Turn off the heat, pour the rice into a sieve, drain off all the water, then tip the rice back into the pan. Cover, and leave to steam for eight to 10 minutes.

aromatic rice pilaf

The simple yellow pilaf served in most Indian restaurants. It is lightly flavoured and a lovely accompaniment to any curry.

220g basmati rice, well washed
2 good tbsp ghee (or 1 tbsp butter and 2 tbsp vegetable oil)
1 rounded tsp cumin seeds
10cm cinnamon stick
1 bay leaf
4 green cardamom pods
4 cloves
1 smallish onion, sliced
½ tsp turmeric
salt, to taste

Tip the rice into a large bowl, cover with water and leave to soak. Heat the ghee in a saucepan. Add the cumin, cinnamon, bay leaf, cardamom pods and cloves and allow to sizzle for 10–15 seconds, or until the cumin is aromatic. Add the onion and cook until it's turning golden at the edges.

Add the drained rice, turmeric and salt and cook for a minute, stirring. Add 400ml water, then taste the water and adjust for salt. Bring to a boil, cover, reduce the heat to its lowest setting and cook undisturbed for 12–13 minutes. Check a grain, it should be cooked. Turn off the heat and serve when you are ready to eat.

serves 4

southern lemon and cashew nut rice

A lovely, fragrant rice which is perfect with coconut curries, as the lemon cuts through the sweet, creamy taste.

Place the rice in a saucepan with enough water to come at least 20cm above the level of the rice, bring to a boil and simmer for seven or eight minutes. Try a grain, it should be soft, if not cook for another minute and taste again. Turn off the heat, pour the rice into a sieve, drain off all the water, then tip the rice back into the pan. Cover, and leave undisturbed for five to eight minutes.

Heat the oil in a large non-stick frying pan and add the cashew nuts. Fry until golden, then remove and place on kitchen paper to blot off the excess oil. Add the mustard seeds to the pan and, once they have popped, add the lentils and chillies and stir-fry until the lentils darken and take on a reddish colour, but before they turn brown.

Add the ginger, turmeric, salt and 2 tbsp water and cook for 40 seconds. Pour in the lemon juice and cook for another minute before adding the rice, coconut and chopped coriander. Stir with a fork to mix well. Taste, adjust the seasoning and serve.

serves 4

220g basmati rice, well washed
4 tbsp vegetable oil
1 handful raw cashew nuts, split in half
1 tsp mustard seeds
1 tbsp split Bengal gram
2–4 dried red chillies, whole
6g fresh root ginger, chopped
⅓ tsp turmeric
salt, to taste
3½ tbsp lemon juice, or to taste
3 tbsp grated fresh coconut, or 2 tbsp unsweetened desiccated coconut
handful of chopped fresh coriander

pea and carrot pilaf

A colourful dish that goes with everything. You can make it just with peas, just carrots, or even add chopped green beans.

Place the rice in a saucepan and pour in water to come 20cm above the level of the rice. Bring to a boil and simmer for seven or eight minutes. Try a grain - it should be soft - if not cook for a minute and taste again. Pour into a sieve, drain, then tip back into the pan. Cover and leave for five to eight minutes.

Heat the oil in a wide frying or sauté pan and add the cumin seeds, cinnamon, cloves, bay leaves and cardamom. Cook until the cumin is aromatic, around 20 seconds. Add the onion and stir-fry until just soft. Add the carrots, peas and salt, then a splash of water. Cover and cook for two or three minutes. The carrots should retain a little bite. Uncover the pan, there should be no water left (if there is cook it off over a high heat). Add the rice and garam masala and stir with a fork to mix well. Taste, adjust the seasoning and serve.

serves 4

220g basmati rice, well washed
4 tbsp vegetable oil
1 rounded tsp cumin seeds
10cm cinnamon stick
4 cloves
2 bay leaves
2 black cardamom pods
1 small onion, sliced
½ large carrot, cut into 1cm cubes
90g peas
salt, to taste
½ tsp garam masala

creamy saffron and nut rice

A rich dish; the nuts and raisins add texture and sweetness.

Tip the rice into a bowl, cover with water and leave to soak. Heat the milk and cream until hot and pour into a jug. Sprinkle in the saffron. Set aside.

Heat 1 tbsp ghee in a saucepan, add the almonds and cashews and cook until golden. Pour into a bowl and add the pistachios. Add the remaining ghee to the pan and, once hot, the whole spices. Once the cumin is aromatic, add the onion and raisins and cook until the onion is soft and turning golden at the edges. Stir in the rice. Add enough water to the saffron jug to make a total of 400ml and pour it in with the nuts. Add salt to taste. Bring to a boil then reduce the heat to really low, cover and cook for 11–12 minutes. Check the rice is cooked, then turn off the heat and leave to steam, covered, for eight to 10 minutes. Serve hot.

serves 4

220g basmati rice, well washed
5 tbsp milk
1 tbsp double cream
good pinch of saffron
3 tbsp ghee (or 2 tbsp butter and
    1½ tbsp vegetable oil)
30g blanched almonds, halved
30g cashew nuts, halved
30g unsalted pistachios
10cm cinnamon stick
5 cloves
1 rounded tsp cumin seeds
1 black cardamom pod
3 green cardamom pods
1 small onion, halved and sliced
3 tbsp raisins
salt, to taste

salads and
raitas

quick carrot salad

You can put this together in an instant, and it's great for cleansing the palate during a rich meal.

2 tsp dry roasted peanuts
2 large carrots, peeled and coarsely grated
salt, to taste
½ tsp sugar
1¾ tsp lemon juice, or to taste
small fistful of chopped fresh coriander leaves
1 tbsp vegetable oil
1 tsp brown mustard seeds

Coarsely grind the peanuts in a good mortar and pestle.

Toss the grated carrots with the ground peanuts, salt, sugar, lemon juice and chopped coriander.

Heat the oil in your smallest pan until hot. Add the mustard seeds and cover, as they will splutter. As they reduce their spluttering, pour them over the salad and toss to mix well. Taste, adjust the seasoning and serve.

serves 2–3

indian chopped salad (*kachumber*)

A wonderfully crunchy salad that is great with any curry.

2 ripe vine tomatoes
120g cucumber (I keep the skin on)
4 small radishes
½ small onion, finely chopped
1–2 green chillies, seeded and chopped (optional)
salt, to taste
1 tbsp lemon juice, or to taste
⅓ tsp roasted cumin powder (see page 55)
handful of chopped fresh coriander leaves

Chop the tomatoes into small dice. Slice the cucumber lengthways, discard the seeds and cut into small cubes the same size as the tomatoes. Do the same with the radishes.

Toss together all the vegetables and chillies (if using), season, stir through the lemon juice, roasted cumin powder and chopped coriander, and serve, or keep at room temperature until you are ready to eat.

serves 4

warm tandoori mushroom, spinach and chickpea salad

A lovely salad with lots of flavours and textures that takes only 10 minutes to make. The mushrooms are marinated then grilled to intensify their flavours, becoming wonderfully deep-tasting. The roasted cumin powder in the dressing is optional so, if you are in a hurry, you can leave it out.

Mix together all the ingredients for the marinade. Keep small shiitake and oyster mushrooms whole, but halve the others. Cut the chestnut mushrooms into 1.5cm slices. Toss the mushrooms in the marinade, making sure each piece is coated, then set aside for 30 minutes.

Heat your grill to high and grill the mushrooms for three to four minutes each side, or until lightly charred; the shiitake and oyster mushrooms will take three minutes and the chestnut mushrooms will take an extra minute each side.

Meanwhile, whisk together the ingredients for the dressing with 1 tsp water.

Place the baby spinach in a bowl, add the hot mushrooms, chickpeas, walnuts and dressing, season well and toss to coat. Serve immediately.

serves 4 as an accompaniment

for the tandoori marinade
2 fat garlic cloves, grated into a paste
8g fresh root ginger, grated into a paste
½ tsp chilli powder
¾ tsp salt, or to taste
¾ tsp garam masala
¾ tsp ground cumin
2½ tbsp lemon juice
5 tbsp olive oil

for the salad
300g mixed mushrooms (shiitake, oyster and chestnut), cleaned
100g baby spinach, well washed
200g canned chickpeas, drained and rinsed
large handful of walnuts, lightly crushed
lots of freshly ground black pepper, to taste

for the dressing
1⅓ tbsp cider, sherry or white wine vinegar
3 tbsp extra-virgin olive oil
good ½ tsp Dijon mustard
½ red onion, finely sliced
⅓ tsp roasted cumin powder (see page 55, optional)

top quick carrot salad, *see page 165*
bottom warm tandoori mushroom, spinach and chickpea salad

mango raita

A lovely sweet, sour and lightly spiced raita which will help temper the heat of hot curries.

Slice the cheeks from the mangoes. Peel and cut the flesh into small cubes (see below for techniques).

Mix together the yogurt, coconut and sugar until the sugar has 'melted'. Add the mango and its juices, a little salt to taste and the chopped coriander.

Heat the oil in a small saucepan, add the mustard seeds and cook until they have popped. Stir into the raita, taste and adjust the seasoning. Serve sprinkled with a little chilli powder (if using).

serves 4

2 small, sweet mangoes (ripe but not soft)
400g plain yogurt
2 tbsp unsweetened desiccated coconut
1½ tsp sugar, or to taste (depends on the sweetness of the mango and sourness of the yogurt)
salt, to taste
a good handful of chopped fresh coriander
1 tsp vegetable oil
½ tsp mustard seeds
¼ tsp chilli powder (optional)

cutting a mango

There are two ways to cut a mango:

The first is to cut the cheeks from the mango then halve them lengthways. Slice the flesh from the skin with a knife, trying to avoid cutting away too much flesh, and cut it into small cubes. You can then tackle the 'wedges' on the sides, though it is hard to get clean slices here as the flesh around the stone can be quite fibrous. I try to get what I can.

The other way is to cut the cheeks from the mango, then slice straight lines into the flesh all the way down to the skin. Give the cheeks a quarter turn and slice again to create squares. Now push the cheek inside out and cut off the squares. Tackle the sides in the same way as above.

top crispy okra raita, *see page 171*
middle mango raita
bottom cucumber and mint raita, *see page 171*

tomato, onion and cucumber raita

This is my favourite raita and the one we eat the most.

Stir all the ingredients together and season to taste.

serves 4

1 small vine tomato, chopped into
  1cm dice
90g cucumber, peeled and chopped
  into 1cm dice
½ small red onion, finely chopped
large handful of chopped fresh
  coriander
¾ tsp roasted cumin powder (see
  page 55)
⅓ tsp chilli powder
400g plain yogurt, whisked until
  smooth
salt, to taste

mint and garlic yogurt

This is a yogurt that I love. It isn't very Indian, but tastes great
with Indian food so I wanted to include it for all the garlic
lovers like myself.

Mix all the ingredients together, taste, adjust the seasoning and serve.

serves 4–5

400g full- or half-fat Greek yogurt
1 garlic clove, grated into a paste
salt, to taste
10 large mint leaves, shredded

apple, orange and mint raita

A lovely, refreshing raita that is perfect for those who like a
hint of sweetness or fruitiness with their meal.

Using a small sharp knife, cut into the orange segments on either side of the
membrane, so the segment falls out. Cut these in half and add to the yogurt.

Add all the other ingredients and stir well to mix. Taste, adjust the seasoning
and serve, or chill until required.

serves 4–6

1 small orange, peeled
400g plain yogurt
1 small, crunchy apple, cut into 1cm
  dice (peeled or skin on, you decide)
large sprinkling of shredded mint
  leaves
1 scant tsp roasted cumin powder
  (see page 55)
salt, to taste
sprinkling of chilli powder (optional)

cucumber and mint raita

A refreshing raita that is really versatile; it's lovely with Indian food but also great with barbecues. I even eat it with my baked potato; delicious and healthy. It's always best to measure out mint leaves, even small quantities, as they can be strong and may otherwise overpower a dish.

200g cucumber (½ a large one)
400g thick plain yogurt
salt and freshly ground black pepper, to taste
8g mint leaves, shredded
¾ tsp roasted cumin powder (see page 55)

Grate the cucumber on the coarse side of your box grater. Squeeze out all the excess water and place the cucumber in a large bowl.

Add all the remaining ingredients and stir well to mix. Serve cold.

serves 4

crispy okra raita

A delightful raita with the subtle flavours of the coast. The crisp okra provides texture to this thick, slightly sweet dish.

400g Greek yogurt
4 tsp sugar, or to taste
salt, to taste
vegetable oil, to deep-fry
12 large okra, topped, tailed and sliced into 1cm rounds
⅓ tsp brown mustard seeds
12 curry leaves

Stir the yogurt until smooth and loosen with 3-4 tbsp water. Stir in the sugar and a little salt.

Heat 5cm oil in a small saucepan, add the okra and fry gently until crisp and just turning colour; stirring occasionally. Spoon out and place on a kitchen paper-lined plate. Toss in a little seasoning.

Pour out all but 1 tsp of oil from the pan. Reheat the oil and add the mustard seeds. Once the noise in the pan starts to die down, add the curry leaves and turn off the heat. Pour into the yogurt and stir well to mix. Taste and adjust sugar and salt to taste, it should be sweet rather than salty.

When you are ready to eat, stir in most of the okra and sprinkle with the rest.

serves 4–5

spices 101

Spices were once more valuable than gold, and their worth in the kitchen remains priceless. They can be seeds (mustard), fruits (mango), roots (turmeric), barks (cinnamon) or even flower stamens (saffron). You need to know the different qualities of each to be a truly excellent curry cook. Some are earthy, others sharp; they can be musty, citrussy, tangy, peppery, pungent, hot or even herb-like. Here's the essential guide to navigating them. Many will require a trip to an Asian store, or a little shopping online (see bottom right). But if you cook curries regularly – and you probably do if you've bought this book – you only need to shop for spices every six months, as they will last well in an airtight container, in a cool, dark place.

common ground spices

Chilli powder *(lal mirch)* The heat of this varies from one batch to another. Generally speaking, the darker the shade, the milder the heat. The mildest is Kashmiri chilli powder (*degi mirch* in Hindi). Chilli powder will add wonderful colour and heat to your dishes but little flavour, unlike fresh chillies.

Coriander *(sabut dhania)* These large, pale, spherical seeds are mild and almost citrussy in taste, with a fabulous aroma. Once powdered, they are one of the most commonly used spices in Indian food, rounding off and softening stronger flavours.

Cumin *(jeera)* This very familiar spice is used all around the world. You'll find it in Mexican, North African and Malaysian dishes, as well as in Indian food. It is earthy and savoury and can be fried or dry-roasted to a darker shade with a nutty loveliness.

Garam masala A famous blend of warming spices that differs from home to home but usually contains cloves, black and green cardamom and cinnamon as well as bay leaves and black peppercorns. Milder mixes will also contain coriander and cumin. It can be added either towards the end of cooking for a real punch of aroma, or closer to the beginning for a more rounded, subtle taste.

Turmeric *(haldi)* This vibrant, mustard-yellow powder is essential in Indian cooking. It is prized both for its colour and for its fantastic medicinal properties. It should be used sparingly as the subtle, musty flavour can be unpleasant in large quantities.

common whole spices

Black cardamom *(badi elaichi)* These large, woody pods have a lovely smoky aroma and are loved by many north Indians. Use in lamb and chicken curries and pilafs.

Black peppercorns *(kali mirch)* This spice needs little introduction... except to say the taste and aroma of freshly ground peppercorns is so superior to shop-bought powder that the latter is not worth buying.

Brown mustard seeds *(rai)* When fried in hot oil, these small brown seeds release a nutty, mild mustard flavour. When powdered, they have a stronger taste. When you grind this spice, be careful to not overwork it or it can become bitter. I very briefly blitz a large amount at a time in a spice blender and then store.

Cinnamon and cassia *(dal chini)* Cassia bark is similar to cinnamon and is more commonly used in India. I prefer to use both whole in my curries or pilafs. I add cassia bark in large shards but, as cinnamon is more delicate, it's best to add it in quills so it breaks up less. The two are interchangeable in Indian food.

Cloves *(laung)* Often used in small quantities in curries, these have a distinct, strong and slightly sweet flavour.

Curry leaves (*curri patta*) These are an important part of coastal food. They are highly aromatic when fresh, but lose much of their flavour when dried. You can buy them fresh in decent quantities in Indian stores and freeze them for future use; they keep perfectly.

Dried chillies Used a lot in India, especially in the areas where fresh chillies are hard to find. There are so many different types, each with its own heat and flavour profile, so be careful the first time you cook with any unfamiliar variety. If you are grinding them, break them in half crosswise and shake the seeds straight into the bin, as these hold most of the heat. You can now buy Kashmiri dried chillies in some supermarkets; these are mild with a lovely dark, rich colour. You can also buy crushed dried chillies, which can be added late in the cooking process to correct a recipe's heat level. This is a godsend if you taste a dish and find it too mild.

Fennel seeds (*saunf*) A sweet, liquorice-like spice that can either be added whole to hot oil or ground.

Fenugreek leaves (*kasturi methi*) These dried leaves have a unique savoury and pleasingly bitter flavour when you crush or crumble them into your curry. They are especially delicious in lentil and chicken dishes, or with spinach and even cauliflower.

Green cardamom (*chotti elaichi*) Gently-flavoured pods with a subtle but unmistakable aroma, used in sweet and savoury dishes, pilafs and in Indian spiced tea. Grind them either with or without their green skins (the skin has lots of flavour but is harder to grind finely).

Green chillies While most westerners think of chillies in terms of heat, I use them more for their flavour. Keeping them whole in a curry, as I tend to, means the heat stays within the chilli and you mostly get their taste. I use the Indian thin finger-like chillies that you can buy in Indian stores; they keep in the fridge for weeks. You can buy green chillies from supermarkets, but they won't have the same flavour or heat.

my top ten unusual spices

Asafoetida (*heeng*) This pungent powder makes food easier to digest; some think it tastes like cooked garlic.

Carom seeds (*ajwain*) A small, dark green seed with a flavour reminiscent of thyme. Use with fish, hard-to-digest vegetables and in some Indian breads.

Chaat masala A blend with a wealth of flavours, such as cumin, mint, carom, asafoetida, mango and ginger. It's tangy and often sprinkled over tandoori dishes.

Dried mango powder (*amchur*) Tangy but not sweet. Use it instead of lemon juice for tartness without liquid.

Dried pomegranate powder (*anardana*) The powdered seeds of a variety of pomegranate. It has a tart fruitiness that's great with chickpeas and lamb (see page 119).

Fenugreek seeds (*methre*) Hard, strong-tasting seeds, these can be bitter. Cook in hot oil until they darken well.

Nigella seeds (*kalonji*) These delicate black teardrop-shaped seeds have a peppery flavour but no heat. Lovely with seafood, vegetables, or naan bread (see page 155).

Panch phoran A Bengali mix of whole seeds including fenugreek, mustard, fennel, cumin and nigella. Often used with fish, vegetables and lentils.

Saffron (*kesar*) The dried stamen of a variety of crocus, with a delicate, musky flavour; a little goes a long way. Store it in the fridge.

Star anise (*phool chakri*) Immediately recognisable, this spice looks like the spokes of a wheel, or a flower. It has a lovely, slightly aniseed flavour and strong aroma.

www.pureindianspices.co.uk
www.steenbergs.co.uk
www.thespiceshop.co.uk

Editorial Director Anne Furniss
Creative Director Helen Lewis
Project Editor Lucy Bannell
Designer Claire Peters
Photographer Jonathan Gregson
Food Stylist Sunil Vijayakar
Props Stylist Liz Belton
Production Director Vincent Smith
Production Controller Marina Asenjo

This edition first published in 2014 by
Quadrille Publishing Limited
Pentagon House
52-54 Southwark Street
London SE1 1UN
www.quadrille.co.uk

Text © 2010 Anjum Anand
Photographs © 2010 Jonathan Gregson
Design and layout © 2010
Quadrille Publishing Limited

Cataloguing in Publication Data: a catalogue
record for this book is available from the British
Library.

ISBN 978 184949 578 3
Printed in China

I would like to thank my husband Adarsh for his support and understanding and for inspiring me, through his own work ethic, to try ever harder to achieve my goals.

Thank you to my family for being there for me and understanding that when I write a book I often neglect other parts of my life! I would also like to thank my friends for cheering me on despite the fact that I temporarily disappeared from their lives, and for knowing that I still love them and miss them.

Thank you Shy for looking through my recipes, pointing out what's missing and reminding me about what other people like to eat and cook. You are always my first port of call when I need clarity.

Thank you Shaleen for your time and patience and for offering your insight about what people want to eat.

I would like to thank my friend and agent Heather Holden Brown, who was the one to say I needed to write a book on curries containing all her - and Britain's - favourite dishes. She was right, of course. I would like to express my continued gratitude to the team at Quadrille who are really supportive and brought this book to life, as well as to Jonathan Gregson for his beautiful, rich photography, and to Sunil Vijayakar, for making the food look so good.

Thank you to chef Kunal at the Leela Hotel in Delhi, who taught me some of his curry recipes. I really enjoyed cooking with you, your food is delicious and has a lot of love infused with the flavours. I hope your dreams come true. And thank you so much to Zareer Lallakakka for his lovely warm hospitality and insight into Parsi food and flavours. Zareer, your old-world chivalry is truly refreshing; I loved meeting you and your family. And thank you for the semolina sweet, which I did finish!